"UNFORG

—Libra

"FASCINATING!"
—Madeleine L'Engle, author of
A Wrinkle in Time

"ABSORBING!"
—*Tallahassee Democrat*

"INTRIGUING!"
—*Booklist*

"ENGROSSING!"
—*Kirkus Reviews*

"EMBER, YOU'RE A VERY UNUSUAL HUMAN BEING,"

he began, carefully, rocking his prayer hands in rhythm with his words. "You're not like everyone else, not exactly. . . ."

She sighed in exasperation. *Tell me something I don't know!* She waited for more, but he hesitated, apparently at a loss for words.

"You said you never met my father," she said.

"No. He and your mother conceived you in the natural way. His skin was golden, too, I'm sure. And I assume they were married in some fashion, according to their culture."

She frowned in confusion.

"Where's my mother? Take me to her now. I've got to see her."

He tapped his prayer hands against his tightly clamped lips. "You don't know how many times I've rehearsed our meeting—what you would ask, how I would answer. But . . . there's actually no easy way to tell you what you need to know."

She gulped. "Just spit it out, then."

He stepped closer and took her hand; his eyes met hers.

"Your mother is dead," he said, softly and clearly. "I found her, buried beneath a glacier on the arctic tundra. She had been dead twenty-five thousand years."

EMBER FROM THE SUN

MARK CANTER

A DELL BOOK

Published by
Dell Publishing
a division of
Bantam Doubleday Dell Publishing Group, Inc.
1540 Broadway
New York, New York 10036

ISBN: 0-440-22430-6

Reprinted by arrangement with Delacorte Press

Printed in the United States of America

Published simultaneously in Canada

July 1997

10 9 8 7 6 5 4 3 2 1

OPM

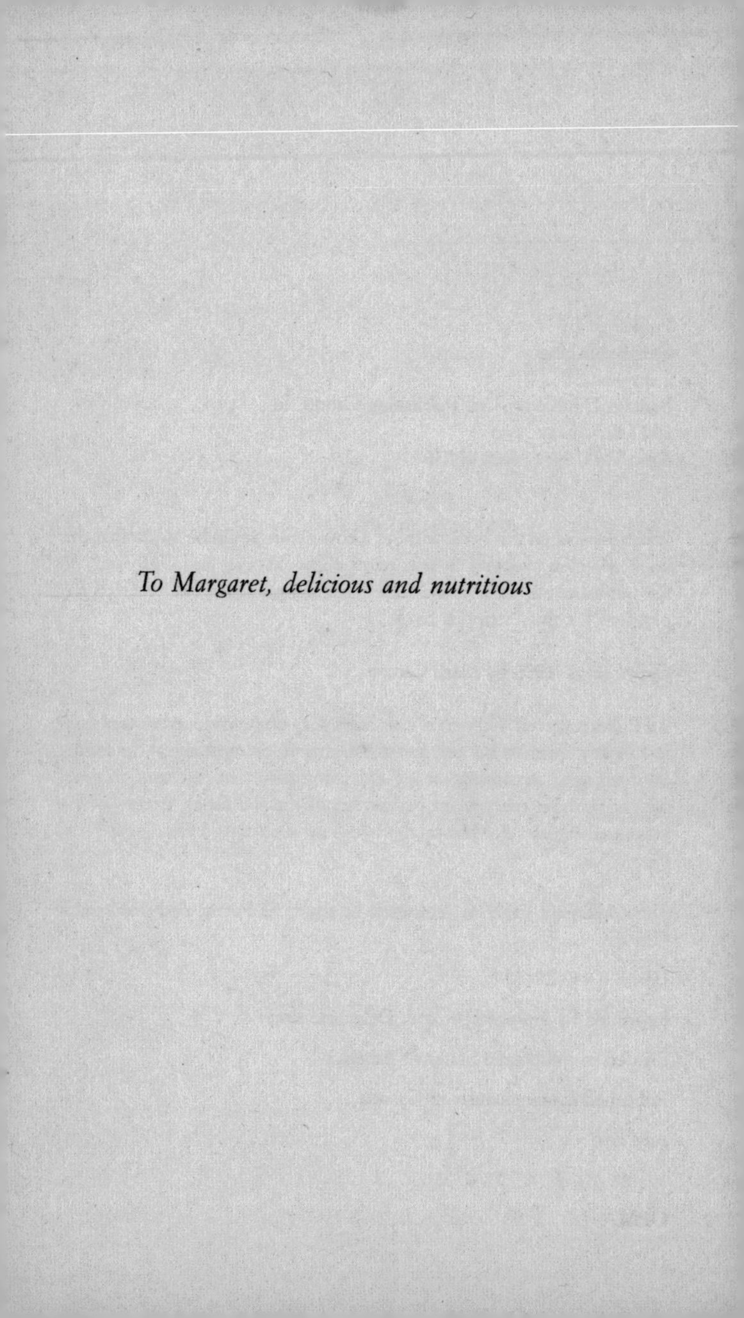

To Margaret, delicious and nutritious

The author thanks Evan Earl Dussia II, M.D., gynecologist, for his technical advice on human embryo implantation; Don Wood, science writer, for his insightful critique of the first draft; Russell Galen and Danny Baror, literary agents, for topnotch representation; and Jackie Cantor, editor, for her suggestions for improving the manuscript and for her golden heart.

PART ONE

(Nahadeh, Yute, *The Neanderthal Papers*, Pacific College Press, Deer Park, Washington, 1987, p. 24.)

One can draw few certainties about prehistoric human lifestyles from the mute record of fossil bones. Consider this: The bones of the goats of the Galapagos Archipelago do not offer the slightest clue that these animals are able to climb trees to eat leaves—a behavior that is readily observed. What unguessable abilities and surprising cultures would Neanderthals display if we could watch them go about their lives?

1

TWO MEN AND a girl tramped across a springy mat of deer moss and tiny yellow flowers scattered to the horizons of the tundra. John Nahadeh drove a team of malamutes that towed a dogcart packed with video gear and digging tools. His daughter, Nika, strode alongside.

Yute Nahadeh walked several yards behind his father and sister, pausing to collect fungi, bearberries, skunk cabbage—any flora that looked edible—and sealing the specimens in plastic sandwich bags. The big man's boots squished the wet moss with a sucking noise as he stooped to work.

A golden eagle spun and swooped, crying a rapid *kak-kak-kak*. Yute glanced up to see a lemming dart into its burrow and the eagle reel away. He lifted a pair of Bausch & Lomb binoculars from their leather case and tracked the bird climbing in a spiral toward the sun.

He smiled and lowered his gaze, letting it drift across the grassy sea. Puddles and sheets of water splotched the thawed ground, reflecting cloudless blue. Knee-high dogwoods and birches stood out among crimson islands of fireweed. Several miles away, dwarf-forested hills jutted from the plain and climbed in giant steps to snow-shrouded mountains.

The air smelled like wildflower pollen and cold mud; a sweet, moist, green scent. And this fragrance, like clay on a bee sting, drew from him an old pain. His homesickness surprised him; he had not felt that way since boyhood, when he left to pursue what his father called "dead-ucation." Now he did not resist the hurt, but allowed it to open his soul to his Caiyuh homeland.

Grandmother, let me love you again. For a long moment he stood still and drank the living air in slow gulps.

Then he returned to his task, and snipped a clump of rice lilies. He pulled the pistils off the purple flower with his teeth and chewed delicately. *Tastes like clover,* he decided, and wondered at the flower's nutritional value. *Did prehistoric peoples sun-dry such foods to eat later, during the long cold?*

"Yute!" his sister called to him.

He looked up, nibbling at a silver lichen, then spit out the bitter stuff. His father had traveled several hundred yards ahead, steering toward the face of a small glacier that spilled from one of the foothills. Nika ran back toward her brother, her black hair billowing.

Yute strode in her direction, reaching behind to

put his botanical specimens into his fanny pack. He peeled off his wool sweater and stuffed it in on top. The air temperature had climbed since the chilly morning; even so, permafrost lay only six inches below the sloshy ground.

"My feet feel like Popsicles," he said when they met.

"Come on," she said, "you know Father won't wait. Run."

They ran side by side. Nika's loose hair draped her back and swept the top of her hips.

"What's a Popsickle?" she asked.

"A frozen treat. Someday I'll buy you one, in Seattle."

"Not if they taste like your feet," she said, and punched his shoulder, then sprinted ahead out of range.

Yute laughed and chased her. He grabbed a handful of her thick hair and tugged it like a mare's mane.

"Whoa down, pony, whoa down, gal."

Ahead, their father stopped the dogs and waited for the two to catch up.

"Can you believe your eyes?" Yute asked.

"He wants everything to go well between you today," she said.

Yute and Nika followed the swath the dogcart had cut through a wide patch of orange poppies. Yellow-and-black swallowtail butterflies flitted near the flowers, and Yute wondered which of the tundra's insects Ice Age people ate. Beetle and bee larvae and termites, certainly . . . but what else?

The dogs crowded in a semicircle and John fed them dried fish heads from a large steel coffee can. The elder Nahadeh was short, but solidly built, his black hair entwined in a fat braid that dangled past the broad yoke of his buckskin shirt.

Yute kept his distance; he was afraid of dogs, even harnessed ones, especially when they were eating. John pointed to a distant peak that peered over the shoulders of the mountains in the foreground. "Denali," he said.

Nika lined up her eyes with her father's pointing finger. "Aaaah," she said slowly. "You see it, Yute?"

Yute aimed his binoculars at the mountain. Long, wispy banners of snow flowed from sharp ridges near the peak.

"Denali—The High One," he said.

"It's rare to see Him so clear," John said. "Usually He hides His face in clouds. Today, He looks straight at us. Something will happen today, I feel. Something powerful."

Nika beamed. "Hear that? Think we'll find another Tundra Man?"

Yute laughed. "Don't get excited. We haven't seen anything so far but fox scat. Tundra Man was like the sky tearing open and God reaching through to hand down a gift to anthropology. How often does that happen in any science?"

According to the grant proposal Yute had written for this project, it was an expedition to videotape his father killing a caribou with a spear hurled from a spear-thrower, a hunting skill the old Caiyuh still used. But Yute had stashed in the cart an insulated body bag with a lining packed with dry ice, in case miracles are granted in clusters.

Two summers ago John and Nika were hunting at

the base of the small glacier beyond where they now stood, when they came upon the remains of a man, sitting in a rock-lined pit that receding ice had uncovered. The pit turned out to be the burial site of a 25,000-year-old Cro-Magnon male.

Anchored in solid-frozen flesh, his dark-blue eyes stared outward from the Ice Age. His skin and dark-red hair were daubed with ocher, a reddish iron-ore pigment. His right hand clutched a reindeer antler staff bored with a hole resembling a mouth, with carved rays of force radiating from the lips; a raised-scar tattoo of the same design covered his forehead. Above a necklace that alternated cave-bear claws and cave-lion fangs, his throat was deeply gashed, the apparent cause of his death. Mud bowls brimming with dried cranberries and blueberries were placed near the body, along with stone tools and weapons. Pollen studies found that armloads of alpine flowers had been strewn about the grave pit, which was roofed over with the shoulder blades of woolly mammoths.

Tundra Man ignited the world of anthropology. He was the most ancient preserved human ever discovered —predating Ice Man of the Austrian Alps by two hundred centuries. Through Yute's efforts and much political maneuvering the corpse ended up at Pacific College, near Seattle, where Yute was a professor of paleoanthropology. A gold rush of specialists followed, and Yute headed the Tundra Man Project team. The information that had poured out of their research would make doctoral dissertions almost write themselves for years to come.

Nika passed him a canteen. "What are you thinking so hard about?"

He smiled and shrugged, then gulped a deep, delicious swig of the clear spring water.

She leaned toward him to take back the canteen, and whispered, "Have you thought about his offer?"

He nodded and whispered, "I'm tempted. But it's a tough choice."

Their father had asked Yute to spend a couple of years in Swift Fork; he could have his grandfather's old cabin. Not only did John want his son home, but he needed Yute to help battle the threat that hung over their way of life. A corporation called CANARD—Central Alaska Native American Resource Developers—was pushing to build a series of gold mines in the heart of Caiyuh hunting land. The first shafts would be sunk in the Kantishna Hills, where the three of them were trekking today.

But moving back to Swift Fork would mean stepping away from his career just as his reputation as a scientist was taking off. First came his research coup with Tundra Man. And now his ideas on Neanderthals were grabbing the spotlight of controversy. Most of the field's experts disagreed with him, a giant improvement from having been largely ignored.

"Father says you're always thinking about something," Nika said.

"I suppose so," he mumbled. "Did you know that Neanderthal brains were bigger than ours?"

"Not bigger than yours, they never would've survived."

He chuckled. "What makes you think they survived?"

"I thought that's what you say—they evolved into us."

"That's not the same as surviving. We're not Neanderthals. They were our cousins, but unlike us."

"There's a book at school that shows them—hunched over, kind of apelike."

He waved the image away. "No, no," he said. "That's all wrong—antique science. They're not down the evolutionary ladder from us. If you dressed a Neanderthal man in a Seahawks sweatshirt and blue jeans, and stuck him on the bus in Seattle, no one would notice anything out of the ordinary—just a guy with a football-player build: big neck, big chest—but not strange looking."

"Just kind of a big oaf."

"Well, big, yes—stronger than an Olympic weightlifter—but not an oaf. Not at all. Remember, I said their brains were bigger than ours. Picture a race not *less* evolved than we are, but *differently* evolved. Maybe a whole different kind of intelligence."

"Different how?"

"Lord, that's what I'd love to find out," he said. "I'd stand anthropology on its head. So please, please, dig up a Neanderthal for me."

She grinned. "I'll do my best."

Yute took another mouthful of water and swished it around his tongue. *Whoever said water is odorless and flavorless never drank from an arctic spring.*

Nika touched his arm. "Yute, if you move back here, we could look for Neanderthals together."

He smiled. "That would be great, wouldn't it?" But he wondered if it would be worth the cost of dropping out for a couple of years.

He studied his sister as he passed back the canteen. Black eyes, black hair, dark skin like tarnished bronze, white teeth. He noticed her shape beneath her clothing; firm breasts under a faded flannel shirt; strong, slim legs leading down from her denim cutoffs. The last time he'd visited, she was a girl; now she was a young woman. Growing up in a muddy little village in the middle of nowhere. She knows how to kick a huskie in the teeth when it barks too much—something he would not dare to do—but what does she know about the wider world? What can she discover, in Swift Fork, of science and the humanities?

On the other hand, these things that meant so much to him—must they matter to anyone else?

Nika lowered her gaze and looked away, but Yute found it hard to take his eyes off her. He thought of women he had dated in Seattle. Some of those women saw themselves as wild; wild like city lights and easy sex and dancing to irresistible music. Nika was wild like the tundra. It lived in her.

John walked over to them and offered a handful of small, dried river trout.

"Eat," he said. "We're on a hunt."

Nika and John munched on the fishes and passed the plump egg sack of a salmon between them, squeezing it and sucking roe from the oviduct. Yute ate two granola bars and the three of them shared the water without talking.

After the break the group hiked the remaining few

miles to the base of a glacier. The ice field splayed into a dozen fingers as it beveled downward to meet the green land.

"Listen!" Nika said. "Do you hear, Father?"

John smiled and nodded, but Yute heard nothing.

"The caribou are coming," John said.

In a moment Yute heard a click-clacking noise coming from around the far edge of the glacier. He had been told that caribou feet click with each step, the sound of snapping tendons, but he had not imagined it was so loud. As a boy, he had never joined his father on a hunt; instead, he was always trekking through books.

"I'm going to break out the equipment and get set up," Yute said. He unpacked the video camera and a large dish wide-range microphone and mounted them on tripods.

John held three spears and a spear thrower in his right hand. He had fashioned the six-foot shafts from fire-hardened spruce and tipped them with double-edged flint blades. The thrower was not his own; it was a cast replica of the reindeer-antler spear-thrower found in Tundra Man's grave: a twenty-inch rod, hooked on its end, resembling a giant crochet needle.

The lead caribou of the herd were coming into view a quarter mile away, and Yute could now hear grunts mixed with the loud clicks. Thirty or more animals were already visible. Through his binoculars he saw they were mostly ragged, shedding cows, maybe a half-dozen calves, a few bulls. But more click-clacking was audible behind the wall of ice.

Yute felt his heart beat faster. "Shouldn't we move in closer?" he asked.

"No need to," John said, "they'll come to us."

From what Yute could see, his father was wrong. The lead animals already had caught sight or whiff of them and were hesitating or halting, some of them trying to turn back, causing a traffic jam of the heavy cows as the herd behind pressed forward. Some animals spread out to go around the impasse, but they, too, stopped. Yute began mounting a telephoto lens on his camera.

John shook his head. "The caribou will soon be nearly close enough to touch."

He moved ten feet forward and told Yute to be ready with the camera. Then he nodded to Nika. She took a small whistle of carved bone from her shirt pocket and blew hard with puffed cheeks. No sound came. The dogs lying around the cart jumped up and barked. She blew again. No sound. She continued to blow the mute whistle. The cart dogs whined and fidgeted and one became tangled in its leather traces.

Suddenly Nika tilted her head back and howled loudly like a wolf. A moaning deep in her throat turned into a high, undulating wail. Yute stepped back, startled. Nika yipped and began to howl again. The dogs joined in, yowling and wailing. Yute felt the hairs stand up on his neck. In a moment he heard the wolves answer from the other side of the glacier.

His chest knotted; he couldn't catch his breath. He was scared of dogs, but he was terrified of wolves. Then he forced a long, deep breath into his tight chest and let it out slowly, willing himself to breathe evenly, calmly. He stepped over to the cart, careful to approach in a line directly behind, where the dogs could not reach him. He fetched a leather holster, unsnapped it, and drew out a

Glock handgun. He stuffed it in a baggy side pocket of his shorts. When he returned to the tripod, the first of the tundra wolves had already appeared in the distance, a hundred yards beyond the caribou.

The lead wolf was all black. A half-dozen mottled gray wolves loped up to form a flank line.

Instantly, the loose-knit caribou herd melted together and surged forward. A few stragglers rushed to rejoin the group, a year-old cow among them.

The black wolf decided. He charged, and the pack followed.

The young cow bolted, but the black wolf steadily closed the gap, its long, slim legs shooting out and snapping together in giant bounds. The wolf ran past and ahead of the cow, then spun in front to cut off its escape. A gray wolf caught up and latched on to the cow's right flank. The cow twisted and slung the gray wolf to the ground, but it rolled and was up and lunged again, in one motion. Four more wolves clamped their jaws on the hind legs, planted their feet, and tried to tug the cow down. It lurched forward, dragging the wolves.

From where he stood, Yute could hear the wolves snarling and the cow bawling. He imagined the whites bulging around the cow's dark eyes. That image—the eyes huge with fear—made him sick; he choked back a sour taste that started up in the back of his throat.

Then he watched the black wolf dash under the cow's belly and between its front legs to grab its throat. The cow tried to trample the wolf, but could do no more than straddle it. Blood gushed from its neck. The cow collapsed on top of the wolf and still the wolf held on with its fangs. In another few seconds the cow's head dropped forward and it rolled to one side, dead.

The rest of the herd headed straight for the spot where John stood. The animals were not in a full gallop, but trotting, pressed in a tight squeeze. The clattering of antlers now added to the clicking of feet, the snorts and grunts, the dull rumbling of hooves. Nika moved back near the cart, squatted near the lead dog, and grabbed its collar with both hands, holding tightly. Yute wanted to roll the videotape, but he froze, his eyes fixed on the wolves as they ripped into their kill.

John held the spear-thrower behind his right shoulder, hook up, and laid a spear on it so that its tail end butted against the hook, the spear tip pointing forward and up. The river of caribou flowed in front of him now, spooked by the wolves into a narrow corridor between the people and the wall of ice. A large bull moved near. John hefted the spear-thrower, took three running steps, planted, and heaved his arm forward; at the last split second of its arc he snapped the throwing rod ahead with his wrist, hurling the spear with great force.

The flint blade sliced deep into the bull, behind and beneath the shoulder blade, cleaving its heart. It bellowed and leapt once, kicking out its hind legs. It was dead as it crashed to the ground. The other caribou stepped around it, not stampeding, not pausing. Nika was shouting rapidly in Caiyuh, whooping and hollering. But Yute was preoccupied with the wolf pack and had missed John's kill; his camera was not switched on.

In another few minutes the herd of two hundred or so animals had moved onward to the east and disappeared behind a finger of glacier. Nika stuffed her hair down the back of her collar as she walked to join her father. They squatted beside the carcass and began carving up slabs of meat with replicas of paleolithic flint blades, provided by Yute. Nika worked nearly as fast as John.

"Cuts good," she said to him. "Sharp as steel."

His eyes smiled. "You mean the Long-Ago People weren't dummies?"

Yute filmed them, using the tripod because his hands were shaking. He kept swiveling his head to keep an eye on the feeding wolves, less than a quarter mile away.

"Some of the young ones among our people don't know how to do this," John said as his blade flicked through the bloody flesh, separating muscle from skin, tendon, and bone. "They don't even want to learn no more." He paused and jabbed the bloody flint at Yute's camera, smiling with big white teeth. "But not my son who lives in the city. He wants to know all about it." He puffed a loose strand of hair from his face and went back to work. "Tell me, Yute, do you plan to hunt many caribou in Seattle?"

Nika looked down and bit her lip. Her hands were slick with blood; she wiped her sweaty brow with a forearm. A warm, pungent smell clung to the air. She finished her cuts along the bull's legs and tugged the hide off in one large sheet. She spread it shaggy side down on the matted moss, knelt on it, and began scraping off the thin layer of shiny fat with a semicircular flint scraper grasped with both hands.

"My mother used to make our winter clothing with caribou skins," John said. "Parkas, pants, mittens, socks.

Boots too; the leg skin is good for making soft boots. And tents. Sled seats. I forgot some of that. Even I forget our ways."

He cut out a dense blob of fat from the bull's rump. With his teeth he tore off a large mouthful, leaving a grease mark on his chin. Then he held up a glistening wedge, tinged pink with blood, offering it to Yute.

Yute shook his head.

"You liked it when you were a little boy and I brought it home to you," John said.

"I'm no longer a little boy, Father."

John cut out the bull's kidneys, the size of large baking potatoes, and handed them to Nika, who walked a few yards toward the wolves. She held the purplish organs in the air above her head and whistled piercingly through her teeth.

"Tlingaluk!" she shouted. "Tlingaluk! Hey! Hey!"

The black wolf looked up.

"Tlingaluk!" She offered the kidneys.

The wolf put its head near the ground and began trotting toward her.

Yute sucked in his breath and shot a glance to John, who had his back to the encounter. Nika crouched and the black wolf closed in, almost upon her. Blood hammered in Yute's head. He grabbed the pistol and braced his shooting hand, aimed and tracked the wolf along the barrel, held his breath, and squeezed the trigger.

The bang made the others jump. The wolf jolted and sat down hard. Nika screamed. The wolf hopped up and fled, wincing loudly, its tail tucked between its legs, dragging a bloody hind limb. The pack scattered, scrambling toward the far edge of the glacier, from where they first appeared. Nika stood up, calling out to the wolf, then bolted after him; her long hair came untucked and flapped on her shoulders as she ran.

John stood dazed with his mouth hanging open. Then he stormed over to Yute, yanked the pistol out of his hand, and slung it away. "Are you so blind?" he demanded. "Why did you do that?"

Yute just shook his head. "I'm . . . I don't know," he stammered at last. "I thought she was in danger."

John stamped the ground. "That wolf was maybe going to lick her face. We give the pack leader the best—the kidneys, the back fat—in thanks. We've hunted with the help of the wolves for longer than anyone can remember—for generations."

"Father . . . I'm sorry." Yute could barely talk past the lump in his throat. "I'm terribly sorry."

John sighed heavily. He looked up and Nika was nearly out of sight around the edge of the glacier.

"Maybe she'll tell her wolf the man who shot him is a Caiyuh—a good man—but he don't know how we live here." He blew out slowly through pursed lips. "I have to go after her. She's strong, but the tundra is stronger."

John took a hatchet and two wool blankets from the dogcart. With his hunting knife he hacked off slabs of white backfat and red muscle and wrapped them in squares of caribou hide. He set the bundles in the center of the blankets and tied their corners together to form a knapsack that he hung from his shoulders as he stood.

Yute stood rooted in the same spot, running his hand through his close-cropped hair again and again. His father walked over to him, laid his callused hands on Yute's shoulders, and looked up into his eyes.

"It wasn't your fault," he said. "It was mine. I wanted to show you our way of hunting instead of explaining it all first, like your books do. I should have told you about the wolves."

Yute could only nod. If he tried to speak he might weep, and he did not want that to happen.

"She calls him Tlingaluk—you remember that word?"

Yute shook his head.

"It means 'Thundercloud,' " John said, and faintly smiled. His hair smelled of woodsmoke. "Take the dogcart back, you can ride in it. The dogs know the way to the village, just let them go. They always trot faster on the way home. You'll be back in Swift Fork by dark. If we're not back by late afternoon . . . well . . ." He gave Yute's shoulders a strong squeeze. "Don't miss your plane, son. He only flies in and out once a month."

John turned away quickly, walked to the dogcart, and began untangling the leather traces.

Yute swallowed. "Tell Nika . . ." he started, but his voice cracked.

"I'll tell her you love her," John said, without looking back. "She'd be more blind than you if she didn't see that already." He turned the dogs and cart toward the village.

Yute repacked and loaded his gear. Then he climbed onto the back of the cart and sat down, straddling the camera and equipment cases. John yelled, and the dogs moved out briskly.

Yute glanced back.

John set out at a jogger's pace in Nika's direction, following the dashes of blood on the moss and flowers.

2

THE DOGS SEEMED glad to be heading home and tugged eagerly at their traces, padding along at a steady trot. They sloshed through a shallow puddle and icy water splashed Yute's bare legs. He hardly flinched. The telephoto lens case slid off the stack and banged his shin, and he grabbed it without looking and set it aside.

Kreeee-ah! A long-tailed jaeger screeched overhead. *Kreeee-ah!* It beat its broad gray wings to hover for an instant, then tucked and dove and snatched a lemming in front of the dogcart and flapped away with the furry rodent jerking in its talons.

The raw power of the vision snapped Yute out of his reverie.

How do I see that violence as beautiful—the feast of nature—but when a wolf kills a caribou, I almost spill my guts with fright?

A grasshopper popped onto Yute's head and he reached to flick it off, but its hind legs caught in his short, wiry hair. He yanked it loose and tossed it, then picked out the leg it left behind. Killing the insect somehow infuriated him. He beat his fist against the dogcart and spat out a loud string of curses at the bug, the wolves, himself. Finally, he gazed out over the arctic desert and, feeling helpless, yelled with all his might.

Then he sighed and plopped his head back onto the wooden frame and peered up into the deepening blue. Long orange streaks smudged the western edge of the sky and the sun no longer lit the tundra flowers like tiny candles. Yute pulled his sweater out of the fanny pack and tugged it on over his barrel chest.

"What a fool I am," he said quietly.

A breeze rose steadily, turning cooler. The dogs did not slow their pace. The cart rolled past a pingo, a steep hillock shaped like a miniature volcano, filled not with lava, but ice. It formed when permafrost squeezed in from all sides of a silted-over lake and shoved the lake ice and earth into a hundred-foot blister.

The pursuit of knowledge carried me away from here. The pursuit of love can carry me back.

The cart rolled through a clump of cotton grass, scattering the puff balls, and Yute remembered himself as a boy dashing through the chest-tall grass and chasing the white puffs as they floated away.

I could stay for two years and study the old ways. A field study, a research sabbatical. I could probably get a grant for it. A smile began to form. *Father and sister need me now. I could devise a study to show how the CANARD mine will disrupt a traditional native society.*

He breathed deeply into his belly and let out a sigh. "The bush pilot can leave without me," he said.

A strand of firs stood out like a fleet of tall-masted ships on the rolling horizon; it marked the halfway point to the village of Swift Fork. He was now about five miles from where he shot the wolf. Yute spun his head around. He wanted to tell his father and sister he was going to stay. He wanted to know that Nika forgave him, feel her throw her arms around him. The prodigal son was coming home.

If he jumped out here and ran back, he wondered, could he catch up with them? He glanced westward. No way. The sun would set in another hour. And besides, the wolves . . .

He watched the trotting sled dogs. Wolves wouldn't come near the big dogs. There was a tarp and some blankets, he could spend the night in the dogcart at the edge of the glacier. Wait there till morning for his father and sister.

"I'm going back," Yute told himself. Then louder, to the dogs: "We're going back."

He tugged at the leather traces of the cart, trying to steer the dogs into a wide U-turn. The dogs pulled harder in the opposite direction, straightening out the path. The cart rocked as it swerved back on line.

Then he grabbed the wooden cart frame and rocked it to one side to force the dogs into a gradual turn. The dogs leaned over and jerked the cart back into a straight line. Several boxes slid off and cartwheeled on the ground.

"Come on, dammit, we dumped some gear. Turn around!"

How does he steer this? Yute stood in the rolling cart, straddled the top of the handlebar, and swung his leg over, stepping down onto the runners on the back side. Then he hopped off at a jogger's pace to keep up. He grasped the handlebar and twisted the rear of the cart to the left and held that position, to force a right turn. The dogs tugged hard to the left, nearly yanking the handlebar out of his grip; the cart whipped back to the right; careened up on two wheels, and rolled over, slinging Yute to the ground. The leader trace twisted off its mooring and the sudden give tripped the dogs, but when they jumped up, they were free of the cart. Yute scrambled to his feet and rushed to grab the loose end of the leather strap, but the dogs turned and growled, baring their fangs, and he backed away, with his hands held high. Then the lead dog took off, and all six malamutes, still linked together, raced for home.

Yute spit out a mouthful of grit and kicked at a clod of moss with his boot. Mud caked his nostrils. With handfuls of cold water he rinsed his nose, and a trickle of blood started down.

"I'm staying, do you hear?" he yelled, and spun in a half circle, facing the big orange sun. "I'll learn the skills. My father and sister will teach me."

He righted the cart and gathered up the camera cases and the tools that were strewn across the grass, restacking them on the cart. Then he folded a small canvas tarp and two woolen blankets, draped them across a broad shoulder, and rested a spade and an ice ax on top.

He wiped his bloody nose on a wet wool sleeve. He knew he had to make it back to the glacier before nightfall so he could see to build a shelter.

He broke into a jog and soon perspired in spite of the dropping temperature. Even if he missed them, he figured, he could make it back to Swift Fork blindfolded. That was no problem. Surviving the night without freezing was a minor problem. Tundra is like desert, the wind chill makes all the difference. The temperature probably wouldn't drop much lower than it was now. But with the wind picking up, the wind chill could kill him.

He planned to dig an ice cave when he got to the glacier, just large enough to squeeze into. He'd be out of the wind, and his body heat would do the rest. *I may not be toasty, but I'll certainly live if I hurry up and get there in time to dig while I can see what I'm doing.* No moon tonight. It was going to be as dark as the inside of a tomb.

The sky had faded to dusk behind the foothills, and Venus twinkled above the glacier, when he arrived. Yute chose a lip of ice that met the ground at the base of a foothill; by digging straight back he could carve out an ice cave with an earthen floor. In the deepening gloom he chipped and shoveled until he could barely make out the deeper blackness of the cave opening. The wind, now gusting, whistled across the cave mouth. Yute crawled in, spreading out the tarpaulin before him on the hard, cold soil. He wrapped both blankets around himself like a cocoon, trying to avoid the icy walls. A piece of debris prodded at his back, but he was much too exhausted to care. In the next minute he was asleep.

At dawn Yute squirmed half awake, shivering.

"Something powerful will happen," he muttered between chattering teeth. He had hoped that meant something more intellectually stimulating than a battle with pneumonia.

He rose on one arm and twisted around. *Where's that damn root that's been jabbing me all night?* He groped under the tarp and his hand touched something instantly recognizable.

A human hand.

His breath caught and he drew back his hand and stared at his own fingers, as if they had gone mad, independent of the rest of him. Slowly, he felt again for the object. A soft hand with icy fingers seemed to reach out for his.

He yelped and jerked away, banging his head on the ceiling. Then he laughed at his involuntary recoil. His eyes grew wide in the dim light and he began to tremble inside.

"Something powerful," he whispered, and flung the tarp aside.

A slender hand poked through the frozen dirt.

For a long moment Yute only stared, panting softly while his heart drummed in his chest. Then he shot backward, feet first out of the cave, and grabbed the ice ax.

He bent over close to the earth, pecking gently with the ax, chipping away flakes of permafrost. In a moment he saw a scalp, with lots of hair. Last night's blind shoveling had uncovered and broken open the edge of a lid made of thatched willow sticks. Beneath the lid he could make out the rim of a rock-lined circular pit. The hand protruded from the space; the flesh was intact and did not even appear to be shriveled or mummified.

Yute sweated in the chilly air. Goose bumps stood out on his neck and arms as he reached gingerly to touch the hand again. The flesh felt ice cold, but pliant, not stiff. The fingers flexed easily.

"How can this be?" His face wore a grimace of disbelief. Somehow the tissues were not frozen rock hard. The vessels of the hand were filled with cold blood, thick as sludge—but liquid, not frozen. In the dark the spade had nicked the edge of the palm and a thin smear of dried blood covered the wound.

But how could anything be in those veins but dust and frost?

Yute gulped and the feeling of awe swelled in him like a wave. He backed out and grabbed the spade. Puffs of vapor shot from his mouth as he stabbed the spade into the ice to enlarge the cave. The sun climbed higher and the day turned bright. Yute worked carefully, but with high energy, and in just under an hour the cave was roomier, with a taller ceiling, wider sides, and twice the depth. Near the rear wall the burial pit was now completely exposed.

He kneeled in front and hesitated, then delicately removed the thatched grave cover.

Slanted sunlight fell upon a young woman's face, angled slightly upward, gazing directly at her discoverer. The light illuminated her dark green eyes.

Yute sucked in his breath. He didn't move or think until he remembered to breathe.

"Behold, woman," he said. "The light of the next world."

The body, dressed in a shaggy sheephide tunic, sat in a knees-to-chest position; its right elbow was braced on its right knee so that the hand was upraised in a gesture of eternal farewell, or, perhaps, greeting. Thick dark hair, woven into many fine braids, spilled over her shoulders and snaked across her bosom. Her facial features were robust: big eyes, broad cheeks, a large nose and full mouth, and a heavy jaw. From these and more subtle clues he knew she was a Neanderthal.

Yute's eyes brimmed with tears. No scientist had laid eyes upon a Neanderthal in the flesh before this crystalline moment.

"You're absolutely beautiful," he said. "Most of my life I've been waiting for this . . . for you."

He glanced up to the horizon. No one to be seen for miles. The sun glinted off the glacial ice. *How long ago did she live and roam this arctic plain here with her tribe?*

"Excuse me, sirs"—Yute's voice took on a formal tone—"Dr. Fischer, Dr. Whitcombe, other learned fellows of the academy; I recall that you gentlemen insisted Neanderthals died out in Eurasia and the Middle East and never crossed Beringia into the New World. Well, it is my great pleasure to introduce you to a Neanderthal woman who is truly a First American."

He looked at her staring green eyes and gave her a name. "Tundra Woman," he said, "you are going to crown my career."

Okay, first things first. I've got to recruit some field

consultants so I don't miss a jot of data from this site. A surveyor, geologist, photographer, preparator, a pollen whiz . . . let's see—Lynn Dreyfus on the pollen studies; need a soil expert, probably Kelly . . . get a crew of grad students on site to sift the earth . . .

He smiled hugely. This was perfect. He wouldn't be able to stay in Swift Fork, he'd need to work mostly from his lab near Seattle, but he could visit the project site regularly, see Nika and his father, and maybe still help out against CANARD.

In a moment his smile faded. "Get real," he told himself. He wouldn't have time for anything else for years to come. This Neanderthal was going to be his life's work, through to the end.

He gently touched her cheek with his fingertips. The cold, soft skin was covered with fine blond peach-fuzz. He shook his head slowly, feeling an odd familiarity, a sense of recognition, like déjà vu. He searched his memory. Had he seen an artist's rendering of a Neanderthal in some textbook or diorama that matched her features? No chance of that. Such conceptions fell far short of the look of high intelligence that was plain even in the woman's vacant gaze. It was as he argued in his papers—evolutionists had grossly underrated her race. But none of the old-school paleoanthropologists agreed with him, he was not one of their club.

His mouth tightened and a decision came to him all at once. He would not call in a team of consultants. He would handle the initial research himself, back in Seattle. Later, the consultants could come and do the fine sifting and add a few pebbles to the mountain of knowledge that he would obtain. But that mountain was his to build, even if it took years. Then he would stand atop it and from on high he would call the world of anthropology to order and make his announcements about Tundra Woman.

He made a low whistle. "What an impact you're going to make!"

Yute crouched near the cave door and swung upward again and again with the ax, chopping deep seams into the ice of the ceiling, until it weakened and sagged. Then he walloped the ceiling with the broadside of the ax head, once, twice, and it cracked with a loud boom and collapsed. He dove out the door as it thudded behind him. The burial pit was sealed under a half ton of white.

With the Neanderthal woman packed in shovelfuls of crushed ice and wrapped in the wool blankets, he dragged the body along the ground, sliding on the tarp. He strode as fast as he could, never slowing. He planned to push the dogcart to the village and catch the bush plane to Fairbanks, then hire another private plane to Seattle. In an hour and a half he reached the cart. He unzipped the body bag and felt that it was still frigid inside from the dry ice in its lining. He carefully slid the body into the white vinyl bag and zipped it shut.

Then Yute sagged onto the damp moss, breathing hard, his back against the cart, his sweaty head drooped between upright knees. And, to his surprise, he began to cry softly, without tears. Choosing to stay with Nika and his father had been a happy moment. But in all his career he never dreamed he would find a Neanderthal in the flesh.

He strained his eyes in the direction of Denali.

3

Tlingaluk's bloody trail climbed into the wooded hills and Nika followed at a run, sidestepping and leaping fallen timber from the head-high evergreens. Finally, she slowed to a walk and had crossed half a dozen hills when she glimpsed a gray wolf that faced her from the crest of the next rise, then disappeared. A scout. That meant the pack was gathered nearby; it had reached the boundary of its territory.

Sweat ran in rivulets down her chest and back, dampening her flannel shirt. She unbuttoned it and took it off as she jogged down the steep slope, tying the sleeves around her hips from behind. Cool mountain air flowed over her bare torso. Her small breasts bounced with each step and sweat drops flew. She swept away long strands of wet hair that clung to her face, gathered her mane together at the back of her head, and tied it in a long ponytail. A clear stream meandered at the base of the hill. She waded in up to her knees, bent down, and scooped the icy water over her head, gasping.

As she looked up she saw the same scout wolf at the top of the next hill. Now she could see he had a black face. She spoke to him in Caiyuh: "Black Face Brother. I'm worried about my friend, your chief, Tlingaluk. How badly is he hurt? Let me come to him to see if I can help."

The wolf turned and was gone. It returned with two others as she was walking up the hill. "Your chief knows me and my father. I played with him when we were both cubs. Let me come to you." The first wolf left. The two others put their heads low, watching her, not blinking. She approached slowly with her arms held near her sides, palms outward. When she reached the spot where they stood, they backed down the hill, then spun and fled, looking over their shoulders.

A lump formed in her throat. *They're scared of me now.*

"Tlingaluk!" she called. "Remember your sister. I'm coming to help you. Hear my heart, and don't be afraid."

Ferocious snarling erupted from beyond a thicket of dwarf dogwoods to her left, and a wolf yelped in pain. She broke into a run and came upon the wolf pack circled around a fighting pair. An all-black wolf was pinned and squirming beneath a big gray wolf that tried to lock its jaws around his throat. She screamed, "Tlingaluk!"

and moved closer, but several gray wolves blocked her way, growling deeply, fangs bared. Her eyes darted around frantically; she spotted a dead limb on the ground and grabbed it up, but more wolves had joined the blockade.

Tlingaluk yelped and winced. She brandished the club above her head and stepped forward.

"*Stop!*" shouted her father, from behind. "Stay right where you are. This is not your tribe."

She now saw that the wolf on top was Black Face. He clutched Tlingaluk's throat in his fangs and shook his head violently, ripping a ragged hole in the soft flesh, spraying blood. Tlingaluk bucked and twisted till he broke free. He scrambled to his feet and faced the big gray wolf, who still clenched a wad of black fur in his red teeth. Then Tlingaluk wobbled and sank back on his wounded leg. He looked straight past Black Face and caught Nika's eyes for an instant. Then he tossed his head back to howl, but only a gargled sound came out. He shuddered and collapsed. Black Face stood over Tlingaluk for a moment, his whole body stiff and his tail held erect.

The wolves that had stood in Nika's way ran over to the new pack leader and clustered around him with their tails tucked between their legs, licking his muzzle and ears. Nika's father came up beside her and put his arm around her bare shoulders. She turned toward him and buried her face in his damp shirt. "Daughter, don't cry," he said in their native tongue, stroking her hair. "The black wolf chose to die."

She looked up into his face and shook her head, not understanding.

"When wolves fight to see who's boss, the loser only has to roll onto his back and give up. The winner won't kill the other wolf unless he refuses to give up. You know that."

"Then why didn't he give up?"

"His leg was shattered. He wasn't going to be any use to the pack as a cripple."

"So Black Face attacked him?"

"Probably the other way around. Tlingaluk was a great chief. He chose the best wolf and picked a fight with him, knowing he was bound to lose, and the other wolf would be the new chief."

The pack milled around Black Face, who kept his eyes fixed on the two Indians. John removed his blanket sack slowly. Then he tossed a large slab of back fat at the feet of the new pack leader. Black Face jumped back, startled, and ran off a few yards, the other wolves following.

"Black Face Brother," John said softly, "today we have lost your trust. Now is not the time to win it back. But over the seasons, let us bring such gifts to your people, that in time we might earn your trust again, as it has been for generations between us."

The big wolf crept forward nervously, sniffing the air, not taking his eyes off John and Nika. He grabbed the caribou fat and retreated with it to a safe distance, gulping it in one blob without chewing—gagging and gulping again. When he was finished he suddenly turned and trotted away. Six wolves followed on his heels and the pack vanished over the next ridge. In a moment Black Face reappeared at the crest, checked on the two people, then headed off again.

Nika started toward the body of Tlingaluk, but her father caught her arm. "We have a long journey ahead of us, and so does he."

They turned around and walked back up the hill in silence.

After an hour's trek they stood on top of a knob with the vast flatness of the tundra spread below. Behind them the sun was dipping to the distant mountains, turning the jagged peaks into glowing gold. Her father pointed to a deep cleft at the foot of two hills. "There's a stream there. That's where we'll camp tonight." Without talking they built a lean-to with pine and spruce boughs propped between trees. John spread the blankets on the ground beneath the shelter. Then they gathered firewood and he chopped out the core of an old pine stump, encrusted with yellow sap. Nika built a large cone of kindling and small sticks around the pinewood. John unsheathed his hunting knife and scraped it across a flint, shooting white sparks onto the hardened sap. It ignited with a loud *whoosh*. He set a dead limb on the blaze as the hills all around grew dark and cool. Nika rinsed their sweat-soaked shirts in the stream and spread them on pine stakes jammed in the ground near the fire.

They sat side by side, staring into the flames. The air smelled sweet, of spruce needles and pine smoke. John tended two hunks of caribou meat on a green wood spit and when it began to sizzle they ate it with their hands, along with the raw, slippery fat, and they passed a canteen of spring water between them. The burning logs popped and hissed. Sparks raced up and vanished toward the river of stars that arched over the hollow. Fat

Snow Fox crept partway around the Tent Pole star before either of them spoke.

"Father," Nika began, looking straight ahead into the fire, "why was Yute so cruel?"

"It wasn't on purpose. He was afraid. He thought your wolf was going to attack you."

"But I was handing him a gift. Couldn't he see that?"

"Not through his fear."

"Then he's stupid."

"Not stupid—but scared."

"I hate him."

"Hate is like fear, Nika. It makes you blind."

"Tlingaluk was a great wolf."

"Love can blind you too. You went running off without taking food, a hide for shelter. No hatchet. No matches or flint. Where were you going to spend the night?"

She thought for a second. "Dig an ice cave?"

"With what? Your teeth? You didn't even take your knife. Your clothes were soaked with sweat, they wouldn't have kept you warm tonight."

She looked down and mumbled, "I would have been all right."

"Why you, Nika, and not others? Others have died out here without food and shelter and a fire. In the summer."

She knew he was right. She looked up and the yellow-orange firelight danced and flickered on his strong face. Wrinkles etched his forehead and crackled at the corners of his black eyes, but his dark skin was rubbed smooth at the cheekbones like river stones. She leaned over and threw her arms around his neck.

"Father, thank you for coming after me."

He held her for a long moment, his chin resting on the top of her head, rocking gently. "Daughter," he said, hoarsely, "I would crawl into a den of grizzlies after you."

"And would you pause first to look for your hatchet and your knife?"

"No. I would jump in with no clothes on, just like you," he said with a laugh. "Come on, wise one, let's see if our shirts are dry."

The shirts were stiff, but dry and hot. The night had turned cool and she shuddered with pleasure as the flannel hugged her skin. High above the dark outline of the hollow the sky erupted with glowing light. Curtains and ribbons of red, green, and violet waved and shimmered in the clear air.

When the fire had burned to embers, Nika gently said, "I don't hate Yute. I miss him already."

John nodded with his whole torso in the Caiyuh gesture of deep agreement. He took her hand in his and they stared into the embers as they cooled and darkened. Then the two wrapped themselves up in blankets under the lean-to and snuggled together for warmth. A snowy owl hooted nearby. Nika closed her eyes, remembering a little wolf cub, a fluffy ball of the softest black fur. She was asleep before the third round of hoots.

The next morning the caribou steaks were cooked and the sun had burned off the fog before her father woke her. After breakfast they hiked down the hill onto the tundra and headed toward the glacier. They waded across a clear-running stream and John pointed out the splayed tracks of a lynx in the muddy bank; bloody tufts of brownish-gray fur were all that remained of its meal, a snowshoe hare. In another spot a small mammal, maybe a marmot or a fox, had urinated; and the freshly shredded bark on dwarf willow branches showed where a moose had nibbled within the past day.

The two paused in a patch of richly laden blueberry shrubs, and bundled up a dozen handfuls of the fruit to eat later.

A rich, damp smell of mud, marsh grasses, and bird guano reached them on a cool breeze. They soon came to a large pond ringed by foot-deep drifts of molted feathers and filled with convoys of young swans, gliding after their mothers. More of the graceful birds circled overhead, calling in muffled, musical whistles. Nika knew they would be flocking south within weeks, as soon as the growing birds were strong enough.

"Father, tell me about your hunting trips with Grandfather."

"Again?"

She nodded.

"You've heard the stories fifty times by now."

"I still like to listen."

He smiled. "Early each fall, after the swans flew south, but before the first keeps-on-the-ground snow, me and my father and my brothers and Billy Broke-Tooth and Jack Anvik and a dozen other men would start on a long hunting trip, up through the hills toward where the Tanana River breaks off into the Kuskokwim."

"And you were youngest."

"I was twelve the first time they said I could go. I got so excited, I think I peed on myself."

Nika laughed. "You always say that."

"You always laugh. . . . We'd sometimes run into a few other bands of hunters—Athapaskans from Telida and Tonzona, or sometimes Inupaks from farther west. Everybody had so many dogs. And the dogs all wore packs until the first snows came and the creeks froze up and the ground smoothed over. Then we built sleds and the dogs tugged those up the hills into the mountains as we followed the caribou and moose and mountain sheep. And everybody always tried to get as many as my father, because he was the best hunter who ever lived, I think.

"We camped in the most beautiful places. And by the time we got to the Tanana, it would be thawing and big chunks of ice would burst loose with a crack and a bang and it would be the mightiest thing you ever saw—fast and cold and white. Like it was alive. And branching off, the Kuskokwim—not much tamer. And we'd sew seven or eight moose hides together with dried sinews and stretch them across a boat frame made out of poplars and willows. Then we'd seal the hides with pine pitch. And all fifteen of us would wedge into one of those big boats with a dozen dogs and all our bows and spears and mounds of frozen meat. And we'd shove off down the rapids whooping and hollering like a bunch of drunks—"

"—But you didn't have no alcohol."

"—Just the river made you wild like that. And it would carry us, wet and near as frozen as our meat, all the way back to the foothills. And we'd walk home from there."

"And Grandmother and all the villagers would run out to greet you."

"We'd sing a noisy hunting song and they'd all come running out, singing of homecoming. It felt so good to be home again, bringing meat to all the families."

"I would give anything to do that."

He sighed. "Well. Those days . . . Now they've got hunting and rafting outfitters, and everybody's got rifles with scopes, snowmobiles, motorboats . . . video cameras . . . And what do you think will happen to our land if CANARD is allowed to mine it?"

"That's why I like to hear your stories of the old ways."

"I know. But I always feel a sadness after I tell them."

They arrived at the glacier. John was the first to spot the caved-in ice shelter. He ran ahead and Nika followed. She found him counting sets of bootprints that went in and out of the cave several times.

Her eyes widened. "Yute?"

He shook his head. "He's not in there—the footprints lead out as often as they lead in." He grabbed up the ice ax lying near the entrance and swung it with great force. "Just pray I'm right."

Nika grabbed the shovel. "Let me help."

"Stay back," he puffed, hacking out big chunks of ice. "Give me room to work fast."

Nika's gut clenched. She had seen a man from her village who fell down drunk one winter night and froze solid on the front steps of his cabin; ice caked his nostrils and his eyes were white with frost. She chewed her lip, and kept her eyes down on the clods of ice that scattered near her feet.

In a few minutes John had chopped out a four-foot-deep tunnel in the collapsed ice. He stopped and rested on his pick handle, breathing heavily.

Nika was afraid to look up. "Tell me, Father."

"It's okay, nobody in there." He stepped back and draped an arm around her shoulders. His muscles felt warm beneath his shirt.

"What do you think happened?" she asked.

"Not sure." He stepped over to the tunnel and squatted to peer inside. "I've never seen an ice cave fall before. I've seen snow caves come down. Snow is tricky. But ice . . ." He turned a chunk over in his hands. "Something's not right. I sent Yute on his way to the village, with the dogs. Why did he circle back on foot?"

John studied the footprints again, this time on his hands and knees.

"Aiyoo! Look over here," he said, pointing to a bed of ice flakes. "Who is this?"

They both ran their palms over the subtle indentation left by a small body that Yute had laid flat on its back. Slender and muscular. Nika thought the outline of the hips traced a feminine curve.

"A woman?" she asked.

He nodded with a frown.

"Out here?"

He looked back toward the tunnel. "Let's see if the cave hides anything more."

He shoveled collapsed ice out of the cave and tunneled along the bare ground. Then he stopped and glanced back at Nika; his jaw had dropped.

"How did he know where to look?" he said.

"What, Father?" Nika crawled in behind him.

"He found another of the Long-Ago People. But I have no idea how he knew to dig right here."

She beamed. "Wa Denali! He was hoping so much. . . ."

"Yes, but *how*? Half the time he's lost out here—can't tell an ice fog from a badger fart."

Nika laughed, feeling baffled, but happy for her brother. "Think how lost we'd be in his city."

The furrows melted from John's brow and he broke into a big grin. "Yute is a great hunter, after all—he tracked his game through solid ice."

"Aiyoo!" Nika shouted, and belted out a high-pitched, rapid yodeling. John clapped a steady beat and ice dust flew from his forearms. The two danced, forward and back, with shuffling steps, as John yelled the hunting song from his boyhood.

Late afternoon sunlight angled into the ice cave. John and Nika finished their snack of blueberries and stood to go. A spear of light pierced the shadow in the burial pit and glinted from an object. They both saw it.

"Go look," he said, but she was already halfway into the cave, crawling on all fours. The shiny thing was round, flat, and smooth, wedged between rocks near the rim.

"It's heavy," she said, squinting as she stepped into the brightness. She held out a metal disk the diameter of a duck egg, strung on a braided leather thong. In the sun's rays it gleamed.

"O, Raven-Trickster," John said in a low voice, "is this another of your bad jokes?"

"Gold" was all that Nika could manage.

John glanced over both shoulders. "We got to keep this secret, Nika. All we need is for CANARD to find out about it. They'll have mines pocking this land from mountain to sea."

The disk appeared to be some kind of amulet, hammered from solid gold. Deep scratches engraved the surface. The etching resembled the grotesque faces found in Eskimo demon masks: lopsided eye sockets, a bent nose, and a toothy mouth downturned in a grimace; a frown wrinkled the knobby forehead.

"A skull?" Nika wondered.

The mouth was filled with rat-sharp teeth, the nose cavity was empty, but in each eye socket were tiny figures. In the larger socket on the right were stick figures of people—adults and children, if proportion meant anything to the artist. Below the stick people she recognized two wolves, or maybe big dogs. The smaller, left socket, contained no people, but two bighorn sheep, two goats, two musk oxen, and a pair of animals that looked to her like shaggy elephants.

"I don't get it."

"Must have something to do with the spirit world," John said. "Two of each animal to accompany the dead on their journey, in order to breed herds in the next world."

"But do you see the elephants?"

"Alufints?"

"There," she said, pointing. "Those two are elephants. They're huge animals with big long noses like a parka sleeve."

He raised his eyebrows.

"I've seen pictures of them in schoolbooks," she insisted. "Bull elephants are five times as big as walruses, with tusks five times as long."

He whistled low. "Grandmother must feed a lot of people with such creatures. But *those* are heaps of frozen meat, draped with sheepskins."

"Oh." She chuckled. Her father had never been to school, but he was right about the piles of meat. Elephants lived only in hot jungles, like Florida.

She took the amulet from his hand and admired it, turning it over. "Look, Father." The opposite side was etched with a V-shaped flight of swans, or maybe geese or ducks. The artwork intrigued her. "I don't think an everyday sort of person wore this."

"Do you like it?"

She nodded. He took it and placed the leather thong around her neck. The gold disk glowed against her cinnamon skin and the waterbirds appeared to fly straight up.

"Wear it for now," he said. "But keep it always hidden when we get back."

She looked down and slid her fingers over its polished surface. "A medicine woman wore this."

"Ah—it whispers to you?"

She yanked her hand from the amulet and shook her head.

"No need to feel shy when the spirits speak," he

said. "It's an honor. If they think you're alert enough to talk to, then accept it and listen."

She gulped.

"My mother talked with the spirits often," he said. "Go ahead. I'm right here."

She closed her eyes and took a deep breath, cupping the amulet over her heart. Almost immediately she said, "She was a kind of chief of the Long-Agos, the First People." After a while she added, "That's it. That's all I feel. The medicine woman and her people . . ." She opened her eyes. "It's strange. I don't see them, but I feel them. It's almost as if . . ." She closed her eyes again.

"Just say it."

"Well, I can't picture them good, but it's almost . . . I can *smell* them. Like when you smell snow coming and it reminds you of winters past, or like smelling Mother's comb makes me sad. There's a certain smell—a people smell—and it makes me feel . . . it makes me almost remember. Like I knew them . . . I almost remember, but I don't." She looked at him. "They were different from us."

He nodded. "Now Yute will take her back to Seattle with him, like a young husband with his new wife. I know him. I know how jealous he'll be of her. He'll keep her hidden, all to himself, or try to. Then one day, years from now, they'll have many children."

"Children?"

He chuckled, without humor. "Papers and books. My grandchildren will be the papers and books that come from the marriage of my son and that ancient corpse."

The setting sun bathed the foothills and distant snowy peaks in molten copper. John hefted the ice ax and shovel and balanced them on his shoulders.

"Are you rested enough to walk back tonight?" he asked.

She nodded. "Let me carry a tool, Father."

He handed her the shovel and they started homeward.

Fat Snow Fox was rising out of his den and climbing into the night sky when an insight flashed into Nika's mind. "Father, the picture on this charm is not a skull."

"What then?"

"It's a map."

"Aiyoo!"

"Those knobs on the forehead are the foothills. The big eyes are caverns. The people and animals are inside caverns under the hills. The mouth of the caverns is toothy—like Wolverine Cave—sharp rocks hanging from the ceiling and rising from the floor."

"Where?"

She shook her head.

"Near where Yute found the woman?"

"I don't know. But I feel the Long-Ago People and their animals are still there, waiting."

"Dead, you mean."

"I know . . . for thousands of years. But, somehow . . ."

"For what do their spirits wait?"

Their boots swished through knee-high grass and Nika inhaled the green fragrance of trampled weeds and flowers, and the cool, dewy air, and the earthy aroma of her own warm skin. And she sensed her father walking alongside, a different breath of sweat and pine smoke. She gazed up into the Great Sky River and sniffed deeply, as if to smell the stars.

"They wait for spring," she said at last, and touched her fingertips to the amulet and its flock of waterbirds, returning home. "When they will be re-born."

4

AT 3:00 A.M., lights shone in the laboratory of the Center for Early Human Research at Pacific College, in Deer Park, a Seattle suburb. Yute Nahadeh leaned over a stainless-steel countertop, typing rapid commands on a computer keyboard. His short black hair fluffed in the cold air pouring from the vent in the acoustical tile ceiling. Dark bags hung under his brown eyes and four days' growth of whiskers roughened his chin. Above the left pocket of his white lab coat, his name stood out in embroidered red letters.

A chair was at his knees, but he did not take time to sit. He stared at the screen for a moment, arms folded across his chest, one thumb clicking the button on a ballpoint pen in and out as fast as it would go. Then he strode away impatiently but was back in a few minutes, his eyes glued again to the screen.

Nearby on the wall hung a framed Latin inscription: *Homo sum: humani nil a me alienum puto.* A typewritten English translation was taped to the calligraphy, because Yute tired of telling visitors what it meant: "I am a man; I regard nothing that concerns man as foreign to my interests."

Behind him, in a windowless room that reeked faintly of Lysol, a row of skeletons stood in chrome frames along a green tile wall. The first of the skeletons was small and chimpanzeelike, with long arm bones and short, bowed legs. Next were several larger, robust skeletons, humanlike, but with sloping skulls and large brow ridges. Second from the end was a heavy-boned, but otherwise modern-looking, human skeleton; it gripped a thrusting spear in its large hand. At the end of the line stood a slightly taller, more frail human skeleton; its cranium was adorned with a mortar and tassel from Pacific College, purple and gold; it clutched a flint ax in a skeletal hand upraised against its neighbor, perpetually set to bash his skull.

A rustling, scritching noise came from a covered glass terrarium that sat on a counter against the far wall. Inside, an irregular mound was draped with what looked like a black satin cloth. Yute crossed the lab and lifted the hinged glass lid. The rustling became louder and the cloth squirmed—hundreds of shiny beetles devouring the last bits of flesh on a Madagascar lemur. He brushed them away with a wire test-tube brush, unveiling a nearly clean primate skeleton the size of a tomcat.

One more day. He closed the lid.

At the computer the amber cursor blinked on a screen that contained a blank grid. He leaned against the back of the chair and let out a long sigh. He took a swig of coffee, then spit the cold, bitter mouthful back into the mug.

"Hurry up!" he barked at the computer.

In a few more minutes, if time would just continue to ooze forward, he was, perhaps, about to solve the riddle of how Tundra Woman had been preserved for thousands of years in her mind-boggling state of freshness.

Temperatures at that latitude should deep-freeze a human body, he knew. And because water expands as it turns to ice, freezing ruins tissues by wrecking the structures inside the cells or bursting cell walls. That is what had happened to Tundra Man. The hard freeze had kept his flesh from rotting, but on a microscopic level his cells were a tangle of debris. Not so with Tundra Woman; her tissues had never frozen. A dozen biopsies showed that her organs were so intact, they might still function if transplanted into a living patient.

An educated hunch led Yute to contact a biochemist at the Department of Agriculture, who researched ways to prevent crops from freezing. The biochemist sent Yute a computer database of proteins called supercooling stabilizers. These specialized organic proteins, found in arctic fish, plants, and insects, worked as a natural antifreeze, allowing tissues to be supercooled to subzero temperatures without freezing. The aggies were having great success injecting these stabilizers into citrus plants and other crops, to prevent freeze damage. Yute waited three endless weeks to receive the database, and had spent the past four days—with only a couple of hours' sleep—checking unusual blood proteins found in Tundra Woman against the models in the database. It was an excruciatingly slow process of analysis, and so far he had checked only six proteins, with no match.

Finally, bright blue dots began to appear across the red grid on the screen. He leaned forward. *Yes. Yes. What do we have?* The dots formed into a jagged graph, a two-dimensional model of a three-dimensional molecule. He examined the graph and entered a command to compare it with graphs from the database.

It matched: a glycoprotein the USDA called AFP2.

"That's it," he whispered. Tundra Woman had eaten foods that concentrated natural antifreeze throughout her tissues.

But was it deliberate? He stared at the door of the walk-in freezer where the body was stored. *How could you have known the right foods to eat?*

A sudden wave of exhaustion passed through him like a fog, blanking out his ability to concentrate. He sat down at his desk and briskly rubbed his scalp and massaged the muscles at the back of his neck. But it was no use. With the major question of the last several weeks answered, the tautness of his body and mind melted, and he could no longer fight his tiredness. He laid down his head on folded arms and fell asleep.

He dreamed of blood, running in a rivulet into a drain in the floor of a slaughterhouse; it made a steady sound, *plip-plip-plip-plip*, as it dripped to the gutter below. A caribou cow lay on its side on the concrete, its jugular slashed. In the background sides of frozen caribou meat hung in rows from sharp hooks.

Yute watched a tall man in a green surgeon's gown use a hacksaw to cut through the caribou's skull. It was not until he read the embroidered name that he recognized the man as himself in his role as professor of comparative anatomy. He looked down at his own body, clothed in the winter garb of a Caiyuh—no, not a Caiyuh—a much more primitive draping of heavy hides crudely stitched together.

A red mist sprayed the professor's gown on each return stroke, and white clouds came from his nose as he huffed. Then the scientist grasped the antlers and lifted the skullcap off like a lid, revealing a tiny golden woman, seated inside in a tight tuck, apparently dead.

Yute gasped. But the professor did not seem shocked.

"This is the little person inside the caribou's head who directed the caribou's actions," he explained. "This cow was extraordinarily intelligent, smarter than anyone could have guessed. Most other caribou only have tinier caribou inside their heads, as you would expect."

"Do we have a little person inside our heads too?" Yute asked.

"Of course," the professor answered. "How else can one be conscious and move about?"

"But who lives inside the head of the little person in our head, to direct *him*?"

"A scientific question. Let's find out."

The professor took a penknife and, bracing with his thumb, sliced in a circle around the top of the miniature woman's head. Brilliant light streamed out along the lengthening seam, glinting off the man's watch. Squinting against the brightness, he plucked off the skullcap. Light flooded the room. He clapped his hand over his eyes and peeked inside the skull through the slit of two fingers. Suddenly, his mouth gaped.

"What is it? What do you see?"

But his other self, the professor, spun around and strode briskly away, not looking back, and as he walked he hunched over until he was trotting on all fours and suddenly he was a massive dark wolf and he began to flee with his tail between his legs, and he kept running till Yute could no longer see him in the far shadows.

Yute moved closer to the light source. He reached into the little skull with his thumb and forefinger and picked up a spark of pure, intense energy. A tingling current buzzed through his hand and up his arm and spread over his body. Then he saw the spark was solid at its core, with an object the size of a pinhead. Through tightly squinted eyes he made out what he held: *a human embryo.*

He awoke from the dream with a start, staring at the metal frame of his computer. A glance at the wall clock told him he'd been asleep six hours. He unfolded from the chair stiffly, trembling inside.

Hunches and dreams, he thought. *Mendeleyev dreamed the layout of the periodic table, making it possible to predict the characteristics of elements not yet discovered. And Kekule solved the puzzle of benzene's structure —six carbon atoms linked in a ring—by dreaming of a snake swallowing its tail.*

"What if my dream means what I think it means?" he asked aloud.

Yute started the coffeemaker brewing and rushed into his office bathroom to shower with steaming water, shaving in the shower to save time.

In the closet he kept a folding cot and a couple of dozen starched white shirts, so he could work around the clock. But he had worn the last of the shirts three days in a row, so he threw on a cardigan sweater over his bare torso, and put on a fresh lab coat. He couldn't recall when he'd last eaten—day before yesterday?—and he didn't want to leave the lab now, so he retrieved half a hard, stale bagel from the trash can and, with a fresh cup of hot black coffee, forced it down. With the help of a second cup he downed twenty grams of vitamin C and a multivitamin. Then he opened a sterile surgical pack, pulled on a paper surgical cap, insulated boots and shoe covers, and a surgical mask. He scrubbed his hands and arms to the elbows and slipped on a sterile gown and gloves. Then he used a disposable sterile towel to pop the door handle of the walk-in freezer, and stepped inside. The temperature and humidity were set at levels typical of tundra winter.

He carefully removed a plastic drape from a dissection table, and the smell of disinfectant spray wafted from the table's four stainless steel planes that sloped gently toward a drain at its foot. A young woman's supine body stood out starkly golden against the polished steel. Yute had not determined if the golden skin-tone was a natural pigmentation, or a byproduct of slow oxidation during 250 centuries of refrigeration. The whole body was covered with blond downy hair, which reflected light and added to the impression that her flesh was made of burnished gold.

The five-foot-two figure was strikingly muscular and curvaceous; it reminded him of the exaggerated female physiques seen in fantasy art of jungle goddesses and Martian princesses—but with large hands and feet. He had not been surprised by her appearance of great strength; Neanderthal bones were thicker and denser by far than modern human bones, and massive skeletons exist only to support powerful musculature. He had penned in his notebook: *Given a modern diet—with cow's milk, vitamin and mineral supplements, etc.—what kind of Amazon would she have become?*

The goddess lay in ghastly disrepair, her uncapped skull a deep empty bowl, the flesh of her face and neck flayed to the bone. He had begun his dissection by removing and preserving her scalp, with its braided coiffure intact. Next he had sawed off the top of her skull at the browline and then spent nearly two months delicately teasing apart the brain, seeking its revelations about human evolution.

Her brain volume was slightly more than 1,500 cubic centimeters, or about 100 cubic centimeters larger than the average modern human brain. He had expected this, for endocasts derived from the skulls of other Neanderthals showed larger brains as well. But what he was able to see for the first time was the distribution of that three-pound world, how its structures were organized. Among other things, he found that her brain's limbic lobe—the area that processes the sense of smell and also memory and emotions—was nearly 70 percent larger than in modern humans, corresponding to a much denser matrix of olfactory nerves in her upper nasal passages.

But the biggest surprise—the one Yute predicted would most shock orthodox evolutionists—was the size of her cerebrum, the seat of advanced behavior, higher thought, and language. The life of this Neanderthal "brute" was directed by a cerebrum that was 18 percent larger than the cerebrum of a typical modern human—and this greatly puzzled Yute, because her speech centers, on the Broca's area of the frontal lobes, were clearly smaller. It seemed to him a biological dilemma: compared to people of the modern world she had more brain area devoted to self-awareness, and yet less brain area devoted to speaking.

Where does that leave her? he wondered in his notes. *With lofty thoughts and a far-reaching imagination—but no means to tell other people, or to be told their ideas? Was she forced to pantomime? Use sign language? Could such an individual, living today, be taught to read and write?*

The anatomy of her tongue and throat did answer one long-standing question in anthropology: Neanderthals had adequate equipment for speech. The shape of her vocal tract, and of the small U-shaped hyoid bone that supported the muscles of her tongue, proved that. With the slightly higher position of her larynx Tundra Woman's voice might simply have been higher pitched than usual for modern humans. Now it was her "wiring" for speech that was in question.

He dabbed her skin with an alcohol-soaked cotton swab and poked a fat hypodermic into the large vein below her collarbone. He popped a vacuum seal on a test tube and drew it one quarter full of cold, dark blood; then he wiped the puncture mark with the swab as he withdrew the needle.

Two months ago, before beginning any other studies, he had started with a broad series of blood assays, gathering data for later analysis. But there was one blood test he had not thought to perform: a pregnancy test.

Now he dashed out of the freezer with the tube of blood and quickly went through the steps of a pregnancy test. After a few minutes a dark blue circle appeared on the test matrix. He only gawked. Then it hit him like an avalanche.

Tundra Woman was with child.

He tried to short-circuit his dizzying excitement. *It's too big, it's a fetus.* If the baby had grown to a fetus, there was nothing more to be done. But if he could find an early-stage embryo in Tundra Woman and implant it in a surrogate mother— *Forget it! It's a fetus.*

Standing in the freezer beside the dissection table, Yute used his foot to roll forward an instrument stand with a set of sterilized surgical instruments, prearranged on the work tray. He held his gloved hands out in front of him. They shook. He breathed deeply and slowly to calm his nerves. But his hand still trembled as he made the first deep incision in her abdomen, just above her pubic bone. A quarter hour later his gloved hands lifted out her uterus and fallopian tubes and placed them in a stainless steel tray. The pink organ was the size and shape of a small pear, with a puffy tube curving downward from each side of its bulbous end. He redraped the body and carried the tray outside to a desk containing a videomicroscope. Inserting the lighted tip of a tiny fiber-optic lens through the cervix into the uterus, he scanned the uterine walls.

No fetus.

He blew out a loud sigh of relief. "So far so good."

Next he switched to low magnification and began to search the walls in a methodical sweep. In ten minutes he examined every square centimeter of the endometrium and did not find an embryo.

He unclenched his jaw and rubbed at his mouth. *Can this really be happening?* An embryo embedded in the uterine lining would be very difficult to remove and reimplant. But an embryo still traveling down a fallopian tube toward the womb would be ideal: it could easily be taken up in a pipette and implanted in a different womb.

He started with the left fallopian tube, inserting the lens with extreme care. Almost immediately he spotted the embryo.

He held his breath.

It was a transparent sphere the diameter of a pencil lead. Through the microscope it resembled a clump of soap bubbles, encased in a larger bubble. The bubbles were cells; he counted eight. The embryo was not muddy or fragmented. Like her other tissues it contained no ice crystals.

"Still viable," he whispered.

A goofy grin spread across his face and he shook his head in wonder. He marked the embryo's location with four arrows drawn with violet dye, then carried the uterus back into the climate-controlled freezer, lifted it from the tray, and gingerly set it back inside the abdomen.

He had no reason to believe the Neanderthal embryo would not keep in the freezer indefinitely. Even so, Yute felt a terrible urge to hurry.

5

A DRIZZLING RAIN rippled a bright green puddle in the tree-lined street. The puddle turned yellow, then red. Air brakes squeaked and huffed. In a moment the puddle turned green again and a garbage truck accelerated with a diesel growl and rumbled by, splashing the sidewalk.

Oily fumes and the sweet stench of rotting garbage wafted through the open drop slot in a Goodwill Industries collection box. Inside the tiny wooden hut Jimmy Ozette perched on a mound of clothes, scoping out the wet day.

"Pyoo-ee," he said, and let go of the metal scoop. It swung shut with a bang, cutting off the gray morning light. It was black inside now, except for cracks of light around the drop slot and the rear door.

"Hey . . ." said the girl next to him.

"Jeez, Chena, how can you read in here anyway?"

She put down the book, one of a dozen children's books that had been tossed inside the box, along with clothing and toys, though the stenciled sign on the outside said CLOTHING DONATIONS ONLY, THIS BOX.

"What time do you think it is?" she asked.

"Early still. And I'm already starved."

"I gotta go to the bathroom," she said.

"Number one?"

"Two."

"Shit."

"That's what I said."

They laughed.

"Okay. I feel like a mole in here, anyway. Let's get out."

They stepped over the scooped-out nest of clothing that had been their bed and ducked through the collection door into the drizzle. Jimmy held the door open so he could check out the clothes in the light. "Any raincoats?"

"I've never seen you wear a raincoat."

"That's true," he said, rummaging through the pile. "How 'bout just a flannel shirt? Mine's getting pretty stinky." He found a flannel shirt with red and black checks, but it was gigantic; the collar tag said XXL. He picked up a thin wool navy sweater, then a gray sweatshirt; same size.

"Think of all those little green kids crying," he said, holding up the sweatshirt. "Must've been the Jolly

Green Giant died." He finally settled on a flannel hunting shirt, neon-orange.

Chena giggled. "That's awful."

"So? It's my size." He changed shirts, tossed his used one on top of the mound, and closed the door. The latch dangled. He took two wood screws out of his jeans pocket and, with the screwdriver blade on his pocket knife, affixed the hasp.

"Now I've really got to go," Chena said.

"Shell station." He took her hand and they started toward the gas station a block away, each carrying a plastic grocery bag.

Jimmy Ozette was thin and small, for fifteen. His black eyes, straight black hair, high cheekbones, and arching nose announced his Indian heritage at a glance. Chena Kynaka was Jimmy's age, an inch taller, and heavier. She was a Quanoot Indian, like him, but had lighter hair, skin, and eyes, because her family's roots had intertwined in the last century with those of Russian and English fur traders.

She was wearing jeans and a dingy pink sweatshirt, the one she threw on when she and Jimmy had taken the afternoon ferry to the mainland a week ago. The front of her sweatshirt depicted a snarling killer whale in a football helmet, the ball tucked under a pectoral fin; above it, in bold letters, WHALER BAY HIGH SCHOOL, and below it, with letters formed out of totem poles, ORCAS. Jimmy said whoever had named the team was a jerk. "No one knows what an orca is," he said. "Why couldn't we have been the Whaler Bay Killer Whales?" Jimmy was always asking, Why couldn't something else have happened other than what did happen?

Jimmy and Chena had known for nearly a year they were going to run away, but they were waiting for Jimmy to turn sixteen in two months, so he could get a job at one of the fast food chains. But last week Jimmy's mother fell down drunk again, this time breaking her other wrist and her collarbone and biting her tongue nearly in two, and he told Chena he wanted to hurry up and get out before she broke in pieces on the ground in front of him.

Chena had five older brothers, all loggers like her father. From an early age her mother expected her to share the workload of caring for all these outdoorsmen, but Chena saw things in a revolutionary light, in which, astonishingly, her own desires counted. *At least Jimmy doesn't have to worry about anybody out looking for him,* she thought.

The gas station was open and the attendant was a young dude who let them have the bathroom keys without a hard time. Jimmy noticed Chena had the storybook with her and he rolled his eyes.

"I'll finish it in the bathroom."

"It's just a kids' story."

"I want to see if the prince gives up his kingdom to save his people. He's selfish, but he might change."

"What age is it written for?"

"Dunno, eight?"

"Then he'll turn good and sacrifice his kingdom," he said, and unlocked the door labeled MEN. "They wait till you're older to start letting you in on how people really are."

After using the toilet Chena tied her sweatshirt around her waist and stood bare chested at the sink. She took a bar of soap from a sandwich bag and washed her hands and face and armpits. She reached for a paper towel, but they were used up, so she dried herself with gobs of toilet paper.

"You were right about the story," she said, and stepped out into the damp morning.

He shrugged. "Let's head to Kwik-Save for some chow."

She took his hand and they walked together, feeling proud of their love, feeling bright. Even though a lid of rain clouds sealed the suburb in a jar of gray. Even though they were not planning to look for something to eat inside the supermarket, in the aisles stacked with foods, but behind the store, in the Dumpster.

Sunlight poured onto the faculty parking lot through a large rip in a sheet of pale gray clouds. Yute Nahadeh wore a blue nylon jacket over a white T-shirt and running shorts. He placed his right foot on a cement barrier in a parking space and touched the heel to the asphalt, stretching his calf. The wind was cooler than usual for early fall, he thought. And brisk; there would be sailboats out on the Sound. He decided to run by the marina, an eight-mile loop.

He leaned over to touch his right knee, stretching his hamstring muscles. In his mind he went over the ad for a surrogate mother that was to appear today in the "Personals" pages of the *Seattle Times* and *Post-Intelligencer,* plus a dozen smaller newspapers and five local college rags.

"Doc, how's it going?"

He looked up to see, strolling toward him, a white-haired man with a pink face and a white goatee. Robert Duncan, professor of art history and a notorious windbag. No way around him.

"Just fine, Rob. How are you?"

"Not too bad." The man paused to chat. He was wearing a light gray suit and a black bow tie and he looked to Yute like the secret twin of Colonel Sanders. "How's the sabbatical going? Hear you've been working round the clock for weeks."

"It's . . ." Yute looked up at the wind sweeping the clouds away. A high-pressure front was moving in fast, turning the sky into a golden autumn playground. "Going well. Beyond my expectations."

"So what's the big secret in your lab? Have you found the missing link or something? Pops tells me he can only clean the place by appointment these days."

Yute smiled and shook his head. "It's a lemur from Madagascar—may be an entirely new species. Guess I'm overly secretive about my research until I publish. Come up sometime and I'll show you the skeleton. I'm learning some important new things from it." Yute stepped past him. "I'd love to chat more, but I'm in a hurry this morning."

The Colonel Sanders–double talked to his back as he walked away. "Retaining every fraction of information that goes into your head, as usual."

"On the contrary," Yute said over his shoulder, "isn't that why we specialize, Professor—because there's too much knowledge for any of us to retain?" He pressed the stopwatch button on his watch and bolted into a run.

"Specialize?" the man called after him. "You know more about art history than I do." Yute was sprinting and in seconds was a quarter way down the block. The other man yelled, "But I know nothing about cavemen!"

Yute did not look back, he turned the corner and escaped behind the limestone building that housed the library. Then he slowed his pace, settling into a smooth, swift stride for an eight-mile run. His long legs moved beneath him in a steady beat in rhythm with his breathing, his running shoes rolled off the pavement with a quiet padding sound.

Eight blocks from the campus he hurdled an anchor chain fence and turned to run along a pathway of Bayside Park that led to a large marina. He easily passed others who were walking or jogging, and liked the feeling. He would pick a jogger in the distance and reel him in until the jogger fell behind in his wake. Three young people stood in the grass beneath enormous elms, flowing in the slow, liquid ballet of Tai Chi. A thin little Vietnamese woman was setting up a parasol over a hotdog vending cart. The salt air took on a more fishy aroma as he came to the wooden docks and turned to run past the boat slips. Seagulls wheeled in the air above a forest of aluminum and wooden masts. In the distance beyond the marina scores of sailboats slid over Puget Sound, their brilliant jibs puffed out like the throats of seabirds in a mating dance.

Yute thought of Tundra Woman and pondered the many questions his research had already raised. What proteins prevent tissue freezing? From what food sources? How did she know which foods to eat? For that matter, he thought, how does any folklore arise?

The Caiyuh and other arctic tribes save the adrenal glands of butchered caribou to give to pregnant women and young children. Chemical analysis found that the gland stores a tremendous concentration of vitamin C, an essential element that is otherwise hard to find in the arctic diet. But that's recent scientific information. The people have lived this way for millennia. How did they know?

Eating carrots helps you to see at night. True. Because carrots are loaded with beta-carotene that the body uses to make vitamin A, which it needs to make retinal, which goes into the light-sensitive pigment in the rods of the retina. Light breaks down the pigment, discharging a signal to the visual cortex, producing black-and-white vision—especially suited for seeing at night. So says modern science. But people have claimed for centuries that carrots are good for night vision. How did they know?

And what about willow bark for pain relief, kaolin clay and apple peels for diarrhea—aspirin and Kaopectate are derived from those folk remedies—and the list goes on and on. But how did the midwife, the granny healer, the medicine man know?

One thing seemed certain. Tundra Woman didn't use the scientific method. It wasn't a matter of observation, hypothesis, experimentation, and theory. Somehow, she simply *knew*.

His stopwatch read 28:05:36 as he turned around for the return leg; he was running seven-minute miles, his favorite pace. He had completed marathons at the same speed. Once the endorphins kicked in at about three miles, he could keep the tempo up forever, it seemed, gliding in a trance of long strides and deep breaths.

Approaching on the sidewalk, a man in jeans and a nylon jacket walked a large black Rottweiler on a leather leash. The thick-necked dog wore a black leather collar with silver studs. Yute crossed the street, slipped between parked cars, and ran along the other sidewalk. Two silver-haired women in pastel-colored sweatsuits strode along at a brisk pace, swinging their arms in long arcs.

They smiled and called out "Good morning!" in chorus.

Yute grinned with his whole face. "It's a fabulous morning," he said.

On a hill in Bayside Park, Chena and Jimmy reclined on a bench, watching scores of colored sails tilting and scattering over the green water of Puget Sound. Children laughed and squealed in a nearby playground while their parents chatted. A high-leaping whippet caught nearly every Frisbee his bearded friend tossed to him. A woman in a straw sunhat stood before an easel, painting a large watercolor of the marina.

Chena got up her nerve and walked over to a tiny Vietnamese woman with long graying hair who sat on a canvas stool in the shade of a parasol that advertised VIENNA ALL-BEEF FRANKS.

Chena smiled. "Hello."

The woman nodded a greeting and slowly stood, but did not return her smile.

"My boyfriend and I were wondering if there was some errand we could do for you in exchange for a couple hot dogs. We don't have any money."

The woman shook her head, frowning, and sat back down.

"How about if we push this heavy cart all the way back up the hill to where you load it on the truck?"

"Husband do that," the woman said, busying herself with a loose thread on a black cotton shoe.

"Well, could we maybe wash it for you?"

"It look dirty?"

No, it looks like you could do brain surgery on it, Chena thought, seeing her reflection in the gleaming aluminum surfaces.

"Give it up, Chena," a world-weary voice called from the background. Jimmy was sprawled on the park bench under a huge sycamore tree, his neon-orange flannel shirt unbuttoned, his jet-black hair spilling to the grass.

A runner in a blue jacket raced past, then turned a buttonhook and walked back to the hot-dog cart. The Vietnamese woman jumped up. "Yes, sir! What you like?"

"Give me two foot-long hot dogs," he said, and turned to Chena. "You like them with sauerkraut and the rest?"

Chena glanced behind her. He was talking to her. "Uh, yeah, I guess."

"How about your boyfriend? He like all the extras?"

She nodded. "Yes, sir."

"Give me two foot-long hot dogs, all the way, ma'am. Load 'em up."

Chena smiled. The man smiled back. He was an Indian, big like her brothers, and handsome, with dark, intense eyes. The vendor handed the man the two hot dogs and he handed them to Chena.

"Hey, Jimmy!" Chena called as she hurried toward the bench with their first hot food in over a week. "Thank you, sir," she called over her shoulder. "I really appreciate it."

"You're welcome. Just take care. And be careful." The man fished into his jacket and paid the old woman. Chena watched him for a moment as he sprinted away; he was a strong, fast runner. He never glanced back to take glory in his deed, which showed he had class.

Jimmy wolfed down his hot dog, but Chena tried to savor every bite. She closed her eyes and chewed slowly. Her long, wavy brown hair hung over the back of the bench, tousled by the breeze. She had never imagined that hot dogs could taste so sublime.

She felt warm fur rubbing against her ankle at the same time she heard the *meow*. A scrawny gray kitten had been drawn to the smell of the steamed frank. Its fur was matted with something tarry like motor oil.

She bit off a piece of meat and fed the kitten.

"Chena, don't." Jimmy groaned.

"She's hungry too. Look at her eat it. She's sweet."

"Go eat at the docks," Jimmy told the cat, and gave it a gentle push with his shoe. "Go on, there's a zillion fish guts there, free." It scampered off.

When Chena finished her hot dog, she licked up

the last specks of chopped onions, sauerkraut, catsup, and mustard that had spilled into the crinkled paper tub. Jimmy crumpled his trash into a ball and high-tossed it toward a wire mesh wastebasket; it bounced off the rim. Chena got up and dunked it in. She plucked a neatly folded *Seattle Times* from the basket and scanned the headlines, strolling to the bench and sitting down without taking her eyes from the page. Jimmy rested his head in her lap, half listening, while she read aloud a few of the articles. Then she turned to the "Personals" section.

"Listen to this one: 'Ruggedly handsome, professional safari guide and large-game hunter, SWM fifty-two, whose life reads like Hemingway fiction, seeks attractive, unconventional, adventurous woman under thirty for action-romance.' "

Jimmy chuckled. "Action-romance? He's gonna turn her loose in the woods and hunt her?"

"Guess so."

A loud buzzing on the sidewalk made them glance up to see a pack of four teenagers gliding by on Rollerblade skates. The skaters wore bright outfits that coordinated the colors of their skates, helmets, and knee and elbow pads.

"Must be nice," Chena said, then went back to her paper. " 'Handsome, successful orthodontist, observant Jew, thirty-two, seeks sex goddess to worship. Must keep kosher kitchen.' "

They laughed. "Hire a maid, and worship her," Jimmy said.

"Oooh," she said. "Here's a weird one: 'Monster fan, SWM twenty-eight, enjoys old monster and horror movies of the nineteen fifties and sixties, seeks female monster fan, eighteen to forty-eight, for acting out unique sexual fantasies.' " She shuddered.

"The guy's a hopeless romantic," Jimmy said. He sat up and put his arm around Chena, snuggled his face against her neck, and kissed her. She giggled and scrunched up her shoulder.

"Tickles!"

Jimmy squeezed her waist tightly and began to read the ads himself. After a moment he asked, "What does *Rub-en-es-que* mean?"

"Hmm?"

" 'Attractive, Ivy League–educated DWF forty-one,' " he read, then hesitated, " 'Rub-en-es-que . . .' "

"Oh, *Rubenesque,*" Chena pronounced.

"Whatever, '. . . casting on the deep for love and laughter and shared visions, quiet talks, opera, classical music, literature, gourmet meals with fine wines. Link between brain and sex organs a must.' " Jimmy said, "Sounds like a rich lady who got burned by her last old man."

"It means fat," Chena said. "Peter Paul Rubens was a guy who painted nude fat ladies a few hundred years ago, way before thin was considered pretty. If you don't want to say, 'By the way, I'm sort of fat,' you just say, 'Rubenesque' and it means the same thing."

"And hope some guy like Rubens is out there reading your ad," Jimmy said.

"Or you can say *zaftig,* means 'hefty.' "

He smiled. "You're amazing. You know who just might want you back more than your folks? Your teachers. They're never going to find another student as good as you at Whaler High, that's for sure."

She felt herself blush. "It's just because I read a lot."

"So I've noticed."

She gave him a little pinch on the arm. Then she put down the paper and hugged him, closing her eyes and breathing in the smell of his sun-warmed hair. It made her feel great when he complimented her, something he did easily and naturally. She never got compliments at home.

Jimmy said, "Maybe I should write my own ad: Single Red Male, under thirty-five, wiry, not bad-looking if you go for Indians, unemployed for now but with high hopes once I move out of the wooden box I sleep in. Seeking financially secure, attractive professional woman who looks great in heels, and has a strong mothering instinct."

"What do you want with her?" Chena asked, putting on a hurt look.

He shrugged. "Just teasing. I'd use her money to get us started on our dream."

Jimmy and Chena had been talking together about their dream nearly every day for half a year—ever since their friendship had burst its bud and blossomed into a love affair. In the original version of the dream they were supposed to have waited until they both turned sixteen, then they were going to run away from home and get jobs to support themselves in an inexpensive efficiency apartment. From there she would get her high-school equivalency diploma at night and go on to night college, while still working. She would earn a good degree, in education or literature or maybe even nursing or some other science, and he would work as a deckhand on one of the trawlers or long-liners until he was old enough to get his captain's license and hire himself out to the fishing fleets and, who knows—if they could save up for a down payment—maybe even someday own his own boat.

Problem was, they couldn't wait any longer for the world to be theirs. Jimmy was being hurt so bad by his love for his stupid mother. He had to get out before his heart exploded, like one of those Mexican things—piñatas—that you just keep whacking and whacking with a stick until it shreds and the good things inside spill out on the floor.

"I could write an ad too," she said. "Single Native American Woman, fifteen, eager to learn and succeed and not afraid to work hard for her dream. Seeks man of similar age to make a life and true love forever. Must be of Native American heritage, preferably of the Quanoot tribe; would particularly like somebody with the same dream, who can appreciate and share her efforts—especially a sweet guy named Jimmy James Ozette."

He smiled at her, starting with his mouth and spreading to his shining black eyes. They hugged for a long while.

Then Chena picked up the paper again. "Let's check the help-wanted ads. There may be some one-day stuff that we can do, like wash windows, or something, where they won't be afraid to hire fifteen-year-olds."

He read, too, but she was ready to turn the page while he was only a third of the way down. He let out a low whistle. "Like I said: They're going to miss you at Whaler."

She spotted the bold print near the top of the next page:

ATTENTION, YOUNG WOMEN
MAKE $40,000 IN 9 MONTHS:

Medical doctor seeking healthy surrogate mother, age 18 to 30, for embryo implantation. Anonymous client will pay $5,000 for undergoing implantation, plus $10,000 more if procedure is successful. After birth, an additional $25,000 will be paid to the surrogate mother, for a total of $40,000 for a full-term pregnancy. No smokers, drinkers, or druggies; blood tests will be required to confirm health status. Respond to: P.O. Box 1467, Deer Park, WA 98121.

When she finished reading the ad, she turned her face straight up to the blue sky and opened her mouth in wonder. Jimmy was a few lines behind her; then he said, "Holy cow." They sat without speaking for a moment.

Then Chena blurted, "It wasn't in the paper yesterday and he doesn't give a phone number, just a post office box, so nobody's contacted him yet."

Jimmy stood up and crossed his arms, staring at her.

"I know I don't look eighteen, but he might not care. As soon as a girl's pregnant, she's an emancipated minor."

He frowned. "You'd be willing to do that? Get pregnant and all?"

"Sure. I'm healthy. No problem. My mom said all her births were easy, that Kynaka women are made to make babies."

"Your dad sure thinks so . . . but . . ."

"But what?"

He looked down. "I mean . . . you know . . . how's he gonna do this to you?"

"Oh, Jimmy, there's no sex to it. I mean like *sex* sex. It's like a turkey baster or something. The doctor just inserts it and . . . really, there's no sex. You can be right there beside me, I want you to be."

He shuffled his feet. "But it's . . . you know . . . it'll be some other guy . . . not with sex, I know, but . . ." He glanced up at her. "You're supposed to be mine."

She grinned. "But that's the beauty of it, don't you see? The baby won't be ours. It won't even be mine, not even half mine. It's an embryo. That means they just implant it, and—bingo—I got somebody else's baby growing inside me. It could be a Chinese kid, anything."

"And you're trying to tell me that you, Chena Kynaka, who gives part of her hot dog to a little kitty, won't get all attached and freak out about giving this baby away?"

"I'll be doing a beautiful favor for some lonely couple that can't have kids."

"But watch, he'll want a white woman."

"I'm part white. Tell him my womb is white. Jimmy, he could pick me. He could."

Jimmy sighed and rubbed at a scar where his mother had broken his nose. "Too good to be true."

"That's the only thing that worries me, it's too good." She read the ad again. Then a third time, aloud. Then she pulled Jimmy close to her and burst into tears.

"I know," he whispered. "I know." He stroked the side of her face. "It's scary. To be staring right at our dream like it could just be handed to us. So easy. But then maybe he won't pick you."

She nodded her head and cried softly against his chest.

"Then again, maybe something this good can happen to us," he said. "Once in a lifetime. Those kids' books . . . all those stories about Sisiutlqua and the Guardian Spirits. They can't be making *all* that stuff up. I don't think. I mean, not from zero. There is something good behind life—I'm hoping, anyway."

He lifted her chin. "Look, even if we don't get this money dropped in our laps, you and me got each other, like we said. True, Chena Hawk?" He called her by her mother's clan name.

She smiled and jumped up, tugging him along by the hand. "True, Jimmy Otter. Let's go."

"Where to?"

"Deer Park is tiny—probably just one post office. Let's go find it and find box fourteen sixty-seven, and wait. When this doctor comes to check his mail, we pounce."

Yute was about a half mile from campus now and he picked up his speed slightly.

He ran past a utility crew working in an open manhole surrounded by a canvas screen. Two potbellied men peered down into the hole, talking to an unseen third worker. They wore yellow hard hats and gray jumpsuits with SEATTLE POWER & LIGHT in white cloth letters on the back.

That was fast, Yute thought. *They weren't here when I ran by before.*

A block from the faculty parking lot, another manhole was open in the middle of the street, directly in front of a parked white Seattle Power & Light van with its emergency flashers blinking. A heavyset man in a red hard hat was speaking into a handheld radio. ". . . not at this end, far as we can tell. Must be at your end. Over."

Yute glanced at the time-temperature sign on the bank. It was dark. No lights in the windows of the office buildings that lined the block, and at the Shell gas station the yellow scallop sign was not revolving. Though he was sweaty from his run, a terrible chill swept over him, as if ice water poured down his back, and he sprinted the last block and turned the corner around the library. What he saw made him wince and grab his forehead. All the lights were out in the college classrooms. The electricity must be off everywhere on campus, including his lab.

That meant the freezer was not functioning.

"Not now!" he screamed, and raced back toward the second crew. The man with the radio squatted near the open manhole, looking down the ladder. Yute shouted from a quarter block away as he sprinted toward him.

"How long has the power been off?"

The man looked up for a second, frowned, then looked down the ladder.

Yute ran up to stand next to him. "How long has the power been off and how long will it stay off?"

The man, still squatting, looked up at Yute and eyed him over. "Who wants to know?"

"Dr. Yute Nahadeh, of Pacific College; sir, I have an extremely important experiment in my lab that requires constant refrigeration."

"Don't you have an emergency generator, like at hospitals?"

"No. I . . . No. Just a battery for emergency lights. It doesn't power the freezer."

Before the last few weeks the walk-in freezer had rarely been used; it had stored only four specimens: two lemurs and two chimpanzees. He'd considered a gas-powered generator to run the freezer during power outages a noncritical expense, and had overlooked the situation in the case of Tundra Woman.

"You oughta get yourself a gas generator for times like this," the man said, then looked away from Yute and spoke into the radio, "Mike, you might as well run the whole series, 'cause we haven't found nothing at this end. Keep me posted."

He stuck the radio into a metal holster on his belt and stood to face Yute. He was a couple of inches shorter, but heavier. "We don't know yet what's wrong. And I can't tell you how long it will take to fix it, but, from the looks of things, my guess is it won't be real soon. Sorry." Static squealed across the radio and he adjusted the volume button. "It can take a couple of hours just to track down the source of an outage like this one. And then another few hours, half a day, to fix it." He was ready to brush Yute off and get back to work.

"How long has it been out?" Yute asked. He read the man's name embroidered over the left pocket. "Please, Mr. Douglas, it's important."

The man leaned over the yellow metal railing and called down, "T.J., when did you get the first call?"

"What?" came a woman's voice from inside.

"Ask T.J. when he took the first call about the blackout."

After a pause she appeared at the foot of the ladder and called up, "He says about an hour ago. He says he needs the blue test kit." She glanced behind her for a moment. "Oh, and a different spotlight—his sucks."

"How long would it take for you to install an emergency generator in my lab?" Yute asked the foreman, following him to the sliding door of the van. The man stepped inside to get the equipment and spoke without turning around.

"Sir, that's not my job. And we're not allowed to use our gas generators for anything other than company business."

"Mr. Douglas, I don't know how to impress upon you the urgency of this situation." Yute held up his hands to the man's bent back. "The world is about to lose a scientific artifact of incalculable value. It is utterly irreplaceable. Can you please help me?"

"I can tell you where to call to buy yourself a generator, who'll install it for you. Call Phillip's—"

"There's no time for that!"

"Look, buddy"—the big man spun around and stuck his head out of the van, directly in Yute's face—"every time the power goes out somebody always flies into a panic over it—'My daughter's wedding is in two hours,' 'We're supposed to have the senator and his wife over for dinner at eight,' 'My tropical fish are worth three times your salary'—I've heard it all. Well, there's nothing I can do about it. I'm not God. I don't store lightning bolts in my hip pocket. You'll just have to wait like everybody else. Sorry. For the future, get yourself an emergency generator. For now, let me do my job, and we'll get the damn power back on for you."

Before the last sentence was finished, Yute had turned without a word and sprinted toward his lab.

"Maybe packing the thing in ice would work," the man called after him. "This repair is gonna take several hours, count on that." He slid the door hard. It slammed shut.

Yute dashed up the stairs to his fourth-floor lab, three steps at a time.

What am I going to find? Tundra Woman was supercooled, not frozen. Thawing is not *what will occur. But what then?* He wished he knew more about the physics of supercooling.

Just let the embryo be all right. Even if the rest turns to mush. Let the embryo be safe. The embryo.

The emergency lights were on. He twisted a key in the heavy padlock on the freezer door handle and it snapped apart with a loud metallic click. Then he hesitated, afraid. With a deep breath he yanked the handle and entered, blowing out his breath in one continuous stream. The frost that normally clung to the walls had melted and left a slick of water on the textured aluminum floor. He pulled off the white plastic sheet that draped the body, still blowing his breath out. The body had the same dark golden skin tone. He touched it. The skin was cool, not cold. Wet. Finally he dared to inhale. There was no stink. There was a smell of wet skin, wet hair. But no decay. Not yet.

"Yes!" he shouted, and did a little skip that splashed the water on the floor. Suddenly he stopped. "Now what do I do?"

I've dissected her brain, pharynx, larynx, tongue: the most revealing anatomy. I've managed to preserve parts of those structures in formaldehyde. My notes, photos, are meticulous. So I've accomplished the most important work. If she decomposes now, nothing radically informative is lost. I'll retain the world's only complete Neanderthal skeleton. I can forget her for now. My business is entirely with the embryo. The living Neanderthal.

He left the freezer and ran to take a quick hot shower and throw on a clean surgical gown. He unwrapped a set of sterile instruments and laid them out on a green sterile cloth on a black Formica lab table. Then he stepped back into the freezer and retrieved the uterus and fallopian tubes, carrying them in a small dissection pan. Just then the lights went back on. The freezer motor began humming.

Still, I've got to go through with this, he decided. *It's the only way. I can't take a chance on recooling this tissue, because the antifreeze proteins may lose their potency after one freeze. Next time, the flesh might freeze solid.*

With a sterile curette he scraped oviduct cells from the lining of the right fallopian tube and dipped the tiny spoon into a sterile petri dish filled with room-temperature Ham's solution, a plasmalike liquid with glucose and an antibiotic. He carried the dish to the microscope bench.

First, he relocated the embryo. It looked undisturbed. He very gently sucked the embryo into a tiny plastic catheter and dunked the embryo into the Ham's solution. Beads of sweat stood out on his brow.

"Long live the queen," he whispered, and his shoulders dropped two inches as he pushed back in his chair.

After a breather he covered the dish with a porous lid and set it in a heater unit that he programmed to slowly climb from room temperature to one hundred degrees, the endogenous uterine temperature, in six hours. The embryo would gradually return to its normal metabolism and would soon begin to divide again and again. Now he no longer had the luxury of time to find a surrogate mother. The embryo could survive in the saline bath for a day or so, he knew, but he couldn't risk waiting longer than that.

He glanced at his watch: 10:39 A.M. *How can I find a suitable mother by tomorrow? Cruise the campuses, accosting every healthy-looking woman I see? Not exactly low-profile behavior, and no guarantee I'd find someone—and, damn!—today's Saturday.*

He paced around the lab. Prostitutes. They sell their bodies on demand; but then I'm dealing with pimps, alcohol, drugs, cigarettes, AIDS. Still, if I can find one young enough, new to the business, not yet ravaged by her lifestyle. No. Wouldn't work. A prostitute would take birth control pills, couldn't be implanted right away. I need someone healthy who is ready to be implanted no later than tomorrow.

He sat down, feeling light-headed, and recalled he had not eaten breakfast or lunch. Suddenly he clapped his hands together. The girl at the hot-dog cart! She was no prostitute, just a runaway. Fifteen or sixteen or so.

Too young for legal consent, but biologically, the ideal age for childbearing. She'll have every reason to keep the secret of how she got pregnant. I can give her, give them both, an apartment of their own as part of my deal.

He was already on his feet, shedding his surgical pajamas and jumping into a pair of black jeans. He grabbed the least-wrinkled white shirt he could find in the laundry hamper at the foot of the office cot. He sniffed a cotton armpit and tossed the shirt back in the hamper. Instead, he threw on a clean, V-neck surgeon's shirt, hospital-green. Then he rushed out the door and bounded down the stairs.

6

YUTE NAHADEH FIDGETED in the tan calf leather seat of his cream 1956 Mercedes gull-wing. It was parked on the peak of Hill Street, across from Bayside Park, providing a clear view most of the way down to the marina. He checked his watch. Over three hours, and no sign of the two street kids. Where could they have gone?

His eyes carefully scanned the sidewalks of the park, starting at the north and sweeping to the south like a search radar. He tilted the seat again, trying for a comfortable position.

He had already trotted throughout the park scouting for the pair, badgered the old Vietnamese lady who had sold him the hot dogs, accosted strangers for any leads. But he only moved in circles like a bloodhound who had lost a scent trail.

He compulsively checked his watch again, then spit a curse and banged his palm on the steering wheel.

Is this the right strategy? Or should I try the whores, after all? There's no way around the birth control pills, but there must be a few women who suffer side effects from the pill, so they rely on a diaphragm and abortions. Trouble is, how do I find such women?

He let out a loud sigh. *It's a hopeless quest.*

Time took on a tangible presence that pressed in on him from all sides, like oppressively thick tropical air. He rolled down the window, even though the evening was turning cold as the sun fell below the edge of the bay. Time was running out, but he did not sense its passage this way, as sand running from an hourglass; he felt it shrinking over him like plastic wrap. He felt that if he failed to find a surrogate mother within the next few hours, the suffocation would be complete and time would have robbed the embryo and himself of their lives.

He adjusted the seat upright and started the engine.

"I'm getting cold, Chena."

Jimmy's hands were shoved in his pockets and his arms hunched tight against his body. He and Chena sat on a concrete park bench across the street from the post office.

"Maybe we could leave a note and come back tomorrow."

"What'll it say? *Hope to be a surrogate mother. Contact me inside the Goodwill Collection Hut on the corner of Spruce and Fir?*"

Through plate glass windows Chena could see the silver post-office box they had located earlier. When customers were in the post office, she had not taken her eyes off it. But now she could relax her vigil because the place was deserted except for a night crew that was cleaning and mopping.

"Well, the guy's probably not going to drop by this late to check for mail."

"How do you know? Maybe it's on his way home from the hospital or the movies or something."

"C'mon, let's head back. The bakery's tossed out their old rolls by now."

"I knew that's what it was—you're just hungry. But look at it this way: If I get this job, we'll be eating all the smoked salmon and yams, quail, dried clams, goat's milk, apples—"

"You're making my stomach hurt."

"—venison steaks, pumpkins, biscuits . . ." She giggled at the image of a wooden feast table heaped with food in the center of a Quanoot longhouse at a traditional wedding potlatch. "I'm going to be the first to talk to him."

"Okay. But I need to hunt for a way to stay warm." He got up. "Be back."

The post office manager had thrown them out earlier, pointing to the NO LOITERING sign. Now the branch had been closed for a couple of hours, but the front door was open to mailbox renters until nine. Maybe after the cleanup crew left, she and Jimmy could go in and just sit down on the floor and rest and wait, sheltered from the brisk breeze coming off the bay.

After a few minutes Jimmy returned with a large folded-up canvas tarp, the kind used for protecting cars from the sun. She didn't ask where he got it. They huddled underneath and snuggled and kissed, giggling all the while. Their body odors reminded her of the dank-earth smell of mushrooms that she gathered in the forest a hundred steps from the back door of her home.

She poked her head out as a classic Mercedes roadster cruised by, a black-haired man at the wheel.

"Hey, Jimmy, look!"

Jimmy surfaced from the dark warmth inside the tarp. The car's taillights brightened at a stop sign. The car moved on.

"Missed it," Chena said. "The guy in that car is the one who bought us hot dogs."

In a half hour Yute arrived in an older, seedier district of Seattle, slowly cruising by the sidewalk, evaluating the streetwalkers. Most of the women looked older than he hoped for. A Filipino teenager in electric-pink spandex pants and a tank top, with a fluffy pink sweater thrown over her shoulders, approached his passenger side window and hung on, walking with the car for a few steps, describing some of the things she could do for him. Right age, he thought, but too petite; a Neanderthal baby might be large. He shook his head and drove on.

Down the block he spotted a tall black teenager with large breasts and hips and an athletic build. He pulled over and stopped. She might do. She was talking with a white woman in gold lamé pants who looked over, smiled, and strutted toward the car. He shook his head and gestured that he wanted the black woman. The teenager tried to hide her surprise. She gave a little laugh and approached the car, but he saw her flick a cigarette to the sidewalk, so he waved her off and accelerated. No smokers.

"Honky queer!" she yelled, and shot him the finger.

This is idiotic, it isn't going to work. He'd now spent nearly five hours in his fruitless search for a candidate for motherhood, and any candidate might fail the blood tests, or prove unsuitable for other reasons.

He stopped at a traffic light. A woman who looked to be in her late thirties, wearing spiked heels, purple bicycle-style shorts, and a low-cut red leotard top stepped over to his driver's window. Maroon henna-dyed hair fell across her face as she bent toward him to advertise her big breasts. She smelled of perfume, cigarettes, and a trace of alcohol: she was the epitome of what he didn't want.

She winked. "Older means bolder, babe. Do things the other girls are too young to dream yet. I don't disappoint."

He shook his head and she shrugged and started to turn away. "Hey, wait," he said. "Do you know a lot of the other prostitutes?"

She turned back. "Lookin' for someone special?"

"Yes, I am."

"You a cop?"

"No."

"Private eye? Somebody's daughter on the street?"

"No, I'm a doctor."

She studied him a moment. "You don't look like no doctor, but I guess you don't look like no cop either. More like an actor from a western."

"Get in," he said, "the light's changing." The light turned green and a cabdriver behind them laid on the horn. She yelled something obscene at the cabdriver as she walked around the front of the Mercedes. Yute pushed open the gull-wing door for her and it swung upward smoothly on stainless-steel pistons.

"Pretty slick," she said as she climbed in. "Does it fly?" She grasped the handle and pulled the door downward.

"Don't slam—" He winced as she slammed the door.

"Sorry, man," she said. "Shoulda warned me sooner." They pulled away from the blaring horn and turned the corner. The cab went straight ahead, the driver screaming at them with a reddened face. "Blow it out your ass, pal," she said, casually flipping the guy a finger.

Yute glanced over at her as he steered. "You may be able to help me—"

"I charge for my information," she said, and slid her fingers over the black walnut dashboard paneling.

"Not a problem. You may be able to help me—"

"Look, if it's special tricks you want, nothing's too kinky for me, believe me."

"Just shut up and listen," he said. "I'm not interested in buying sex. Not from you or anyone else. A client of mine is seeking a professional surrogate mother.

He's hired me to implant an embryo in a young, healthy woman. I'm desperate because I have only one more day to find the right young woman and implant the embryo before it expires."

She frowned. "You wanna make a working girl pregnant?"

"I can pay her forty thousand dollars for nine months."

"A girl with a great bod who knows this business already makes that much."

"Yes, but she'll be off the street. She gets pregnant, and no more hustling for nine months. Her womb does all the work, while she gets a vacation. And I can provide a small apartment, groceries, as part of the bargain."

"Pretty weird," she said, twisting her scarlet lips. "But . . . sounds like a maybe. I think some girls might be interested."

"I'm looking especially for someone who's just beginning, maybe who's trying to come out on the street, but she's young and new to it, or better yet, she's still just —thinking about it."

"Always a few of those hanging around."

"I'm trying to find someone who doesn't smoke or drink or use drugs."

She let out a husky laugh. "And, let me guess—a vegetarian who eats only organic granola and stuffs a date pit up her twat for an IUD." She laughed again and began to cough hoarsely. Then she hacked and rolled down the window and spit.

"You're right, I'm being a jerk," he said, and slowed the car. "My mistake." She was still coughing quietly when he pulled over to the curb and stopped.

He felt helpless. "Look, if you were homeless, where would you go at night," he asked, "a cold night like this?"

"Homeless, I'd go to one of the shelters. But you're talking about a runaway, right? Then I'd steer clear of the shelters, 'cause my daddy might look for me there."

"I'm not a father. But I am looking for a couple of Indian kids I met earlier today in Bayside Park."

"Well, I do have a pretty good idea where to look," she said, and turned the handle on the gull-wing door. It glided upward with a barely audible hiss.

"Where?"

She stepped out of the car.

"Oh, right. Forgot." Yute reached into the back pocket of his slacks and pulled out a black leather billfold. He leaned across the bucket seat and handed her a twenty. "Here."

"Come on. You're a doctor. You make twice that much every time someone pees into a plastic cup."

"I'm a forensic specialist. I don't work with living patients."

"Good for you, you save on malpractice insurance." She rubbed her thumb against her fingers. "More."

He handed her another twenty.

She stuffed the bills in her purse. "If I were a runaway, 'bout now, I'd probably be Dumpster-diving with my pals."

He shrugged and shook his head.

"You know, scrounging for food. The Dumpsters behind supermarkets are the best. They toss out a ton of stuff every evening near closing. The street people practically form a chow line."

His eyebrows shot up. "Kwik-Save!"

"Near where you saw those kids today, right? Even homeless kids don't wander too far from the kitchen."

"Right . . . that's right. Thank you."

"Easy money," she said with a smirk. "Guess that's what they call *oral* sex." She reached up and slammed the door down, hard. Then she turned and strutted back in the direction from which she had come.

Kwik-Save, he thought. *Please. It's my last slim, ridiculous chance to save the embryo.*

Chena and Jimmy hurried, shivering, their sleeves pulled down over their hands, from the post office to Kwik-Save. Each night around eight the deli tossed out bags of stale rolls and breads, and the other departments chucked decaying fruits and vegetables and expired goods. They rounded the corner of the big brick building that housed the grocery.

"Damn, we waited too long," Jimmy said. A couple of older street people were rummaging through the Dumpster. A woman in a turtleneck sweater and filthy overalls stood inside the large metal box and handed out a pinewood crate to a thin man with long, stringy gray hair and a scraggly beard. The crate held two or three bunches of spotted bananas.

"Missed our chance," Jimmy muttered.

But the skinny man smiled, showing bad teeth, and

waved them over with bananas in his hand. "Plenty here," he said. "Share and share alike."

"Yeah," the woman said from the doorway. "We don't bite or nuthin'." She strained to press her weight up onto her hands, then she straddled the door, swung the other leg over, and jumped down to the asphalt.

Chena and Jimmy thanked them and took the bananas. They strolled over to the edge of the parking lot and found a grassy spot under an elm to sit down with their supper. A few of the fruits on the bunch were nearly perfect, just split or squashed near the ends. Chena grinned when Jimmy attacked a banana the same way he had wolfed the hot dog earlier. It was the only other food they had eaten today.

"Monkey," she said.

He grinned back, with stuffed cheeks. "You bet I am."

The two teenagers ate in silence. The other couple sat on a concrete barrier near the Dumpster talking quietly. Then the man and woman ambled over to them.

"There's still a few bags of rolls and it looked like a box of oranges in the Dumpster," the big woman said. "Why don't one of you climb in there and hand them out?"

"Sure." Chena stood up. "I will."

The woman winked at Chena and jerked a thumb at Jimmy. "Always let the man get dirty, hon."

Jimmy was already walking toward the Dumpster. "No prob," he said, his mouth full of his fourth banana. "Where are they? It's hard to see in there."

"Toward the back wall," they both answered.

Jimmy hopped up onto the sill, then swung his legs

over and dropped down into the smelly darkness. The bearded man rushed forward and banged the door shut and swung down the retainer bar; the woman grabbed Chena from behind and clamped a dirty hand over her mouth. Jimmy screamed a string of curses and pounded the walls of his trap; the steel rang dully, like a gong.

Chena's heart jumped under her breasts. She tried to yell through the meaty hand that muzzled her mouth. "What are you doing? Stop! You're hurting my arms!"

The woman dragged her, kicking and bucking, into the shadows behind the Dumpster. The man glanced all around and followed after them.

"Share and share alike," he said, and mashed his toothy mouth against hers. Sweaty strings of his hair flapped in her face. Then the man bent forward to tug down her sweatpants. Chena drove up her knee with all her strength and felt and heard it thud against his eye. He howled and sank to his knees, hands cupped over his eye, his chest heaving.

"Stupid bitch!" the woman screamed from behind, and wrapped the crook of her arm around Chena's windpipe and shoved her head forward, mashing off her air supply. Chena fought and kicked and squirmed, but couldn't break the choke hold.

The man's head wobbled, then he winced loudly and stood, stiffening his whole body until it shuddered. He leered at Chena and sucked in a long breath through his teeth. In the shadows his ruined eye was a dark orb and the other eye was wild with rage. Chena's vision blurred and a strange calm washed over her as she understood she was going to die.

Suddenly, from behind the man, a big hand shot

forward, clamped his face, spun him like a doll, and slammed his head against the Dumpster. He slid down the wall into a heap like a pile of dirty laundry. The woman let go of Chena and fled. Chena's knees sagged and she staggered backward and sat down hard. The husky silhouette of her rescuer hovered above. A strong hand reached down under her arm and scooped her up to her feet and led her out into the white glare of high-beam headlights.

She blinked to believe her eyes. The man from the park.

"You all right?" he asked.

She nodded, catching her breath. "Get Jimmy out."

Yute threw open the Dumpster door, and Jimmy leapt over the sill and fell onto the asphalt and scrambled to his feet in one motion, spitting curses like flames.

"Chena, what the hell they do to you?" His black eyes were big and shiny wet.

"I'm all right, I'm okay." But as she said it, the stench of garbage and sour sweat and tooth decay clogged her nostrils and with a jolt she retched.

Jimmy hugged her and burst into tears. "Oh, Chena, I'm sorry, so sorry, so sorry."

"Shhhh, it's okay now," she said, crying with him. "They tried to . . . but they didn't get far." She stroked his long black hair. "Shhhh, it's okay, I'm all right now."

After a long moment Chena said, "Jimmy, look who saved me."

Yute stood, backlit, in the funnel of brightness.

7

CHENA SAT ON a wooden stool in a lab with green floor and wall tiles and stainless steel counters. To her surprise she didn't feel nervous. Jimmy sat next to her, rubbing the scar on his nose. He wore a pair of surgical pajamas with the sleeves and cuffs rolled up in wads; she was engulfed in a navy-blue cotton bathrobe.

She smiled at him and squeezed his hand, then leaned over and kissed him. Their clean, damp hair smelled wonderful from the rosemary shampoo and their warm skin was fragrant from the peppermint oil soap—all part of the world's most pleasurable hot shower.

"Relax," she whispered. "I want to do this. It's the door to our dreams."

Little white cartons of Chinese food lay opened, spread across a countertop. Jimmy had devoured two cartons of garlic shrimp and rice. Now Chena sniffed a curious bouquet of shampoo and soap, garlic and hot mustard, Lysol and alcohol, and something else—formaldehyde, she decided.

She thought of the way things had worked out and it left her feeling almost dizzy. Events had surged together magically, as in the old Quanoot tales of spirit guardians; how the invisibles pulled strings for you. She and Jimmy and Dr. Nahadeh had been looking for each other. *It was meant to be.*

Yute worked with his back to them, opening packages of blood-test kits and arranging them on a counter. He paused to rub the back of his neck. *He seems more nervous than Jimmy,* Chena thought.

Yute turned around to face them. "All right, I'm ready to begin. Is everybody okay?"

Chena nodded. "I'm ready."

"Did you get enough to eat?"

"Plenty, it was delicious. Thank you."

"Real good," Jimmy said.

"I'm glad." Yute prepared a hypodermic and syringe. "First, I need to draw some of your blood."

Chena rolled up her right sleeve, made a fist. He wrapped a rubber strap around her upper arm, wiped her elbow fold with alcohol, and withdrew two test tubes of blood; then he popped off the tourniquet and stepped over to the counter and busied himself with the test kits.

"Leave the sleeve up, please, I'd like to check your blood pressure next. This will only take a few more minutes; I'm running a series of rapid-assay screens for infections that would endanger a fetus."

Jimmy frowned. "Don't worry, nothing wrong with her."

Yute returned to her with a blood pressure cuff and put his stethoscope to his ears. After a moment he removed the cuff from her arm.

"Excellent: one ten over seventy."

"You going to listen to my heart?" she asked.

"Right now, in fact." He placed the stethoscope to his ears again.

She spread open the front of the robe, baring her breasts.

"That's okay," he said, and folded the robe back. He bent forward and pressed the stethoscope against the cloth. "You're definitely fit. You've got a strong, slow pulse."

"Told ya," Jimmy said.

"Now, as you can see, I have no exam table. I'll go get some bath towels to pad the lab table and make it more comfortable for you to lie on."

He turned and walked into his office.

Chena turned to Jimmy. "Hey, don't be a jerk. He's not doing anything wrong, he's just being careful."

He nodded, but looked away.

"You want to own a fishing boat someday?"

"Sure."

"Well, if this works, 'someday' is going to get about twenty years closer."

He sighed.

"I know," she said. "It is pretty weird. I'm about to get pregnant."

Yute reappeared with an armful of neatly folded white bath towels and a pillow. He arranged them on the black Formica tabletop.

"How do you want me?" Chena asked.

"You can just sit where you are for a moment. We're waiting on the last few test results." He ran his hand through his hair. "So far, so good."

He stood at the counter looking over the dishes and strips and tubes. "No alcohol, no nicotine, no cocaine, no herpes, no hepatitis, no gonorrhea, no syphilis, and"—the beeper on a timer went off. He picked up a white plastic disk and studied it closely, then let out a big sigh of relief—"no HIV."

He laughed and spun around to her and gave her a little hug. "This might all work out."

"Of course it will," she said. "It was meant to be."

"Okay, can you hop up on the table for me?"

She lay back on the towels and he placed the pillow under her head. She swiveled to look back at Jimmy. He appeared to be counting the floor tiles.

"Jimmy, will you rub my temples?"

"Sure," he said. "Got a headache?"

She only smiled to herself. He dragged his stool over to the end of the table and began to rub her temples in a slow and soothing way.

Yute put on a headband light and retrieved the petri dish from the electric warmer. Using a low-power magnifier, he counted the embryo's cells: sixteen now.

"The cells are dividing," he said. "It really is alive."

"Hope so," Chena said.

He picked up an instrument that ended in a sterile

gold wire, thinner than a human hair, and, with the magnifier in his other hand, bent his head over the petri dish.

"What are you doing now?" she asked.

"Embryo transplantation is a hit-and-miss procedure," he said softly as he worked. "I'm improving the odds by poking a few tiny holes in the outer envelope, which the embryo has to shed in order to implant in your uterine wall."

He unwrapped a sterilized speculum and smeared it with a sterile lubricant. With her hands Chena drew her knees up toward her chest. He gently inserted the speculum into her vagina, then expanded the instrument to reveal her cervix—the neck of her womb. At its center was an opening the size of a small pea.

"Hold still, one moment," he said.

He spun his chair to the counter and dunked the open end of a tiny plastic catheter with an attached syringe into the solution in the petri dish. He drew up the plunger and carefully sucked up the embryo into the tube, then spun back to Chena.

Sweat glistened on his forehead. "Now, please—don't move at all."

He lined up the catheter, inserted it through her cervical opening, and deposited the miracle in the fundus of her womb.

8

FLURRIES OF SNOW whipped around the corner of the federal courtroom building in Fairbanks. Nika Nahadeh tipped her parka's hood over her head, knowing in a few minutes she would have to yank it off again, because it was a winter parka, much too warm for October. She had sewn it out of caribou hide and lined it with arctic fox fur, and she wore it today, along with her hide pants and boots—even though it was only small-dry-flake-snow cold—because it was her best traditional clothing. Now, in spite of the chill gusts whistling past her ears, she felt her torso baking slowly, like a trout wrapped in wet dogwood bark and buried in red coals.

John Nahadeh, her father, stood next to her on the

courtroom's granite steps swaying back and forth to a rhythmic chant. He wore a ceremonial moosehide parka, bleached white by repeatedly smearing it with wet limestone paste and drying it in the sun. The roomy hem of the parka hung below his knees; it was bordered with diamond-shaped crimson designs painted with cranberry stain. With a padded stick he pounded a round hoop drum fashioned from willow wood draped with the thin, taut skin of a deer. He looked like a snowy mountain standing there, overflowing with spirit.

Other Indians from Swift Fork, Slow Fork, Telida, and as far away as Little Mud and Big Mud villages—many of them dressed in traditional garb—stood gathered on the courtroom steps, or strolled back and forth on the sidewalk, picketing with various signs. A row of four University of Alaska students spread a large banner that bore the flying ducks logo of CANARD—Central Alaska Native American Resource Developers—and the corporate slogan in black print, REAPING ALASKA'S RICHES FOR HER NATIVE PEOPLE; but two words had been edited with red paint, so that it now read: *RAPING* ALASKA'S RICHES *AND* HER NATIVE PEOPLE.

Nika's father turned to her and spoke in the Caiyuh language. "Nika, sing with me. We need every voice to join together now."

"Tell me what to sing, Father," she said, as he put his arm over her shoulder and drew her to his side. "I don't know the songs."

"I don't know any either," he said. "I make them up as I go."

"You know the hunting and fishing songs, the birth song . . ."

"Yes, a few. But think how many spirit songs were lost because I was too lazy as a boy to let my grandparents teach them to me." He looked down at her. "I don't know any spirit songs that can speak right now for the land, for the animals, against these greedy Indians and businessmen. So today I'm making the songs up. Listen, I've been singing like this."

He sang in a wavering falsetto, the chant weaving a simple melody over the heartbeat of the drum:

> "Grandmother is alive and you must not harm her.
> If you cut open her heart, you cut open my heart.
> Grandmother is alive and you must not harm her.
> Thieves, you don't belong here; she says she don't know you.
> Grandmother is alive and you must not harm her.
> When you hurt her, you always hurt yourself."

Nika sang with her father, softly at first, but as her passion overcame her shyness, her voice grew bolder until it rang from the granite walls like a reed flute, high and clear.

CANARD planned a gold-ore-mining operation in the foothills near her home. Most of the Indians in the neighboring villages strongly welcomed the project. It meant jobs. And that meant being able to afford beer, cigarettes, rifles, dirt bikes, bass boats, snowmobiles—and for the mine foremen, even a Jeep, or a new mobile home.

But most of the Caiyuh, of Swift Fork and Slow Fork villages, clung as well as they could to their old ways and were dead set against the mine. Lately, several environmental defense groups had come to their support after a *National Geographic* cover story on Tundra Man contained a short piece on the mine proposal that threatened the Caiyuh hunting grounds.

Now a young Chilkakot man in a bright orange ski jacket and wraparound mirror sunglasses yelled at John and Nika. "Hey! Go home and play Injuns! You wanna be native, go live in the woods with the fucking bears!"

John ignored the man and kept on singing, but soon a dozen young Indians surrounded them on the steps, screaming insults at them. Several of them carried silkscreened signs featuring the CANARD logo along with the words THE MINE IS MINE! Finally, the mob settled into a chant: "Go home, throwbacks! Go home, throwbacks!"

Nika felt her face get hot and her throat tighten until she could not sing. *Just don't cry,* she thought, biting her tongue hard. She felt her father's callused hand take hers and he led her through the hecklers into the foyer of the courthouse, where a federal marshal stood in front of the tall brass-plated doors to the courtroom. The officer stared ahead and did not acknowledge them.

In a private hearing inside his chambers the district judge was about to rule on a request for a three-year moratorium on the mining project to allow time for further environmental and social impact studies.

"Father," Nika whispered. He bent his head to hers. "Why can't they see that the land is ours and leave us alone?"

"Is the land ours?"

"You said our ancestors settled between the river forks longer ago than anyone can remember."

"Grandfather used to say that the stars are nicks on a burnt counting bone, one star-nick for each generation of Caiyuh that has fished the rivers and followed the caribou and tracked the mountain sheep."

"So we were there first, long before the Inupaks and Chilkakots and Athapaskans, let alone the whites."

"No, daughter. The land was there first. Then the Caiyuh came along, sprouting up like poppies on the tundra. The land doesn't belong to us; She gives us our lives. We belong to Her."

"Then why do so many Indians want the mine?"

He shook his head. "If things go our way today, we get three more years to convince them that a gold-smelting mine will hurt the tundra, bad. Time enough to get more ecologist people to back us up. Then we can demand another break; keep stalling, keep fighting it."

From behind the closed doors of the courtroom came murmurings and footsteps. In a moment the heavy doors flew open. Two non-native men and a Chilkakot Indian dressed in crisp dark gray suits and red ties swept out of the wood-paneled room. The white man in the lead froze opposite John and Nika and scowled. Frizzy blond hair raked from ear to ear across his bald crown. His tie bore a repeating V-pattern of flying golden ducks. The man trembled with anger and pursed his lips as if he were holding back from exploding. The second white man, who carried a shiny aluminum briefcase, grabbed his arm and pulled him along. The Indian man's face was a dark moon adorned with a black walrus mustache. He walked tall and showed no emotion, but nodded to John as he passed.

John returned the acknowledgment.

"That pink-faced man was Rex Kaiser, the big boss at CANARD," John whispered. "He don't look too happy with us. This looks real good." He kept his eyes fixed on the doors.

"Chief Willy looked like a phony in that suit."

"Hush." John shot her a sharp glance. "Do not speak of people you know nothing about. He's a good man."

Nika was taken aback. "You know him?"

"We met years ago, in this city."

She knew then he was talking about the months he spent in an alcoholic rehab center run by the Salvation Army. He ended up there the year after her mother died giving birth to her. He had left Nika in Swift Fork in the care of her grandmother.

"You can't blame him for what he's doing. He cares about his people."

"But he wants the gold mine."

"You have to see it from his point of view. When he was a boy, he and most of his friends were sent away to an Indian boarding school in Seattle. He learned a lot of useless stuff, and when he got back to Telida, he and the other boys were unable to help their dads hunt and fish. The girls were just as lost. If you said 'Go dig up some wild potatoes,' they'd have to ask 'What do they look like? Where do I find them?' "

"That's terrible."

"Yes, well, the boys took it hardest. They couldn't get jobs, unless they left home and went out to work on the pipeline, or moved to the cities. So a lot of them hung around, feeling worthless, and got drunk, got into fights."

"He was an alcoholic?"

"Yes, but he straightened himself out fast, same as me. We talked a lot back then. He told me his goal was to lead his people into the modern world. You got to admit he's done that."

"Then the mine is his dream come true."

John nodded and appeared lost in thought. "I remember the counselors read the Bible to us every day. Not much of it made sense to me, but one line stood out: 'What does it profit a man to gain the world and lose his soul?' "

A blond woman, wearing a navy-blue dress with a single strand of pearls, stepped out and rushed over to John, lifting her briefcase triumphantly; the logo of the eco-defense group One Home Planet was silkscreened on the black canvas.

"It passed! We won!" she said. "They get to continue geological research, but they can't start mining for three years."

"Aiyoo! Thank you, Linda, thank you so much!" John said, shaking her by the shoulders so that her short hairdo bounced. *"Aya hey, Wa Denali!"* he shouted, and his voice broke with emotion. *"Aya hey, yo aya hey, Wa Denali!"* It echoed from the marble floors and walls. Tears streaked his face. Nika had seen her father cry only one other time, when her brother, Yute, had come home for the summer during a break at medical school. Tears spilled down her own cheeks. *Aya hey, Wa Denali,* she said silently.

"You must stay the night with us," John said to the lawyer, laughing now and wiping his eyes on his parka sleeve. "Big party! Salmonberry moon. We'll go ice fishing, the whole village."

"Well . . . sure. Sounds wonderful. First I've got to get back to my hotel room, put on some clothes for the real world." She twiddled her pearls. "What do I need to bring?"

"Just dress warm. We got everything."

Two crews of TV news reporters huddled around them. Nika squinted into the glare of a television camera light.

"Can I get a statement from you?" a reporter asked the lawyer.

"Talk to Mr. Nahadeh," she said, smiling. "He and his tribe are the real winners today."

The reporter turned to John. "As leader of the mine opposition, what do you want to see happen to the foothills?"

"Nothing. I don't want nothing to happen to them. I want them to stay the way they've been forever, heaped up under the sun, full of people, with Denali standing above—beautiful."

"Full of people? What do you mean?"

"The four-leggeds and the winged and finned people, the trees and grasses . . . all the tribes that live on Grandmother. Not just to humans She is home."

The other reporter thrust his microphone in front. "Is it true you've received death threats, warning you to drop your fight against the mine?"

John shrugged. "I once got death threats from my father when I broke his best hunting knife. Just means they're angry—they want the mine and I don't. But the Athapaskans and Chilkakots and my people have been neighbors for a long, long time. At heart, we're brothers, not—"

"Thank you. Good enough." The reporter turned to his cameraman. "Did you get the girl? She'll make a good mug for a voice-over." The cameraman nodded, and the bright light was again in Nika's face. "C'mon. Let's get some sound bites from the demonstrators before it breaks up." The two bolted through the outer doors, while the other television crew hurried off in the direction of the CANARD men.

The lawyer frowned. "And you wonder why people don't get in-depth coverage of the issues," she said.

John arranged to pick her up later at her hotel. Then he and Nika stepped out into the street to join the other protestors and board the school bus that would take them home.

In the courthouse parking lot a large crowd of pro-mine demonstrators surrounded a small group of Caiyuh. The CANARD supporters were waving their fists and chanting, "The mine is mine! The mine is mine!" Someone in the crowd shouted something and a hundred heads turned at once and the mob surged toward John and Nika.

"Stay behind me," John told Nika as he stepped in front. "Just relax, and don't let go of my hips. We're going to do the shadow dance."

She squeezed his baggy parka and grabbed his hips with both hands. John moved forward in an easy stroll, saying nothing, looking straight ahead. The mob met and pressed around them, yelling and cursing.

"Hey, you fucking retards! Old-Ways is past. We want jobs now."

"Get off our jobs, Grandpa. You don't belong in the modern world."

John didn't slow and didn't hurry, but only shifted his center here and there to cut through the arms and legs of the crowd; Nika held on and blended with his movements, as when they did the shadow dance at home in front of the fire. She felt his power as he parted the crowd; not the iron force of a wedge splitting firewood, but the steady flow of a raindrop wending its way through a woodpile, rolling over and around the logs. Someone slapped the top of her head so hard, she saw stars; she did not look, she held on. Someone screamed in her ear; she saw only her father's broad back and held on.

After what seemed a terribly long moment, they were out of the pack and walking alone down the slushy sidewalk. Nika didn't look back, but she could hear that the mob was not following. Fifty yards ahead the small group of Caiyuh walked toward them. It was not until she was standing in the midst of her friends and her father patted her hands that she realized she was still clutching his hips.

"You're a very good shadow dancer," he said.

She took a deep breath and put her head down, crying without a sound.

"No tears now, daughter," he said softly, lifting her chin in his rough hand. He smiled with his eyes and they shone as bright and warm as a campfire. "We're safe. The hills are still safe. And tonight we go full-moon ice-fishing in the way of our ancestors. *Aya hey, Wa Denali!*"

9

CHENA AND JIMMY parked their shopping cart beside a row of wooden tables heaped with fresh fruits and vegetables in the open-air farmers' market. A crowd of shoppers wound through the narrow alleys between food huts and produce bins. Thai and Filipino and Chinese and Italian and Greek foods were boiling, sizzling, baking, roasting, in the little white huts, spicing the cool air with rich aromas. High above, silver flakes of clouds covered the May sky like the scales of a mackerel.

Chena inhaled deeply. "Mmmm, smell. . . ."

"It all smells great," Jimmy said.

"Tonight, I'm gonna cook you a supper that'll send you floating off to Old Man Land."

She chuckled at the image. It had been a long time since she'd thought of that expression. Old Man Land was a real locale, a tiny wooded islet near Whaler Bay Island, but it had taken on the feel of a mythic place—a spirit world. Supposedly it was always shrouded in fog and lost in *tsitsika*, "twilight time," when nothing is quite real. Old Man, a shaman, had lived there alone for as long as the oldest villagers could remember, and there seemed to be no end to far-fetched stories about him.

"Ooh, there it goes again," she said. She took his hand and placed it over the firm hemisphere of her belly. "Feel that?"

"Wow. You got a World Cup soccer player in there. So that's the big secret—it's a clone of Pelé."

Dr. Nahadeh had told them the donor of the embryo was an anonymous client, a mystery even to himself. He had given them the first $15,000, and they would get the rest when the baby was born and her job was done. Their part of the deal was simply for her to stay healthy and stay put and for them both to keep quiet about the whole thing. But between themselves they speculated and joked about the baby's identity: a test-tube child from a geniuses-only sperm-and-egg bank; a baby Jesus, cloned from skin cells scraped from the Shroud of Turin. Who knows? But certainly, a special kid. Otherwise, why all the secrecy?

Nowadays, Dr. Nahadeh dropped by the apartment about once a week to check on her and Jimmy. He was downright motherly about her health, even Jimmy's.

He planned to deliver the baby himself, right there, in the apartment.

Three weeks to go. Her breasts felt heavy and full; her whole body hummed with life. She closed her eyes and smiled.

"Chena, you should see yourself right now," Jimmy said. "If you stepped into a dark room, you'd glow like fox fire."

She laughed. "That's just the way I feel."

They loaded a canvas bag in their shopping cart with apples and pears. They strolled on, past a stall with whole ducks turning on metal skewers and another with strings of sausages dangling alongside waxed blocks of round cheeses. They came to a row of low wooden bins heaped with crushed ice and many kinds of fresh fish, and again, Chena breathed in deeply and the oily, cold, raw smell of the sea seemed to expand, not only her lungs, but her heart.

"You like the smell?" asked a dark-skinned Chinese man behind the counter. He wore a white apron streaked with fish blood. His whole face crinkled into a smile that narrowed his eyes into slits and revealed two gold front teeth.

Chena nodded. "I like it a lot."

"I like it too," he said, grinning and nodding vigorously. "Most folks think that people like you and me are crazy. But my father and uncles, cousins, everybody, was fishermen in Taiwan, and fish smell good to me, like home."

"Me too. Where I come from, if you're not a logger or a fisherman, you're a bum," she said. "Or a housewife, I guess. My family, we're all loggers, but we love fish. Eat it all the time. My brothers—you should see them eat. They're all huge guys."

As soon as she said it, she felt sad. It seemed to her that she had flicked the surface of a pool of hidden sorrow. Curious, she tested the water again. It was surprisingly deep, and for the first time in eight months she allowed herself to slip into homesickness. She looked away from the Chinese man as her eyes misted, busying herself with choosing a fish.

I'm going to be my own woman—or at least well on my way—before I go back home. Home? *So it is home, after all. But I'm with Jimmy now. That's the way it's going to stay.*

She selected a whole herring, which he wrapped in white butcher paper and stuck in a plastic bag. She held out a five-dollar bill, but he waved it away.

"I many time miss my home too," he said in a softer voice, still smiling. "You two enjoy this fish, come back see me, okay? Show me new baby."

She swallowed hard and thanked him with a deep nod.

"What was that all about?" Jimmy said as they walked on.

She shrugged.

"You mean you're as homesick as I am?"

Her eyebrows shot up. "Oh, Jimmy!" She hugged him, with her big belly squeezed between. "Let's go home!"

"All right, okay, listen to this: In three weeks, you have the baby, we take the money and we go back to Whaler Bay. Nobody knows any different. We get married and get our own place. I start running trout lines from my own boat. You go on to nursing school. And maybe, later on, we start our own family."

She smiled. "And we live happily ever after."

"Exactly. Just like in the kids' books."

PART TWO

(Nahadeh, Yute, *The Neanderthal Papers*, Pacific College Press, Deer Park, Washington, 1987, p. 76.)

The usual notion is that Cro-Magnon peoples invading from the east slaughtered the less sophisticated Neanderthals of the west. But this scenario is not likely. The Neanderthals, with their larger brain size and massive brawn, would have been able to defend themselves mightily against aggressors on their home turf. It is far more plausible that Neanderthals evolved into modern humans—and thus "disappeared" by becoming something new.

Speech is the evolutionary engine that drove the rapid change of Neanderthals into you and me. Speech would be an inestimably advantageous tool for humans to acquire;

thus nature and society would delete the genes of less gifted talkers from the gene pool. As Neanderthals began to rely more on talking, the pharynx grew larger, the voice box descended in the throat, and the base of the skull (the ceiling of the voice cavity) became more arched. As this arch became more vaulted, it gave the entire head its modern shape: the longer, lower Neanderthal skull with its more outthrust face was drawn in and up into a shorter, taller skull with a more vertical face.

In this light our modern species might be more appropriately named **Homo loquitur,** Man the talker.

10

As Chena's due date neared, Yute worried daily about all the things that could go wrong during birth, the many dangers to her and to his Neanderthal child. But here he sat at her bedside, six hours after her water broke, watching her labor progress smoothly, in text-book-perfect stages. He felt his shoulders relax for the first time in weeks.

Chena sat upright in the bed, wearing a sunflower print nightshirt, pulled up to expose her beachball-round belly. Her hair was sweaty, her face flushed, but her eyes shone brightly, with no signs of tiredness. She was young, tall, and big boned, with flexible joints and elastic muscle tone and a strong heart and lungs. It was as she told him the day they met, "Kynaka women are built for birthing babies."

Jimmy sat behind her, propping up her torso, leaning back against the headboard. He wore a pair of denim cutoffs and a T-shirt with a Mako Fishing Boats logo. He rubbed her lower back during her contractions and gave her sips of Gatorade from a sports drink bottle when she rested. The two squeezed hands and talked softly. In the background blue and pink lambs hopped over rainbows —the wallpaper was Chena's idea.

Her contractions arrived faster—every two minutes. She let out a loud groan, and her round belly squeezed into an oblong shape.

She glanced at Yute. "I'm getting a really strong urge to push."

"Okay, but not just yet," he said. "Let me check you real quick first."

He squeezed a glob of lubricant jelly into his hand and smeared it over his fingers. He waited for the contraction to end, then checked the cervical opening of her womb. She was fully dilated.

He smiled at her. "Great, Chena, go ahead and push on the next one. You're ready to have this baby."

With the next wave of muscle contractions she grunted and bore down; her face reddened and sweat popped out on her forehead. Wave after wave of contractions followed, with only brief rest spells between.

Chena had pushed for most of an hour when the top of the baby's head appeared. Wet hair plastered its scalp in thick swirls.

Yute hopped out of his chair. "It's crowning!" he shouted. "Look at all that hair!"

Chena grimaced, eyes squeezed shut; Jimmy helped her reach down and touch the baby's wet hair. "Oh! It's so warm!" she said. When the contraction eased, she tilted her face up and Jimmy bent his head down to kiss her.

Yute reached into his medical kit for a hand mirror that he held between her legs when the baby crowned again.

"Wow," Jimmy said. "Chena, open your eyes, you can see the whole top of its head."

Yute touched the dark head of hair with his whole hand and felt the heat through his surgical glove. Anticipation surged through him like live current. A Neanderthal—a time traveler across twenty-five thousand years—was being born into his world.

Chena pushed again and the baby's head crowned further. "*Oowww.* It hurts."

"You're doing great," Jimmy said.

"No, it hurts bad."

"You're almost there," Yute said, and squirted lubricant jelly from a white tube onto the baby's head. "It's going to hurt, can't get around that. Just a few more pushes and it'll be over."

The contractions continued powerfully, and the baby crowned each time, but the head did not move down steadily through the birth canal. Yute clenched his teeth; his doubts were back, redoubled.

"Oh, it's coming, here it comes!" Jimmy said. "Push with all you've got, Chena."

Chena growled from deep in her throat and contorted her face into a fierce expression, like a Quanoot warrior. The baby crowned all the way to the brow, then the rest of its head slowly exited, facedown.

Yute cupped his hands around the baby's head, to catch the birth on the next push. Chena bore down again, shaking with exertion, but the rest of the body did not slide free.

"*Owww, owww,* I can't!" she yelled, and grabbed Jimmy's arms. "It's breaking my bones."

"Hey, do something, man—the baby's stuck," Jimmy said, his black eyes huge.

Yute's mind raced. In the past weeks he had practically memorized an obstetrical manual for medical personnel working in the Third World, far from hospitals. But his only hands-on experience had been delivering twins in a taxicab in the hospital parking lot—six years ago, when he was a medical resident.

He worked his jaw muscles. *What is the complication here?*

Chena screamed in pain with another contraction, but the baby didn't move down.

Adrenaline shot through Yute and his body jerked. *Shoulder dystocia—a double-mortality emergency. The baby's shoulder lodges behind the mother's pubic bone and can't budge, while the walls of the birth canal compress the umbilical cord, cutting off the baby's blood flow.*

It's a pop quiz, you fool. In his mind's eye he reviewed the manual's diagrams depicting a trapped shoulder. *All right, by the book. What first?*

"McRobert's maneuver," he said aloud. He grabbed Chena's legs and pulled her down to the end of the bed so that her buttocks slid off the edge. "Jimmy, pull her legs all the way back. Get her knees as close to her shoulders as you can."

Chena pushed again with a deep grunt and then a shriek of pain. Yute gripped his hands on either side of the baby's head over its ears and tugged downward with a steady, strong pressure. The tiny body did not yield; it was as though he were trying to pull a stump out of the ground. The baby's face was turning blue.

"Okay, Jimmy, make a fist and push straight down over her pubic bone. No, right there, right there. Try to push the baby's shoulder underneath the bone while I pull."

He tugged again. Sweat snaked down Chena's torso in rivulets.

"You pushing, Jimmy? Push down *hard.*"

"I am, it's not working."

"All right, Chena, I'm going to give you more room down here," Yute said, and dove into his doctor's bag for a pair of surgical scissors. Without taking time to inject a painkiller he wedged his fingers between the baby's neck and Chena's tissue, slid the scissors in deep, and snipped once. Chena yelped.

Next step: Wood's maneuver.

"I'm going to reach my hands inside you," he told Chena. "It's the only way."

He squeezed his hands past the baby's head into the birth canal. He pressed one hand against the baby's back and the other against its chest and tried to rotate the baby. It would not budge. The baby's face darkened to the shade of a blueberry.

"I'm calling nine one one," Jimmy said, and started to scoot out from behind Chena.

"Too late for that," Yute said. "Stay put, I need you here."

"Too late for the baby, maybe—"

"If you want to save Chena, sit your ass back down."

Jimmy drilled Yute with his look. "Man, you better be right."

"Lift her under her arms, help me slide her back onto the bed," Yute said. "Chena, I need you to roll over onto your hands and knees."

She shook her head, without looking up.

Yute took her face in his hands and tilted it up so that their eyes met. "Don't quit on me now, Chena. Please. The next few minutes count like nothing else ever will."

She nodded.

"Jimmy, help . . . I've got her legs . . . okay, lift her up and turn her over." Chena cried out as they spun her and set her down onto her hands and knees.

Next step: Free the opposite shoulder. Yute pushed his fingers inside to loosen the shoulder at the perineum, opposite the trapped shoulder. It swiveled an inch or two, but the problem shoulder still did not dislodge; muscular contraction pinned it against the pubic bone like a powerful current jamming a swimmer against a rock.

Next step . . . and last resort. Yute gulped at the thought. *Break the baby's collarbone.*

He groped until his fingers touched the clavicle of the trapped shoulder. He pinched the bone between his thumb and two fingers, and twisted hard . . . harder . . . *dammit*! He sucked in his breath and twisted with the force it takes to snap a thick wooden pencil; his fore-arm bulged and trembled before the bone fractured with a loud *pop*. Instantly, the shoulder hunched forward and slid free of its snare.

"It worked!" Yute shouted. "It worked!"

He caught the limp baby as it slipped out, trailing the umbilical cord. Its bluish skin was coated with white, cheesy vernix and smeared with Chena's bright blood. It was a girl, and she was not breathing. Yute placed her on her back on the bed and put his big hand over her tiny chest; he felt a weak heartbeat.

"Jimmy, get Chena down on her back, prop her feet up with a pillow. Keep her warm. Talk to her. I'll be with her as soon as I can."

"Is the baby okay?" Chena asked in a weak voice.

Yute suctioned the baby's mouth and nose with a bulb syringe, then placed two plastic clamps on the slippery cord close to the belly and cut between the clamps with scissors. Sweat droplets from his face splashed onto his hands. He wrapped the newborn in a baby blanket and dried it vigorously, to stimulate blood flow. It did not make a sound.

"Jimmy, grab that oxygen gear for me."

Yute tilted the little head back as if she were sniffing the air and put his mouth over her nose and mouth and gently puffed, praying that her snapped clavicle had not punctured a lung. After two quick puffs he cocked his ear close to her nose and heard her make a reflexive effort to breathe.

"C'mon, c'mon, c'mon!" He puffed twice again and listened. "C'mon, kitten, you can do it." He was about to puff again, when, with a little gasp, the baby began to breathe on its own.

Yute moaned with relief. He bent his head close to the baby's face and whispered. "That's it, keep it up. Good job. We call that breathing. You're going to be doing that on your own now, your whole life long."

Chena stared at the baby with wide-open eyes.

"She's okay, she's coming on strong," he said, and then, suddenly, he was crying. He held the oxygen mask over the infant's face and shuddered from head to toe.

He sniffed. "You doing all right, Chena?"

She nodded. "A little girl," she whispered.

Yute pressed his stethoscope to the baby's chest and heard the rhythmic swish of two tiny bellows. Her lungs were inflating on both sides—no punctures. Her skin tone pinked up, spreading from her chest to her face and then outward to her limbs. Again he briskly rubbed her skin with the blanket and this time she began bawling in loud yelps, her little mouth a circle of trembling lips.

"Let me hold her," Chena said, reaching for the baby.

Yute laid the newborn on its belly on Chena's chest. She held the baby close, talking to it sweetly in a high, singsong voice. It stopped crying and opened its eyes and appeared to listen intently.

"Jimmy, she knows me," Chena said.

The newborn's skin tone now became a rich, deep pink, with a hint of gold suffused through it.

"Look at her color," Chena said. "She's beautiful. And her hair . . . and she's got eyebrows and eyelashes already."

Jimmy frowned and said nothing.

"We need to keep her warm," Yute said, and unfolded a receiving blanket.

"She's toasty," Chena said.

"Standard procedure," he said, and covered the infant with the fluffy blanket.

"Is she all right? I heard something go *pop*. Was that me or her?"

Yute felt a chill in his gut. "I had to break her collarbone to get her out."

Chena gasped. "Oh, you poor sweetie," she said, and kissed the baby's cheeks. "Does she need to go to the hospital?"

He shook his head. "You don't need to do much for a simple fracture of the clavicle—maybe immobilize the arm in a sling—but usually even that's not needed." He leaned down and gently palpated the baby's shoulder girdle. "Good. Yeah, that looks real good. She should heal just fine all by herself." He sighed. *And I'm damn lucky it* was *a simple fracture and it didn't stab through her lung.*

"Thank God," Chena said. "Did you hear that, sweetie? You're gonna be just fine." She kissed the baby again. "She smells so fresh, like rain."

The newborn bobbed its head, rooting for a nipple. Chena helped it to find the dark smooth target. It latched on and nursed.

"What a strong suck." She smiled at Jimmy. "Little whale calf!"

Jimmy leaned his head against hers and watched the baby nurse.

Chena talked and cooed at the nursing baby, and

only winced once when Yute delivered the placenta. Then he injected Xylocaine into her muscle tissue and sewed together the episiotomy incision.

Yute cut the thread above the last knot and glanced at his watch—almost 8:00 A.M. He stood and pulled off his surgical gloves with a snap.

Mother and child were resting. His Neanderthal was alive and well, but he was too drained to think clearly or to feel much joy. He badly needed sleep. Tomorrow would be for science, for elation. This morning he felt relieved that his curiosity and ambition had not killed them both.

Chena awoke in the early afternoon. Jimmy brought her waffles with fresh-sliced peaches on top, scrambled eggs, and orange juice. He perched at the foot of the bed.

"Thanks," she said, sitting up. "I'm so hungry."

She balanced the plate in her lap and ate, gazing at the infant dozing on its belly beside her. The little thing really did have the longest hair for a newborn—past her shoulders—and it was unlike any hair color Chena had seen: so darkly red, it looked black, but when it caught the sunlight from the bedroom window it glowed like an ember.

Ember. It was the perfect name for her.

"What do you think of naming her Ember?" Chena said.

Jimmy frowned. "I hate to keep reminding you, Chena, but it's not ours."

A lump the size of a crab apple rose in Chena's throat. She put the fork down on the plate and set the half-eaten meal on the end table. Tears welled up in her eyes.

"Aw, Chena," Jimmy said, and let out a sigh. "This is what I knew was going to happen."

"It's not his either."

"He already told us that—"

"And you're the one who told me not to believe him."

"Well, turns out he was telling the truth. If that's an Indian baby, I'm a white man."

"So if we kept it, it's not like we'd be stealing his daughter. It's not his child."

"Chena. Get real. When he comes back tomorrow he's going to give us the final twenty-five thousand dollars and take the kid. We'll go back to Whaler Bay and start a new life together."

"He mentioned letting me nurse it for a few weeks —extra money."

"Bad idea. You'll only get more attached."

The baby stirred and lifted its head to look at Chena, twisted around to see Jimmy, then flopped its head down again.

Chena gave a startled laugh. "Did you see that?"

"What's the matter?" Jimmy said.

"She raised her head."

"So?"

"Newborns aren't supposed to be able to do that. Watch—*there*."

The infant lifted its head again and looked around

the room with shiny eyes. Then with a little lunge, it rolled over onto its back and started to cry.

"Look at that," Chena said. "Newborn babies just don't roll over." She scooped up the infant and cuddled it against her bosom, rocking gently. It stopped crying and began nuzzling with its mouth, whimpering. Chena felt a liquid warmth surge deep in her breasts. She guided the baby's mouth to her leaking nipple.

The baby sweated from the effort of nursing, and Chena took off its one-piece flannel pajamas. The sudden heat of its skin touching hers startled her, and in the same instant a current of life flowed tangibly between herself and the child.

"It's two way, isn't it, Ember?" she said, and stroked the long, soft hair. "You're feeding me, too, somehow. I don't know how . . . I just feel your vitality. We Quanoots say: 'The river runs strong through you.' "

She gazed at the little face, at the red Kewpie-doll lips sucking hungrily, rosy cheeks and skin ever more golden. Sadness closed around Chena's heart like a seine. She swallowed and pressed her lips together.

"Who in the world are her real parents?" she asked in a shaky voice.

"Beats me. She doesn't look white or brown or black or—"

"She's golden. Ember is golden. And if her parents love her at all, where are they? Why aren't they here?"

In a moment the baby's eyes fluttered and closed; her long, dark eyelashes stood out against her cheeks. In her sleep she continued to nurse.

Chena sang a Quanoot song to Ember. She sang it

to Jimmy too. It told the story of a man from a village of hardworking fishermen who trapped a sea otter and how the otter bargained with him, promising him a great gift for sparing his life. The man agreed and set the sea otter free. Later, when the man's wife gave birth, he recognized the humorous spirit of the sea otter in his baby girl. She taught him how to laugh and play and have fun; and then she taught him how to make music and dance, carve and paint, and tell stories and jokes. Together, he and his little daughter showed the whole village the joyful arts that balance work.

"Jimmy, you sure you want us to have kids?"

"*Someday.* I've told you that."

"You'd make a great dad." She smiled with her big gray eyes.

He rolled his eyes. "Aw, Chena, here we go . . . you're doing it."

"Doing what?"

"What I knew you were going to do."

By the time Chena shifted Ember to her other breast, she and Jimmy were wrestling over the pros and cons of returning home to Whaler Bay Island with a new daughter.

11

YUTE SAT IN front of his computer, running protein analyses using the USDA database. His research had found three different types of antifreeze proteins in Tundra Woman's blood and a dozen unidentified oddities.

A stereo receiver on the countertop was tuned to a National Public Radio news program, and a small television set was tuned to CNN, with the sound muted. Every now and then, when he saw TV images that interested him, he muted the radio and unmuted the television.

In a spiral-bound notebook he wrote copious research notes in his hybrid of cursive and printed letters. He looked up at the TV and groped with his left hand for the remote. He listened to part of a split-screen dialogue—Barbara Walters interviewing herself. Then activity on the computer screen grabbed his attention; a molecular model rapidly took shape.

"Outstanding," he said. "Number four."

So far, each of the antifreeze proteins identified in Tundra Woman's blood had matched with a protein produced in some arctic plant or animal. Two were from freeze-resistant lichens, one from an ice worm that burrows cozily through glaciers, feeding on dissolved minerals. The protein now on the screen—the USDA labeled it AFP16—matched with one found in a species of tiny arctic frog that spends each winter encased in pond ice, then hops away when the ice thaws in the spring.

Yute marveled at how a prescientific person could have selected to eat the necessary plants and animals to prevent tissue freezing. Or had it merely been coincidence, just a normal part of her daily diet?

But suppose she had concocted an antifreeze potion—say, boiled the stuff down and made it into a concentrated paste—it raised the most mystifying question: Why did she decide to preserve her body, unfrozen? *Why?*

"Perhaps it was an aspect of Neanderthal religious belief," he said, and flipped open his notebook and jotted down the idea.

He checked the time. In a quarter hour an opera program would begin, and he would switch on the four big speakers positioned around the lab. Tonight's program featured his favorite performer, Angelica de Venicia, at the Met. He adored her voice, for she was the rarest of songbirds in the opera forest—a mezzo—with a darker, denser tone than a soprano's.

It had taken him several years to fall in love with opera, after being introduced to it by his first college roommate. Actually, the music had thrilled him from the start, but it was tough to overcome his disgust with the pretentiousness that engulfed the opera scene. He did not admire the white ties and tails, chandeliers, limousines, and narcissism of it all. He'd once heard of a week-long Colorado River raft cruise in which opera singers sang to the boaters around the campfire at day's end. That was the kind of opera environment he could appreciate: beautiful music and wonderful voices—and bury the rest of it.

He had bought a bottle of country Merlot to celebrate the birth of his living Neanderthal, and he uncorked it now, with a bright *whup*! It was not an expensive wine, but he preferred its flavor to most of the high-priced grape he had tasted at faculty parties. There were no wineglasses in the lab, so he poured the dark liquid into a small, clean beaker.

He glanced at his watch, reached forward, stored the data, turned off the computer, and flicked on the speakers. In a few moments Venicia was singing Rossini, her voice flying up and down the scales like a burst of sparrows through a sunlit orchard. He turned the volume up and leaned back in his chair, stretching his legs and propping his running shoes on the counter beside the keyboard. He pictured the youthful virtuoso in a white cotton tank top, khaki shorts, and hiking boots; singing to him by a campfire. A ruddy glow danced across her features. Her voice spilled forth as effortlessly as her dark mane tumbled over her milky shoulders, or as the sweet wine flowed down to warm his belly. He splashed another few fingers of Merlot into the flask.

While he gloried in the sensual pleasure of the music and wine, he began doodling in blue ink on the back cover of his notebook. Stars and spirals and swirls, mindless forms and patterns, as he lost himself in the music. He sighed as the singer soared through a breathtaking aria, and he lifted his pen and danced it in the air like a conductor's baton.

When his eyes returned to the notebook he noticed he had sketched a man's rugged face. Now he wrote above it, *Neanderthal*?

He tried to remember when he first became interested in Neanderthals. He couldn't pinpoint a time; even as a boy he had often sketched similar faces and Stone Age scenes. Yet he never understood the depth of his fascination; it was simply a kind of hunger to learn more.

He shook his head and swigged the wine.

It was as if some secret about Neanderthals always hovered beyond the range of his knowledge. *As if—as if* . . . he rolled his eyes upward, searching for the thought.

The other power. He blinked in surprise as the words popped into his awareness.

Other power? What other power?

Nothing occurred to him. He tried to feel the question with his whole being, but no concrete answer came forth, just a vague sense of some great loss, and a need to regain what was lost.

The other power . . . the *other* power . . .

He finished off the wine in the flask.

Other than *what*?

This time an image leapt into his mind: a mouth with lines of force radiating from the lips. He frowned. That was the tattoo on Tundra Man's forehead. Now he added the design to his sketch of the rugged face. It made a likeness of the prehistoric man discovered last year.

But what does Tundra Man, a Cro-Magnon, have to do with Neanderthals? He stared at the portrait, trying to find its link to his subconscious mind, but he drew another blank.

He shrugged and tossed the notebook on the counter.

"Wine talks, but it babbles."

He tugged off his sweater, and filled the flask to its neck. The ornate music decorated the room.

For now, he thought, *I'm going to enjoy this magnificent coloratura, this human nightingale, and not try to figure out my Neanderthal fixation. The baby is here. A three-year sabbatical to raise her at my cabin gives me time to observe and examine and test her. Then I'll announce what I've accomplished—publish my findings in every relevant journal—and call in consultants from around the world to study the child with me.*

The anticipation of profound discovery was at once exciting and calming. He put the flask to his lips and gulped the wine, feeling immensely satisfied.

The phone rang. He answered without turning down the music volume. It was Chena.

"How are you feeling?" he asked. "How's the baby? Listen, I've been thinking that I'd like to hire you to be her nanny."

"I'm calling you from Whaler Bay Island," Chena said.

"You're *where*?" Yute snapped to attention and yanked his feet down off the counter; the chair legs screeched. He grabbed for the remote controller and knocked it to the floor. He lunged and cranked down the volume by hand.

Chena told him of her decision. She and Jimmy were back home to stay. They didn't want the rest of the money; they were going to keep the baby.

"We had a deal!" Yute shouted.

"You said you'd give us five thousand for just trying, plus ten thousand if it worked. Well, it did, and we're keeping that money—for now, anyway—I mean . . . maybe we can pay you back someday."

"I don't give a damn about the money. The baby is mine."

"That's not true," Chena said. "She wouldn't be alive if not for me. I'm her mother, surrogate or not, and . . . I love her. She's staying here with Jimmy and me. I'm sorry. That's just the way it is."

"Wait . . . Chena, wait. Let me think . . ." Yute put a hand to his forehead. His mind swam from the wine, and he felt out of breath. *What the hell am I supposed to do now?*

"Look, Chena, you're a good kid, a real good kid, I like you. Honestly. But do you think that I'm just going to lie back and let you do this? I can't. I'm coming to get the baby."

Jimmy's voice came over the line. "I think not, Doc. Not if you want to keep your precious secret. Anyone can see this kid is special; how special, we don't know; we don't want to know. You don't hassle us, and we won't tell a soul where the baby came from; no one will come snooping around your lab asking a lot of questions, stuff like that. But if you give us any trouble, you're gonna earn yourself a Ph.D. in trouble before it's over. So you've got no choice."

"Jimmy, please listen to reason—"

"Chena and I are sorry it had to end this way, but . . . well . . . we're real sorry. We all shoulda seen it coming. Thank you for your help and all. Good-bye."

The phone clicked dead at his end.

Yute banged down the receiver, then leapt from his chair and ripped the cord out of the answering-machine unit. He swung his body and hurled the phone across the lab against the freezer door. It shattered in a confetti of plastic and the tape cassette skittered over the green tiles to rest at the feet of Tundra Woman's skeleton.

12

THE DOWNPOUR ON the cabin's tin roof filled the room with a trembling gel of sound. Chena stretched out on a sleeping bag atop an air mattress on the cedar plank floor. She read from *Dr. Spock's Baby and Child Care* by the silvery-white glare of a gas lantern hanging from a rafter.

Ember slept beside her, wearing only diapers; she fussed and screamed if Chena tried to dress her in pajamas.

"Ember keeps kicking off her blanket," Chena said. "That's about the tenth time."

Jimmy sat with his back to the room at a workbench near the rear wall, outboard motor parts spread before him. His black ponytail poked through the hole at the back of his baseball cap and hung past the yoke of his denim jacket.

"She's like one of those little electric hand warmers," he said. "If it's warm enough for you and me, it's plenty warm for her."

"Yeah, I guess," she said, touching Ember's golden skin.

"You guess? She's trying to say, 'Mommy, will you keep that tortilla off me? I'm no bean burrito.' "

Chena laughed and went back to her reading. Every now and then she read aloud a passage to Jimmy and they talked about it.

"You remind me of him," she said.

"Of who?"

"Dr. Spock."

"I remind you of a bald white guy in his eighties?"

"He seems really kind, like you."

Jimmy turned around and met her eyes for a moment. "Everything's going to be all right, Chena."

She nodded. "I hope so." She gently stroked Ember's back; it was silky soft, with almost invisibly fine blond peach fuzz. "Do you think Dr. Nahadeh will leave us alone?"

"He better."

Chena snuggled next to Ember to smell the dark garden of her hair; she closed her eyes and rubbed her nose against the baby's warm head.

"Have you got enough light?" Jimmy asked, "—'cause I don't. I lost a carburetor screw."

"Come take the lantern, I'm going to go to sleep anyway."

A knock sounded on the cabin door.

Chena sat up and Jimmy hopped off his stool. They shot looks at each other. She scooped up the baby and moved to his side.

"Couldn't be him," he said, and jabbed his fingers into a can of Goop hand cleaner. "No way the ferry ran in this storm." He rubbed the white cream around his blackened hands and wiped off the grease with a red rag.

"And how could he know where to find us?" she asked.

"Unless someone down in the village told him," he said.

He dragged a wooden crate out from under the workbench and lifted off the lid. Chena winced. Her father and brothers were avid hunters, but since childhood she had hated guns.

The knock sounded again, louder.

Jimmy reached into the crate and pulled out his grandfather's harpoon rifle. He grabbed a two-foot-long stainless steel harpoon with a barbed head that looked like a grappling hook tipped with a sharp nose cone. He loaded a powder cartridge into the rifle's firing chamber, then folded the hinged barbs of the harpoon and slid it inside the short, fat barrel. The tip of the nose cone poked from the end.

Someone now pounded on the door. *Bam bam bam bam.*

Jimmy pointed and Chena rushed over and huddled behind the cast iron woodstove in the room's center. He strode to the door, lowered the harpoon rifle to chest height, turned the wooden handle, and kicked the door wide.

A tiny old Indian man stood there, nose to nose with the harpoon. He wore traditional Quanoot clothing: a tunic and pants of woven, pounded cedar bark. A wet mop of white hair plastered his head, and his brown face was rust-tinted like the sheet of rain that poured off the eave behind him.

"Expecting whales on this mountain?" the man asked, and his black eyes tossed back the glow of the lantern.

Jimmy lowered the rifle. "Sir, get in here, you're soaked."

"Thank you." The old man stepped inside the one-room cabin and shut the door. In the bright light his face looked as wrinkled as a doll face carved from an apple and shrivel-dried in the sun. His straw-colored clothing dripped and a puddle formed around his bare feet.

Chena laid Ember, still sound asleep, on the sleeping bag, and began rummaging through a pile of clothing for a sweatshirt and sweatpants for the visitor.

"You must be cold," she said. "I'll start a fire in the woodstove."

"I'm never cold," he said. "I'm like her." He nodded toward the sleeping baby.

Chena glanced at Jimmy, who stared with big eyes at the stranger. There was no need to ask him who he was. He was the legendary shaman, Old Man.

"Would you like dry clothes?" she asked.

"Yes, that would be nice."

"They're yours," Jimmy said, and took the sweatsuit from Chena and handed it to Old Man. "Please keep them. I hope they fit."

"Thank you," he said, and, without hesitation, began to undress. Chena followed Jimmy to the workbench. He ejected the cartridge from the firing chamber and carefully replaced the harpoon rifle in its crate. Old Man spread his bark clothes over the top of the black iron stove.

Chena returned with the wooden stool, the cabin's only furniture. But Old Man waved it away and sat cross-legged on the sleeping bag next to Ember. A navy-blue sweatshirt hung loosely on his thin frame. WHALER BAY H. S. ORCAS appeared in silkscreened red letters across the chest above a black-and-red traditional mask of a killer whale.

Old Man ran his fingertips over the whale mask and smiled at the couple. *"Wasco,"* he said. "My family totem."

Jimmy took off his denim jacket and draped it over Old Man's shoulders like a cape.

"Please keep that too," he said.

Old Man reached up and squeezed Jimmy's hand.

"You're going to be a good fisherman, Jimmy Otter."

Jimmy's mouth dropped open, then he laughed nervously. "Yes, sir. Thank you."

Old Man patted the sleeping bag beside him and Jimmy and Chena sat down. He gently picked up Ember and hummed softly into her ear. She instantly opened her eyes and turned her face to his. He smiled and she smiled back. Then he propped her, sitting up, in Chena's lap. He clapped his hands together loudly, placed his left hand over his heart and his right hand over Ember's chest, spoke a blessing in the singsong Quanoot tongue, then bent and kissed her forehead.

Old Man then stood to leave.

"Spend the night," Chena said. "You can sleep in the sleeping bag. We've got blankets for ourselves."

Old Man smiled and shook his head of white hair. "The rain has stopped. The tide will be turning soon; I'm going to ride it all the way home."

"Would you like anything to eat first?" Jimmy said. "We got a cooler. I could fix you a sandwich."

The shaman paused at the door and turned to them. "Thank you both. I bless your new marriage."

Chena rushed forward and grabbed his thin, ancient hand. The wrinkled skin felt hot, like Ember's. In their nests of creases his black eyes blazed beyond age.

She swallowed. "Old Man, did I do the right thing? Was it fair of me to keep her, according to Qua-noot-cha?"

He took both her hands in his. "Chena Hawk, it is not a matter of right or wrong. The way that can be strayed from is not the Great Way."

"Who is she? You came all the way here in the storm to bless her?"

He arched his eyebrows. "I came to be blessed *by* her. I've waited a long time for her birth." He smiled, and the deep lines of his face made whorls around his eyes, like grain patterns in cedar. Old Man raised her hands to his lips and kissed them, and turned and stepped outdoors into the tingling air of the rain-freshened Earth.

13

EMBER RAN HER fingers through a thick cascade of wavy hair and twirled its reddish-black strands in her fingertips. Her chest felt tight. She didn't like the brightly lit room or the thin gray-haired woman in the green dress. The woman's perfume and hair spray fogged the room, and within that cloud of aroma she detected undernotes of antiperspirant, polyester, cotton, chalk dust, coffee on top of mint toothpaste, and fainter traces of baby powder, a pee-soaked diaper.

"Dr. Jackson is an expert on how children learn," her mother was telling her. "She's going to help us find out why you have trouble talking." Chena's tone was cheerful, almost singsong, but Ember sensed her uneasiness.

"You teach babies?" Ember said, perched on Chena's lap.

"What, dear?"

"She asked if you taught babies," Chena said, with a nervous chuckle.

"Oh. No, but as a matter of fact, my last client was a young mother who brought her baby with her. How did you . . . ?"

"She has a very keen sense of smell," Chena said.

"*Keen* isn't the word for it," Dr. Jackson said. "Come closer, honey." She extended a brittle-looking hand. "Promise, I won't bite." Her eyes glanced up at her gray bangs. "And I'll remember to wear less hair spray and perfume next time."

"Just do your best, sweetheart," Chena whispered, easing her daughter off her lap. Ember stood in front of her, facing outward but holding on to Chena's knees. Dr. Jackson smiled at her, but Ember didn't budge. Dr. Jackson sat down at her desk to wait, still smiling.

Ember's eyes kept going to the bookshelf behind Dr. Jackson's head. On it stood a small bronze statue of a centaur and a clear plastic model of a horse that revealed the organs and skeleton inside.

Dr. Jackson took the centaur statue down and held it out to Ember, without crossing the room. "Have you ever seen one of these romping in the woods on Whaler Bay Island?"

Ember shyly stepped forward and took it.

"My daddy only hunts deer," she said thickly.

"She says her daddy only hunts deer."

Dr. Jackson laughed, a little melody of five notes. "That's called a centaur. It's really just a make-believe creature, honey, but I've always liked them."

Ember studied the centaur, turning it over in her hands. Then she handed it back and pointed to the Visible Horse model on the shelf. Dr. Jackson took it down and handed it to her. "Do you like horses? My father was a veterinarian and horses were his specialty. I love horses."

Ember pulled the two halves apart and touched the painted plastic parts inside. Pinkish and purplish and gray and yellow and crimson, with red and blue lines wiggling through.

"Ember, *ask*," Chena said.

"No, it's fine. She's welcome to play with it." Dr. Jackson took her hand and led her to a child's table. Ember sat down in a bright blue plastic chair and took the model's parts out one by one, feeling the shape of each part with her fingers. She saw how the parts snuggled together like a set of camping utensils. She had watched her father butcher half a dozen deer and she saw that the toy horse's insides were much like a deer's. She recognized the heart, kidneys, lungs, stomach, and liver, because her family ate those parts of a deer. She lifted the skeleton and all the bones moved. She glanced back at her mother.

"Like a Halloween horse!" she said.

The top of the skull popped off and out rolled something that looked to Ember like a squiggly misshaped football, painted the color of scrambled eggs; by its color and texture she knew it was the brain, because they also ate that part of a deer at home.

She didn't know the names of the other parts, but she remembered by their color and shape how they fit together. She put the brain back inside its hiding box. She set half of the rib cage into one half of the transparent frame. She laid in the lungs and nestled the heart between them and fit the liver into its nearby space; over these she placed the second half of the rib cage. She arranged the other plastic organs in their spaces in a cushion of muscles. Then she had to take some parts out again to set the kidneys in first. Finally she placed the clear shell over its opposite side and snapped the sides together.

"Well, I guess that makes our first test look pretty darn silly," Dr. Jackson said, and gave a melodic laugh. "I was going to ask you to sort some shapes into a box." She put the horse back on the bookshelf.

"Ember, you are very, very talented at what we call 'pattern recognition.' That means you recognize shapes and colors and textures and how all these things fit together into larger patterns. I'll bet you're terrific at solving jigsaw puzzles."

"Oh, you should see her," Chena said. "Her dad took one of those big thousand-piece puzzles and sprayed it solid black, to give her a little more challenge. Hardly slowed her down."

Dr. Jackson smiled. "Oh, what the heck. Let's do the first test anyway. I'm curious."

On the table sat a bright yellow plastic box. Each of its six sides had three holes for fitting various shapes. Dr. Jackson opened a lid on the box and dumped out eighteen plastic shapes. "Ember, put these shapes back in the box as fast as you can—wait, don't start yet. Wait till I say 'Go.' " She took a stopwatch from a pocket in her green dress. "Go!"

Ember's hands darted over the table, snatching the plastic stars and crescents and other shapes and stuffing them through the slots in the yellow box, twirling the box on its corners to expose all its sides. In less than a minute the last shape, a triangle, hit with a clunk.

"Good girl," Dr. Jackson said as she stopped the watch. "Thirty-six seconds."

"Is that good?" Chena asked.

"Unheard of for a five-year-old. I timed myself on this task once. Best I managed was fifty seconds, and that was on the third try."

Ember took a deep breath and her shoulders dropped a little when she breathed out. She glanced at her mom. *At least I doing okay so far,* she thought. Dr. Jackson now led her to a bright yellow plastic table. On its top was a small candle and a cardboard box of tacks. On the wall beside the table was a corkboard. Ember sat down in a bright red plastic chair and Dr. Jackson explained the game: Arrange the objects so that the candle, when lit, would not drip wax on the table.

Ember pantomimed that there were no matches.

"You don't have to light the candle, honey," Dr. Jackson said. "Just show me how you would go about it."

Ember studied the objects for a few seconds.

"There's no right or wrong way to do it," the woman said. "Just do it any way you think would work."

Ember picked up the box of tacks and emptied it. She stuck a tack up through the bottom of the box into the base of the candle to hold the candle in place, and set the box back on the table. It was top-heavy and fell over, so she pushed four tacks downward through the inside corners of the box to stand it on tiny metal legs. It was still too wobbly, so instead, she tacked the box, with the candle inside it, to the corkboard.

"That works," Dr. Jackson said, smiling. "Nice. Very creative."

"It's a creativity test?" Chena asked.

Dr. Jackson nodded. "It shows creative problem-solving skills. Ember, you're the first person I know who tacked the box to the corkboard. Some kids put the candle inside the box. Most kids just try to balance the candle on top of the box."

"I can do some things better than the other kids," she told Dr. Jackson, focusing on shaping each word clearly. Even so, she heard her words come out as thickly as when kids made fun of her by speaking while holding on to their tongues.

"What's that, honey?"

"She said she can do some things better than the other kids," Chena said. "Actually, she can do most things better than kids her age. She's faster, stronger, better, at any kind of sport—even better than the boys—and also games like jigsaw puzzles, or games that involve memory."

"I understand she is adept at American Sign Language."

"Oh, that's quite a story," Chena said, smiling at Ember. "My other daughter, Kaigani, got scarlet fever when she was three, and it left her almost completely deaf."

"I'm sorry," Dr. Jackson said.

Chena nodded. "It was the worst nightmare our family's been through," she said. "Anyway, my husband and I went to special classes to study sign language, with the idea of teaching it to the girls. We were sitting in the kitchen and practicing from a workbook. The girls were three and four years old. Well, little Ember remembered every sign she saw us use, and was showing them to Kaigani that night. We ended up teaching Ember every sign from that workbook in two or three sessions. She retained them all, and within a couple of days she was talking in signs; not hesitant about it—fluent. She taught Kaigani, just naturally, while Jimmy and I practiced for months. The people at the school had never heard of anyone—at any age—picking up signing that fast."

Ember shrugged. "But the kids still make fun of me," she said, "because I'm retarded."

"Well, listen here, Ember," Dr. Jackson said, kneeling to be face to face with her. "I'm an expert on how 'smart' kids should be at every stage of growing up. I've been studying these kinds of things for years and years. Okay? And based on the tests Mr. Lewis gave you, or even on the few minutes we've spent together, I already know you're definitely, absolutely, not retarded. Okay? The fact is, you're way ahead of most other children your age. Do you believe me?"

"But I can barely talk."

"Yes. Well, a lot of things have to work together just right in order for us to talk easily. Sometimes, people have certain conditions that make it hard for them to talk or to read. But we can work with those conditions. It doesn't mean you're stupid. Not at all."

Ember looked down.

"Look here at me." Dr. Jackson gently lifted Ember's chin. "I'm a full professor at this university. I've written three textbooks. I give talks around this country and in several other countries. But would you believe that when I was your age I could hardly talk at all? Only my mother could understand me—maybe half of what I tried to say."

Ember's eyes grew bigger.

"That's right," Dr. Jackson said. "Do you think maybe I was retarded?"

Ember shook her head.

"Maybe just sort of slow?"

Ember shook her head more vigorously.

"Wacko?" Dr. Jackson made a funny face, her tongue to one side.

Ember giggled.

"No, of course not. The fact is, I had an unusual condition in my brain that made it hard for me to put words together in the right order."

"How did you learn?" Ember asked.

"How did I work?"

Ember shook her head. "How did you *learn*?"

"To talk," Chena said.

"I studied with a speech therapist—that's what Mr. Lewis is—a person who is trained to help children who have trouble talking. My therapist helped me a lot. And just growing up helped a lot too. See, some of these troubles in the brain begin to fix themselves as you get older. By the time you're a teenager they may be mostly gone."

"That old?" Ember frowned. "I can't wait that long."

"She says she can't wait that long."

"Yes, I'm beginning to recognize her speech pattern," Dr. Jackson said. "See, Ember, that's another thing I'm good at: I can understand kids even when they don't talk so well."

"Mr. Lewis couldn't get me to talk any better than I do now."

"Well, let's just say that I'm older and more experienced than he is. He was one of my students, that's why he sent you to me. I'm considered one of the best speech pathologists in the world. Can you believe that?" She laughed her little tune. "I think you and I will be able to do a lot of good therapy together. What do you say? Do you trust me?"

Ember nodded. She had decided she liked this wrinkled old lady after all.

"But there's one thing first," Dr. Jackson said. "You have to pay me something up front, before we begin."

Ember's stomach knotted and she began to twirl a strand of her dark hair. "But I don't have any money . . ." she said in a little voice.

"No, no. Not money, sweetie. That's taken care of. And my work with you might end up making me even more famous—that means I get to go to Paris more often." She laughed again. "But I want you to give me something you're holding tightly to, keeping right against your heart."

Ember touched her chest and raised her dark eyebrows.

"Hand over to me that sad, scary idea you have of yourself—that you're stupid, not good enough." She held out her hand, palm up. "Come on." She wiggled her fingers. "Give it up. You pay me up front, before we work."

Ember's eyes misted with tears. She closed them for a moment. Then she spread her fingers over her heart, feeling the hurt there. When she opened her eyes, Dr. Jackson gazed at her with soft pale-blue eyes and nodded slowly. Ember handed over her most private pain to the thin gray-haired angel in the green dress. Dr. Jackson cupped her hands tightly over the burden, stood, and carried it into the adjacent bathroom, leaving the door open, so that Ember could hear the toilet flush. It made a loud *ka-woooosh*.

14

YUTE NAHADEH SQUIRMED on the gray wooden bleachers at the Whaler Bay Middle School baseball diamond. He lowered his video camera and stared, feeling helpless. Less than thirty yards away stood a Neanderthal girl, winding up on the pitcher's mound. Ember wore a black T-shirt, yellow soccer shorts, yellow soccer socks, and black soccer cleats. She would be ten years old next week. All the other players on the field were boys, some of them older than she.

Yute put his eye to the camera and recorded the pitch. He wished he could set time on pause mode, and while the baseball hung in the air, he could step up to her and touch her golden skin, and get a long, close look into her green eyes—into her mind. She was a trove of information about human origin and evolution, packaged in a lithe and rugged frame under a banner of ruddy black hair.

Now through the eyepiece frame he regarded her as an astronomer would regard a newfound planet: as an object of unsurpassable scientific beauty, but viewed across unbridgeable space.

For the first couple of years of Ember's life Chena had been willing to talk with him on the phone every few months and answer his questions about her development. But that ended abruptly.

"You tell us who she is, who her parents are," Jimmy had demanded. And when Yute had tried to steer around the issue, Jimmy said, "Okay, then don't bug us about Ember. We don't want to tell you anything more, and we don't even want to know about her other parents any longer. She's with me and Chena and her little sister now. We're her family. We won't be talking to you again."

Yute set down the video camera and picked up the binoculars.

Sweat ran down Ember's temples. She tucked her baseball glove between her knees and pulled her ponytail tighter through a red hair band. She had pitched a no-hitter until this final inning, when a runner doubled on a line drive that the shortstop fumbled.

Kunk! The sound of an aluminum bat meeting a baseball. Pop fly. The catcher looked up, whipped off his mask, took three steps forward; the ball hit his mitt and he dropped it. The batter easily beat the throw to first base. The other runner now stood on third.

Come on, Ember, Yute thought. *Show 'em who they're up against.*

Ember looked tired. She rubbed her shoulder between each pitch. She walked a batter to first, and one runner scored: four to one, Ember's team in the lead. She struck the next two batters out, walked another. Bottom of the ninth, two outs, bases loaded.

A lanky kid, about twelve years old, swaggered to the plate, brandishing his blue bat. He spit into his palms and rubbed them together. The outfielders stepped way back to the fence as the batter took a few warm-up swings.

"Slug one into orbit, Tom," someone yelled.

"C'mon, Gigger," the batter taunted. "Gimme a challenge."

Her first pitch was an outside curve. The boy swung with a lot of torque, but the ball whizzed under his bat.

Ember smiled.

The batter sneered at her. "I get two more strikes, remember? I'll smash a line drive and knock a hole through your gut."

Ember cocked her right arm back and her left leg high, and as her whole body snapped forward and down, she shot her arm along the same line of energy like a whip, hurling the baseball at the summed peak of force. The ball smacked the catcher's mitt while the batter was in midswing. The catcher dropped his mitt and shook out his hand, wincing.

Yute chuckled. "Good girl, Ember," he whispered. "That's a hell of a fastball for a ten-year-old."

Ember grinned.

The batter grimaced. "I'm gonna knock those big Chiclet teeth right down your throat."

"Hey, watch your mouth, kid, it's only a game," Yute said, unexpectedly loud.

Tom glanced over at the bleachers and gave Yute a one-finger salute. Ember looked at Yute and squinted slightly; she tilted her head up, almost imperceptibly, and sniffed the air once.

Damn, I wish I'd caught that on video, Yute thought. *Got to make a note of that.*

"Quit smelling your boyfriend and play ball," Tom said.

Ember returned her gaze to the batter. "Tom," she said, "I'm going to throw a strike. Just a little warning, so you'll be prepared."

Ember threw an inside curve that broke far to the left of the plate and at the last instant whipped right through the strike zone. Tom saw too late that the ball would be a strike and he swung furiously, barely clipping the ball as it went past. It popped up in a lazy arc, and fell toward Ember.

Tom ran toward first base, his eyes fixed on the fly ball. Ember's eyes tracked the ball's trajectory; she stepped to the left, and at the last instant she spun and caught the fly in her bare hand behind her back.

Tom broke from the baseline and ran over to Ember and shoved her. She staggered back.

"Trying to make fun of me?" He shoved her again. "Trying to start something?"

Kids from both teams surged toward the pitcher's mound and ringed the two inside.

"Stop it!" Yute shouted, and bounded down the bleachers two rows at a time. "Cut it out!"

He broke through the circle of boys, and saw Ember and Tom wrestling in the dirt. Ember twisted her body free and leapt up and Tom scrambled back to his feet and lunged at her again, but Yute stepped between them and gave the boy a stiff arm. He lurched backward and fell, hard, onto his butt. Some of the other boys laughed.

Tom sat on the ground and glowered at Yute. "Who the hell are you, her bodyguard?" He stood and tried to step around Yute to get to Ember. "Get out of the way, this ain't none of your business."

Yute grabbed the boy, spun him around, and gave him a little push in the opposite direction. "Calm down, kid," he said, "it was only a game. You lost—big deal. Now try to be a good sport about it."

"He wouldn't know how," Ember said, from behind Yute.

Tom glared at the two through slitted eyes. "I'll get you for this, Gigger. You, too, mister."

He turned and shoved through the ring, walking quickly away. Several of his teammates followed. Then the rest of the boys began talking at once as they gathered up their gloves and bats and ambled off the baseball field in the direction of a jangle of bicycles leaning against the white clapboard wall of the school.

Ember hurried past Yute. "Thank you, sir," she said, over her shoulder.

"You're welcome, Ember."

She glanced back and stopped. "How do you know my name?"

Yute's heart pounded. *Should I be talking with her? If she tells Jimmy and Chena about meeting me, they might find a way to prevent me from coming to the island to observe her.*

He shrugged. "The other kids . . ."

She eyed him warily. "They call me Gigger."

Yute gulped. He was blowing it already.

"Hey, asshole!" Tom shouted. Yute turned around. Tom was calling to him from the bleachers. "This stuff yours?" He held up Yute's video camera and binoculars.

Before Yute could answer, Tom held them by their straps and slammed them both against the steel railing. Plastic parts crunched and glass tinkled. Then he tossed the broken equipment to the gravel.

Tom yipped like a coyote, and jumped down from the back of the bleachers and sprinted to a dirt road, where he hopped on a motocross motorcycle and gunned the engine. He raced off, spitting dirt clods from the back tire, popping a wheelie in the first three gears.

"I'm sorry," Ember said. "This is my fault."

Yute looked over at her. Her green eyes had misted.

"No, it isn't your fault," he said. "Not at all. He's the one who broke my things, not you. You didn't make him do it. So you don't need to feel sorry."

He smiled at her. "Okay?"

She nodded.

The coiling dust trail now climbed high up the steep dirt road, and the whine of the two-stroke engine rolled around the wooded mountains.

"What kind of parents that guy have?"

"No mom," Ember said. "And his dad, I think,

kicked him out . . . he lives with his grandmother, or something. He's the main troublemaker in the whole school. Most of the kids are scared of him. Teachers too."

"But you're not?"

"Why were you videotaping a little pickup game?" she asked.

It doesn't matter if she tells Jimmy and Chena. This remoteness is too frustrating. I want an intimate study of the Neanderthal on every level, and for that I need her to want it for herself.

"My name is Yute Nahadeh, I'm a doctor and an anthropologist. Have your parents told you about me?"

Her eyes grew big and she nodded slowly.

"Actually, I was videotaping you today. Someday we'll meet again, and I'll explain everything about who you are."

She stepped back. "Gotta go," she said, and turned and broke into a run toward the school building.

He held her in the core of his vision. From a distance she turned and stared back. Then she hopped on her bike and stood on the pedals and sped away.

"Only I can help you find out who you are," Yute said softly. "You'll come to me. I may wait for years, but you'll come."

Ember quietly eased herself into the bed between her sleeping parents and lay on her back. Her father grunted and rolled over without waking. But her mother opened her big gray eyes in the silvery light spilling through the window. Outside, a three-quarter moon lit the tops of the pines covering Big Drum Ridge. Chirping crickets and tree frogs spread a thick blanket of sound beneath the piercing dialogue of two great horned owls.

"Bad dream, sweetie?" Chena whispered.

Ember nodded.

"Same one?"

"Yeah," Ember said in a hush. "But this time I woke myself up before the people bury themselves in the ice cave."

Her mother draped an arm over Ember and snuggled closer. "When you understand what the guardian spirits are trying to tell you, the dream won't be necessary anymore."

"That's what you always say, Mom."

Chena closed her eyes. "Because it's true."

"The salmon are running," her father said clearly, in his sleep. Ember giggled and whispered, "Catch a truckload, Dad."

It felt cozy and secure between her parents. The heat of their bodies soaked into the firm muscles of her arms, shoulders, and chest. She inhaled deeply and let herself melt into the warmth.

Jimmy Ozette's skin and long hair carried fragrant traces of fish and dried sweat, tobacco from hand-rolled Bugler cigarettes, pinesap and cedar, gasoline and leather boots and denim, and a whiff of his black Labrador retriever, Chinook. Ember smiled. His outdoorsy odors evoked the immense love she felt for him. Chena Ozette smelled like herbal soap and rosemary oil shampoo and spearmint toothpaste and warm cotton and her own version of the earthy aroma that Ember identified with all grown-up women.

The Nose. That's what Nahvi and Ona call me. But how am I supposed to turn it off? I don't know why I can smell things no one else can. I don't know why I'm so different from everybody. Only girl in fourth grade who got her period; only one in fifth grade with boobs, except for Chawnee—and hers are just because she's so fat.

And it's all the rest. How come I'm so muscular? Not another girl, not even in high school, looks as strong —is as strong—as me. And probably only Bobby and Sook, and maybe John . . . no not John . . . I guess, really just Bobby and Sook; only two boys in the whole middle school are as muscular as I am—and they both lift weights.

"Mom," she whispered, "are you awake?"

"Mmm-hmm."

"I don't know why people are so mean. If I was a normal person and I saw somebody like me, I wouldn't hate them and call them names and stuff for no reason, just because they're different."

Chena opened her big almond eyes and touched Ember's face with her long fingers. "Everyone has to be who she is," she whispered. "You're lucky you're a person with a big heart. Some people have to get by without a heart for a long, long time—dead inside—until they learn to care about others."

Ember sighed and stared at the fat wedge of moon. Its glow outlined shadowy shapes in the room. The cedar chest with a carved beaver's face, the birchwood chair and desk. The closet door stood ajar and inside she could make out the dim ghosts of Quanoot warriors crowded in single file, paddling a big cedar war canoe, going out to meet the first Russian sailing ship on the horizon. Shadows of tree branches swayed on the ceiling and walls.

Ember thought about her recurring dream. The people in it had skin and hair the color of hers, and they were very strong-looking, even the women and children.

"Mom, how come we never see people with golden skin in real life? A million people have told me they've never seen skin my color before. Mr. Boniface said he's been all over the Orient and he's never seen skin as golden as mine." Chena's breathing was becoming slower and deeper. "Mom, you still awake?"

"Mmm."

"Remember that giant chart and all those pictures —and nobody was golden. You guessed maybe one of my parents was Samoan and the other was Han Chinese. . . ."

No way, Ember thought, pulling a thick strand of wavy hair down in front of her eyes in the dark. *My hair is unique; my face is unique. I'm a zoo of one. A weirdo. No one else like me in all the world.*

"Tom and Bobby and that whole gang call me Gigger," she whispered. "I finally asked them what *Gigger* was supposed to mean; said it meant 'golden nigger.' So then I had to ask what *nigger* meant." She grimaced. "Makes me sick that people can think like that. Why should anyone care about another person's skin color? It's just *skin.* I'm golden, Kaigani's copper, Dad's more like dark, rusted iron, you're kind of a light cinnamon; other people are dark brown, or kind of pink, or the color of straw. Who gives a you-know-what?"

A fat shape swooped into the tangled shadows of branches on the ceiling. *Hoo-hoo-hoo-hoooot.* Barred owl.

"I'm not scared of guys like them. That's the truth. I mean, not fight scared. They make fun of me, so I always get kind of tight in my stomach when I see them. But I'm not fight scared. Sometimes I really *want* to fight."

She noticed her voice growing louder and she returned to a whisper. "It's like, I get the feeling Bobby and Tom, all those guys, are scared of *me.* Because I'm good at baseball and football and running and stuff. But that's so stupid!

"Really, all the kids seem nervous around me, Mom. I hate that! Just because I'm . . ." Ember swallowed hard and put her hand to her face, felt her large nose and mouth and jaw.

Different. And I'm always going to be different—no matter how good I can talk.

A wave of sadness spread through her chest like a gush of cold seawater. She drew back from the feeling and tried to rise above it. Then she saw herself as a timid little sandpiper fleeing in darting steps from her own pain. She gave up with a deep sigh, and let her loneliness flood over her. Tears spilled from under her eyelids and rolled down the sides of her face, her chest heaved and her shoulders shook, but the only sounds she made were little gasps between her sobs.

After a while she made herself stop. So much for crying making you feel better, she thought, sniffling. Her mother breathed evenly and her father snored lightly. He had rolled toward the middle and Ember was wedged between her parents, but she did not nudge them; she needed to feel their breath mingling with her own. She took her mother's warm hand and placed it over the wound in her heart, pressing her hands on top of it.

I love you and Dad. And Kaigani. But I don't know how much longer I can take not knowing who I really am.

She thought of the man she had met today at the baseball diamond. Yute Nahadeh. Her eyes hadn't recognized him, but her nose gradually did, and then she had suddenly linked his aroma with her past, her birth.

He knows who I really am. She shuddered at the thought.

The only thing more terrible than not knowing who I am would be to find out for sure that I'm something I don't want to be, someone nobody could love. Then I'll know *that I'm all alone, forever.*

She watched the moon shadows slowly traverse the room until they faded into a brightening pink light. Then she slipped into an exhausted sleep.

The dream came again.

15

THE RISING SUN cleared the peaks of the Cascade Range and splashed warmth across a wide summer pasture on Dr. Martha Jackson's Lost Weekend Ranch. Lazy wisps of fog evaporated from the hollows. Gilded light silhouetted a dozen grazing horses.

"It's even more beautiful than I imagined," Ember said.

Dr. Jackson nodded. "Isn't it just heaven? I love it here. We're flanked on the north by Tolt Reservoir, on the east and south by Snoqualmie National Forest, and on the west by apple orchards that roll away clear to the horizon. So we're protected—it's not like we're about to have a suburb butting up against us."

"We?"

"Ha. Me and my horses."

"They're all yours?"

"Actually, just four, I board the others; I've got a big stable and there's plenty of rye and alfalfa in these pastures."

"Ooh, look at him," Ember said. A gray-and-white mottled stallion pranced back and forth, holding his head high; brown spots the size of apples dotted the soft white hair over his rump and loins. "I like the spotted one the best."

"You've got an eye for horses," Dr. Jackson said. "He's an Appaloosa. He's mine, and he's my favorite. Named him Apple, that's what he loves to eat."

"Even his hooves are pretty—vertical stripes."

"The striped hooves and the spots are features of the breed," Dr. Jackson said. "The Appaloosa came from the Palouse Indians, a tribe that lived here and in Idaho. They're a rugged saddle horse, and he's a fine one—look at the muscles ripple in his chest."

"He seems so proud."

"Proud and stubborn. He's the only horse here who isn't saddle broken. The others are good riding horses. If you'd like, we can go for a ride around the reservoir—it's gorgeous, lots of wildflowers."

Ember smiled. "I'd love to."

Dr. Jackson wore jeans and a rodeo shirt with pearly buttons, and western boots and a Stetson. Ember thought her speech therapist looked terrific—even with gray hair she was the perfect cowgirl. Ember wore a red cotton tank top, denim cutoffs, and running shoes; she adjusted her own Stetson, a gift from Dr. Jackson for her fourteenth birthday, yesterday.

"You couldn't break him?"

Dr. Jackson laughed. "Me? I'm too brittle to train horses. I hire a man to do that, but in Apple's case . . . I don't know . . . he was such a wild-spirited colt, I just didn't have the heart to tame him. He's free. I love to watch him, that's enough for me."

The grass at their feet was strewn with apples from a Crispin tree that stood just beyond the pasture fence. Dr. Jackson bent down and picked up two big rosy-yellow ones and stepped up to the barbed wire.

"He can be a sweetheart," she said, "if you've got an apple in your hand." She held out an apple to Ember. "Want to feed him?"

"Sure."

Ember took the apple and held it in her open palm over the wire fence. Dr. Jackson whistled and the horses turned to stare. Some of the horses started toward them, ambling, but Apple charged the fence at a furious gallop and stopped so short, his hooves kicked up dirt against Ember's bare shins.

"Wow!" Ember shouted. "He's beautiful!"

"Girl, I can't believe you didn't even back up," Dr. Jackson said. "He uses that trick to scare new folks, and they fall on their butts. You're no fun—did you even blink?"

"I . . . it's strange. . . ." Ember shrugged, feeling surprised at her felt connection with the stallion. "It's like I could read his body, what he was going to do."

"I knew you'd be a natural with horses. I really did. I would've been amazed if it had been otherwise."

The Appaloosa munched the apple from Dr. Jackson's palm, dripping sweet juice from his lips, then turned and ate Ember's apple. Ember reached up to pat his forehead, but he bucked his head and batted her hand away.

"Told you he's feisty," Dr. Jackson said.

The other horses arrived. Ember stooped and grabbed another apple and offered it to Apple, but when he reached to eat it, she turned and fed it to a sable mare standing at his shoulder. He snorted.

She gathered two more apples from the ground. "If you want to eat this juicy, yummy apple"—she held one up and Apple's big brown eyes followed it—"you've got to let me touch you. Just once, your hair looks so soft. I won't hurt you."

Apple lowered his head to take the apple and Ember put her hand up to touch his forehead. He jerked his head and knocked her hand aside.

"Okay, this apple goes to your girlfriend," she said, and fed the apple to the sable mare again. She stroked the white star on the mare's forehead. "See, Apple? She likes it. I pet her gently, I'm nice."

She held forth the second apple. The stallion lowered his head to eat it and Ember laid her hand upon his soft hair. He flinched and she yanked the apple out of his mouth as he stepped back.

"Uh-uh. No apple unless you let me . . ."

She held out the apple again. The Appaloosa thrust his big head forward, plucked the apple from her open palm, and lurched back; then he munched the fruit out of arm's reach.

Ember laughed. "You stinker!"

Dr. Jackson laughed too. "That's the spirit I was telling you about. He's full of it."

Apple gulped the last of the fruit, then threw back his head and neighed, staring straight at Ember. She laughed again. Then she threw her head back and neighed, imitating him precisely.

Dr. Jackson's eyebrows shot up. "Said you've never been around horses."

Ember shook her head. "Haven't."

"Ha. I think you used to be one."

"Come on, Apple," Ember said, holding out another Crispin. "Free of charge." She fed the Appaloosa three more apples, without trying to pet him. He smelled wonderful, a warm, dense aroma she wanted to wrap around her body like a velvet robe. She felt a sudden urge to run alongside him, to race with all her strength.

"Can I cross the fence?"

"He might bite," Dr. Jackson said.

Ember was already climbing a fence post. "No, he just wants to play."

"Be careful," Dr. Jackson said.

Ember hopped down on the other side. The startled horses backed up. Apple neighed and turned and bolted away. Ember jerked the chin strap tight on her Stetson and chased after him in a headlong sprint, leaning forward, feet flying over the ground, and when she caught up, she slapped his rump. He kicked and bucked. Ember whistled and sprinted in the opposite direction as fast as she could go. Apple spun and galloped after her.

Ember turned and stopped in her tracks, facing Apple as he charged upon her.

"Look out!" Dr. Jackson shouted.

At the last second the stallion braked short, and Ember sidestepped and slapped his shoulder and raced away toward a stand of shade oaks. Apple galloped after her. But when he got to the trees, he slowed to a walk and swiveled his head, looking for her. He tilted his head and flared his nostrils, sniffing the air.

Ember giggled. "Apple! Up here!"

The horse glanced up. Ember swung herself down from a low branch and jumped to the ground behind him and slapped his rump again, then made a mad dash for the fence. Apple chased her all the way and Ember grabbed a post and scrambled up, kicked her legs over the wire, and jumped down the other side.

Apple snorted and neighed and pranced back and forth on his side of the fence, not taking his flashing eyes off Ember. Veins the size of ropes bulged in his neck. His breast heaved.

Ember picked up an apple and held it over the wire for the stallion. She neighed to him in a clear, high voice.

Apple lowered his head and trotted over. He took the big yellow apple and crushed it in his teeth and the sticky juice sloshed out.

Ember and the stallion held each other's gaze for a moment, both of them still breathing hard. Then he pushed his handsome head and neck over the fence and let Ember stroke the soft mottled hair of his forehead and stand on her tiptoes to run her fingers through his coarse dark forelock. He let her rub her nose against his sweaty neck, and press her face against his face and kiss him.

Dr. Jackson let out a low whistle. "Girl, it's not

that you used to be a horse," she said, "it's that you are one now."

Cool mist clung in tiny beads to Ember's bare arms and legs. Dr. Jackson pulled on the hood of her jacket against the chill. A fishy aroma mixed with the diesel fumes from the chugging engine of the late-afternoon ferry. The clouds in the direction of Whaler Bay Island hung to the sea like a purple curtain, hiding the setting sun.

This morning they had finished their last speech therapy session. Even after eleven years of their working together Ember had trouble enunciating u's and l's and r's, but at today's session they never got around to doing much exercise on vowels and consonants. Instead, they talked about all kinds of things. Dr. Jackson told her more about growing up on racehorse breeding farms in Lexington, Kentucky, and they recalled their fun over the past couple of years at Lost Weekend Ranch. Ember told the doctor about her secret place in the inland forest on the island. Dr. Jackson had scheduled the afternoon off, and she took Ember to lunch, and later, for ice cream. They talked and laughed and the time dissolved, and now Dr. Jackson was at the ferry dock to see Ember off.

Ember dreaded saying good-bye to her frail old teacher; a sense of loss weighed upon her; she sensed in her body that she would never see her friend again. Now they stood together, but Ember found herself looking down at her rubber rain shoes. The lump in her throat made it hard to swallow, let alone talk.

Dr. Jackson finally broke the silence. "You've come a long way, dear," she said quietly. "I'm so very proud of you. What's left is just a matter of practicing on your own—living your life and talking to people."

Ember nodded.

"You know, it's a rare and wonderful thing to be seventy-three and have a close friend who's sixteen. Our bond was strong right from the beginning. I . . . well, you know . . . I never had a daughter of my own. . . ."

Ember pressed her lips together tightly, but the tears leapt out and started down. Her whole body trembled as she handed over her gift.

"For you to remember me . . ." she managed to squeak out.

Dr. Jackson peeled off the gift wrap. A cardboard box held a clear plastic model Ember had customized and assembled from parts of the Visible Man and Visible Horse model kits.

"A visible centaur!" Dr. Jackson said. She looked up from the gift and laughed her five-note melody. "Girl, you are really something else!"

". . . never forget you . . ." Ember choked on her words. She wanted to say a thousand things at once —*"for loving me the way I am; for everything you've done for me"*—but she only said, "I love you, Dr. Jackson."

Their eyes met in a timeless space. "Ember, I love you too."

They drew each other into a hug, and wept. In that embrace Ember felt the other's bodily confession: Dr.

Jackson knew she was dying. Ember ached. She wanted her liquid heart to spill its youth into her friend and fill her with new life.

Then the window of truth closed, and it was time again for the polite drama of two parting friends.

"We'll still see each other," Dr. Jackson said. "Your dad can take us fishing again, or you can come out to the ranch. You know Apple is in love with you. No one else can ride him; no one else ever will."

Dr. Jackson smiled brightly even as tears ran from her blue eyes. "In fact, I tell you what—I'm giving him to you. As of today Apple is your horse—how about that?"

Ember nodded and made a big smile. The ferry's air horn blasted a long *tooooooooot.* The running lights shone red and green. Ember hurried down the aluminum ramp and a crewman started an electric winch that drew the ramp into its stowage.

Ember waved. "I'm going to miss you, sweet lady," she shouted. "So much!"

Dr. Jackson waved as the ferry slipped away from the dock. The engines roared to full ahead and churned the green sea to white, and the dock receded in the deepening dusk. Ember's teacher, still waving, melted into the sea spray.

Seagulls circled and dipped, mewing and crying, *kee-er kee-er kee-er.* Ember closed her eyes, remembering a five-note melody and the unforgettable fragrance of a true friend.

16

SUNLIGHT POKED THROUGH the rain-forest canopy of Whaler Bay's inland forest, casting slanted shafts of gold onto a moss-draped tangle of roots and dead branches. Ember sprinted uphill past seedlings sprouting on rotting logs, among towering, straight red cedars that stood a foot tall when Columbus was born. A pair of ruby-throated hummingbirds hovered near a cluster of wild lilies, then the tiny birds buzzed off, zipping among velvety trunks laden with mistletoe, lichens, and ferns.

Ember wore a red tank top with WHALER BAY H. S. TRACK printed on it, denim cutoffs, white ankle socks, and running shoes. Her biceps bulged with each arm thrust, and the muscles in her thighs rippled and rolled with each lunge of her legs.

She glanced over her shoulder and could no longer see Kaigani, but it felt so good to run and run and run with her heart pounding and her lungs aching that she didn't want to slow down. She could circle back for her sister after she reached the crest. She smelled the grove of virgin spruce hidden in a deep pocket on the far side of the ridge. The hill became steeper and she pumped her arms harder to climb without slowing.

She pushed herself until the ache in her lungs began to burn and then she decided the fiery feeling was not pain but pleasure and she ran faster. Then she knew that Nanehla, the Mother Spirit, who sometimes takes on the form of a fleet-footed doe, had taken over her form; and it was Nanehla who burst into the sunlight at the top of the ridge and fell to her knees, heaving with deep breaths and laughing.

After a moment she started down the hillside. Kaigani appeared a couple hundred feet below, framed between huge red cedars, jogging up the slope, her straight black hair flowing behind. As she came closer, Ember saw Kaigani's cheeks flushed pink through smooth copper skin, her red lips puffing out with each breath as she ran. Kaigani was slim and graceful and long legged, and she looked so beautiful running among the mossy evergreens that Ember again laughed out loud.

Kaigani reached the top and leaned over, hands on knees, breathing fast and hard. She smiled at Ember, stuck her tongue out, and panted like a dog. In a while she straightened up.

"I am so slow makes you laugh?" she signed.

"So beautiful makes me laugh," Ember signed. "Come on," she said, pointing. "My secret place is at the bottom of that hollow."

The two sisters headed down into a spruce grove whose sweet fragrance filled the air. They followed a clear stream that flowed along the valley floor until the valley narrowed and the stream squeezed between the twin faces of wooded hills. In the V formed by the hills there was only enough room to walk single file along the bank. The stream angled downward steadily and the gurgling water turned into gushing white foam. From up ahead came a steady roar.

Kaigani tapped Ember's shoulder. "I feel it through my feet," she signed.

The hillsides became more vertical and rocky and the view ahead suddenly opened into the sun-dappled space of a deep rocky gorge. The sisters peered down from a granite ledge. The stream shot out over a twenty-foot cliff and plummeted with thunderous splashing into a carved-out pool below. The water boiled white where the falls struck, but elsewhere was a deep emerald green, the very hue of Ember's eyes. Beyond the pool the stream continued, surging over rocky shallows and disappearing into tall shadows where the gorge tapered into wooded hills again.

Kaigani's bright gray eyes were lit from within like smoked-glass lanterns. "Wonderful!" she signed.

"Tsasanawa," Ember said with a big smile. She'd found it—the mythological paradise of the Quanoot.

Kaigani smiled back but shrugged her shoulders—she had not read Ember's lips. "Tsasanawa," Ember repeated, forming the letters with her hand. "Complete with waterfall," she signed.

"A real paradise," Kaigani said. She slurred the words, for from the age of three she had learned to speak without the aid of hearing her own voice. "How did you find this place?"

"I've been everywhere in these hills, it was just a matter of time and luck. Found it five summers ago." She caught a look of hurt on her sister's face, and she touched her hand. "I always knew I'd share it with you someday. But I needed a private place—to go and be alone with Nanehla." As she said "Nanehla," she crossed her hands over her heart, then lowered her right hand to the Earth as she raised her left hand to the Sky.

Kaigani nodded. "You were gone so much, Mom and Dad and I thought you'd married a bear."

Ember laughed. "Almost did, but that's another secret." She looked up suddenly and pointed. A flock of a dozen red-winged blackbirds zoomed straight over their heads and dove with the waterfall to the floor of the canyon, pulling up inches above the frothy water and skimming down the stream until they disappeared in the distance.

"I see animals do stuff like that all the time," Ember said, "and I can't see any purpose for it other than sheer fun—which is what I'm in the mood for."

She began peeling off her tank top and shorts and running shoes. Kaigani followed her lead and stripped to a one-piece swimsuit. But Ember stood naked. Her compact body was curved and scooped and sculpted by sharply defined muscles. Firm, round breasts bulged atop a deep, broad chest. A hint of corrugations showed under the roundness of her belly. Her thighs were sinewy and solid. Fuzzy blond down covered her golden skin everywhere. Red-black wavy hair heaped up like a dark headdress that billowed past her shoulders and hung to the middle of her back.

She smiled at Kaigani. "In paradise you don't have to wear anything."

Kaigani scanned the tops of the cliffs and looked up and down the stream.

"Keep an ear out for people coming."

She slipped off the shoulder straps and stepped out of her swimsuit. The smooth skin of her shoulders and small breasts glowed in the overhead sunlight; the jet-black hair that hung to her hips gleamed with a bluish tint. Kaigani stood six inches taller and weighed several pounds less than Ember.

Ember knew her willowy sister was the most beautiful girl on Whaler Bay Island, probably in the world. She stepped to the ledge and looked back at Kaigani and grinned. Kaigani shook her head forcefully and frowned, pantomiming a broken neck.

"Don't worry, it's deep," Ember said. "I've done it a hundred times. Watch." She bent her knees and shoved straight out from the ledge. For a weightless instant she hung in the cool mountain air like a swan, back arched, arms widespread like wings, then her body arced downward and she knifed into the water.

The chill of the water made her want to gasp. She opened her eyes as she swam upward and saw a solid cloud of bubbles rising to her right where the falls crashed down. When her head broke the surface she let out a loud "Whooop!" and shook her wet hair out of her face. She heard applause and looked up to see Kaigani smiling.

"Come on!" Ember said, beckoning with big gestures.

Her sister gestured back about their clothes; how to bring them down.

"Leave them. We're alone," Ember signed.

Her sister backed out of view, then she charged off the ledge and shrieked the whole way down. When she came up, she pressed one hand between her thighs.

"The water shot straight up me."

"Ouch." Ember winced. "Safer to dive in."

"Only if your brains are in your feet."

The water was stinging cold, but they stayed in awhile playing in the turbulence at the edge of the falls, letting the outer sheet of water tumble on them. If they got too close, it smacked with enough force to knock them under. Finally, they swam to the pool's edge and climbed out onto a big slab of rock.

"You don't even have goose bumps?" Kaigani said, shivering in the sun, her nipples hard. She sat with her legs drawn to one side and pulled her dripping black hair over her right shoulder to wring it out.

The steep walls of the narrow gorge towered over them. The noon sun bounced off the rock walls and brightly warmed the boulder where they lay basking.

Ember gazed at the warm red glow on the inside of her eyelids and felt the heat of the rock against her back. She relaxed deeply, letting herself soften and settle with each breath, and soon she noticed an odd sensation, as if the boulder had begun to drift in the stream; she smiled and let herself float with it, wherever it might take her.

Then she seemed to expand and rise like sun-heated air, through an atmosphere of warm red, breathing light and the tinkling of wind chimes, the buzzing of bees.

The vision came suddenly.

Ice and snow. Someone loudly trumpeted a ram's horn alarm. The Killers have come! Everybody inside—hurry! Golden women draped in animal furs ran toward a cave mouth with a bundled child under each arm. A boy with muscular arms and legs sprinted with his baby sister bouncing in a fur pouch strapped to his back. Golden men with red or blond beards herded shaggy goats and woolly oxen into a giant cavern with walls of blue ice.

Inside, people gathered on mats of fur or woven grass placed on frozen tiers. Bluish light reflected from children's smoke-smudged faces, their eyes big and scared. No one uttered a word, though some communicated with animated signs. Finally, several men and wolves herded two huge woolly mammoths into stalls with walls of hard-packed snow, and secured hemp-mesh doors in place.

U-Ma, the Vision Mother, stood silhouetted in the snow-bright glare of the cave entrance. A big white wolf stood beside her. U-Ma raised her right hand. Everyone's eyes were glued to her. The only sounds were the wind whistling at the cave's mouth and the deep snoring of the mammoths, who had been fed the sleep milk. With hand signs and body language U-Ma spoke to her people.

"The Killers have arrived on the far edge of our hunting grounds. Our scout may have been seen. It is time."

U-Ma and her helpers began passing out the sleep milk from dried mud bowls. In an adjoining cavern others fed the sleep milk to the wolves and goats, sheep and oxen.

A second group of helpers passed out an extra ration of the bitter black paste everyone swallowed daily; it would enable them to sleep without freezing solid like the walls of the cave. Many of the people were crying and embracing; women lay down in a huddle with their children and husbands.

A toddler hurried over to U-Ma and clung to her leg; a young woman pulled him away, kicking and screaming, his shouts echoed around the cavern. The woman clapped her hand over his mouth and then gave him her breast to soothe him as she lay down on a mat beside a red-bearded man.

"Breathe in all of this," U-Ma signed, "and remember the aromas of our life; we will not wake up again in this world. A great shaman from the next world will return to us to restore us. Sleep now, my people, like the winter bear—until spring, when the sun returns."

Then U-Ma and her white wolf left the cave and climbed to a large mound of snow dammed above the entrance. She collapsed the stacked tree branches and a thundering white avalanche plugged the cave mouth.

The Killers will find no one to slaughter. The ice womb of the Great Mother will preserve her children until they are reborn.

Ember sat up with a jerk and found herself shivering uncontrollably.

Kaigani sat up with a worried expression. "*You* cold?" she signed. "Getting sick?"

Ember shook her head in a kind of daze.

"What's wrong?" Kaigani said, and put her arms around her. Ember began to cry softly and Kaigani squeezed her tight and rocked her for a while. Then she gazed into Ember's eyes.

"The bad dream?"

Ember shook her head. "This time it was . . . I wasn't asleep—I was *there*." Her vision blurred with tears.

"I *felt* the people—I *smelled* them. Oh, I wish you knew what that's like. . . ." She covered her heart with her hand. "In my dreams I've just seen the goldens. Seen things. But this time I smelled them, and when I smell something that way, it's like . . . I suddenly *know* it . . . like smelling and knowing are the same thing: I smelled their fear and sadness, felt those emotions like I feel my own—not from a distance at all. And I touched every one of them *at once* . . . it's hard to explain . . . but it was as real as this boulder, as real as touching you. Now I *know* there are others like me. My people. They aren't just a dream—I know their aromas. They're here, somewhere, in this world. But I don't know where." She bowed her face into her hands. "They hid themselves from a band of murderers . . . it's horrible."

Ember wept. Her heavy, wet hair wrapped her arms like living strands of red kelp. Kaigani stroked Ember's head, combing her slender fingers front to back.

The ice womb of the Great Mother will preserve her children until they are reborn.

Ember looked up at her sister. "There's a terribly urgent mission . . . something I'm supposed to understand, to do," she said. "But . . . I don't remember the secret; I don't know what it means at all." She shook her head slowly. "I feel responsible—like it's up to me. *My* people . . . they're depending on me for—for . . . it's almost like"—she shut her eyes and rocked her torso, calling forth the feeling, the knowledge—"for their *rescue*. Their rescue! But I don't know how to save them."

Kaigani nodded, her face open and soft. Then she reeled back in fear, pointing over Ember's shoulder. Ember turned her head and saw a large black bear ambling toward them, splashing through the rocky stream. A breeze was blowing downstream, so she had not smelled it, and she had been too distracted to hear it coming. A few yards away a moss-draped cedar had blown over from high above and tumbled into the stream and the bear paused there and made loud, low grunts, staring at them. Kaigani backed off the rock into the water, tugging on Ember to hurry.

"It's okay," Ember said. "Don't be scared. That's Doka; she's my friend."

She slid off the rock into the water and waded slowly toward the bear, her hands outheld, palms up. Kaigani crouched in the water behind the boulder. The bear sloshed forward and put its head down like a dog; Ember scratched hard behind its ears, digging her fingers into the coarse black fur.

"Hey, Doka, I missed you." The bear half closed its eyes and made low, whining sounds of pleasure; its breath stank like fish. "Keeping your belly full, old girl?" Ember had named it Doka—grandmother—because of its gray muzzle. It had taken her three summers to win the trust of the old bruin, by feeding it much fish and affection.

She knelt down and hugged its thick neck, then she walked with it like a big tame dog toward Kaigani.

"Come and meet my sister."

Kaigani slowly stepped out from around the boulder and stood still, staring with big eyes. As Ember and the bear drew near, she held out her hands as Ember had done. Just as Kaigani reached for Ember's hand, the bear's nose tilted up and twitched, sniffing. Ember smelled it a second later: men coming.

The bear whipped around, knocking Ember and Kaigani down, and splashed away in a fast, lumbering gait. Ember shot a glance up at the ledge of the waterfall, but couldn't see anyone.

"Someone's coming," she signed. "Follow me."

She dived into the pool and swam underwater around the edge of the falls, leading her sister toward a hidden shelf of rock behind the cascade. Ember and Kaigani climbed out on the slippery granite, drenched in constant spray.

"Whoopeeee! Naked girls!" a male voice shouted above the din of the crashing water.

Damn. "They found our clothes," Ember signed.

"Who?" Kaigani signed.

Ember shrugged, her lips drawn tight.

"Hey, Gigger, we know it's you. Recognize your shoes, Bigfoot. Where'd ya'll go? Don't we get a peek?"

Bobby Kynaka. She spelled out B-O-B-B-Y with her right hand.

"Ugh." Kaigani grabbed her upheld thumb in her opposite fist and yanked it down and out, the sign for *asshole*.

"Two assholes," Ember said, holding up two fingers. "I hear two voices." She set her jaw. "Wait here. I'm going to find out."

Kaigani grabbed her arm. "I'm scared," she said.

Ember looked around for a weapon. "Be back in thirty seconds." She swam off and returned with a branch of smooth driftwood the length and heft of a baseball bat. "Hang on to this. Just like getting a hit off Dad's fast pitch. Any guy who sticks his face in here, knock a home run with his skull. I'll be back in fifteen minutes, slugger."

"Hey, Gigger, where's Kaigani? You two why they call this a *virgin* forest?"

She swam back across the deep pool and scrambled out where the stream became shallow and ran down the streambed as fast she could, taking high choppy steps through the ankle-deep water.

"Whew! Look at her go! Buns of steel!"

"Okay, run away—but you won't get your clothes back. Ask Kaigani what she'll do to get her clothes. It's a long way home." As soon as the rocky walls began to taper off and flatten out, Ember darted out of the stream and scurried up a rock face into the dense cedar woods. Then she turned and sprinted toward the high ground, her heartbeat hammering in her chest.

How dare you show your ugliness in my beautiful secret place, Bobby Kynaka!

"Hey, we're gonna sell your panties to Mr. Boniface. They say he pays ten bucks for ripe ones, and you can't get much riper than these! Now I know what ape pussy smells like!"

Approaching the top, she crept forward in a crouch and hid at the base of a large cedar near where Bobby and Tom Luc stood. Both wore cowboy boots and jeans and were bare chested, with their T-shirts stuffed through a belt loop in back. Bobby was tall with broad shoulders and muscular arms, a thick neck, and a belly that bulged over the belt loops; his black hair was cut very short on the sides and spiked on top. Tom Luc was also tall, but skinny, with darkened acne scars covering his face and chest and back; his shiny black hair was pulled back in a ponytail. Tom leaned forward over the ledge, peering down, searching. He held Kaigani's swimsuit in his hand.

Ember lunged from the tree line and in three strides rammed into Tom with a powerful shove that sent him flying off the edge, his arms and legs frantically paddling the air for balance; his torso tilted far forward. She heard the smack of his belly-flop above the roar of the falls. She buttonhooked to position Bobby between herself and the granite ledge. Without taking her eyes off him, she reached down and grabbed the rest of Kaigani's clothes and her own from the mossy bank.

He stood with hands on hips, glaring. "Got no qualms about fighting you, Gigger; it's not like you're a normal girl."

"Glad to hear it," she said, backing farther away, then tossing Kaigani's clothes behind her and quickly yanking on her cutoffs and her tank top. "I'd hate for this to end with a friendly handshake."

"Ain't you a brave little fuzz face. Come on!" He beckoned with both hands.

She moved toward him in a semicrouch.

"Come on, ape-shape." He wiggled his fingers. "Come on and get your ass kicked."

She lunged so fast, she was halfway to him before he began to draw his arm back to punch her. She let loose with a furious snap kick and the instep of her foot connected between his legs at the seam of his jeans as if she were punting a football over the treetops; the heels of his boots popped off the ground. He bellowed. And as he crumpled forward she brought her knee up hard into his chest. He wheezed. Then she cocked her knee again, grabbed the back of his head, and whipped his head down as her knee shot up to his nose. She felt and heard a loud crackle, like stepping on a walnut shell.

He reeled backward in blind pain and she charged in low, slamming into him like a linebacker, driving him backward toward the edge. He scrambled wildly to keep his footing and flattened out at the lip of the ledge, clawing at the rocky surface.

"Don't!" he wailed. "Please! I can't swim!"

He looked at her with blood running from his nose, his eyes rolling with pain and fright. She backed off. Then, in spite of her anger and without intending it, a deeper part of herself melded with a deeper part of him in the same way she had touched the golden people in her vision. Before she could break the connection, she felt the rush of Bobby's fear and hate and pain; and beyond that she tapped his history of self-doubt and failure and despair; and deeper still, below his mind, she began to merge with his heart in a space where there was no difference between "Ember" and "Bobby."

She yanked her attention away from the fusion and it instantly ended.

Bobby had been lying prone on the granite with his hand over his broken nose, moaning. But now he looked up at her with a bewildered expression. His hand slid off his nose and touched his heart, and his mouth opened as if to speak, but he shook his head and looked down again.

Then a cold revulsion came over her that filled her cells as suddenly as her heated rage had before. Her shoulders slumped and she felt as if she was going to vomit. *I don't want to merge with people like you, Bobby. I hope nothing like that ever happens to me again. You can keep your darkness to yourself.*

Even so, her anger was spent and she felt ashamed; her violence had disturbed the peace of this canyon as much as Bobby and Tom had. Maybe it would have been better to have stayed hidden, like the goldens from the Killers.

But that didn't seem right either.

What can you do, then? How do you wage peace?

She sighed deeply and sat down. "My dad's big brother is an ex-Marine, and he taught me how to fight," she said. "Because I'm so different—as you've been reminding me since kindergarten—he thought I might need to stand up for myself someday."

He spit a wad of blood, but didn't look up.

"Tell me, Bobby. Why have you always hated me so much? I mean, before I caved in your face?"

"You're as funny as kickback on a chainsaw."

He got up on all fours, panting through his mouth. A bubble of dark blood hung from each nostril, but the flow had stopped; his eyes were already starting to show the classic raccoon bruises.

"Do you get along this well with all your cousins?" she asked.

"*You?* You ain't my cousin. You're a freak."

He crawled forward until he was well away from

the ledge. Then he eased back onto his butt with a groan and looked up at her. "Chena is my aunt, but you're some kind of weird medical experiment."

"What are you raving about?"

"You're a mutant, created in a lab somewhere, that's what my family thinks. That's what everybody I know at Whaler High thinks."

She swallowed. "Well, whatever I am . . ." Her voice wobbled; she cleared her throat. "Look . . . I don't know who my real father and mother are, but I'm not a mutant. Whatever I am, there are others like me."

"Bullshit. Nobody's ever seen one. Not even in books."

"Even if it were so—do you automatically despise anyone who is different than you?"

"You tore my family apart."

Ember felt her stomach flutter. "My mom's told me everything. But she says it had more to do with her running away from home and marrying my dad, than with me. She's tried to patch the split. She's really tried. But she says you Kynaka loggers never liked my fisherman dad, and you can't accept that she chose to adopt me."

"Well, that's not so tough to figure. You're not one of us. You don't belong here. And like I said, you ain't my cousin." Bobby groaned and stood up, supporting his crotch with one hand. "You're *nobody's* cousin."

Ember winced.

He turned and walked away in mincing steps, bent slightly, one hand holding his abdomen.

Tears stung her eyes. *Why should I want someone as cruel and crude as you to accept me? I should take it as high praise that your kind reject me*. But getting angry at Bobby and at herself did not deflect the pain that stabbed through her.

Let me belong somewhere, she prayed inside the cave of her heart. *I am somebody's cousin, somebody's daughter. I'm a golden. My vision of the goldens holds the truth about me. Please let it be so.*

"Bobby, I really want to know something," she said to his back. "Why did you and Tom hike all the way out, two days, to come to this place?"

He turned his head. "Why did *we* come? This has been our secret place since we were kids. We come here and just be ourselves. Free. Nobody in the world to bug us. But you and Kaigani messed that up." He began to limp off again.

"Bobby."

He stopped and turned, frowning. "What now?"

"You and Tom can have it all to yourselves in spring and fall and winter. Let Kaigani and me come here alone in summer—and I promise not to tell anyone I broke your nose."

He looked at her and tenderly touched his ballooning face; his eyelids were starting to puff up, leaving little slits. He nodded. "Deal."

Then he walked back to the ledge. "Now don't push me off, goddammit, I really can't swim. I just want to call out to Tom." He stepped toward the edge, eyeing her warily, with one hand held out to ward off her charge. She put her hands up and walked away from him, picking up Kaigani's clothes.

"Tom, come on! Let's get the hell out of here."

No answer.

"Hey, Tom!" he shouted again.

Ember felt her chest tighten. Something was wrong. How could she have been so stupid? If only she could call to Kaigani, but her sister would not be able to hear.

"Tom!" Bobby yelled. "Where are you? I'm leaving, man."

Ember started toward the ledge to dive into the pool, but spun toward a tramping in the underbrush. Tom Luc dragged Kaigani along, one arm hooked tightly around her neck. The other hand held a knife.

Ember's heart froze.

In a moment Tom stood before them, his soaking jeans clinging to his lanky legs. His ponytail had come loose and long strands of hair hung in his face. A smear of watery blood covered his forehead from a gash at his hairline. He held Kaigani's head bent toward his chest with his fingers clutching her thick black hair. She was naked and shivering; her eyes darted from Tom to Ember and back. Now he jerked her head back to expose her neck, and pressed a big hunting knife, serrated on its spine for gutting fish, against her bare throat. Kaigani closed her eyes, but all the while Tom's black eyes burned into Ember's face.

17

"BITCH WAS HIDING behind the waterfall," Tom snarled. "Hit me over the head."

"What the hell you doing?" Bobby said. "Take it easy. Put down the knife."

"Kiss my ass. Just look at you. Gigger do all that? Or did you smash into a tree trying to run away from her?"

"Put the knife down, Tom. Come on. Think about what you're doing. It's not worth it."

"That don't sound like you, Bobby. What'd you do? Take a wimp class while I was gone?" He glared at Ember. "By the time I'm through," he said with a sneer, "it'll be worth it."

Ember's eyes were fixed on the knife edge creasing Kaigani's skin. She felt as if she couldn't get enough air into her lungs. "What do you want?" she heard herself ask in a small voice.

"When I hit the water it knocked the wind out of me, I just about drowned, you little cunt. My skin's still stinging. And my head's bleeding. I figure it's payback time."

"Man, count me out of this shit!" Bobby said, holding up his hands and turning half away. "When the cops ask what happened up here, I didn't have nothing to do with it."

"Yeah, sounds like a big chickenshit who gets his nose busted by a fuckin' girl who barely comes up to his chest."

"And you're the kind of brave dude who holds a knife to a girl's throat? Man, I've known you forever and I never guessed you'd do something like this."

"Yeah, well, I never had a girl do to me what's been done," he said, glowering. "Now listen up, Gigger." He jerked Kaigani's hair and she grimaced. "I'm gonna slit your sister's throat like a trout fillet—unless you do exactly what I tell you to do."

Ember swallowed hard and nodded.

"Come over here—on your knees—and unzip me."

"Tom, man. Don't. Let her go," Bobby pleaded. Ember sank to her knees and crawled forward, still eyeing the knife.

"Stop it, man," Bobby said. "This is dead wrong."

"Quit your fuckin' whinin'," Tom snarled. "You're standing there with a broke nose and you don't even have the guts to take the upper hand when you got a chance."

"You don't have to hurt her," Ember managed to say as she unzipped Tom's wet jeans.

"All right, monkey, undo the top snap and tug my pants down a bit. That's enough. Hoo—look at the big boa grow! Guess he likes you more than I do."

Bobby stepped forward. "I said stop, goddammit."

Tom took the knife away from Kaigani's throat and pointed it toward Bobby. "Gonna make me, Cherry?" Bobby said nothing but kept coming.

Ember saw her chance. She slammed her body sideways into Tom's shins and sent him sprawling on his face, while Kaigani staggered backward. Bobby dove for his knife hand. Tom curled into a ball, screaming and rocking in pain, his hands clutching at his chest.

Ember grabbed Kaigani's hand, lifting her off her feet, and rushed with her fifty feet into the woods before she glanced back.

"You got the knife?" she yelled at Bobby.

"Oh, God," he said, and knelt near Tom.

Kaigani covered her face and burst into sobs. Her knees wobbled and Ember made her sit and then held her close.

"I'll get your clothes," she signed. Kaigani nodded. Ember hurried off and returned with her sister's swimsuit, cutoffs, socks, and shoes. She hugged her again and signed, "Okay?"

Kaigani gulped and held her thumb up; the hand trembled and her face was streaked with tears.

"Hurry, he fell on his knife," Bobby said.

Ember ran back to him. "How bad is it?"

"Dunno. Not good." Bobby's eyes were big and scared.

Tom lay on his side in a tuck, and she could see the knife, buried to the hilt, protruding from the right side of his chest. She kneeled close to him. Only a small amount of blood was seeping from around the hilt. That seems like a good sign, she thought. Then she remembered about internal bleeding.

"The knife's in his right side, so it missed his heart," she said. "At least, I think it did. But it's stabbing straight into his lung—who knows how much he's bleeding inside."

Tom's eyes were screwed shut, his face a mask of pain as he rocked back and forth, panting and whimpering.

Bobby stood up. "Look, we got dirt bikes at our campsite about a quarter mile from here," he said. "At the foot of the mountain, where the dirt road ends, there's an emergency phone for rangers. I can get there in about an hour and the rangers can radio a helicopter to fly him across the bay."

"An hour?"

"Maybe a little less."

She stared at Tom and shook her head.

"Maybe forty-five minutes," Bobby said.

Tom was motionless now, still on his side tucked in a ball. He was beginning to wheeze.

"*Go.* Hurry."

"I'm outta here." He took off at a run, limping slightly.

Tom's dark-skinned face grew pale. He breathed more rapidly and shallowly.

Damn, he's going into shock, she thought, straining to remember what she knew about such things from talking to her mother. "Keep the person warm," she told herself aloud. "Elevate his legs slightly, and—and . . . what else?"

Tom's face relaxed into blankness, and it frightened her.

Everybody talks about how warm my body is. Guess I've got to do it.

She swallowed her revulsion and made herself lie down beside him and hold him close to keep him warm. *Talk to the person, reassure them. Yeah, right.*

"Tom . . . don't die on me. Just don't die now." *Even though you brought this on yourself.* She took a deep breath and sighed, trying to cope with her anger.

She remembered her dream of the goldens and how she experienced all of their emotions directly, as if her heart were the hub of a sunflower and the other people's minds radiated from it like petals. But she didn't want to touch Tom's heart in that way, it was far too intimate; it was to *become* the other person. She recalled her brief link with Bobby and it made her shudder.

"Tom, hang on. Bobby went to get help, so just hang on."

Now I understand why the goldens hid from the Killers. They didn't want to fight. They could feel the pain of the people they fought. They were heart joined with their enemies, so they only wanted peace.

"Come on, Tom, you gotta hang on."

His skin grew cool. He began to gasp.

"Nanehla, Mother Spirit, what should I do?" Ember whispered. She touched the Earth with her right hand and raised her left hand, palm up; she shut her eyes and listened with her whole body for guidance. Not a voice, but her intuition, spoke.

Forgive him and heal him.

I don't know how to heal him.

Forgive him, then you'll know.

But I don't forgive him.

Touch his heart with yours and you'll forgive.

I'm too scared of his darkness.

Forgive yourself for being scared.

Ember took a deep breath. "Mother, keep me safe."

She projected her presence with all her heart. *I am here, Tom. You can feel me with you now. Stay with me. Don't leave.*

His body twitched and suddenly she was experiencing a primal level of his awareness. It was a heavy, numbing feeling that appeared in her mind's eye as a dull-gray leaden sea at dead calm. Not a trace of breeze stirred. It was night, overcast. A weak red glow in the sky throbbed in a slow double beat. The clouds curdled and began to sink. The air itself seemed to solidify.

She felt that she was suffocating and she panicked and recoiled from the vision, gulping breaths. Now she was certain Tom was dying. It seemed only a matter of minutes.

O Great Mother, I surrender. Lend me your power.

An image came to her: the hot, bright sun lighting and warming the Earth, energizing all its creatures. With the image a cascade of knowledge flooded her awareness and she felt guided to act.

She turned her attention within her body, just below her navel, and encountered a center of power; it appeared to her as a fiery seed of light and heat. She focused on this energy point, opening herself to it with each breath until it blazed and her whole body ignited with its radiant force. Her flesh became hot and sweat ran down in droplets. She then transmitted the heat and energy to Tom, not from without, but by directing it to shine within him. As this went on, she felt his awareness return to his body. The vision of a lifeless seascape in a desolate night gradually brightened into a green ocean, blue sky, white clouds, all lit by a golden sun, and its warmth and power were connected to her own breathing, as if she were breathing for Tom, feeding him vital force.

She had grown completely unaware of her surroundings, and did not snap out of her trance until the helicopter's rotors beat the air and whipped the leaves on the trees into a frenzied rustling.

Two paramedics descended on slings. In minutes they had placed an oxygen mask over Tom's nose and mouth, started a bag of plasma dripping into a vein, and loaded him in a stretcher covered by a wire mesh cage.

"It's a miracle he held on this long," one of them shouted to the other over the whine of the jet engine and the gale from the rotors. Ember cupped her hands around her eyes to guard them from flying dust as she watched the stretcher ascend, winched into the hovering aircraft. Her hair whipped and buffeted like the wild leaves.

One of the paramedics put his arms through the yoke sling, snugged it under his armpits, and rode the cable up.

The other man yelled near Ember's ear, "You girls gonna be okay?"

"We're fine," she yelled back. "We're camped nearby."

"Need food, anything?"

She shook her head.

"Sure?"

She smiled at his concern. He smiled back. She knew it would make him feel better to give her something.

"Got any chocolate?"

"You bet. Always carry it for emergencies." He dug into a zippered pocket of his orange nylon flight suit and produced two Hershey bars.

She thanked him and waved as he rode the sling up into the open door of the helicopter. Seconds later it climbed, banked, and disappeared over the ridge in the direction of Seattle.

When Ember lowered her eyes, Kaigani was gazing at her with a beatific expression, as if beholding an angel. Ember blinked and forced a little laugh.

"What are you staring at?"

"I saw what you did with Tom," Kaigani signed.

Ember shrugged. "Kept him warm with my body, that's all."

"You kept him alive. The man said so."

"No, he didn't."

"I read his lips," she signed. "He said, 'It's a miracle he held on this long.' "

"So?"

"I was sitting over there and I felt your spirit pouring into him. I've never felt anything like that before."

Ember shook her head. "No, it wasn't me. It wasn't."

Kaigani nodded emphatically. "I *felt* it, Ember," she signed. "It was the most beautiful thing I've ever felt, like all the rays of the sun focused into one beam." She spread her arms and fingers wide, then brought them together until her index fingers touched and pointed as one.

"It was Nanehla. She did it all."

"Yes, but the Mother Spirit came through *you*—not the trees, not me. It kept Tom alive."

Ember felt somehow guilty. All her life she had been different on the outside. Strange-looking. Not normal. She had always wanted to blend in and not exploit her differences. Now this was far more alienating—she was becoming different on the inside.

"Please don't set me apart, Kaigani. You're my best friend. I'm closer to you than to anyone in the world. Please don't start treating me any differently—it's just me—Ember."

"I'm still your best friend," Kaigani said. "And I love you even more."

"But I don't want you to love me even more." Ember choked on the words, and a tear ran down, leaving a wet track. "Just . . . you know . . . be my sister. Don't love me more or less than ever."

"But you aren't the same. There's still a sort of glow around you right now. I can practically see it. I always felt you were meant for something special. . . .

Look at you! Your time has come. Some kind of change has started."

"Shhh. Don't say any more." Ember held her fingers to her sister's lips and buried her face in her soft shoulder and wept.

The Hershey bars melted in her hot palm.

18

MIKE LEE JABBED the delete key to kill what he had typed on the computer screen. He stared at his scribbled product notes, hoping an idea would leap from the page like a pop-up greeting. He frowned and tapped a pen against his chin, then typed:

> *If you thought the Super-Speed Shaver was a sharp idea, wait till you see Giorgio Chicarro's new line of men's grooming products.*

"Stinko." He zapped the sentence and shoved his chair back from the keyboard.

He rubbed his face, then flopped his head back

and stared at the acoustical tiles on the ceiling. His lanky frame slouched against the cool, smooth leather, until his eyes leveled with the aquarium on his teakwood desk. He watched the pas de deux of two purplish-black fantails: ballerinas of minimum brain, maximum peace of mind.

He had rearranged his office so that he sat with his back to the door and faced windows overlooking Trinity Chapel from midway up the John Hancock Building, the tallest in Boston. Over the last months he had surveyed every angle and shadow and smallest detail of stone in the centuries-old baroque-style chapel. Too often these days he caught himself chapel gazing.

A woman's voice came over the speaker phone on his desk. "How's it coming, Mike? Almost done?"

He jerked upright and repressed a reflex to look busy. "It's coming, Liza. You'll be the first to know."

"Hurry," she said. "Stein's in one of his moods."

"Which one? Excedrin or Maalox?"

"Both, I think. Better get a move on."

"Roger," he said. "Wilco."

Mike straightened his purple-and-yellow silk tie and buttoned his double-breasted yellow Italian sport coat, then returned his attention to his notes. What to say . . . what to say . . . something punchy, surprising, maybe scientific—*about underarm deodorant.* Hoo boy. His mind felt like a receiver switched to an unavailable channel.

"Okay then, jock-itch powder . . ." He rubbed the corners of his eyes. "Jock-itch powder . . . uh . . . clam chowder?"

He laughed at himself. *It's a philosophical problem:*

Chicarro has a new line of products, and I don't give a damn.

He looked out the window at the dark stones of the chapel, fifteen stories below. The beauty of the building ran deeper than the lines of its architecture. He imagined quarrying and transporting and cutting and setting the big granite blocks. *Is anyone alive today who could work stone like that?* He pictured how, over the years it took to build the chapel, the stones had shaped the men who shaped the stones. The granite still worked its craft, even on him.

Mike blew out his breath in a long sigh. He ached for the *something-more-to-life* that great architecture and art and music reflected to him. A deeper essence existed; he didn't need proof of that. No day passed that he didn't recognize it in some brief, small moment: the chapel in the rain and a flight of white doves against the wet black stones. Oh, yes, the world possessed a spirit—or rather, the spirit possessed a world. But too often he felt that he stood outside the essence of life, peering in. He longed for *connection*, to be able to meet all things at the heart.

Today it seemed that an invisible heavy band was squeezing his chest, and he found it harder than ever to concentrate on creating breathtaking ad copy.

He clicked the mouse twice and a logo for *Mountain Bike* magazine reappeared on the screen. He called up an article on mountain bike trails in the vicinity of Seattle. The article provided maps and photos and a short video clip; he had watched the clip a couple of dozen times over the last two days. It showed a legendary rider, Randy McDaniels, jumping his bike across a ten-foot-wide stream, his rear tire kicking up dirt where it touched down with a foot to spare.

Randy. During his college days the two competed in some of the top eastern mountain bike races, on steep, twisting trails with names like Hamburger Helper. But nothing in the East, not even in the White Mountains, matched the knobby-tire challenges awaiting in the Cascade Range. It was like the difference between surfing four-foot chop at Atlantic City and riding the big blue Pipeline at Waimea. Twice more he watched the man in the fluorescent colors leap the stream.

"Mike!" Liza said, from behind. "Are you trying to get fired?"

"Probably," he mumbled, and aborted the screen. He swiveled his chair to face her. "Just looking for a little inspiration."

"*Stein*. Rhymes with *time*."

"*Da*, comrade worker." He saluted. "Committing I am now to greater productivity."

She chuckled, but as she walked away she whispered, "Tick-tock, tick-tock, tick-tock, tick-tock."

He turned back to the blank screen and twisted his mouth, rubbed his hands hard. *Get fresh*. He slapped his cheeks the way a trainer slaps a punch-drunk prizefighter. *Come on, Mike, knock 'em out*. His fingertips poised on the home keys.

"Um, Giorgio Chicarro's new line of men's grooming products . . . May nothing less kiss your skin . . ."

He frowned. Then he typed: "My heart is not in my work today; it will not be in my work tomorrow. I am in exile from my own spirit. Reunion begins the moment I can no longer tolerate the separation."

He read his words and a crazy grin spread slowly across his face. He loosened his tie and walked to the floor-to-ceiling window and pressed his forehead against the glass. A radiant spring afternoon warmed the pane. Kids kicked a soccer ball in the brick plaza far below.

Reunion begins the moment I can no longer tolerate the separation.

"Then let it begin," he said. "From now on, when my heart calls, I listen and I follow."

With that promise to himself the tension and weight dropped from his chest like shedding a diving belt. He knew then, bodily, what to do. He returned to his chair and began typing a letter of resignation; the words easily came to mind.

Three hours later Mike strolled down the plush burgundy carpet toward the office suite's elevator, carrying a leather briefcase and an art portfolio case. He did not look sullen and pouty like the suntanned men in the giant framed advertising art on the walls; he had worried about this moment for months, but now a smile would not leave his face.

The elevator bell rang and the doors slid open. A woman in a sharply pressed gray wool suit stepped out and briskly strutted down the hall in black high heels. Mike turned around and took one last look at the reception desk of the advertising firm of Stein & Wittingham. He backed into the empty elevator.

On the way down he sized up his situation. He had just quit a good-paying job that other guys in their twenties would kill for, and he didn't have the foggiest notion where or when his next paycheck would appear. Yet by the time the car reached ground level, he was riding on top of the world.

He pushed through the revolving doors of the John Hancock Building into the angled sunlight and shadows of Copley Square. Pipe organ music leaked from the thick walls of Trinity Chapel; he recognized Bach's "Sleepers, Awake." The soccer ball sped his way and he stopped it with a tassled loafer and kicked it back.

Suddenly, a rush of freedom rose from his heart and he filled his lungs and belted out, *"Ya-hoooo!"*

Pigeons burst aloft and the kids glanced up from their game. Mike's shout echoed between the chapel and the skyscraper.

19

Mike Lee sideslipped the bike's back wheel around the shoulder of the rocky knob and saw the trail ahead drop sharply for twenty yards. *Here we go,* he thought, and his gut tightened. He leveled the pedals, slid his butt off the saddle to keep his center of gravity low over the back wheel, and rolled over the brink. He let the bike fall first, then followed it, with straight arms and legs, squeezing gently on the front brake handles, keeping his belly tucked into the back of the seat. Ahead, he saw the trail abruptly climb another hill, so he released the brake and yanked up on the handlebar to merge with the rise, lifting himself over the seat and leaning far forward in one motion. He pumped hard to get up the incline, laughing exultantly.

Up ahead a small log lay across the trail. Hopping a log while climbing a hill was tricky—it required popping a wheelie without flipping onto your back. He tugged up on the handlebar to skip the front wheel up onto the log, crunched his upper body down, and as the front wheel rolled over the top, he leaned far forward and thrust his hips ahead hard; the bike shot frontward until the rear wheel smacked into the log, then he hopped the rear wheel up and over with another body jerk and half-pedal stroke.

Cleaned it! Stand back, folks, I'm radioactive today!

At the crest of the hill he saw the long drop: fifty-five yards with a hairpin switchback to the right at the bottom, disappearing into scrub pines. He braked to a stop at the lip.

Aw, man. Sex Changer. What's around the curve? . . . if I make the curve. Oh, well. Wimps need not apply. He checked the snugness of his helmet.

"Look out below!" he shouted, hands cupped to his mouth. "Bike on trail. Coming through!"

He set his jaw and shoved off, sliding his butt backward off the seat as the front wheel dropped out from under him.

Lightly applying the front brakes and keeping his arms and legs straight, he dove in a semicontrolled plunge. As he hit the level patch at the switchback he squeezed the rear brake, planted his right foot, and whipped the rear wheel around in a sideslip to hug the trail and not smash into the trees. The bike skidded at a crazy angle, spraying loose dirt and pebbles all the way around the curve.

Suddenly he was staring at a girl in a bright yellow T-shirt and red shorts walking in the center of the trail in front of him. Her eyes flashed wide and she froze. A gaggle of kids was close behind.

"MOVE!" he screamed, and mashed both brake handles with all his might as he laid the bike on its side, still skidding. At the same time someone grabbed the girl from behind and snatched her out of the way. He and the bike slid over the embankment and separated as they tumbled down the steep slope. He managed to do three shoulder rolls before he lost control and bulldozed through a clump of bushes, crash-landed facedown, and plowed to a stop in a sprawl.

After a moment he heard a woman's voice. "You okay?"

He groaned and slowly rolled onto his back. Bright silver stars floated in his vision when he opened his eyes. He blinked. She stood above him, but from his head-downward position on the slope, she seemed to be leaning away from him at a forty-five-degree angle. Same bright yellow T-shirt and red hiking shorts the kids wore. Her calves and thighs were very muscular and her skin was an unusual color; from his upside-down vantage the bulge of her breasts mostly hid her face. She kneeled and peered into his eyes.

"You okay?" she said, sounding worried.

Thick, wavy hair tumbled over her shoulders like a dark avalanche. The sun backlit her head with a halo that made her hair glow red, and his blurry eyesight added to the effect.

She reached over and unfastened his helmet strap; the Fiberglas shell had split in half and she pulled the pieces off his head. His auburn hair and beard were cropped close. Green-and-purple biking shorts and a matching tank top clung to his lean, sinewy body.

"Good thing you were wearing this," she said. "I heard a terrible crack and I thought it was your skull." She stared into his eyes again and furrowed her brow. "Are you all right or not? Can you talk?"

"I can talk," Mike said slowly. "I'm just . . . relaxed. . . . Think I got knocked out. Are all the kids okay?"

"They're fine. Nobody was hurt. Just lie still for a bit."

He gazed into her emerald eyes. An expansive warm sensation rose in him, as if he were facing the early-morning sun. The fog in his head lifted, his vision cleared.

"I'm not so groggy now," he said. "I'll be all right."

Ember turned and waved to Kaigani standing on the ridge twenty feet above in a huddle of a dozen kids; she gave her the "okay" sign with her thumb and forefinger.

She turned back to him. Now he noticed that her arms and cheeks were softened by the same ultrafine peach fuzz that covered her legs. A large, wide, high-bridged nose would have dominated her face if not for its other oversized features: big almond-shaped eyes; thick, dark eyebrows; high, arching cheekbones; bright teeth in an abundant mouth that protruded slightly over a heavy jaw—and all of it framed in that midnight-mountain of hair.

What struck him most now was her skin color—gold, as when you hold a bottle of dark stout up to the light—just that color.

"Better lie still for a few more minutes," she said.

"Can't."

"Why not?"

"Because I'm stretched out on top of a sticker bush."

He scrunched his long torso into a sit-up. Prickly stems from the flattened bush were sticking through his nylon tank top into his skin. He reached behind to pull them out and she helped. Wet blobs of purplish-red juice mixed with thin smears of blood from dozens of scratches.

"Blackberries," she said, holding up a stem with a few uncrushed berries on it.

"Ahh. First aid, please," he said, holding out his palm. She pulled off four ripe blackberries as big as the pads of her thumbs and dropped them in his hand. He popped them into his mouth and closed his eyes as the sugary juice burst on his tongue.

His eyes shot open. "Crap. My bike! How mangled is it?"

"Well, what do you expect, screaming down the trail like that into a blind curve? We're all lucky no one was more hurt."

"I yelled for people below to look out. I yelled, 'Bike on trail. Coming through.' Loud. You guys deaf or what?"

"Everyone in the group is deaf except for me. It's a camp for deaf kids. My sister and I are counselors."

His mouth dropped open. He now recognized that the tiny hands printed across the top of her T-shirt formed letters of the deaf alphabet; below the hands a silhouetted figure in a canoe paddled on a lake at the base of a snowcapped peak.

"Oh . . . I'm sorry . . . hey, I'm really sorry. . . ."

"Just be more careful, okay? These trails belong to hikers as much as to bikers."

"You're right. That was stupid of me: I had psyched myself into a daredevil mood and I was staring down the slope only thinking of the adrenaline rush. Wasn't using my brain. I apologize."

He smiled contritely. "So much for first impressions," he said, and put out his hand. "Mike Lee."

She clasped his hand and half smiled. "Ember Ozette."

Her hand was surprisingly warm, and bigger and stronger than he'd expected.

"Thank you," he said. "For coming to my aid."

Their eyes met again and for an instant he felt the same expansive feeling as before, then an electrical current surged from her fingers.

"Whoa!" he said. "Did you feel that?"

She dropped his hand and drew back as if he'd glimpsed her in the nude.

He shrugged. "Just static electricity. Odd that it didn't discharge when we first touched."

She swallowed and nodded.

Why is she suddenly shy? Is there some Indian superstition about trading sparks with someone you've just met?

He tried to make out the hand-formed letters on her T-shirt. "Camp . . . ?"

"Buena Vista."

"Is it really on a lake at the foot of a snowy mountain?"

"It's on a lake, a beautiful lake. And you can dayhike to a lookout point to catch a great view of Mount Rainier. We were heading back from there when you almost ran us over."

"I learned my lesson." He rubbed the welt at his hairline. "Let me check out what's left of my bike."

She stood first and gave a tug with one arm to help him to his feet. He popped up like toast.

"How long you been bodybuilding?" he asked.

She turned and walked toward his bike. He followed, limping slightly from a sore left knee.

"Is it a secret?"

She shrugged. "You won't believe me."

"Give me a hint."

"I've never done any bodybuilding."

He chuckled.

"It's true. I've never touched weights. Played a lot of soccer, ran a lot of track. No weights."

The muscles of her arms and legs moved smoothly under her skin as she walked, giving him the image of a graceful golden cougar. Her dark mane bounced with each step as if it contained its own springy sinews.

"No free weights, you mean."

"No machines either."

"Wow. That's hard to believe."

"What'd I tell you?"

The bike had come to a stop against a spruce tree thirty feet below them. Mike discovered it was in good shape overall, but the front wheel was warped like a potato chip.

"Can you fix it?" she asked.

"Not out here. Unless some friendly bear can lend me his trueing rack and a new set of spokes."

"What are you going to do?"

He looked up the steep hill at the trail. "Walk back, I guess."

"But you're limping. How far?"

"Twelve miles; fourteen, maybe. I rode up from a campground near the town of Longmire."

"You better come back to the camp with us. It's only three miles. You'll be lucky if you can make it that far without your knee swelling and locking up—that's a nasty bruise developing." The top of her head reached only to his chin, so she tilted her neck back to talk. "The camp nurse can take a look at your knee, and I can give you and your bike a ride back to where you're going. She might say you need a ride to the nearest doctor."

"Sounds reasonable. Thanks."

The kids and Kaigani spilled down the bank to take a closer look. There were eight kids, five of them girls. They looked at Mike and giggled and signed excitedly to each other. Mike blushed and busied himself reexamining his bike. Kaigani came and stood next to Ember. Tall and slender, rich copper skin, gray eyes, and black hair in two long braids.

"Mike, this is my sister, Kaigani."

"Hi." He was staring at her.

"Hello." She smiled with her eyes.

Her beauty stunned him. He noticed he held his breath and he made himself look away.

"You ready?" Ember asked.

He nodded.

"Here, use my walking stick to give your knee some support," she said. "Let me take the bike."

"You'll have to stand it up and roll it along on its back wheel."

"I can handle it," she said, pivoting the bike until it was vertical.

Ember and Mike started down the slope with Kaigani and the campers behind. When they reached the switchback below, they turned left to follow the trail that cut through the evergreens and wound among hills and cliffs studded with granite slabs and boulders.

After half an hour they came to a patch of wild blueberries strewn among the rocks in a small clearing. The kids raced off to pick the berries they had missed on their first go-by. Mike used the walking stick to ease himself down, wincing, to a seat on a flat boulder. Ember leaned the bike against a pine and sat down next to him.

"How's the knee?" she asked.

"Well, I'll have to miss the tap-dance marathon," he answered, gently rubbing the swollen joint, "but I'll live."

Kaigani came and sat on the other side of Ember, and asked him the same question in pantomime. He started to gesture that his knee was going to be all right.

"You can talk normally to her," Ember told him. "She reads lips so well, you'd think she can hear you."

"In a couple weeks it'll be as good as new, and I

can go back to selling stair-climbing machines, door to door."

Kaigani laughed and said something with hand signs.

"She says she's glad you're still in one piece," Ember said. "She's sorry about your bike."

He looked at the women.

"You two don't look anything alike."

"I'm adopted," Ember said.

"What tribe do you belong to?"

Ember nodded at Kaigani. "She's a Quanoot."

"And you?"

"Adopted," she said flatly.

The children strolled back from the clearing with bluish-purple lips and fingers. The sisters stood.

"Here come the kids," Ember said. "Ready to move on?"

She helped him to his feet, then handed him the walking stick. The warmth of her hand startled him again. She tilted the bike onto its rear wheel and they headed down the trail.

"Just one more question," he said. "Did you grow up with the Quanoots of Sea Lion Cove or Whaler Bay Island?"

"Whaler Bay. How do you know so much about Quanoots?"

"In the fall I'll be teaching freshman English and Communications at Whaler Bay Community College."

"Really?"

"Yeah. I've been researching Quanoot history and folklore on the Internet."

"Then you probably know a lot more than most of us. At least the ones my age."

"How old are you?"

"That's two more questions," she said, then laughed. "Just turned eighteen. You?"

"Twenty-three."

"What part of the South are you from?"

"You can tell? South Boston."

"Boston?"

"Just kidding. Been working for the past few years in Boston. I'm from Charlottesville, Virginia."

"Where are you going to stay on Whaler Bay?"

"Don't know yet. All summer I've been camping out in national parks. That's what I plan to do for the rest of August."

"Well, the faculty dorms are these big cinder-block shoe boxes. Really ugly. You should maybe rent a cabin on the west side of the island. That's where the salmon fishers live, farthest from town. The east side is more developed and crowded and it's mostly logger families, so a lot of the hills on that side are stripped of big trees. It's pretty sad."

"Thanks for the advice. I'll look into it."

They walked along in silence for several minutes.

"My dad may even rent you his hunting cabin."

He raised his eyebrows. "Yeah?"

"My dad's got a summer cabin that needs some repair, but the location is breathtaking. It's on a hill right above West Bay. From the porch you can watch whales sounding. And Otter Creek runs behind it, about a quarter mile below Otter Falls."

He whistled. "Sounds ideal. That would be a dream come true."

"I'll talk to him," she said. "I'm going to be a student at the college this fall."

"Hey, that's great. Maybe you'll wind up in my class. There's a good chance of it, in fact—freshman English is required and there are only two faculty members teaching it."

His limp was growing worse. Ember beckoned to her sister and Kaigani came and took the bike from her. Then Ember stepped next to Mike.

"Here, put your arm around my shoulder. We've got about another mile."

"Thanks, it's really starting to throb." He slipped his left arm across her shoulders and immediately felt her support on that side, solid as a tree trunk. Her right arm wrapped around his back at the waist. The warmth was not only in her hands; her body seemed to be running a fever.

"Bet you never get chilled in the winter."

"Not yet."

"Ever catch cold?"

"One or two."

"A season?"

"In my life."

"Ha. I believe you," he said. "And about the bodybuilding too."

They stepped around a bend in the trail and a silver mountain lake appeared through the trees. They turned off the main trail onto a smaller footpath that sloped down toward the water.

His knee suddenly sagged. She caught and upheld his weight with her arm around his waist. Again he felt an electriclike current move through him in a burst. This time he wasn't so sure it was static electricity.

20

MIKE AND EMBER sat cross-legged on the grass beneath an immense red cedar in the Plaza of the First Americans, surrounded by the classroom buildings and library of Whaler Bay Community College. In the plaza's center stood a replica of a two-hundred-year-old Quanoot totem pole, carved from a single cedar trunk. A raven crowned it, perched atop a beaver, shark, killer whale, otter, and bear; clan emblems painted the traditional red, white, and black.

Nearby, a gray-haired woman knelt on a wool blanket. She wore a long dress made of stone-hammered, woven cedar bark, and she held a small loom in her lap. A small crowd watched as she wove cedar bark and goat hair into cloth. Another group sat near two musicians who played guitar and bamboo flute, while a steady stream of students and teachers passed by on a pentagram of sidewalks.

"I want to get something nice for your dad to thank him for taking me fishing," Mike said. He pulled two wrapped sandwiches and a pint carton of milk out of a brown paper lunch bag. "I told him how much it meant to me."

Ember munched a crisp green apple. She wore a short-sleeved cotton knit blouse with tiny beads of many brilliant colors, and denim shorts and sandals. Mike bet she was the only one on campus dressed so lightly on this cool and blustery October afternoon. He wore a plum-colored wool sweater over a blue denim Oxford shirt and plum tie, black denim jeans, and leather hiking boots.

"He likes you a lot," she said. "He told me you worked hard and took to it like a Quanoot."

He smiled. "Calls me Jagdaw—what's that?"

"Means 'long fish'—a nickname for someone who's tall, like calling a buddy 'the big guy.' "

He folded up the paper bag and stuffed it in the back pocket of his jeans. The sun glinted off the colorful beads of Ember's blouse; the amber color of the cloth magnified her skin tone.

"By the way, your blouse is really gorgeous. Kaigani made it?"

She nodded. "She's getting so good. I keep telling her she should try to market her designs."

"She's definitely got the artist's eye, the rainbow eye." He opened the milk carton and took a swig. "Did you know the word *iris*, the colored part of the eye, comes from Iris, the Greek goddess of the rainbow?"

"That's pretty. The Quanoot word for it is *laa*sheh*." She clicked her tongue between the syllables. "Means 'little sunset.' Same idea—lots of colors."

"Laasheh?"

"*Laa*sheh*. You gotta get in the click."

*"Laa*sheh,"* he clicked. "*Laa*sheh*. That's tricky."

She chuckled. "Listen to this." She sang a bright melody with a couple of dozen words that seemed to be made up almost entirely of tongue clicks and pops.

"Wow. I love that."

"It's a Quanoot tongue-twister, a nursery song. Took me five years and a speech therapist to get it right."

"Sing it again?"

He listened to the little tune as he unwrapped a peanut-butter-and-jelly sandwich and took a bite, chasing it with milk.

"I want to record that."

"My mom says it's ancient."

"I read that the Northwest Coast natives had hundreds of languages, more than all the nations of Europe, and the languages were more distinct from each other than European ones."

She nodded. "That's what I heard in high school. The tribes traded together with a jargon based on Chinook."

"I can picture mommas in these islands singing that little song to their babies long before Mother Goose waddled ashore."

He washed down another glob of peanut butter and seven-grain bread with the milk.

"Want one?" he said, holding up the wrapped sandwich.

"Me? Peanut butter?" She made the sign for vomiting, thrusting her forearm up and then out and down.

He laughed.

"I love learning to sign," he said, "the fact that it's nonverbal. It's sort of like written Chinese, all pictograms."

"Pictograms?"

"Picture-words. Like the pictogram for virtue, *teh*, is made of symbols for *road*, *eye*, and *heart*—virtue is the road to seeing with your heart instead of looking only with your eyes—all that in a few swoops of a brush on paper."

"You can read Chinese?"

"Ha. I wish."

They ate their lunches and Mike handed a part of his second sandwich to a tame squirrel who immediately ran across the lawn and scurried up a pine tree, chattering about its prize.

"Hope he's got some milk in that tree, to wash it down," Mike said. In a moment the squirrel discarded the sandwich and it plopped in the midst of pine cones scattered on the grass.

"See?" Ember said. "Peanut butter is disgusting."

Her smile instantly turned into a tight line. Mike turned to see a tall, wiry, pock-faced man striding toward them from across the plaza. He carried a bundle in his arms.

"Trouble?" Mike said, sitting up straight.

She took a deep breath, nodding.

"Who is this guy?"

"Tom Luc."

"Old boyfriend?"

"Hardly," she said. Her body tensed.

Tom knelt in the grass at her feet, a pained look on his bony face. He spread a huge bouquet of wildflowers on the ground in front of her sandals.

"Forgive me, Sisiutlqua," he said, bowing his head to the grass. "I didn't know the legends were true. I'm grateful to have learned what you are, even through my sin—that's your mercy."

"Tom, get up," Ember said, glancing around. Some people had stopped to stare.

He rose to his knees.

"I've quit drinking and smoking and partying. Tell me what else you want me to do."

"I'm glad for you, but please, just leave me alone."

"Bobby and I are telling others about you. He realizes what you are too."

"I'm not Sisiutlqua!" she said in an angry whisper.

"We hold *tsuka* at sunset on Bird Rock every evening, more than a dozen of us now. The others sent me to ask you to come and bless us."

"But—"

"Will you please come this evening and touch us? Some of the people are in bad health."

"But I'm not Sisiutlqua. Damn. What happened to Gigger?"

Tom winced. "Forgive my cruelty. I was blind, and I'm ashamed. But I'm willing to live Quanoot-cha now. I believe it now. You came to us because we need you so bad."

"Tom, I know you're sincere," she said. "But so am I when I tell you I'm not Sisiutlqua . . . I'm just not. I don't know what else to say. . . ."

"But I felt your light. I saw it. I was dying, I was sinking out of my body into a black whirlpool, and then your light shone, strong, like a white cord, it caught my soul and reeled it in."

Mike looked from Tom to Ember with wide-open eyes. A group of gawkers gathered to watch.

Ember closed her eyes and shook her head.

Tom began to cry softly. "Please. I've been messed up all my life, been hurt a lot and caused a lot of hurt. I want to change all that, turn my life around. Come to the *tsuka* . . . please."

Ember did not look up at him. "I can't, because you've got the wrong person. What I did, or how I did it, I don't understand myself. But"—she sighed—"how can I be Sisiutlqua? I'm not even a Quanoot. Look at me and you know that. Tell the others what I've told you. I'm sorry."

"You can't hide your power," Tom said. "Grandma Kynaka told us that Old Man came to visit you when you were newborn. I believe he knew you'd be a great Soul Catcher." He bowed to the ground again. "You'll come to us when our Quanoot-cha is pure enough. I know it."

He got up quickly and left, pushing through the small crowd and crossing the plaza in long strides. After he was gone, the group turned as one to stare at Ember.

Mike grabbed her book bag. "C'mon, let's get out of here." He led her down the sidewalk toward the humanities building.

Inside his office she slumped onto a lumpy orange couch and stared at the wall, her arms crossed in front. He sat sideways next to her.

"Want to talk about it?"

She shook her head and bit her lip.

"Can I get you some water?"

She nodded.

He returned with a white coffee mug filled with cold water. Her face was buried in her hands and her broad shoulders trembled. Mike felt tempted to gather her up in his arms, comfort her, tell her how much he liked her. Instead, he left to grab a box of tissues, then he sat on the floor and waited quietly.

She stopped crying and looked up with a crooked smile. "Sorry," she said, and dabbed her eyes.

"No need to be. What was that all about?"

"Mistaken identity."

"So I gathered. Who's Sisiutlqua—however you pronounce it?"

"Can we go back outside? I feel like I can't breathe, I need to move."

In a moment they were walking briskly along the campus jogging path as it wound through evergreens near a duck pond. Joggers passed them in both directions.

"What was that about a cord of light?"

"Is it okay if we don't talk about it?"

"Sure, whatever. . . ."

A male runner with a sparrowlike build pulled up alongside Ember, jogging in place.

"Hi, Ember, coming out again for track?" he said, puffing slightly.

"Not this year."

"No competition?"

"No time."

"Too bad. You're the only threat we had to offer."

"You didn't do bad last season."

"Not bad. But you were the quad killer, the one to beat." He smiled with small, perfect white teeth. "See ya." He waved and sprinted ahead and disappeared around a bend.

"That guy was my one friend on the team."

A moment later she said, "Know why?"

"Why what?"

"Why Frank was my only friend? I think he's gay."

"You didn't dent his machismo."

"That's my guess."

At the duck pond a woman was leaving and gave them the rest of her bag of stale bread. They tore off bits and tossed them and the ducks converged, quacking loudly, to stab at the food before it sank. Mike and Ember laughed as one little duck kept darting under the huddle of taller necks and grabbing the bread. Finally, a big white drake chased the little duck away, yakking and nipping at its tailfeathers.

Ember settled back on the grass, hands behind her head; her dark red hair spread out over her muscular arms. Mike glanced over, worried about her. He tossed more bread to the small duck. "I'm naming this little guy Duck-under, the Underduck."

"Mike, it really amazes me how much you know."

"*Seem* to know. Don't let it fool you."

"You do know a lot."

He shook his head. "I read too much. And I have

this gift—or curse—of remembering just about every factoid I come across. But storing up a ton of information—so what?—doesn't amount to real knowledge."

"What's real knowledge?"

"Insight. Or at least practical know-how, like your dad's fishing skills. He's the best."

He lay down sideways next to her, his head propped on his hand.

"Reminds me of a cartoon," he said. "A patient is lying on a couch talking to a psychiatrist and he says, 'In my real life I'm an English teacher.' And the psychiatrist says, 'What's so real about being an English teacher?' "

"But you must've done great in school. When was the War of 1812?"

He laughed.

"Oh." She rolled her eyes. "Okay, that was dumb. See, that's me. I wasn't even trying to be funny. All right, then, World War One. . . ."

"Let's see. . . . Congress declared war April sixth, 1917. Germany signed the Armistice November eleventh, 1919. The German fleet surrendered to the British November twenty-first, and the last German ground forces surrendered in East Africa on November twenty-fifth."

"See, you're like an encyclopedia."

"I've got a kind of memory called eidetic imagery. A picture sticks in my mind after I see something, especially after I read something. Sometimes I can even go back and reread a page in my mind. It's as if I'm staring at it somewhere. That's what I did just now; I looked up and saw the dates printed in black and white."

"So why is that bad?"

He shrugged. "Aw, I don't know. . . ."

"You said it was a curse."

He sat up and fed the last few crumbs to the ducks. She sat up too.

"See, I'm a know-it-all," he said. "You've noticed. And my dad's a know-it-all, and my three big brothers are the same. They all seem perfectly happy—three of them are doctors and one's a law professor. But I don't like being stuck in my head, and that's how I tend to be most of the time, hung up in a bunch of facts and abstractions."

"You'd rather be a feel-it-all than a know-it-all."

"You got it."

"And that's why you go dive-bombing down these mountains without a parachute."

A smile spread across his face. "You'd make a good shrink."

"Know what my mom always tells me? 'You have to be what you are.' "

"Sounds good on paper."

"I know . . . it's hard."

A bell rang in the distance for the next class period. Ember sat up. She seemed about to say something.

"What?" he said.

She let out her breath. "Never mind. Gotta get to class." She picked up her book bag.

"Hey." He touched her hand. "Trust me."

She looked into his eyes. "Do I look like a Native American to you?"

"No," he said. "You've got the high cheekbones, but that's about it."

"Have you ever seen anyone who looks like me?"

"No."

"Not even in photos?"

He shook his head.

"What race would you guess I belong to?"

"I've been wondering that ever since I laid eyes on you."

Her shoulders sagged. "Everybody wonders," she said. "I'm a walking, talking genetic mystery."

"I find your looks fascinating."

She turned her face away. "I should charge admission."

"Sorry, guess it gets old."

"*So* old! People always staring and whispering, but only the little kids are innocent enough to say what's on their minds—'Mommy, is she half *animal*?' " Her green eyes were big and misty. "I had my fill of it a long time ago, but it's just going to go on and on, all my life."

He was quiet. Again, he wanted to put his arms around her, squeeze her, but he couldn't make himself act. Finally, he said, "Must be lonely."

"Not so terrible . . . I've got Kaigani and my mom and dad—and nature." She waved her arm at the duck pond.

"But who are your real parents?"

"God knows. I belong to a race that only I've seen."

"You've seen them? Where?"

She hesitated. "They're golden, like me."

"Where?"

"In dreams . . . and visions." She watched for his reaction.

"It's okay, I believe you."

"I really gotta get to class." She stood and slung her canvas book bag on her back. He stood too.

"Thanks for the company," she said. "Liked your class today."

"You like Kazantzakis?"

"I like Zorba."

He nodded. "Me, too, he's sort of my hero," he said. "What've you got next?"

"Gym. Where the guys hate me because I'm too . . . whatever . . . and the women are scared I'm a lesbian mutant. Got half the locker room to myself." Her lips smiled, but not her eyes. "So long." She waved and turned down the path.

"Ember, wait." He caught her arm and she looked back. The afternoon sun gilded her face. His heart beat faster. "How would you like to go out with me sometime?"

"Go out?"

"You've heard of it? People get together and eat dinner and talk, go to a movie, have a good time." He folded his lanky arms and forced a little smile. "I guess you don't know me that well yet. . . ."

"No, it's not that. I like you a lot. In fact, I've been trying to think of how to get you and Kaigani together."

"Kaigani?"

"She reads lips perfectly. And I could spend some time with the two of you and translate for her. You're picking up signing real fast. It's easy."

"But—"

"See, I've been wanting to be a matchmaker for Kaigani for a long time, but I haven't come across any decent guys. She's an incredible person; she's fun, she's loving, she's smart, she's beautiful. . . ."

"She's way too beautiful."

"Oh. But you'd be comfortable with me?"

"That's not what I meant, not at all. I find your looks—"

"Fascinating. You told me."

He sighed. "What I mean is, I really *like* your looks. I've never been attracted to women who look like Barbie dolls. You're beauty is . . . unique."

"Not many women covered with fur."

"So?" he said. "So what? Look at me—all arms and legs. Not the perfect specimen of male splendor."

"You've got nice eyes and a great smile."

"Yeah, well"—he blushed—"I'm also notoriously shy. And Kaigani—she's perfect. I mean, she *is* the epitome of female splendor."

"You ain't seen nuthin' yet! Wait till you see her in an evening dress, with her hair flowing down—"

"Ember, I'd rather go out with you."

She looked away and her eyes seemed to follow the clouds over the duck pond for a moment.

"I'm going through a big upheaval these days," she said. "Sometimes it feels like there's an earthquake shaking down the walls inside of me. I think I'd be too weird."

"That stuff about Sisiutlqua?"

"Look, I happen to know that Kaigani thinks you're cute and sexy."

"She told you?"

"Remember all the giggling girls back on the trail? They were in on it from the beginning."

"Ah. The Secret Hand Code."

"And I could go with you, say, to a party. Kaigani and I are really close. I could interpret for a while until you two can communicate better."

He was silent.

"Not only is she gorgeous, Mike, but she's the nicest person I've ever known. She's a poet too—you should read her poems."

"Really?"

The second class bell rang. They were both late.

"Think about it," she said. "Gotta run." She turned and jogged down the path in the direction of the gymnasium. The book bag bounced on her back and she cinched the straps tighter and broke into a sprint.

He yelled, "All right—if she wants to."

Ember gave him the thumbs-up sign without turning her head. He watched her run at full speed until she dashed around a stand of yellow cedars.

Powerful and graceful. She did seem half animal.

21

MIKE AND EMBER and Kaigani were among a hundred guests at the wedding potlatch, yet the longhouse was not crowded. The big cedar-plank lodge was a model of pre-European Northwest Coast architecture; it served as a community center for traditional Quanoot ceremonies.

Inside stood one large rectangular room. Elaborately carved cedar trunk pillars rose from each corner to support crossbeams that held the gabled roof two feet above the tops of the outer walls. Candlefish-oil lamps flickered from the crossbeams and logs blazed in a central fire pit; the smoke drafted up and out through the roof gap into the slate-gray autumn dusk. Low benches lined the walls, leaving the center of the room open for dances and ceremonies around the fire. Woven cedar-bark mats covered the plank floor.

A carved, painted killer whale's face adorned the planks of the left wall; a bucktoothed beaver stared at it from the opposite wall. Across from the duck-through doorway a thunderbird with widespread wings perched on a totem. Gifts were piled in a mound around the totem's base, like packages under a Christmas tree. Nearby tables were stacked with many different foods.

Mike and the two sisters sat on one of the benches.

"Show him, Ember," Kaigani signed.

Ember swiveled her head, discreetly sniffing the air. "That guy with the mustache?" She nodded toward a man in his early twenties whom Mike often saw hanging around the campus plaza selling handmade jewelry. His face was classically Indian, but he had light brown hair and dark blue eyes. "He's got a joint or two in his jeans, left rear pocket, maybe. Smells burnt, so he's already smoked part of it."

"No way," Mike said. "You can smell that from here?"

A middle-aged couple strolled by, holding hands. He wore a denim jacket over jeans and western boots, she was dressed in a traditional button robe of blue wool decorated with hundreds of buttons sewn in geometric animal shapes.

"He smokes tobacco," Ember said. "They both do. They've had a few beers. And they've already made love tonight."

"You're serious?" Mike looked at Ember and Kaigani, then he laughed. "You two are yanking my chain."

Kaigani laughed, but shook her head, making the sign of the cross.

"When I hugged Linda a little while ago?" Ember said. "She's pregnant."

"Come on. How can you tell?"

"Her breasts, her skin, there's a certain smell . . . I can't explain. It comes into my mind as a smell picture . . . if that makes any sense."

Mike nodded slowly. "But I had no idea . . ."

Bone sticks whacked a hollow wooden drum to sound the beginning of a ceremonial dance. The three friends looked across the big room to the source of the rhythms.

"It's starting," Ember said.

The bride and groom stood near the center of the longhouse, dressed in sleeveless knee-length wool tunics, his red, hers blue. Their bare legs were adorned with anklets made of combed white dog fur. His robe was belted with dozens of horizontal strips of thinly hammered copper, and on his head he wore a woolen crown tufted with a ball of snowy-owl feathers. The bride's tunic was decorated with rows of white tubular dentalia shells, the kind that had been harvested off these coastal islands for centuries and used among the tribes as money, called "hy-kwa" or "wampum," all the way inland to the Western Plains. She wore a centuries-old shell headdress that cupped her head like a skullcap and hung to the middle of her back with alternating rows of dentalia and Viennese melted-glass beads, which the British had traded for sea-otter pelts.

Six dancers dressed in demon costumes surrounded the couple, shaking skull-faced rattles and howling fiercely. One dancer wore a painted wooden ghost mask that opened its jaws wide to reveal a second wooden face, which then stuck out its tongue. With a yew bow and invisible arrows the groom quickly slew each attacker and they crumpled to the floor. The wedding guests cheered.

Then another group of dancers wearing killer whale, bear, and salmon masks danced around the couple and the groom killed them with harpoons, bows, and spears, and they lay down in line behind the bride to be prepared for a feast. More cheers.

Finally, a man dressed as a woman with huge breasts and hips pranced around the groom, trying to entice him away from his betrothed.

Ember laughed. "That's Mr. Kent."

The groom picked up a whaling canoe paddle with a painted eye on both sides of the leaf-shaped blade, and swatted the would-be seducer on her bottom, then yanked off her wig, revealing the cross-dresser to be the local high-school principal. The crowd laughed and applauded.

"Fooled me," Kaigani said. "I was sure it was her dad."

"Mr. Kent's awful cologne."

Mike noticed a trio of couples at the other end of the room, staring at Ember and chattering. Ember must have noticed, too, because she turned her back to them and he saw the muscles in her jaw stand out. It seemed that in the past few weeks he'd been seeing more and more of that sort of rudeness. *Haven't these people gawked enough in eighteen years? Why can't they just let her be?*

He glowered at them. They looked away, suddenly busy with things at their end of the room. Ember touched his hand and gave a tiny shrug. "Don't mind them," she said.

Mike smiled at her. "I'm in awe of this ability of yours."

He told her what he knew about the anatomy of smell. Only smell and taste, which amplify each other, are processed near the center of the brain, the place of emotions; the brain areas for hearing and seeing and touch are peripheral. Smell, of all the senses, conjures the strongest emotions and recollections.

"So it all points to smell and taste as the most primal senses," he said, "in terms of evolution."

"Meaning what?" Ember said. "I'm primitive?"

"No, but just . . . we're all influenced by aromas all the time, more than we think," he said. "It's below our awareness, but it puts us through changes. For example, they've proven that the reason women who live together tend to menstruate on the same cycle is because they smell each other's sexual aromas."

Ember and Kaigani glanced at each other, and Kaigani half smiled.

"See, the pituitary gland—it's called the master gland because it directs all the other hormone-secreting glands—is located in the same area of the brain that handles emotion and smell. That says a lot about the power of smell over the mind and body."

"Mom told me when Dad gets up early to go fishing she rolls over to his side of the bed to snuggle up with his aroma," Kaigani said.

"They've done studies with salamander embryos,"

Mike said. "If they shift the nose-bud cells to the side, the brain reorients itself and grows sideways in the skull; the whole reptilian brain is oriented toward smell."

Ember flicked her tongue and darted her eyes like a lizard.

"It's not just reptiles," he said. "You know, when I first walked in here, the aroma reminded me of climbing into my grandmother's cedar chest to hide, when I was about three or four. I'd totally forgotten about that, but one whiff of all this cedar and—bang—I was right there in Nana's chest when my mom threw open the lid, crying. She was scared and mad because she'd been looking for me all over the house and yard."

"That's what I mean by a smell picture," Ember said.

"Oh, I gotcha," Mike said. "But how can you pick out distinct odors in a room like this? There must be a million scents in here."

"Same way you instantly spot a familiar face in a crowd, or pick out a familiar voice when you pass a roomful of people talking."

"Tell him about you and Dad at Raven's Nest," Kaigani said.

"Oh, brother . . . the beginning of my legend."

"Raven's Nest?" Mike said.

"A little bar used to be up the hill at Humpback Point. When she was seven and I was eight we spent the day with Dad setting out trout lines, and on the way back we stopped at Raven's Nest. Wasn't much more than a shack; in fact, that day it was raining and the roof was leaking, so everyone had crowded to one side to get away from the drips. Mostly fishermen grabbing a beer on their way home. They were playing *kun-kun*, heard of it?"

He shook his head.

"An old betting game. You set down fifty scallop shells—the Quanoot word for them is *kun*—and each one has a design, like a cross or a square or a circle, scratched on the bottom and each design is repeated on one other shell. You get a few seconds to look at the arrangement, then the designs are turned facedown. The game is to turn over a shell and find its mate; every time you match, you get another turn."

"Concentration," Mike said. "Card game I played as a kid, same idea."

"So these guys were playing *kun-kun*, and the pot had gone up to forty dollars and this big logger named Rocky Hoh had won. He dared my dad to put in ten dollars and play him for the fifty. My dad took out a ten and asked if I could play the game for him. Everybody just stared. A lot of people thought I was retarded, because I had a hard time pronouncing words.

"Rocky said, 'It's your money, Fish Man.' So my dad sat me on his lap and Rocky scattered the shells on the table, then turned them over. I went first, and I made a match and another and another until all the shells were matched. He never got his turn."

"Wow, you've got a photographic memory," Mike said.

"No, it's not visual—or at least that's not the main part of it. Rocky got all pissed off and slammed the table with his fist and said that we'd cheated somehow. So my dad bet him another ten dollars that I could do it with my eyes closed."

"Are you serious?"

"That's what they all said. Everybody got in on it. The pot jumped to two hundred forty-five dollars."

"I was shaking in my boots," Kaigani said. "I didn't see how she could do it."

"You should've been in my boots. I thought Dad was nuts. Then he said, 'First, she gets to hold each shell.' Everybody grumbled, and he said, 'Don't worry, when she plays the game she won't touch a shell unless she turns it over.' So I held each matching pair up close and inhaled and let the scents imprint in my memory. Then I closed my eyes and they blindfolded me with two bandanas. Rocky spread the shells out on the table and mixed them up. My dad made everybody move back, which helped, because these guys were pretty rank. I waited a moment and inhaled slowly and deeply. Bingo. The whole pattern on the table lit up in my mind like a color chart. I turned all the shells over, two by two."

Mike made a low whistle. "You really ought to have some scientists take a look at this. You know—test it, measure it. It's an amazing gift."

Ember grimaced. "The last thing in the world I want is to be somebody's salamander in a lab."

"But a memory like yours . . . how far back does it go? Can you remember being in the womb?"

"The wedding's about to begin," Ember said. She stood and pulled Mike and Kaigani to their feet.

22

THE WEDDING GUESTS joined hands in a triple circle around the couple. The bride sang a traditional Quanoot wedding song to the groom, which Ember translated in whispers to Mike. The bride told the groom she was a good woman and could make healthy babies and she was looking for a good hunter and fisher to provide for a future family. She asked the groom if he was brave as an eagle, resourceful as a raven, loyal as a dog, and playful as an otter. Finally, she asked if he loved her enough to leave his mother's longhouse and move in with her clan. He sang to her, yes, he was all of these things and he loved her enough to want to be her husband this very night. The bride agreed with a big smile.

The bride's mother, a fleshy pumpkin of a woman in an orange button robe, stepped forward and embraced the groom as her new son and tied a woven grass cord from his right wrist to her daughter's left wrist. The newlyweds kissed, the guests ooohed and closed into a huddle to congratulate them. The bride's mother reached under her glasses to wipe at tears.

The groom's father wore a knee-length vest made of cedar bast and goat hair, and a wide-brimmed woven bark hat encircled with tree-frog silhouettes. With the help of his wife and several others he passed out the gifts stacked under the thunderbird totem to the guests. Jars of elderberry and gooseberry jams, pumpkin and apple pies, bottles of homemade brew, cartons of cigarettes, boxes of fish hooks and shotgun shells and sparkplugs, spools of tackle, saw chains, hatchets, axes, wedges, knives, whetstones, heavy work gloves, wool socks, wool knit hats and flannel shirts, and more.

Ember told Mike the history of the *potlatch*, the Chinook word for "give-away." Before the arrival of Europeans the Northwest Coast, lush with food and building materials, was the most populated area of North America. Tens of thousands of natives lived in many large villages throughout the islands and inland rivers. The chiefs of the various clans built their reputations by throwing big feasts in which they gave away loads of blankets and clothing and other gifts to show off their wealth and status. The custom eventually rose to a competition, with each chief or village trying to outdo the others with how much they could give away.

When the whites came on the scene, trading factory goods for sea-otter pelts, the pressure among the natives to maintain social ranking became exaggerated to an extreme; the hosts of the potlatches killed dozens of slaves, shattered copper money plates, burned canoes, and threw blankets and carvings and baskets of candlefish oil into the fire, to prove that their wealth was unmatchable. Finally, the encroaching white settlers outlawed the potlatch.

"And the rest is colonial history," Mike said.

"That about says it."

A young girl handing out gifts gave Ember a silver hairbrush, and Kaigani a carved wooden box filled with shell beads, and Mike a palm-sized whale tooth with a killer whale engraved upon it.

"Intaka pah hneh," the sisters said, nodding. Mike thanked the girl.

"Intaka . . . ?" Mike asked when the girl had moved on.

"Intaka pah hneh," Ember said. "Means, 'The gift must move' . . . it won't get stuck with us, we'll give it away again to someone else, or give something else away of the same value. Maybe I'll give her back the hairbrush at another potlatch."

Mike saw that the handle of the hairbrush was tarnished.

"It's not new," he said.

"Probably an antique—it may have been passed back and forth in potlatches for a hundred years."

"That's excellent," he said, and wondered at the history of the scrimshaw in his hand. "The gift must move."

"It's where *Indian giver* comes from. The whites

couldn't figure out why we were always giving things away and later expecting them back in some form."

The groom's father held out a carved wooden ladle and poured candlefish oil into the fire and the flames turned orange and roared ten feet into the air. The strong smell of burning fish filled the room.

He shouted, "Let the feast begin!"

A group of men brought in several sides of goat that had been roasting on spits outdoors. The food tables were brought to the center of the room, filled with plates of smoked clams, salmon, and trout; steamed shrimp; fried squid and octopus; dried halibut; salmon and herring roe; pickled quail eggs; boiled or pickled kelp and other seaweeds; and a large iron pot of thick, lumpy white soup. Hot dogs and hamburgers were stacked on serving trays next to bags of pretzels and potato chips.

Mike planned to taste everything, and started with a big spoonful of the soup. "What is this?" he whispered to Ember.

"Yellow-jacket larvae stew."

"Had to ask," he said, and gulped it down. He was surprised by its sweetness, like a hot, salty vanilla milkshake. "Ugh. Not bad." He ate another spoonful. "Ugh again. Okay, what's next?"

"Try one of these," Kaigani said, and held out a pickled quail egg the size of a walnut. He tried to take it from her hand, but she shook her head and opened her mouth.

When he opened his mouth she stuffed the whole egg into it. "Hey, I like it," he said with his mouth full. "Remind me of dem good ol' deviled eggs us southern boys thrive on. What do Quanoot wash quail eggs down with?"

"My dad's wild plum wine," Kaigani said, and grabbed one of several bottles of deep purple liquid from the table.

The three sat at their bench with more strange foods for him to sample, and they laughed and signed and talked and drank the very sweet wine straight from the bottle.

"How'd you wind up in Boston, from Charlottesville?" Ember asked.

"Well, my apartment mate and I—"

"Male or female?" Kaigani said.

"Female. But we weren't lovers or anything, just fellow starving writers, we met at a workshop at UV. Anyway, we entered a TV-ad-writing contest, put on by Saab. My ad won. I only meant to grab the money and pay some bills, but a job offer came with it. I'd never been to Boston, so I thought, what the heck—Adventures in Beantown."

"What was your ad?" Ember said.

"Okay. Picture a guy underneath his car's hood, and a buddy drives up in an old Saab and toots the horn. 'Hey, Sam, wanna play a few rounds?'

" 'Can't,' Sam says. 'Gotta find out why my engine keeps stalling on me.'

" 'Shoulda bought a Saab, buddy—this baby's been purring for sixteen years.'

"Sam grumbles and ducks back under the hood. A little while later another friend comes by in an even older Saab. Same sort of dialogue. Finally, a guy pulls up in the latest Saab sports coupe, toots the horn, and Sam slams down the hood on his own car and yells, 'That's it, I'm playing golf—and I don't wanna hear your Saab story.' "

"I saw that ad a bunch of times, years ago," Ember said.

"Yeah, it actually won some awards. Beginner's luck."

"I'll bet," she said. "Kaigani thought up a TV commercial once, for deaf people."

"Let's hear it."

She shook her head. "For deaf people."

"Right. Describe the images."

"A man and woman are kissing," Ember said, "but all you see are two sets of shoes, because the camera is at ground level. A man's expensive dress shoes and a woman's fancy high heels come together, and one of her feet lifts out of a shoe. Then the man slowly draws back —all you see are his wingtips turning and walking away. In a moment a bouquet of flowers flops on the ground by the woman's shoes, and she turns and walks away too.

"Then you see two rental convertibles drive away from a deserted Last Chance gas station, and disappear in opposite directions down a long, lonely stretch of road, with the sun setting. Then the words appear on the screen: Love *Hertz*."

Mike laughed. "That's cute. Might even be able to sell it for you, if you want."

Kaigani smiled and nodded and then pantomimed tying a necktie and checking her watch, lugging a briefcase to the office. Mike smiled back at her.

He watched Ember and Kaigani signing as if he were enjoying a fine play. They slowed to quarter speed for him, but with each other their hands seemed to move in a blur, and their faces and bodies animated a spontaneous, rich language.

Kaigani wore a tube dress of her own design, woven of turquoise and silver threads with patterns of tiny sparkling purple beads at the neckline, sleeves, and hem. Her hair was combed to one side and it spilled over that shoulder like a black ink waterfall in a *sumi-e* painting. Her eyelashes and eyebrows were as black as her hair and they accented the bright paleness of her clear gray eyes. A Navaho-crafted silver-and-turquoise earring dangled from the uncovered ear and matched a choker necklace and bracelets.

Ember wore a glittery blouse that Kaigani had knit for her, over a thin wool culotte. Her wavy hair was triple braided and hung in one soft cable. Yellow orchids were pinned in her braids. A deep bruise and scratch traced one high cheekbone, and that side of her bottom lip puffed out.

"You should've seen your sister today," Mike said. "She rode like a scary monster."

Ember grinned and touched the scratch on her cheek with her fingertips.

He had built a mountain bike for her, putting new parts on a Diamond Back Ascent frame. This morning he surprised her with the gift and they pedaled up into the hills together, where he meant to demonstrate the basics of off-road cycling. It soon became clear that she could learn any skill he could teach, so he ran through his repertoire of advanced moves. On the first two or three tries she was performing maneuvers that had taken him weeks to master—months, even. By noon they were riding along rocky fire trails, doing wheelies, uphill switchbacks, hop-and-climbs, near drop-off descents, and high-speed compressions.

"The toughest thing is to leap a ditch or stream," he told Kaigani. "I made the mistake of telling her that."

"You should know by now. . . ." Kaigani said.

"So here we are at the top of this rise, overlooking a stream that's got to be at least eight feet across, maybe ten."

"Rusty Creek," Ember said.

"I've never jumped anything wider than about five feet. So I'm straddling my bike, eyeing this . . . Rusty Creek, and I'm thinking, *I'm gonna break my bones on that lovely sparkling water way down there*. And I'm about to tell her, 'Hey, forget it. Let's eat lunch.' When, *voom*!" He shot his hand out like an arrow and pantomimed clutching the handlebar grips. "She's over the crest and diving down the hill, and she's pedaling hard for extra speed. My mouth drops open, my eyes bug out, but I almost don't want to look. She hits the bottom of the hill and I scream, 'Flatten the cranks and bunny-hop with all you've got!' And she takes off like a metal eagle, in an arc like this"—he drew the trajectory with his hand—"and she a-a-a-l-l-most makes it—*splash!*—jonestown.

"Then she stands up and waves. 'Come on, it's a blast!' So, what can I do? I'm supposed to be the mountain-bike guru, not a wimp. So I roll off the ledge, and it's like dropping into a big Hawaiian wave on a surfboard. I'm leaning way back off the saddle to keep from doing a cartwheel and I straighten up just as I bottom out and I've got a half second to get the bike in the air and suddenly I'm sailing high over the stream with plenty of momentum, gonna clear it for sure. And I do.

Only, my bike is back at the other side, where it jammed a rock. I crash and burn, split the seat of my biking shorts, pepperoni on each knee, and she's standing in the water laughing her ass off."

"Sorry," Ember said, wiping at a tear. "The look on your face . . . it was Wily Coyote when he realizes he can't walk on air." They talked and laughed and passed the wine bottle around. Mike found that he liked herring roe on kelp, "Quanoot sushi," and he went back for thirds.

He looked at the sisters across the room. It was the fourth occasion the three of them had spent time together, and the contrast between Kaigani and Ember still struck him as some kind of mythic art. Willow and Oak. Nightingale and Thunderbird.

Earlier today, when Ember wiped out in the creek, she flipped over the handlebars and the bike bounced up and crashed down on top of her. It had scared him, but she'd gotten right up and waved. Then, after his own spill, he saw that she was bleeding from a gash on her cheek and a split lip. She'd stood there, up to her hips in the icy creek, laughing, teeth pink with blood, her wet bike clothes painted on her torso, nipples erect. She'd lifted her bike out of the water and held it over her head like a dripping trophy, her eyes as bright as the mountain.

Now he watched Kaigani, the valley spirit. Some of his former clients would have paid big bucks to capture her smile for a toothpaste ad, her slender fingers to make diamond rings look classy, her long legs to sell lacy stockings. And she was as gracious as Ember had promised, and talented. He liked the clothes she made, better than most of the designer lines from the accounts he'd worked for in Boston—a lifetime ago.

He sighed. Falling in love was something he'd wanted for a long time. But with two sisters at once?

Mike ambled back to the bench and took another swig of the wine, emptying the bottle. A warm, fizzy feeling percolated up his spine. Kaigani and Ember were signing, rapid-fire, and Kaigani did a brief impersonation of her mother getting dressed for the wedding: it was Chena Ozette, exactly.

"Do me," Mike said.

She shook her head.

"Aw, come on."

"You won't get upset?"

"Too mellow to care."

She mimicked the way he folded his arms and half smiled when he felt shy, capturing the slight scrunching of his shoulders and the subtle tension around his eyes.

He looked at his clone. *That's really me? Good grief.*

Kaigani put her hand on his knee and smiled. "I've been shy most of my life too."

"You are so unreasonably pretty," he said, and as soon as the words were out, he realized he was drunk; but her eyes held his with a look that was sweeter than wild plum wine, and the blood sang in his ears.

He started to fold his arms.

She leaned toward him, caught his hands in hers, and softly kissed his mouth. Her hair smelled like rosemary and cloves. He sucked in her fragrance through slightly parted lips, then pressed his mouth against hers. Her taste was all he knew, all he cared to know.

When he remembered Ember, he glanced over and she had turned her back and moved away from them. Kaigani opened her eyes and looked at Ember too.

A men's game was under way in the center among several contestants who each tried to walk the length of the room while balancing on his head a wooden plate stacked with pine cones; midway across they ducked under a four-foot-high rope stretched across the path. To the survivors of each round another pine cone was added and the rope was lowered an inch.

One man, wobbly drunk, lost his balance as he squatted to clear the rope, and sat down hard, sending pine cones flying. The audience laughed.

Suddenly Ember stood up and strode into the center of the room, and the laughter died. She picked up the fallen man's pine cones, set them on his plate, poised it on her head, and moved smoothly across the room, under the rope, and to the other side. The crowd was now quiet. Mike could hear the pop and snap of the logs in the fire pit.

The other players had stopped and were glaring at her. She knelt and set the plate on the floor, stacking half a dozen more pine cones on it, making a tall, scraggly pyramid. Then she centered the plate on her head, carefully stood, and made her way slowly back across the room, gliding now, as if she didn't have joints but ball bearings. At the rope she turned and flowed beneath it backward. The pyramid of cones could have been a headdress on a prima ballerina with yellow orchids in her dark red hair.

Ember thrust the plate at the drunk who still sat on the floor, his mouth open; the pine cones spilled into his lap. Then she whipped around and stormed out of the longhouse.

23

Ember's footsteps crunched rhythmically in the shell road that led from the longhouse through a wedge of forest to town. Tears blurred her vision as she ran. She turned at a black cleft in the wall of cedars and headed up a steep dirt trail that climbed to the granite bluff called Bird Rock.

She flopped down near the ledge of the rock shelf and gazed out over the Pacific into an endless gray void. The moon was full, but it was trapped with the stars behind a solid screen of clouds, and it made only a pale wound in the sky.

Below in the distance to her left, she saw the string of lights that lined the main street of Whaler Bay Village, and past the village the lanterns of a few hunting cabins twinkled in the woods along the ridge above the rocky coast. Most of the mountains beyond were clear cut, but tonight the moon was not bright enough for her to make out the stump-dotted slopes.

Below to her right all was dark. Cliffs jutted straight up from the sea and bent sharply around to the northeast where the coast gradually flattened into a miles-long shoreline. Out of view around the bend, nestled in the cedars along the shore, stood the fifty-odd cabins of the families who, like her father and his ancestors, took their living from the sea.

Whaler Bay Island. Home, but not home.

She had turned down five full scholarships, one for swimming, one for soccer, and three for track, because she hated the idea of being away from Kaigani and her mom and dad, of having only the constant company of her loneliness.

But where am I heading now? Where do I belong?

A jetliner blinked red and green near the horizon, soaring away from her world, across the Pacific to a different world with different people. *But in that other world, as here, there are no people like me.* The dim thunder of the engines faded into the sigh of the waves lapping on the shoreline.

Why did I wreck the men's game like that? To prove I'm good enough? This is the only home I've got, why make things worse for myself?

A flock of crying seagulls flapped by below the cliff edge, sharply white against the backdrop of the night sea. In the far distance a foghorn belched a low rumbling tone, and another answered.

She thought of the fun she had today with Mike on the mountain bikes, how much she liked his company, his conversation. He always did his best to relate to life from his heart and body and mind; not many people bothered to function at all three levels. And in spite of his bashfulness he was really very masculine and sexy . . . those bright hazel eyes . . . his warm aroma . . .

Kaigani.

Now, there's a woman of heart and body and mind. She and Mike are perfect for each other. I wish them well. I do.

Tears started down her cheeks and she twirled a thick coil of loose hair in front of her face. She smelled her own sweat and her own sex and she tasted the salty tears and the salty sea and she wept out loud.

By the time she stood to leave, the wind had picked up and the clouds were scattering and the silver moon peeked through. She untied her braid and shook her hair loose and it billowed around her face. She combed both hands through and came up with two fistfuls of yellow orchids, which she flung off the ledge.

Go back to the longhouse and apologize to everyone. What the hell else can I do?

Moonlight fell on a cairn of rocks at the far side of the granite shelf. The rockpile was not there a month ago. When she walked over to it, the shadows at its base turned out to be flowers and apples and oranges—which raccoons had strewn about—and unopened bottles of beer. Stuffed between the smooth, rounded rocks were sticks of burned sage and folded pieces of paper. She opened one of the notes. It was typed.

Sisiutlqua,

My baby girl is sick and the doctors can't say what's wrong with her. We are Quanoot, full blooded.

I believed in Jesus when I was little, and I still "respect" him, but he can't (or won't) help us.

My husband and I don't go to church now, since we learned about you.

We are Quanoot, and my great grandmother is teaching us about Quanoot-cha, to live right. We are Quanoot, and we believe in you.

With respect,

Tilly and James One-Boot

P.S. Our little girl's name is Kelka Marie. You went to high school with James, two classes above you.

Ember's gut knotted. "Damn you, Tom! Oh, what have you done to me?" She unfolded another note, written by a shaky hand.

Sisiutlqua, I'm eighty-nine years old, so I don't need to ask you for nothing. I want to thank you for coming to us, to give us back some of our dignity. I'm old enough to remember when the government tore down the last of our totems and forbade us to speak our language. The social people came and took me away to a school on the mainland. Mostly I remember my father crying. I found out later he never got over it. And even though the government people have given back some of the stuff they stole, to put in our village museum, it don't do much good because we lost our spirit.

I believe you are hear to teach the young people Quanoot-cha. Not the words, but the feeling of the Way. I missed out on it, in the white schools and all, but the boys and girls coming up now don't need to miss it, if you help them.

Please help them.

And, I guess there is one favor, after all. If you see my wife, Grace, in the spirit land, tell her I love her and miss her and I'll join her soon.

Gratefully,

Thomas St. John (Kose Chinokanok)

Ember felt as if one of the heavy, round rocks had lodged under her ribs. There were dozens of notes. She read five or six more until she came to a message handwritten by Tom Luc:

Dear Ember/Sisiutlqua,

I've been fasting on water for two weeks now and I feel weak, but real clean. Bobby and I built a sweat lodge next to the stream up the hill behind his mom's house and we sweat every night with a few others and sing the canoe maker's song and the whaling song over and over (we don't know any others yet) and then wash in the cold stream. It feels like washing our bad times away. No cigarettes, drugs, or booze for the last eleven weeks, and none ever again.

Grandma Luc and Grandma Flower are showing us what they remember about the Way.

By the night of Ron and Chanee's wedding I'll be pure enough to tell everybody what you did for me, to announce you to the village. You're *here*! And that's the best thing that's ever happened to me, and to our tribe.

*Quanoot-cha *ki layo me, de ene poi hok.*

Your servant, Tom Luc

Ember heard the angry voices coming from inside the longhouse as she sprinted toward it on the shell road. Her heart pounded in her throat and she froze at the low door and did not go in. She put her eye against a chink in the planks and saw Tom standing in the center of the room; his face was gaunt and cratered, but his eyes were as black and shiny as obsidian; he wore his long hair pulled over one shoulder, in the old style of the whale hunters.

"Sisiutlqua is with us, here and now," he said to a balding man in a rodeo shirt who had taken center stage with him. "To deny that is to deny your own heritage."

"Quanoot heritage is the same as white man's heritage—sin and death!" said the man. "She's no savior, even if she is Sisiutlqua. The only savior is Lord Jesus Christ."

Some people mumbled approval.

"Well, he didn't save me when I was dying. Never showed his face. But I saw her light reach out in a dark sea and grab my soul and tow it back to shore. Now, is that being a savior or not?"

People in the crowd shouted agreement.

"Hand Jesus a harpoon and he wouldn't know which end was sharp," Bobby Kynaka said, from the left side of the room. He had lost weight and grown his hair long, which he wore in the whaler's style. "He is for the whites, for the philosophers and book writers. He's no warrior. Believe me, Ember is a warrior," he said, and rubbed the bridge of his nose. "Living the warrior way makes me feel proud to be a Quanoot again."

Everybody started talking and yelling at once.

Jimmy Ozette, her father, stepped into the center of the lodge house. Gray streaked his black hair and beard; a pale diagonal scar etched his broad nose and right cheek where a chainsaw had kicked back in his face a dozen years before. He held up his hands and the crowd hushed.

"Look, I'm gonna ask you all for the second time. Please go home and cool off, think about this some more before you go off making claims one way or the other. I think Ember deserves some say in all of this, don't you?"

That was her cue. She ducked through the door.

"I'm not Sisuitlqua," she said in a loud voice. The roomful of people turned to stare.

Her mother and Mike and Kaigani rushed to embrace her. They escorted her to the center of the room to join her father. Some in the crowd reached out to touch her hair as she walked by, others pressed forward to sit on the floor in a circle near her.

The room became quiet and she looked around

slowly, glancing at each face; some frowned at her and others trembled with silent tears.

"My name is Ember Ozette and you all know me. Some of you know me well. I'm not any different now than I ever was. That day on the mountain, I kept Tom warm . . . I have a lot of body heat, people joke about it . . . but this is all a big mistake."

She looked at Tom, who was kneeling at her feet.

"I don't mean to deny the Quanoot-cha. I think it's good that you and Bobby and the others are taking up the warrior way. But, I'm not Sisiutlqua. Everybody needs to know that." She reached out her hand to him. "Come on, now, get up. It's me, Ember."

Tom bowed his head.

"She's Satan in drag, that's who she is!" yelled a woman, setting off a cascade of shouts and counter-shouts. A tall, bony gray-haired woman stood up from the circle at Ember's feet and looked her in the eyes. It was her grandma Kynaka.

"Ember, I know who you are, exactly," she said. "On the day after my daughter, Chena, returned home, eighteen years ago, Old Man climbed up to the cabin by Otter Creek where she was staying with you, just a newborn. He had not been off his island for as long as anyone could remember, but he came to the little cabin to see you. He said you would grow up to be a great *kasko*—Sisiutlqua. And he kissed you on the forehead, and he left. That was it. Now we all can see you aren't like one of us. You're special. Old Man knew. He knew."

Chena frowned. "Mom, I've told you a hundred times, I have no idea what he said to her." She looked at the crowd. "That's all just rumor—Jimmy and I don't speak the old language. We don't know what he said."

Tears flowed down Grandma Kynaka's cheeks. "Chena, you gave birth to Sisiutlqua," she said, her voice choking. "Old Man knew. Somehow, it was all part of a great plan. It's going to bring our family back together." She clapped her hands and whispered, *"Quanoot-cha *ki layo me, da ene poi hok."*

Tom and Bobby and a score of other voices in the room repeated the affirmation. Ember found it hard to breathe.

"Tom, you started this," she said. "You've got to stop it. Please—you've got to."

"Sisiutlqua would test the warriors, make sure their faith is alive. Well, mine is."

"Damn it!" Ember shouted. "If you people make me, I'll leave Whaler Bay. I'll move away and not come back . . . a school in L.A. wants me, one in Florida. Is that what you want? To drive me away from my home and family with all of this?"

"Take it easy, honey," her mother said, massaging her shoulders. "Take a deep breath."

Tom stood up, a wounded look on his face.

"What are we not doing that you want us to do?" he said, his shoulders shaking. "I've been fasting for weeks. I've changed . . . I've really changed. Tell us what you want. We need you to guide us, Sisiutlqua."

"That's it. I'm leaving the island," Ember said. "I'm gone."

She shoved through the circle at her feet and strode toward the door, parting the crowd as a wedge splits a log.

"You want faith?" Tom shouted. "Here it is!" He ripped his shirt open, sending buttons flying, and unsheathed a big Bowie knife. The crowd sucked in its breath.

Ember was near the door, and spun to see.

"You saved me before. I have faith you'll save me again."

"Don't!" she screamed.

He pressed the point of the blade against a fat pink scar on the right side of his chest. Mike lunged and with both his hands grabbed the knife arm at the wrist and twisted it away from Tom's chest. At that instant Jimmy swung a canoe paddle broadside and clubbed Tom in the back of the head. The paddle blade splintered with a loud crack. Tom's neck jerked forward, his knees buckled, and he pitched headlong to the floor.

"See what happens when you run with the Devil?" a man said.

"I tell you, she's Satan in drag!" a woman said.

Jimmy brandished the canoe paddle above his head. "The next person who calls my daughter Satan is going to get this paddle up his ass. Now, everybody, shut up, and *GO HOME*!"

Ember slumped onto a bench and her sister and mother sat on either side and put their arms around her. People filed out the door, gawking at her and mumbling to each other.

"You can press charges against him for harassment," Chena said. "Get a restraining order."

"It's not Tom," Ember said in a squeaky voice, shivering. "It's me. I'm different from everyone, outside and inside. Even you, Mom, even Kaigani. You can't know what it's like. Maybe I am Sisiutlqua . . . I don't know . . . I don't know anything, except I'm scared."

"Oh, baby." Chena squeezed her. "Talk to me. What are you afraid of?"

"That my visions will take over, and I'll turn into some kind of freak." She gulped at the painful lump in her throat and her voice broke. "And . . . even . . . you . . . guys . . . won't love me."

Chena laid Ember's head on her fragrant bosom; her braids fell over her daughter's neck. "I'll stop loving you," she said, "the day the moon quits loving the sea."

Kaigani kissed her sister's face and cried, too, and the three of them hugged and gently swayed like a cradle on the tide.

After a while Chena said, "There's someone you need to visit."

Ember sighed. "I'm scared of what he might tell me—but I want to know. I want to go tonight."

"It's late."

"The moon is full, you can read by it."

"Old Man will be asleep. Dad can take you there in the morning."

Ember said nothing, but only set her jaw.

24

MIKE SPRAWLED ON his back on the bed, staring at the animal shapes among the shadows cast by the iron stove. The moonlight caught his belt buckle draped over the chair and threw a silver rectangle of light on one cedar log in the wall.

A family of mice skittered around in the kitchen cabinets. Down the hillside toward the sea, gulls mewed, punctuated by the occasional high-pitched *chip*s of a goshawk. Much closer to the cabin the basso profundo of bullfrogs, *uh-grummit, uh-grummit, uh-grummit,* underscored the tremolo falsetto of tree frogs, *breeep-breeep-breeep.*

The bullfrogs would abruptly hush, simultaneously. Pause a moment. Then one would begin, *uh-grummit, uh-grummit,* a second would add his voice, a third, and then every bullfrog on this side of the island would croak his throbbing three-chambered heart out.

Didn't matter. He wasn't about to fall asleep anyway.

Ember and Kaigani. Binary stars, orbiting each other, exchanging star matter when they came close. How do you love one without the other?

And what's with this wacko cult? Sisiutlqua—that some kind of warrior goddess? And what's going on with Ember, what's she hiding? How can I help her if she won't trust me? And even if she does trust me, how can I help her?

His mind chirped away like the tree frogs.

He got out of bed and stretched his arms above his head; his fingertips just touched the low ceiling. He threw on a pair of jeans, a sweatshirt, canvas shoes, and a leather bomber jacket and made his way down the path to West Bay.

A breeze of seaweed and salt greeted him, breathing against his beard. Silvery light gleamed on tangles of slimy kelp, broken shells, and smooth pebbles.

He had never seen so much bioluminescence as in the water tonight. His footsteps in the wet sand made little bursts of blue light. A glowing sheet of water gushed ashore, and sandpipers scattered in the bright foam, trailing tiny wakes of sparkles.

A giant boulder, blanketed with moss and topped with wind-twisted bonsai-like pines, squatted on the beach ahead. He had found a scooped-out throne in the rock that was a magical place to sit and mull things over

—or to sit and not mull things over. On the dry side of the boulder he kept his canoe.

The Quanoot, along with the Haida, Makah, and Nootka, were the Vikings of the pre-European native world; they raided other tribes along the coast for plunder and slaves, in huge sea canoes paddled by dozens of warriors. It was a smaller model of such a canoe that he and Jimmy Ozette had crafted. They did everything the ancient way. It took a full day to chop down a broad red cedar using stone axes. They split the trunk lengthwise with stone wedges, then widened and deepened the crack with scrapers. Then they filled the groove with a few inches of water and shoveled in fire-heated rocks. As the steam softened the wood, they pried the sides apart using wooden rods as spacers, bending the trunk into a wide canoe shape. The upturned bow and stern pieces were carved separately and glued with tree resin to the dugout. Then they shaped and smoothed the hull and painted it with otters, the Ozette family crest. Jimmy named the canoe *Jagdaw*.

As Mike neared the great hunk of granite, he saw someone dragging his canoe toward the water.

He broke into a run, shouting, "Hey! What are you doing? Stop!"

The figure looked up and the moon shone full in her face.

"Ember?"

"I'm going to Old Man Land."

"At two A.M.?"

"Yes."

"No, you're not."

"I'm going, Mike."

"Forget it, you'll be paddling against the tide."

"I can handle it."

"Three miles, in a two-person canoe, by yourself?"

"I said I can handle it."

"Why didn't you take the Zodiac?"

She didn't answer.

"Because your dad's got it locked up, and he doesn't know you're pulling this stunt."

"Mike. Go away."

Her face wore the same expression as when he'd told her that jumping streams on a mountain bike was dangerous.

"Okay," he said. "I'm going with you."

"I don't need your help."

"Yes, you do," he said, and tossed his leather jacket in the bottom of the canoe, lifted out a life vest, and buckled it on.

"Let me put it this way," she said. "I don't want you to come along."

He dragged the canoe toward the water's edge; when it reached the wet sand it left a track of quickly fading blue light.

"Mike, this is a personal thing."

"I know. If anything happened to you, I'd hold myself personally responsible." He grabbed a wooden paddle. "Get in and I'll shove us off."

She blew out a loud sigh, then climbed in and picked up a paddle. Soon they were gliding over the shiny black sea with Whaler Bay Island shrinking behind them. Each stroke of their paddles produced glowing blue whirlpools that reflected from the sides of the canoe and slid past them in a swirling wake.

"What makes you think this guy likes to be wakened in the middle of the night?" Mike said from the stern.

"I feel him calling to me."

"How do you know he doesn't own a gun? He doesn't know us. This might be like the Marines landing at Iwo Jima."

"He likes visitors. Mostly old people, who believe in the old ways, go to see him. He counsels them and helps them out."

"I thought he was a hermit."

"He is, but he's also Sisiutlqua."

Mike missed the beat with his paddle and icy water sloshed his arms.

"Hold on, I'm confused. A lot of people back there think you're Sisiutlqua."

"It's not a person, it's a title—means Soul Catcher. In the old times there were certain *kasko*—you know that word?"

"It means, like, shaman?"

"Shaman. And they could heal the sick and foretell the future and even bring people back from the dead, if their death was unnatural."

"How do you mean, unnatural?"

"An evil spirit trying to steal the soul away to use as a slave or mate in the spirit world," she said. "When a person was sick, the shaman would fall into a deep sleep and travel to the spirit villages to track down the patient's soul. If he found that the soul was meant to stay there, he'd tell the relatives it was the patient's proper time to die, but if he found that the soul had been stolen, the shaman would do everything in his power to call the soul back."

"So if the guy recovered," Mike said, "it was to the shaman's credit, but if the poor slob croaked, it was never the shaman's fault. Those guys had malpractice insurance beat to hell."

"Soul Catchers were the most powerful of the *kasko*, they came along only every few generations, and they ministered to many tribes, not just their own. The last of the Soul Catchers was named Iwaka—means 'waterfall.' He lived at the time when the Indians caught the Cold Sick and started dropping like flies. He couldn't stop it."

Mike had read about the terrible influenza epidemic of the summer of 1829. The coastal Indians had no immunity to the virus, and its victims literally died within hours of feeling sick. Flu, along with smallpox and tuberculosis, wiped out ninety percent of the native population in ten years.

"There weren't enough people left in the villages to bury the dead," Ember said, "so they abandoned their villages."

"Let me guess—that's when the missionaries stepped in and tore down the totem poles, stuck up the crosses."

"How could anyone stop them? Their magic was deadly."

"What about Iwaka?"

"He didn't die in the epidemic, but he went away to live by himself in the islands—"

"Old Man?"

She nodded. "Old Man."

"No way. He'd have to be—what?—pushing two hundred."

"Nobody knows how old he is. A lot of people think he's Iwaka."

Sweat ran down Mike's back in the chilly night air. Ember took her sweatshirt off and wore only a white leotard tank top. Moonglow glistened from the sweat on her shoulders and upper back, and he watched her muscles flex with each stroke. He breathed hard, matching her pace. The canoe rose and dipped on gentle swells, surging ahead in rhythm with their paddles.

"So why does Tom think you're a Soul Catcher?"

She told him about the incident with Tom and Bobby and Kaigani at her secret place in the mountains.

"It was this . . . bright heat, or like electricity, a fiery energy . . . it seemed to ignite way deep in my belly and spread through my body. It shone the strongest from my hands and eyes . . . it just took over."

She glanced back at him. "Sound totally crazy?"

"I think you were doing an advanced kind of yoga."

"You've heard of this thing before?"

"Read about it," he said. "The Tibetan yogis, up on the roof of the world, developed breath-control techniques called 'tumo' to heat their bodies in the cold."

"Tumo?"

"Tibetan for 'inner heat.' I don't know much about it, really. But I read that in one monastery, the students were graduated when, among other things, they could sit down and concentrate and melt the snow in a circle around them."

Something rippled and splashed in the water, making zigzags of light.

"The most famous adept—*whoa*!" Mike ducked as a big fish sailed over the canoe and smacked down on the other side. "There was a master yogi named Milarepa—means 'white cotton'—all he ever wore was a thin white cotton robe, even in the worst Himalayan winters."

"You'll have to show me where to read about that. It really makes me feel better to know that somebody else has experienced it."

"But it came to you naturally, that's what I can't get over. These monks sit around and practice mind and body disciplines from kindergarten age, and it takes them years to master this stuff. But you saw Tom dying, and you somehow zapped him with a thousand volts. That's really something."

"I don't know how I did it."

"Could you do it again?"

She shot a glance back to him. "I don't want to."

He nodded. "I understand."

They paddled on against the drag of the inflowing tide. Mike could just make out the dark lump on the horizon that was Old Man Land.

"Tibetans," Ember said, "—are they golden, like me?"

"No, they look a lot like Han Chinese, the color of straw, dark straw."

A half hour later Mike thought he saw the flicker of firelight in a low spot on the jagged silhouette of the island. He grew excited about meeting an authentic Indian shaman, like stepping into America's past.

"Ember, tell me about your dreams."

She told him about the blue ice cave and the vision in which she smelled the people and animals.

"Someday, somehow," she said, "I'm going to go on an expedition to look for others like myself—in Siberia, I think, or Mongolia."

"What about records of your biological parents? You must've checked those out by now."

"No records. The doctor who implanted the embryo claims the donors were anonymous."

"Which you don't believe for a minute."

"I . . . I don't know. Sometimes I think I'm a cross between a human and an orangutan."

"Why do you say things like that? I think you're beautiful."

She stopped paddling. "What?"

"You heard me."

She turned to look at him. Even in the half-light her eyes were jade.

He smiled shyly. "You really are very beautiful, you know."

Her bushy eyebrows gathered. She faced forward and paddled more slowly.

After a moment she said, "Kaigani is falling in love with you."

He made no comment.

A noise like sizzling began in the water a dozen yards to their left. It quickly grew louder until it sounded like raindrops spattering in a giant hot skillet. A great blob of vibrating light swelled upward and then the surface boiled with thousands of small fish.

"Whales rising!" Ember shouted.

Six or eight whales nosed upward at the same time, in a ring, maws agape, blowing jets of air, hissing and squealing. Shiny silver herring leapt and flipped and thrashed, reflecting moonlight like tossed coins. After a minute or two of gorging the whales submerged and a glowing blue mist settled on the sea.

"Humpbacks," Ember said. Mike sat motionless, eyes wide, too amazed to speak.

Suddenly a mammoth black shape thrust out of the sea, up and up like a black geyser, then fell back on its side with a thunderous splash and explosion of blue light. Another black mountain erupted skyward and crashed down so close that the wave rocked the canoe.

"Holy shit!" Mike yelled. "Don't they stay in their lanes?"

A few yards off the bow another sizzling ball of light took shape.

"Back-paddle!" she yelled, and their blades jammed against the water like brakes and brought the canoe to a stop.

The pod punched up through the school of fish and waved their cavernous maws side to side, scooping gallons of frothy water. A band of seagulls showed up, circling and swerving and dipping, adding their loud cries to the chaos. After a minute or two the whales sank below.

"Let's get the hell out of here!" Mike yelled, and they leaned into their paddles, hard and fast, and shot forward toward the island.

"Steer right!" Ember yelled, and angled her paddle to swerve the bow away from a swiftly rising ball of light.

A whale lunged upward and stood on its tail, as big

as a bus tipped on end, then began to topple toward the canoe.

Mike screamed, "Jump!" and they both dived over the right side. As Mike hit the water, he heard the canoe splinter behind him. He popped up gasping from the stinging cold.

"Ember!" he shouted.

"Right here, I'm okay." She was bobbing in her life vest a few yards to his left. He swam to her and grabbed her life vest with one hand.

"Damn, it's cold," he said.

"Let's stick together, we've got about a half-mile swim."

"Right. Don't get lost. Every few strokes, make sure we're still together."

Mike turned toward Old Man Land and reached in long, even strokes toward the shore. The cold burned his fingers and his hands were soon numb. Ember swam alongside, trailing light.

After a few more minutes his arms felt rubbery. Ember pulled ahead slightly and he stroked harder to keep up. His bones began to ache from the chill.

"You okay?" Ember called from a few feet ahead, treading water.

"C-c-cold. Th-that's all."

They swam alongside for a while, then Ember waited again for him to catch up. A pleasant tingling spread through his body, and gradually he began to feel relief from the cold, as if thick cotton wrapped his brain, padding it from all sensations. An odd euphoria took over and he giggled.

"Mike, take some deep breaths," Ember said, looking worried. He tried to say *I'm fine,* but it came out garbled, which made him laugh. She grabbed his vest and began towing him.

"Kick your feet," she said. "Keep moving. We're almost there."

Leave me alone, let me sleep, he wanted to say, but his tongue wouldn't work. He closed his eyes.

A loud sizzling rose from beneath them; they were suddenly in the midst of a glowing circle of blue light.

"Get out!" Ember shouted, and yanked him backward, racing toward the edge of the cauldron that now churned with shimmering fins.

They didn't make it in time.

Whale heads popped up all around them. Seagulls milled above. Silver fish flip-flopped in every direction, cutting his face and hands with their fins. He gulped seawater. Then the whales slid below, the foaming stopped, and all was quiet for a moment.

Three black walls shot up and blocked the moon; they hung against the sky for an instant, then keeled over, and the waves bounced Mike out of the water. He saw three flukes rise over his head like smooth black wings, and he sloshed in the wake from the whales as they dove under his feet.

Everything that happened afterward was filtered through dense padding and a terrible need for sleep. He struggled to keep his eyes open, even as Ember screamed in his face and slapped him.

At last, exhausted past all caring, he saw the gaping mouth of a whale, felt himself dragged inside, then darkness, blessed heat, so soft and so comforting.

He gratefully slept.

25

EMBER AWOKE IN a white mist. The fog was so thick, she was not sure if the sun was up. Dew dripped from the craggy ceiling of the hollow tree that sheltered them.

Her head rested on Mike's chest and his heart thumped steadily against her ear. He was asleep, nude like herself, and she was draped over him like a blanket.

Last night, when he became hypothermic in the water, she towed him to the island and dragged him across the beach to a broad totem pole with a killer-whale face carved at its base, jaws open to a scooped-out mouth. Mike's lips were blue and he no longer shivered. She had hurriedly tugged off their soggy, icy clothes and snuggled against him. Then she was forced to reach down into her power and use it.

Tumo. But maybe her power was more than *tumo.* Mike had said nothing about the blending of souls that takes place. Now she knew she loved him, for the same masculine spirit that she often glimpsed at the surface—in his eyes, his laugh—she had embraced at its core.

The aroma of his warm skin intoxicated her. He grew rigid in his sleep, and every time he stirred or his eyelids fluttered, she felt her heart beat faster. But she knew it was taboo, the wetness between her thighs, her hungry heart, all forbidden. They had already melted soul into soul; it seemed that loving skin to skin would be less intimate—and for them to make love would betray Kaigani.

Mike shifted underneath her and opened his hazel eyes. His mouth parted in shock at their naked closeness. He started to speak and she put a finger to his lips. He took that hand and kissed it, then grabbed her sides and slid her up his chest till their lips were an inch apart. She turned her face away.

He took her face in his hands and turned it back to him and kissed her full lips. She let him, but only for a moment, just enough to taste him. Only for another moment, and just another moment—and then she wanted his mouth on her body, everywhere.

"Mike, no." She pulled back, her chest heaving. Her hair fell across her face.

He bent his head and licked the salt from the peach fuzz on her high, round breasts. She gasped. He nuzzled his face between them, then pressed his hot mouth onto her nipples.

"Oh, no, no, no," she said, shuddering.

Strong, gentle fingers caressed and squeezed her neck and shoulders, stroked the long hills of her back, swept over her muscular hips, and slipped between her legs. She sucked in her breath and arched her back. Wetness ran down, slickening the inside of her thighs.

Kaigani had been with lovers and shared with her every detail of those sexual encounters, but she had not imagined it would be so magnetic. She yearned for him to be inside her, and there could be no stopping if she did not stop now.

"Mike . . . oh . . . we can't, we can't." She pushed away from him again, rolled off his sinewy frame, and reached for her clothes. Her skin was rosy-golden and hot, shiny with sweat, and red sand clung to her sides in rusty beads.

"You love me too," he said. "We both know you do."

"And I love Kaigani, and so do you."

He froze, confusion on his face. Then he let out a big sigh and flopped his head down.

She wrung a puddle from her sweatshirt and shorts and wriggled into them.

"Maybe," he said, "maybe we could all make love together. A triad."

"We're sisters, not saints. And not whores."

"I'm sorry." He ran a hand through his damp hair. "Sorry. I'm pretty mixed up. . . ."

"Me too, so don't worry about it. Here, put your clothes on."

Through the low doorway she saw a man squatting

on the pebbly sand twenty feet away, as silent as a totem carved out of the mist.

"Old Man," Ember said, tilting her head at the door.

Mike lurched up and cracked his head on the ceiling. He clutched his scalp with one hand and tried to cover his nakedness with the other. He wrung out his cold, soggy jeans and shivered as he tugged them on; but in his aroused state he could not fit inside or zip the fly.

"You go," he said.

Ember ducked through the opening.

Old Man smiled and stepped forward, chattering in Quanoot. He wore a short-sleeved dog-wool robe with a fringed, knee-length hemline, dyed dark purple with mussel-shell ink. Slung over his back was a wide conical woven cedar-bark hat adorned with killer-whale designs. His thin, bare legs ended in a pair of battered Nike running shoes, mummy-wrapped with strips of red cedar bark. Two yellow gourds were hooked to a cedar bark belt by their spiral stems.

Ember introduced Mike and herself, and Old Man took her hands and kissed each palm, and offered his palms, which she kissed. He looked up with a big grin, gaps in his teeth like a harmonica. She realized she had been too distracted to detect him before, for he reeked of campfire smoke and fish.

So this was Old Man, Sisiutlqua. He was tiny; the top of his head could nestle below her chin. Beneath a seaweed patch of white hair his face wore the wrinkled dunes of time.

Mike ducked through the hole and stood up, folding his arms in front of his bare chest.

"Why was he spying on us?" he said.

Ember spoke to Old Man and he laughed. As he talked, his face and hands danced along with his words.

"He says he wanted to watch us make love," she said.

"Well, to hell with that. Tell him that really pisses me off."

Old Man spoke again.

"He says he's watched whales make love, eagles, sea otters, bears—"

"—great, he's a Peeping Tom naturalist—"

"—but he's never seen people make love. He was curious."

"Tell him—tell him . . . has he ever heard of privacy? Tell him some things in life are supposed to be kept special."

The Quanoot language clicked and popped between them. Old Man nearly danced in place as he spoke; his black eyes twinkled inside their nests of creases. She began to smile.

"He says, 'What's so special?' Every day he sees the sky and mountains and sea do erotic things—trade all kinds of energies and pleasures—and they don't hide their joy from him." She laughed. "He says, 'You got only a little bitty thing compared to a humpback whale—not so special.' "

Old Man beamed at Mike, and stretched his arms apart as far as he could reach. Then he dropped his elbows to his sides and spread his forearms as fins; he seemed to float on the ground, buoyant on his tiptoes, and he blew out a long hiss of breath and sucked in fresh air, arching his supple back and waving his fins gracefully in the sea swells. He made raucous squealing sounds, bending high notes into deep bass like a slide trombone, the song of the humpbacks.

It was uncanny; he had taken on the essence of a whale before their eyes.

Mike smiled.

"He's a cute little cuss, I'll give him that," he said, and he relaxed his shoulders and unfolded his arms.

Old Man motioned for them to follow, and he led them through tall evergreens half hidden in gauzy mist, to a low, wide cove. The tide was out and the sandy flat was stained in black streaks of iodine runoff from twisted strands of shiny purple kelp. Big and tiny crabs skittered in all directions, clattering over smooth, wet rocks that sheltered orange sea urchins, pink-and-blue anemones, and red starfish. A sandpiper cocked back his head, trying to choke down a starfish, but the meal refused to slide down its gullet and the bird regurgitated and tried again and again.

Old Man took a woven bag from his belt loop, scooped out a clam from under the sand, and dropped it in; within ten minutes the three of them had added a couple dozen. Then in one motion Old Man snatched up a crab bigger than Mike's hand and smacked its shell on a rock. He stuffed it in the bag, and soon added another.

Ember grabbed a big crab from behind, as Old Man had done, but it twisted in her fingers and she dropped it before it gave her a pinch. In a flash Old Man bent and plucked up the crab and dashed its shell on a rock. Ember tried again, this time matching Old Man's speed and circular motion: she snatched up a crab from behind and batted it against a rock. Old Man smiled and nodded as she put the food into the bag.

Then they followed Old Man up a hill, winding around moss-shrouded rock formations and sheer granite cliffs that plunged to the sea. Ember smelled fresh water and they soon came to a clear, gushing stream. Old Man dipped the bag to wash the food, and filled the gourds with water. Then they climbed on, to the island's flat peak, where, in a clearing, stood a longhouse, with a raven's gaping beak for a doorway.

Inside, in the central fire pit red-hot rocks lay in a bed of glowing coals. Old Man filled a watertight cedarbark basket with a few inches of fresh water, grasped the fire-heated rocks with bone tongs and laid them inside, placed the seafood on top, and covered the basket with a lid.

Then they sat outside on split log benches and ate the steamed clams and crabs with their fingers. The food was delicious, even without any seasonings, and the stream water was ice cold. At their elevation the fog was beginning to clear, while below them the sea was a broad white cloud.

Old Man's eyes met Ember's. He seemed in no hurry to look away or to do anything else this morning but to see into her. Ember smiled, but shifted on the hard bench, and was glad when Mike pointed out an eagle's nest at the top of a blue spruce.

What can he see? What does he know about me? And do I really want to find out?

She flicked a glance at Old Man out of the corner of her eyes. He was completely focused on her.

Yes. I've got to know.

"You have come to find out why you are different from your family and friends," Old Man said, in clear English.

Mike spun his head at the sound of his own language. "Good grief," he said.

"You came to Whaler Bay," Ember said, "eighteen years ago, when I was a newborn."

"Has it been that long?" Old Man said, and shook his head. "Time gets lost in the fog of this place."

"They say you came to bless me because I would grow up to be . . . Sisiutlqua. But how did you know about me? What do you know? Where are the others like me? Am I a Soul Catcher?"

He held up his palms.

"I will tell you all that I can," he said. "But first, let us bathe, and then, let us dance."

"Huh?" Mike said.

"Quanoot-cha," Ember told him. "It's traditional, before telling or hearing important news, to 'open your body to the truth'—by bathing and dancing."

"All three of us?"

Old Man stood and set off at a stroll toward the midmorning sun.

Ember stood to follow him.

"Look . . . I think I'll just wait this one out," Mike said.

"You're in Quanoot territory," she said, and her green eyes flashed. "When in our land, do as we do, and don't dishonor our ways."

"No, I don't mean to be insulting, I'm just . . . you know me. . . ."

"Yeah, I didn't mean to sound harsh either." She

took his hand. "Guess I'm afraid to admit I need your support. Come on."

He stood. "But I can't dance worth diddly."

"Well, you can bathe worth diddly."

"With you and him?"

"We've kissed and touched, why be shy now?"

He shrugged. "Bad wiring?"

A hundred feet up the trail Ember smelled the sulphur and heard the babbling water. At the island's tip the slopes converged into an extinct volcanic cone, fifty yards from rim to rim. The crater was filled to the lip with water that blossomed with steam. On the far side it overflowed to form a shallow spring that trickled along a bed of pumice and disappeared down the hill. Old Man had peeled off his clothes, and he sat on the edge of the crater and then slipped in with a loud sigh.

Ember crossed her arms and lifted off her sweatshirt and she saw Mike's eyes dart away as her head popped through the neckhole. On a silent signal they both stepped out of their pants, examining the rocky ground around their bare feet. Slowly, timidly, they raised their eyes.

Mike was sinewy, elongated. His auburn head and beard matched the color of his chest hair, but his curls down below were a shocking red. He wore a crooked grin.

"Like I told you before," he said softly, "you're a beautiful woman."

"I like your looks too," she said. "Like a heron."

"Someone told me I reminded her of a wolfhound. I think I like heron better."

They gingerly eased into the hot water.

"Uhhhhhhhm." Mike sighed. "Boil me bones." He rested his neck against the ledge.

Ember and Old Man performed a cleansing ritual, first washing their hands and faces, then splashing the water over their chests, then cupping the water over their eyes, and finally, sucking it in and spitting it out. Mike copied their actions.

Old Man climbed out. His dark skin was as wet and shiny as a seal's. He dressed quickly and disappeared down the hill alongside the little spring. Mike and Ember put on their clothes and followed.

Down the trail a drum sounded a perky rhythm; then a dozen drums added their voices, then a hundred drums beat at once, like raindrops splattering on a tin roof. Ember hurried toward the music, feeling her own heartdrum pound faster.

"How's he doing that?" Mike said, right behind her.

A large array of log drums of many sizes and shapes stood in a narrow clearing that sloped toward the sea. From a ridge high above, spring water trickled through bamboo pipes and rained fat droplets onto the rows of drums. The drops thumped the wood and the drums sang through a slit in each hollow log; from the deep bass voice of the long, broad drums to the high treble of the short, slender drums.

Old Man was already dancing, eyes closed. He would begin with a slight movement of his head that spread through his neck to his shoulders, arms, and hands, and down through his torso to his hips and through to his knees and feet, until his whole form was being played by the drum music. Then that dance would seem to pass through his body into the ground, and he would become still, utterly calm. After a moment his head would sway again with a different motion, and new expressions would cascade through him, dancing down to Earth.

For a while Ember couldn't take her eyes off Old Man.

Then she shut her eyes and surrendered to the music. The rhythms throbbed through her heart and head and moved her muscles and she gave in to the dance as it came. It was hypnotic, ecstatic. She ate the music, and it swallowed her. She began to sing; not words, just sounds, moving up out of her belly, opening her soul like a lung. She heard Old Man intoning, also, and she opened her eyes and he was dancing with her, his face shining, an ancient little boy.

Mike threw himself around, rolling on the ground and hopping up again, doing karate kicks and punches in the air, shouting and laughing.

After a timeless moment Old Man replaced the plugs in the bamboo tubes and the drums stopped beating, one drum at a time, until the last of the hundred rhythms was no more. The island seemed perfectly silent.

"Sit here, both of you," Old Man said, pointing to smooth, flat stones at the edge of the clearing. He sat before them, cross-legged.

"Listen now. I will tell you a very, very old story," he said. "It has come down to our people, passed from storykeeper to storykeeper, but the tale is much older than the Quanoot—even much older than these trees."

Ember and Mike leaned forward.

26

"LONG AGO, IN the time of the First People, it was very, very cold," Old Man said. "Much of the land was covered with ice, and even much of the sea was frozen. It was so cold that no one could talk, because everyone's tongue was frozen stiff.

"Because no one could speak with his tongue, everyone spoke from his heart. And because people could hear each other's hearts, there was no lying, and little misunderstanding in those days, and there was no war.

"People could even listen to the animals and plants with their hearts, and the living things told the people their secret uses, like chewing willow bark to ease a headache, and eating white clay to stop the bowel water.

"Lifetimes passed and the summers started growing longer and the ice that covered the world began to melt. One day a boy named Talu noticed that his tongue was not frozen like everyone else's. He began to try out his gift, saying 'Kak-kak,' like the eagle, and 'Hoo-hoo-oop,' like the owl. Before long he made up his own sounds, and soon he had built a storehouse of words and knew that he was very smart. The others noticed, too, and as soon as he sprouted whiskers, they made him their leader.

"Before long, more children were born with thawed tongues and they jabbered and chattered at each other as they do today.

"But Talu noticed that most of the children could not talk as well. And he pointed this out to the other talkers. Before long, the people no longer lived as equals, because there were two classes: those who talked well and those who could not talk so well. Talu called those like himself 'Water-Talkers,' and he mocked the others, calling them 'Frozen Tongues.'

"But secretly, Talu was jealous, because the Frozen Tongues still had the ability to talk with their hearts, without opening their mouths, and they could talk this way over great distances, and even over lifetimes, for you see, those who could talk with their hearts could remember the hearts of all their ancestors."

Old Man made a point of meeting Ember's eyes. She trembled, outside and in.

"Talu wanted to keep the power of all his words that set him above the others, but he also wanted to regain the magic of talking with his heart. But try as he might, he was unable to relearn the secret of their heart-talk.

"Time passed, and now great-great-grandson Talu was chief of the Water-Talkers. By this time the split between those who could talk with their tongues and those who couldn't had gotten worse. Talu made a law that Frozen Tongues could not mate with Water-Talkers. The Talkers made the Frozen Tongues their slaves.

"After it went this bad way for a long time, it got uglier. By now the Water-Talkers did not look like the others any longer, because they had not bred together for generations. The people were no longer one family, but two. And now those who could not talk were called the Beasts. The Talu of that day declared that the Beasts weren't even fit to be slaves and that they had to go away and live far apart from the Water-Talkers, forever. And this they did. Whenever a child grew up with a frozen tongue, they either killed it or banished the child to live with the Beasts."

Ember felt the hair stand up on the back of her neck.

"More generations passed, and Talu's many-times-great-grandson led the Water-Talkers. Except now they also called themselves the Wise Ones and all sorts of glorious names, for they could explain many things to themselves with all their words, and they were proud that there was not a thing in the world that they didn't have a name for. But they also could lie and cheat each other. And they could gossip and spread terrible rumors. Worst of all, they could hate, because they no longer saw heart to heart."

"Like the story of the tower to the sun," Ember said.

Old Man nodded.

"Tower to the sun?" Mike said.

"Long ago," Ember said, "all the tribes came together to build a tower to reach up to the lodge of the sun, to snatch an ember from its fire pit. With such a prize they would never have to struggle again to build fires in the rain or cold or dark. An ember from the sun would give everlasting fire and warmth and light.

"The tower grew up and up, made of trees and whalebones and mud, but the builders started arguing over the way it should be constructed. They got angrier and angrier, and their harsh words twisted and knotted their tongues, till they weren't even speaking the same language—they couldn't understand each other at all. Finally, one misplaced twig collapsed the whole thing."

"That's the Tower of Babel story, almost exactly," Mike said.

"There are many tales about it," Old Man said. "I'm telling you what happened to the First People, who then spread everywhere in the world, and took their history with them."

"Please go on," Ember said.

"Well, the peace that exile brought didn't last. The Water-Talkers had come to fear and hate anyone who could speak with his heart. So they hunted the Beasts and began to kill them, band by band."

Ember shuddered and rubbed her upper arms, rocking gently back and forth.

"Couldn't they defend themselves?" she asked in a shaky voice.

"They were far outnumbered by the Talkers. Not that the Beasts were weaklings. Some of the ancient stories dwell on their physical strength—arms and legs like tree limbs wrapped in hide. But because they naturally felt into the hearts of others, killing people did not come easily, so they were terribly vulnerable to men of less sympathy."

Ember covered her heart with one hand; Mike took her other hand and squeezed.

"One band of the Beasts called themselves O-kwo-ke, the Listeners," Old Man said. "They escaped by trekking north into the land of the ice, much farther than anyone had ventured before. They found a narrow stretch of fertile hunting ground and followed it for many weeks, until a huge wall of ice blocked their way. Most of the old ones and children died on the journey.

"In that distant land the survivors lived in safety for several generations, until they knew in their hearts that all the other bands had been murdered. With great mourning they accepted that they were the very last of their kind.

"And they knew also that one day Talu and his killers would find them. So they joined hearts to plan for that dreaded time. It was decided in silence.

"Years passed in peace, but then the terrible moment arrived. The Water-Talkers, led by the latest Talu, wandered into their territory and spied them."

Ember held her breath, feeling dizzy.

"The O-kwo-ke did as they had planned. They retreated into an ice cave, where they joined hands and waited, while their Great Shaman Mother dislodged a tray of logs and caused an avalanche of snow and ice to seal the entrance."

"Oh, my God!" Ember leapt up, wide eyed, her hands on top of her head. "I knew it," she said. "It was no dream . . . I smelled her . . . all my people."

Old Man nodded solemnly.

"But that's . . . it's unbelievable," Mike said.

Ember slumped to the ground in front of Old Man and pressed her forehead against his knee, her eyes screwed shut, hardly daring to think. If the people in the cave were her ancestors, then she was proof that they survived.

"Please," she whispered. "What happened to those in the cave?"

"They thought of it as going to sleep," Old Man said, gently stroking her hair, "like the winter bear."

"Better than getting clubbed to death," Mike muttered.

"How did they get out?" Ember said.

Old Man shook his head in silence.

"But I'm right here." She turned her wet face up to search his shiny black eyes. "Look at me." She smiled and tears ran into her mouth. "We made it. I have a mother and father somewhere, maybe even brothers and sisters. Where are the others like me, the descendants of the O-kwo-ke?"

Old Man's own tears started down and forked and branched along the creases of his dark skin.

"The story tells that Talu hunted the Shaman Mother as she fled up the hill above the cave, with her wolf companion. The wolf turned back and leapt upon Talu and they both tumbled and slid down the icy slope.

At the bottom the wolf was dead, and Talu sprawled, moaning, while the snow around his throat turned crimson. As he lay dying, the Shaman Mother performed a great sacrifice. She laid her hands on Talu and allowed his heart and her heart to become one."

He paused and looked closely at Ember.

"Imagine the pain," he said, "of merging with your ruthless enemy, the murderer of your loved ones, destroyer of your whole race. Her courage and compassion is beyond words."

"It would be like a death-camp survivor rendering aid and comfort to the dying Hitler," Mike said.

"I did not say she gave him aid," Old Man said. "That would only make her a saint. I said she joined her heart with his. She became him, in order that he could become her."

Ember made a little gasp. Tears traced the ridges of her cheekbones and rolled down her face.

"Her light passed into Talu and illuminated the well of his own heart," Old Man said. "And Talu *remembered.*

"He remembered the meeting of hearts that the Water-Talkers had left behind. He remembered their common ancestors. He remembered everything. He felt his loss and her loss, and he wept bitterly over what he and his forebears had done. But it was too late."

Ember went limp, her face blank.

"It was the dying Talu who commanded his people to preserve the story of the O-kwo-ke from generation to generation, forever. And the storykeepers have done just that."

"The people in the cave . . . ?" she asked in a weak voice.

Old Man leaned forward and whispered into her ear. "Their Shaman Mother promised them . . ."

Ember barely breathed. All that Old Man had said was like a barbed stinger that worked its way deeper into her heart.

"Am I . . . their savior?" she whispered.

Mike cocked his head at Ember and frowned. "Whoa, back up," he said. "Let's analyze this."

"Sisiutlqua," she said, barely audible. "Not for the Quanoot . . . but for my own people, the Listeners."

Old Man clapped his hands together loudly, then placed his left hand over his heart and his right hand over her heart.

*"O-kwo-ke *ki layo me, da ene poi hok, Sisiutlqua!"* he said, and kissed her on the forehead. "Return, and restore us to life."

27

"OLD MAN HAD the sensitivity to give me some time to be alone," Ember said. "Why can't you do the same?"

She walked fast up the path toward the longhouse. Mike hurried to keep up.

"Because you're not being rational," he said. "You need my help to sort this stuff out logically."

She bent an overhanging pine branch out of her way and let it fly. It swatted Mike, and she kept going.

"Dammit! Cut it out. Listen to reason."

"There's nothing reasonable about it. How reasonable was it when you caught a whiff of cedar and flashed back to hiding in a trunk as a kid? It was a vivid memory, it took over; you didn't make it happen and you couldn't have stopped it. I smelled the people in the cave and it caused a flood of memories—a lot more than I can put into words or understand."

"But the people in the cave, you're saying were your ancestors?"

"Yes."

"That's what I mean—are you trying to tell me you *remember* something that happened before you were born?"

"Yes."

"*Who* remembers?"

"Spirit remembers. Life remembers. I don't know, I said it wasn't logical. It just is."

"So, you're saying, none of it makes sense, but that's okay."

She stopped and spun around on the trail and they almost collided.

"Okay, then, let's hear your logical analysis," she said. "I had a vision—no, I *smelled* a scene, an event—that fits exactly with the story Old Man told us. He said the story of the goldens is older than the forests."

"Correction." Mike raised his finger. "He never said they were goldens."

"Why are you so suspicious? What's the big conspiracy?"

"Not suspicious, as in paranoid," he said, "but skeptical, as in rational. I get this way when things violate common sense."

She turned and strode away.

"I'm going to find out where the other goldens

are," she said. "At least some of them made it out of the cave, I'm proof of that. They survived."

"Look, Tom thinks you're some magic Soul Catcher who's here to resurrect the Quanoot Warrior Way. Is that true?"

"No, I never said it was."

"But now you're ready to believe you're the savior for some tribe that got wiped out, sounds like back in the Ice Age."

She slowed her pace.

"That whole story of the First People is allegory, like the Tower of Babel. It's myth, it never happened. Don't you see? It's about how the development of language turned us all into head-trippers, how we lost our gut feelings. It's no more historical than Raven stealing a cloud from the sky and turning it into the first fog to trick his friends. Are the Raven stories proof that birds could talk in the old days?"

"Hey, here's a piece of illogic for you," she said, and turned to face him again. "Old Man came to Whaler Bay and foretold that I would be a Sisiutlqua."

"I intend to ask him about that in more detail."

"Doesn't compute?"

"I admit I don't know what to make of it yet."

She turned away and continued up the trail.

"But wait a minute. It only has significance if you really are a Sisiutlqua—it's a logical fallacy to use it as proof of what you are. You can't say, he foretold that you'd be purple, therefore you are purple. If, and only if, you are a Sisiutlqua, is the prophecy true."

"Mike, thanks," she said. "Now I'm more confused than before I left Whaler Bay."

Mike said nothing. They reached the clearing where they had eaten breakfast. Ember ducked into the house and came out with two gourds of spring water. She handed one to Mike. She closed her eyes as the cool water trickled down her throat and quenched her thirst; it was a simple pleasure she wouldn't have sold at this moment for a handful of rubies.

"You know, I've been doing a lot of thinking," Mike said, and wiped his mouth. His eyes seemed touched with sadness.

"Uh-oh. There's more?"

"I have to preface what I'm about to say with this —it doesn't change the way I feel about you at all."

"Like hell. Just say it."

"You may not have any ancestors."

"What's that supposed to mean?"

"Maybe there were only a handful of others like you ever born, and they're all about your same age. . . ."

"Yeah, you're the expert on nonsense, all right."

"Ember . . . look, I don't want to upset you . . . but . . . well . . . I think it's possible . . ." He made a big sigh.

She gulped. "Spit it out, I've probably heard it before anyway."

"It's not easy to tell you . . . but it's possible . . ."

She looked down at her feet. "Most of the people on Whaler Bay think I'm a test-tube mutant."

Mike shook his head. "No, no, I wouldn't use those terms . . . but . . . I have to agree . . . you were intentionally created, designed. . . ."

She looked up into his eyes and he sighed again. "Ember, I'm saying I think you were genetically engineered."

She turned her face away.

"I'm really sorry," he said gently. "But think about it. It makes more sense than anything you've heard today. It fits every piece of evidence."

"Aw, forget it, you don't know anything," she said in a hoarse whisper.

"Look at the facts," he said. "You're eighteen. That means you were born a few years before somebody blew the whistle on HuGen Tek."

She frowned. "What?"

"It was a big scandal when I was little, my dad talked a lot about it. These government lab coats were way ahead of the Human Genome Project—they were already experimenting with manipulating genes in human embryos. They were exposed and shut down, and supposedly none of the altered embryos was implanted—but, you know, they always deny everything."

"What kind of experiments?"

"Department of Defense funding—top secret."

Her throat tightened and she swallowed, feeling sick at heart. "Making better soldiers."

"What else? Stronger, fitter, faster—"

"And you think some of them were born, and I'm one of them."

"Yes. I think this Dr. Nahadeh was in on it."

She turned her back to him, fought her rising fears.

"I can't believe you kissed me," she said. "How the hell do you know I wasn't designed to be a cannibal, to eat the dead on the battlefield? I might have bit your eyes out."

"I wish I wasn't the one to tell you this," he said in a small voice. "I know it must hurt." He put his hands on her shoulders.

She twisted away, violently, and spun toward him. "Keep your distance," she barked. "I'm hardwired to kill first, think later."

He spread his arms wide, his eyes soft. "I'm really sorry, Ember."

She bit her lip. Then a dam in her heart cracked and she burst into sobs and fell into his arms.

"It's not true," she cried. "It can't be. . . ."

He stroked her hair that spilled down her broad back. "Shhhh. It's okay. It's okay. . . ."

"It's not okay, it's a nightmare. It hurts so much . . . you can't know." She buried her face in his chest and gritted her teeth as she wept; her nose ran with tears.

Suddenly she pushed back.

"Wait—the blue ice cave . . . ?"

"Maybe you were given extra-sensitive smell for detecting chemical weapons, or whatever. The slightest whiff of pollen or who-knows-what might sometimes trigger vivid hallucinations."

She hung her head. "Please go away now. Leave me alone."

He nodded and started toward the lower trail.

"No, don't go. Stay." She ran and threw her arms around his waist from behind. "Mike, I'm so scared and lonely."

He turned toward her and hugged her tight for a

long while. Then he peeled her hands from around his torso and gave them a squeeze.

"I'll be back soon," he said. "I'm going to go talk to Old Man by myself. I need to ask him a few more questions."

28

OLD MAN STRADDLED a big log, carving a totem pole. His adze struck a steady rhythm, *clink, clink, clink,* on the dense wood.

Mike walked up from behind. "Old Man."

The little Indian lifted his legs and spun on his butt to straddle the pole in the reverse direction, facing Mike. He set down his adze and motioned to the log with his open palm. The sea breeze had freshened, and over his robe Old Man now wore an orange jacket with KITISOOK CHAINSAW SERVICE embroidered on a white patch over one pocket and DAVE over the other.

Old Man tapped his head with his finger. "Questions?"

Mike nodded. "If that's all right."

Old Man shrugged. "Like Ember's mother says, 'You have to be what you are.' "

"How . . . ?" Mike squinted. "How do you know she says that?"

"Isn't that what all mothers tell their children?" He smiled broadly, showing several missing teeth. "Now, what do you need to ask me?"

"First off, did the O-kwo-ke have golden skin, like Ember?"

"The stories don't say. Maybe everybody was nearly the same color back then, so there was no point in mentioning it."

"Back then. How old do you think these stories are? Stone Age?"

"When was that?"

"Way, way back, when people used stone tools."

"That's only six generations ago for my people."

"Well. Paleolithic, the *Old* Stone Age—ten thousand years ago and more."

"Oh, yes, they're very, very old. The storykeepers told three classes of stories. Homeland Tales, that began in these islands; Beyond-the-Horizon Tales, that were borrowed from other tribes inland and to the south; and First People Tales, that our ancestors brought with them when they trekked to these islands from the North, too long ago to imagine."

Mike thought of the nomadic hunters who migrated across the Bering Land Bridge during the last two Ice Ages. They settled the coast first as they headed south, because it was the warmest land, with abundant food from the sea.

"So you truly believe Ember is a descendent of the O-kwo-ke?"

"Yes."

"Where are her people now?"

"Waiting for her to find them."

"How do you recommend she go about searching?"

"She is a daughter of the Listeners. She'll find them."

Mike frowned. "I don't understand—"

"—how she can restore life to an ancient race," Old Man said, using the exact words Mike had in mind.

"That's it."

Old Man gazed over the treetops to the north. The overhead sun had burned off the fog and the sky was a cloudless vault of blue.

"What did the Shaman Mother mean when she said a savior would come?" Old Man said. "Remember, she didn't speak in words, but in sign language and feelings. And stories do not remain unchanged over thousands of generations. They evolve. The stories I learned as a boy say that the savior of the O-kwo-ke is a man: He-Who-Returns."

Aha, now it starts to leak, Mike thought.

Old Man looked at Mike with unwavering clear eyes. "Try not to worry about the words, so much, my friend. If the stories were only baskets full of leaves, we would not have carried them with us for so many lifetimes. Hear what is beneath the words."

Old Man sat quietly. Lines etched every contour of his weathered face, like a topographic map. Mike was surprised that he could look into the bright black eyes and not feel bashful. He wondered what it would be like to speak, not in words, but in feelings. Old Man smiled warmly, and Mike smiled too. He could not remember his list of questions.

Old Man flicked open a pocket knife and trimmed a bit of wood scrap from the smooth round eye of a wolf's head that stared out from the log between them. He rubbed the eyeball with his thumb to test its smoothness, then closed the knife and put it back in his pocket.

Mike ran his fingers inside the wooden mouth of the wolf, over its canine fangs and around the curves of its face. Its furry ears stood upright, alert. Its eyes appeared to be watching keenly.

"Beautiful," Mike said. "You have a lot of talent."

"I have always loved to carve things; it was how I played as a boy; it's how I play, still."

"Ember told me some people think you're the old shaman, Iwaka. Do you claim to be him?"

Old Man chuckled. "I never thought of it as making a claim. Eniawataw is the name my mother gave me; my baptismal name is Christopher; when I was fifteen I started calling myself Iwaka; and for many, many years everyone has called me Old Man. All one and the same."

He stuck out his hand and Mike shook it. It was small boned but strong; callused, but supple.

"But . . . how do you account for living—?"

"I can't even account for one instant of this day alone. How am I here at all? How did this ant get here?" He blew a carpenter ant off the back of his hand. "The Giver gives. We float like foam on the river."

"But . . ." Mike shook his head, at a loss for words.

Old Man smiled at him as one might smile at a child who cannot grasp adult conversation.

"Will it make you more comfortable to know that I won't live much longer?"

"What? You expect to die soon?"

Old Man nodded. "When I told the story to Ember, I had the feeling that everything I was here to do in this life is now done. I won't be here another month."

"How can you be so sure?"

"Because I won't eat another bite of food for the rest of my life."

Mike felt stunned. "You seem so . . . calm about it."

"The part of me that was afraid to die, died a long time ago. No, I expect it to be a pleasure, like shedding a tight pair of boots."

"What about all your stories?"

"Ah, my friend, you've touched my wound." He put his hand to his heart. "My one regret is that I have no one to pass the great stories to. I fear I am the last of the storykeepers."

"Hey, I know what," Mike said. "I could bring out a video camera and record every one of your stories on tape."

Old Man grimaced. "Does blood run through the camera? Will it laugh at the funny parts and cry at the sad parts?"

"Of course not. But people will, when they watch the video. The stories will be saved. I could make copies for libraries and museums."

"Thank you, but no. I saw a TV once; a head talking inside a box. Saving the stories that way would be like killing your best friend and stuffing him so that you can always keep him near.

"My grandmother was the tribe's storykeeper before me, and I learned the legends from her. That's what makes the tradition what it is—each story goes back along a great human chain to the very beginning."

Mike nodded. "I guess I can understand your feelings about it."

The two sat in silence. Mike liked this beautiful old Quanoot, whether he understood him or not. It seemed to him that the shaman was wrapped in an invisible robe of peace, yet he did not seem monklike, withdrawn. His eyes shone; his body was relaxed; Old Man was at home in the world.

"Tell me how you got to be . . . you know . . . the way you are today," Mike said.

"Like all of us, I was born this way," Old Man said. "But I soon forgot my nature and it took a while to return to it.

"My father was an Anglican missionary, from London; my mother was one of his schoolgirls. He had a wife back in England, so my parents never wed, but he took a liking to me and made me his altar boy. He filled my head with Protestant dogma and English literature, while my grandmother filled my head with Quanoot-cha and all her old tales.

"In those days, when a boy reached his twelfth winter, it was time to go into the deep woods and wait for his guardian spirit to come. He would fast and wander, and bathe in the manner we did today, except in icy streams. After days and nights he would fall into a delirium and a spirit would enter him in the form of a bird, or a wolf, or whatever, and teach him his own magic song and spirit dance, and give him guidance to learn the skills of canoe maker, hunter, or fisherman, when he returned to the village."

"Career counseling," Mike said.

Old Man nodded.

"What spirit came to you?"

"That first winter, nothing. My head was filled with conflicting beliefs. I almost died from hunger. My uncles came and found me and carried me home. So I decided to specialize. The second winter I focused on Christianity and its teachings."

"And?"

"It did not fit, and I realized for me it had never fit. So the third winter I abandoned such notions and devoted myself only to Quanoot-cha."

"What happened?"

"I could not get past the feeling that it, too, did not fit. Quanoot-cha was in my ears, but not in my marrow. I had not been afraid the first two winters, not even when I was starving, but then I became terrified. I had nothing to believe in, not a jot of truth. I didn't know the right way, and now I had lost the only ways I knew. Now I was nobody at all, a total failure.

"How could I endure such hollowness? I decided to die, to fast until death, since I was already starving.

"So I climbed over the top of a mountain ridge and followed a valley stream, until I overlooked a steep-walled rock canyon, where a waterfall spilled into a deep green pool. I sat down on a large rock shelf. 'A perfect place to die,' I told myself, and I breathed out with my whole spirit, surrendering everything. I became so relaxed, I think I swayed like a leaf.

"A kingfisher rattled on a nearby perch. I saw the biggest trout I have ever seen leap out of the rapids below. The mist and blow from the falls chilled my face and ruffled my hair; and the air was lush with the refreshing smell of clear, cold water. Then the sun broke through the clouds and a rainbow arced through the spray. So far, dying was beautiful.

"Next, I had to pee. So I stepped to the ledge and added my little stream to the roaring cascade."

Old Man's eyes crinkled into a smile.

"All at once I understood the joke. And I started to laugh, and I laughed so hard, I almost slipped off the ledge."

Mike chuckled. "The joke?"

"The waterfall," he said. "It was like the mighty, gushing flow of life itself, and my tiny stream seemed to me like the concepts that we add to it. We try to make meaning, a philosophy, something to believe in—because we're afraid. We refuse to dive in. We know the mighty current will sweep us away and that will be the end of our little selves. I had been tormenting myself, trying to sum up everything, to turn life into a conclusion, and suddenly my struggle was laughable. It was a recoil from mystery, the river of life.

"It was plain that I did not know what anything is. That was the simple truth. The trees, the canyon, the crashing water, the cold mist—I had no way to interpret any of it. It was all naked wonder. And the feeling dissolved me with such force that I suddenly knew I really would die, for I had no way to hold on to the world or to myself.

"The knot in my heart flew open and I passed beyond all knowing. And there I stood: stark, free—*whole*—breathing down to the tips of my toes."

Mike felt a tingling over his skin. Old Man's joy was contagious. He seemed even now to be the teenage boy who had come unraveled in beauty.

"You're saying 'Truth is within,' " Mike said.

"That sounds like something Jesus said, not me."

"Then truth is in the things that you accomplish in this world? The good that you do?"

"That sounds like Quanoot-cha."

Mike knitted his brow. "I don't get it."

"Neither do I get it. I have never grasped it." He waved his fingers and hands and arms in graceful, swirling waves. "There are no handholds in a waterfall. No footholds. I don't own the life power, I go with it, wherever it takes me."

"And it guided you to become a shaman."

"Yes, and so I am, even still."

Then Mike remembered that Old Man claimed to be two centuries old.

"What about the Cold Sick—you were, what? About twenty-five or so."

Old Man took a deep breath and closed his eyes for a moment, rocking slightly.

"Since that time by the waterfall," he said quietly, "I've never been able to close my heart to pleasure or pain. The depth of them both is beyond speaking." He let out a long sigh.

"It started out a beautiful summer. Salmonberries,

blackberries, raspberries—so heavy on the bushes, they sagged toward the ground. My wife and I camped across the water in the mountains with our twin girls, picking and drying basketloads of berries. We had sunny weather for days at a stretch; it was even prettier than most summers."

"Near Mount Rainier?"

"We called it Uliah-keh."

"Snow King," Mike said. Ember had told him the Quanoot name.

"Every morning we picked; my wife with Nani in a sling on her back, and I with Nene on my back. The girls gobbled up the sweet berries like fat little cubs. Their cheeks were red, their lips purple. The meadows were filled with flowers and butterflies. I didn't think my happiness could increase. Then my wife—Awahni Uwahni was her name—so lovely—she told me she was again with child, and we both cried for joy.

"After three weeks we canoed back toward the island, and from a distance we smelled the death stink. We became very afraid. I turned around and took them back to hide in the forest, then went on alone to check on our family and friends, find out what had happened, see if I could help.

"The village was one big grave, rotting to the black sky. My mother, aunts, uncles, were already dead—not a single person left in my family, and no one left in hers. There had been more than six hundred people in our village; there were about fifty living. The survivors tore out fistfuls of their hair and fell on their knees and begged me to leave. They didn't want any more punishment meted down to them from the jealous Bible-God.

"So I left and fetched Awahni and the girls and brought them to this island."

"You came with your family?"

"Within a couple days they got the shivering fever and died. Awani was Quanoot-cha, so I followed her way; I burned their bodies at the top of this hill." He pointed with a nod. "The girls were together in a sling on her back. Quanoot-cha says *Kiawa o nee, nee o tibane*. 'Ashes to soil, soil to flowers.' You should see the flowers that bloom there now."

The shaman rubbed his eyes, then stood up stiffly and stretched and rolled his neck and shoulders. He no longer seemed to be a young man.

For the first time Mike saw what Old Man had been carving above the wolf head at the crest of the totem pole: a standing figure of Ember. The stunning likeness was bare breasted, wearing only a carved fur skirt; from a leather thong around her neck hung an abalone-shell amulet with a design that resembled a flock of flying geese.

Once, while backpacking through Europe, Mike had stopped in Rome to view the Pietà. Michelangelo had miraculously transformed green marble into soft skin and flowing folds of cloth. Here, too, Old Man had made the statue's skin appear warm to the touch. It was a work of genius.

"It's wonderful," Mike said. "Really terrific."

Old Man beamed his gap-toothed smile. "I used golden birch to match her color."

"But . . . ? Now, wait a minute," Mike said. "You just met her—it's not possible to work so fast."

"Of course not. I've worked on this piece for half a

year now." He rubbed his palm in circles on a wooden breast, buffing it smoother. "It's my very last carving."

"But how?" Mike's mind spun. "How could you know her looks?"

"Ever have an inspiration come into your mind all by itself?" Old Man said. "Say, when you're almost asleep and your head isn't filled with words?"

"Yes."

Old Man opened his pocket knife and added more wavy lines to the details of Ember's mane. "Well, my head is never filled with words. Inspirations rise up in me and make themselves at home."

"But . . . you carved this based on—on *visions*?"

"Actually, I did not carve it. She was hiding in the tree; I only cut away the wood that encased her."

Mike's eyebrows shot up. "That's what Michelangelo said about his sculptures!"

Old Man grinned. "Then, my friend, he enjoys playing as much as I do."

Mike stared at the little Indian with joy and amazement. Then a brainstorm struck and his words spilled out. "Old Man, listen! There's a man on Whaler Bay named Tom Luc. He's desperate to learn Quanoot-cha from a real teacher. He wants to know the songs, the dances, the warrior-whaler tradition. He's perfect. Tom can be the new storykeeper. He could come here, learn the stories from you. You don't have to die without passing them on."

Old Man closed his eyes. "I have felt his longing. Someday he will be a man of quiet strength, but now he's much too raw. He is the kind who would become fanatical about Quanoot-cha, who would be willing to kill or die in the name of his path. No, Tom is not perfect. He's dangerous."

"But . . . it's an unbelievable waste . . ." Tears welled up in Mike's eyes. "Please don't stop eating. Give me a little time, I'll think of someone."

"Consider, my friend," Old Man said, and peered into Mike's eyes with a penetrating gaze, "—the storykeeper must be a person who can learn Quanoot-cha and all its tales, but keep the path alive and supple—in perspective—so that Quanoot-cha will always help, not hinder, the modern tribe."

Old Man's shining expression stoked a fire that brightened deep in Mike's heart. Mike gasped and pointed to his chest with both hands. "*Me* . . . ?"

Old Man gathered Mike's hands in his strong grip. "Storykeeper, remember this moment, and add it to our tales."

29

Kaigani waited with Chena on the rocky shore, straining her eyes toward Old Man Land for a glimpse of her father's Zodiac. Her mother touched her shoulder and signaled she heard the outboard motor. The inflatable boat came into view on the horizon and a minute later it became clear that Ember and Mike were aboard and they were okay. Kaigani let out a deep sigh of relief and saw her mother do the same.

The tide was rolling out. Kaigani waded into the chilly water to her shins and helped Mike and her father drag the canvas boat across the tidal flat onto dry sand. Her black hair swept in front as she leaned forward, and it nearly brushed the pebbly sand.

Mike glanced at Kaigani with a little smile and looked away again. He seemed subdued. Probably her dad had chewed him out big time. Ember walked past them without a word.

Mike's hair was disheveled and his neck had sprouted whiskers below the tidy border of his beard. Kaigani watched the way his eyes followed Ember up the beach and she felt a sudden knot in her gut. Ember broke into a run, heading toward home.

Her father watched Ember for a moment, and Kaigani saw the muscles of his jaw twitch. He looked angry and worried. Last night Ember had made her promise not to tell what she was up to. This morning when her dad woke and found Ember gone, he had hit the ceiling. The veins had stood out on his neck and his long hair shook and it didn't take lipreading to see that he was stringing curse words together in a long row, like hooks on a trout line.

"The whales are feeding out there this time of year," he had yelled. "You both know that as well as I do. You let your sister paddle off into the middle of pods of feeding whales? She could get clobbered."

Now her parents started home, talking together, his arm around her shoulder and her arm around his waist. The sun dipped toward the darkening water, and the boulders and rocks on the beach stretched long shadows over the sand.

Kaigani turned to Mike. "What happened?" she said, signing that Ember looked completely unhappy.

"Will you walk up to my cabin with me?"

Her answer was an instant smile, and she gushed with hope that Mike remembered the thrill of last night's kiss, that he was attracted to her even half as much as she was drawn to him.

On the way he told her about being capsized by the whale and about meeting Old Man, and he recounted the legend of the O-kwo-ke. He faced her as he spoke and did his best with signing, and she had no trouble understanding him.

"He's remarkable," Mike said. "I've never been so touched by anyone, especially someone I just met. You know, I had this friend, Carlos, very smart guy, who went to India and met a guru and . . . well, I couldn't quite relate to him after that . . . and yet . . ."

"And yet . . . ?"

"I don't ever want to have a guru, and Old Man, he's no guru, but . . . am I making any sense?"

She nodded and shrugged.

"Old Man is so . . ." He shook his head. "You know, I quit my advertising job hoping to meet real people." He chuckled. "No—to become more real myself. Old Man is *real*. His heart is free."

They left the beach and started up the trail toward the cabin. The low-angled sun lit Mike's hair and beard so that they seemed spun of red and gold threads.

"Kaigani, Old Man chose me to be the new storykeeper." His eyes searched hers. "Isn't that strange? I told Ember, too, but don't spread the news, okay? I couldn't tell him no, but . . . I feel . . . odd." He shook his head. "I don't know what he sees in me. I'm no Quanoot, and I'm—I'm too . . . you know, *rational* . . . for all that soul stuff."

He frowned. "Fact is, I told Ember not to take the

story of the O-kwo-ke literally, but now I'm not sure at all."

"Her dreams," Kaigani said, "—the story seems to fit."

"Yeah, maybe you're right . . . but, good grief, it reeks of classical myth. Other cultures have similar tales. Why should this particular legend be true, while the others are just allegory?"

"Maybe all the legends *are* true in some way," she said.

He ran his hand through his hair. "I don't know if I did right . . . I told Ember that, most likely, she came from a genetically altered embryo."

"Oh, Mike, you told her that?"

He nodded. "It seemed the most plausible explanation."

"But . . . how did she take it?"

"Not well," he said, and his mouth tightened. "I'm worried about her. I tried to tell her it doesn't really change anything, she's still Ember. . . ." He blew out his breath. "So much has happened to Ember and to me in one day."

A knot tightened in the pit of her belly. "I wish I'd been there," she said.

She walked on for a while, trying to stop the images that poured in, ashamed of her jealousy. She did not want to ask what she was about to ask, but she couldn't leave the subject alone.

"What happened after you two swam ashore?"

"She kept me warm, I would have died if not for her."

"You both had your clothes off?"

"Had to, they were soaked in icy water."

"So you woke up . . . snuggling naked . . . and you just, what? Put your wet clothes back on?"

He cast his eyes downward and pointed out a jutting root in the path; they stepped around it. The trail switched back to climb the steep upper half of the ridge. In places Mike had staked log steps into the footpath.

"Look, Ember and I are friends," he said. "We're friends, not more than that."

Nothing happened, Kaigani told herself. *They didn't make love.* Still, in her mind's eye she watched them making love—Ember as free and wild as a mountain cat, Mike moaning as he lost himself in her hot embrace. It would be impossible to compete with her sister's sexual power. She panicked.

The cabin was in view when she blurted, "Goodbye, I gotta go home." She turned and walked away quickly, not waiting for his reaction. She hurried, and as soon as she was down the hill and her feet struck flat sand, she sprinted homeward, chased by her thoughts.

Her sweatshirt was damp by the time she reached the house. Her dad's pickup was gone. She paused in the driveway to catch her breath, then she marched into the bedroom that she shared with Ember.

Two desks with built-in bookshelves were set against opposite walls in the space between their twin beds, Ember's mountain bike hung by the back wheel from a ceiling hook in the corner. The far wall was dominated by two large windows that Ember had opened wide; the mountains loomed black against the mauve twilight. Ember was dressed only in underwear in the chilly room, sitting on a stool at her desk, writing. She did not look up.

"Congratulations," Kaigani said, "on your new intimacy with Mike."

Ember glanced over her shoulder with a frown; she puffed at the comment, then returned to her writing.

Kaigani tried to keep her voice from trembling. "Do you want to be with him now?"

Ember put down her pen and turned to face her. "I got you two together, remember?"

"Were you already with him?"

"What?"

"Did you two make love?"

"No."

"Didn't you even kiss?"

Ember swallowed.

"What happened between you?" Kaigani said.

"We had our clothes off. Yeah, we kissed, for a moment. But we stopped—we thought of you."

"Don't let me stop you."

"Look, Mike is in love with you—"

"He told you that between kisses?"

"When I dragged him ashore, he wasn't even shivering. When a person stops shivering, he's in hypothermic shock. Would you feel better if I'd just let him die?"

"And the morning? Did you have to kiss him to save his life?"

"I'm sorry that happened. We got carried away, but we stopped—we stopped—that's the truth."

Kaigani began to cry without a sound. Ember stood and touched her sister's shoulders.

"Look, I found out that Mike has been falling in love with both of us. But it's straightened out now. We talked. He chose you."

"He chose me, or you made the choice for him?"

"He loves you, and you two belong together."

Kaigani shook inside.

"You're the most beautiful woman in the world," Ember said, and wiped a tear from her sister's cheek. "Don't you know that? You're a hundred times prettier than I am."

Kaigani rolled her eyes. "Here we go again. . . . Why do you insist you're ugly?"

"I'm no *Penthouse* centerfold."

"Oh, so that's the measure of beauty, centerfolds?"

"You know what I mean. You'd never want to be a pinup girl, but you could be, Kaigani. Not me."

"Fuck pinup girls."

"A lot of guys would like to. . . . The point is—"

"The point is, you *are* beautiful, like a wild mare—"

"You know, I've noticed something, that for all your poetry, you always tell me I'm like some beautiful animal, never a beautiful woman. See, that's the difference between you and me. You're a lovely woman. I'm something not quite human."

"But I . . . no, it's just that you're so strong, a wild mare—it's an image of strength and freedom."

"Yeah, I'm strong as a horse—a woman who looks like a horse is ugly."

"I didn't say you look like a horse. You remind me of . . . Your strength is part of your beauty. There aren't any weak beautiful horses. Horses are strong—

you're strong. God, you don't know how powerful you are. Sometimes I feel weak alongside you."

"Weak? You? You're one of the best athletes on the island."

"And you *are* the best," Kaigani said.

"You shouldn't compare yourself to me," Ember said, turning away as she spoke. Kaigani missed the last part of what she said. She touched Ember's shoulder.

"Hey, I read lips, remember?"

"Just mumbling to myself."

"Don't compare myself to you—why?"

"Because I'm not even a natural human being, I'm a feat of bioengineering."

"You really believe that?"

Ember nodded. "I'm starting to admit it's true, yes, totally."

"Well, I don't. Not for one second."

"Oh, yeah, then how do you explain a person like me?"

"I don't even try."

"Spoken like a centerfold."

"Gimme a break."

"It's not a problem for you, gorgeous." Ember tapped her chest. "I'm the weirdo on this planet."

"Look, I'll make you a deal," Kaigani said. "I'll stop comparing myself to you, and you can stop comparing yourself to me. Okay? Let's try."

Their gaze met and held for an instant, then they glanced away.

"I lasted half a second," Kaigani said, and smiled crookedly. "How about you?"

Ember chuckled. "The same." She flashed a white smile.

Kaigani breathed easier. *To hell with jealousy.* The moment was not as she would have planned it, but she decided to say what had been on her mind for weeks.

"Ember, I want you to heal me."

Ember's face hardened and she stepped back.

"Lay your hands over my ears and make me hear."

"What? Now you think I'm Jesus Christ?"

"Just try. If it doesn't work, it doesn't work. But you have the spirit power . . . let it act on me."

"This is what you promised you wouldn't do—forget who I am. Treat me differently. Why are you looking at me that way? Like Tom does."

"I want to be able to hear Mike's voice. And Mom's and Dad's. I want to hear the birds, the thunder—"

"Kaigani, I can't heal you. Look at me, for God's sake, I'm a soldier." Ember raised her arms and flexed them, and her biceps bulged up as big as eggplants. "I was designed for killing people, not healing them."

"That's not true. Please, Ember, if you really love me . . ." Kaigani reached out and grasped Ember's hands to place over her ears.

"Leave me alone!" Ember twisted her wrists hard, breaking Kaigani's grip. Kaigani bumped the desk and an anatomical model of a horse tipped off the bookshelf and struck the floor, scattering plastic entrails over the floorboards.

Kaigani felt desperate. "You can't heal me, or you don't want to?"

Ember plopped down on the wooden stool and

blew out her breath forcefully. Her whole body sagged. "I feel really insulted and hurt by this crap from you. You're my sister, my best damn friend in the world. . . ."

"Well, then, just try to heal me. Try. I've seen your power. You've got the power. Ember, look at me. Look up. You know you've got the power."

Ember shot a fiery glance at her. "I'll show you my goddam power." She scooped up the red heart and purple lungs of the horse from the floor and squeezed them in her fist until the plastic organs burst like walnuts in a nutcracker. She hurled the fragments down and leapt to her feet.

"Behold!" she roared, arms spread wide. "HuGen Tek's new, improved *Viking*!"

She turned to her desk, raised her fists above her head, and with the full force of her body drove them down on the desktop like twin sledgehammers. The wood splintered and the desk collapsed as a leg snapped off.

"Stop, are you crazy?" Kaigani staggered back, holding her face in her hands.

"Set me on a battlefield and watch me go!" Ember yanked the wooden stool off the floor, flipped it in midair, and caught it by two of its four legs. She tugged the legs in opposite directions, and grunted loudly, flexing her deep chest muscles. The cross braces popped out of their leg joints and the parts of the stool plunked onto the broken desk.

"Stop it!" Kaigani screamed. "You're scaring me!"

Ember spun on her, her face gone dark and her eyes like the green flames copper gives off when it burns.

Her nostrils flared; veins stood out on her forehead and neck. "I'm the warrior goddamn queen," she growled, and in one stride stood so close that Kaigani was wrapped in the cocoon of her body heat. "*That's* my power," Ember hissed. "*That's* what I was made for." Kaigani backed against a bed frame. Ember pressed forward until her breasts meshed below Kaigani's breasts and her hot breath brushed Kaigani's lips; their chests heaved and their heartbeats drummed a duet, and for one instant Kaigani thought Ember was going to grab her hair in both hands and kiss her. Kaigani glanced away, breaking the spell. Ember stepped back with a curious look of shock.

Kaigani was speechless. She had always sensed that she and Ember were like opposite poles of a magnet, but their polarity had never before flared into sexual energy.

"This is my fault," Kaigani said softly. "I—I shouldn't have pushed you."

Ember knelt and gathered the plastic parts of the transparent horse model. Kaigani knelt next to her and helped. Their shoulders rubbed and Ember shied away. Kaigani noticed that the room was dark and cold. She got up and turned on the overhead light and shut both windows.

When she turned back, Ember was watching, her face a grimace of sadness.

"Kaigani, I'm all screwed up. I can't help you or anybody else, isn't that obvious?"

Kaigani forced a little smile, not sure how to react. She wanted to reach out and touch her, but hesitated.

"I don't know what came over me," Ember said.

"Just . . . so much frustration. It won't happen again, I promise." She gulped. "Can we forget about it?"

Kaigani nodded, but she still felt shaken.

Ember caught her breath, her eyes grew wide, and she signed that their parents had arrived home. She leapt up and threw on a black sweatshirt, khaki shorts, and red Converse tennis shoes.

"Where are you going?" Kaigani said.

Ember's eyes swept the floor, then she dropped down and looked under both beds. She reached under Kaigani's bed and came up with the letter she had been writing, folded it, and slid it under Kaigani's pillow. Then she jerked open a stuck drawer in the collapsed desk and took out a small address and telephone book and stuffed it in her hip pocket. Her jaw was clamped tight as she hurried.

Kaigani swallowed. "Ember, where are you going?" She felt a vibration as the front door closed.

Ember put her finger to her lips. "Shhhhh." She slipped into a denim jacket that had been folded over the foot of her bed, and slung on a canvas backpack that was stuffed to bulging.

"Please don't go," Kaigani said. "Dad'll just be mad for a little while. He can't stay mad at us, you know that. You don't have to go."

"It's got nothing to do with Dad, believe me," Ember said. "I'm not worried about his temper, I know he loves me." She tugged the straps on the backpack tighter. "And Mom loves me—"

"Ember, I love you," Kaigani said.

Ember paused for an instant, and met Kaigani's eyes. Tears sprang up, then she continued to hurry. "So the problem really is, *I* don't love me. That's been my torment all along."

"You have such a big heart—but it's clenched like a fist when it comes to accepting yourself."

"I'm torn in two, like the fortune dancer's mask: one eye, hope, and the other eye, fear," Ember said. "Half of me fights to be normal, because I can't bear to admit I can never be like everyone else. The other half, the side that always scares me, drives me to find out who I am, even if the truth turns out to be a nightmare."

Ember pulled on her biking gloves and strapped on her helmet.

"For a long time I thought the half of me that wants to be normal is my eye of hope," she said, "but now I realize it's my eye of fear. Finding out the meaning of my dreams and visions is my only real hope to be whole, no matter how dangerous that hope is."

Through the floorboards Kaigani could feel her parents' footsteps crossing back and forth in the kitchen as they put away groceries. She could race into the kitchen and grab Dad. She turned and eyed the bedroom doorknob and pressed her lips together.

Should I?

Ember strode across the room, lifted down her mountain bike from the corner and threw open the lefthand window, popped out the screen, lowered her bike outside, and jumped to the ground.

"Where?" Kaigani asked.

"To find Yute Nahadeh, the doctor who made me."

Kaigani leaned over the sill. "Ember, don't. Don't do this."

"Tell Mom and Dad . . . just . . . tell them not to worry too much. Oh, and I took twenty dollars from your stash, but I swear I'll pay you back double."

"Damn, you're nailing me again. You're putting me in a position where I'm not supposed to squeal."

"No way—I was long gone when you got home. That's the way I planned it, anyway. All you found was the letter hidden under your pillow. Give me a chance to catch the seven o'clock ferry—half an hour—then show them the letter."

"But they're home, I'd be showing it to them now."

"You didn't find the letter yet because . . . you were soaking in the tub."

Kaigani glanced back at the wreckage of the desk and stool. "And I just strolled right by that mess, into the bathroom?"

Ember slapped her helmet. "Uh—you didn't notice it until you got out of the bath, because . . . uh . . ."

Kaigani sighed. "I had my sweatshirt pulled over my head on my way to the bathroom."

"Yeah, good. Hey, I really owe you for this."

"When you find the doctor, what then?"

"Learn everything I can, find out if there are others like me," Ember said, and gave her a pained smile. "And then maybe I'll break his goddam neck."

She shot Kaigani the hand sign for *I love you* and Kaigani waved good-bye the same way—palm upright, with little finger, index finger, and thumb extended, the other fingers folded—forming the letters *I*, *L*, and *U* of the deaf alphabet. Then Ember hopped on her bike and dashed down a rutted dirt road in the direction of the ferry dock.

A half hour later the moon hung over the mountains like a scrimshaw pendant, white as whale ivory. Kaigani wished she were on a rocket ship heading there now. The breeze felt cold on her long hair, damp from her bath. She turned from the window and walked slowly toward her parents' bedroom, two hundred thousand miles from the Sea of Tranquillity.

PART THREE

(Notes for an essay, *The First Americans*, by Yute Nahadeh, M.D., Ph.D.)

Roughly 25,000 years ago, during the Wisconsin Ice Age, the total land area of present-day Canada, extending south about 600 miles beyond the Great Lakes region, was solidly sheeted with glaciers up to a mile thick. With so much water trapped in ice, sea levels had dropped about 400 feet, exposing a 1,000-mile-wide plain we call Beringia, that connected present-day Siberia and Alaska. Neanderthal and Cro-Magnon hunters trailed mammoths, musk oxen and caribou eastward across Beringia until an unbroken wall of ice blocked their way. This icy barrier arose within view of Mount McKinley and the Alaska Range, near where Tundra

Man was discovered in 1988, and Tundra Woman, in 1989.

Later, about 15,000 years ago—just before the ice sheets melted and drowned Beringia—people migrated across this bridge into North America on a much larger scale. But it is fascinating to consider that Tundra Man and Woman belonged to the first wave of humans to set foot in the New World.

30

YUTE NAHADEH SAT on the edge of a burgundy leather swivel chair at a honey maple desk in a large office. His square shoulders did not betray his middle age, and his silvering black hair showed no hint of thinning. Wrinkles creased the edges of his eyes, but their brightness had lost no wattage. A blue denim shirt and brown corduroy trousers fitted well on his muscular frame. His leather hiking boots rested on a Persian carpet, rich in plum and red, and atop his denim shirt he wore a plum-and-red silk tie.

On the wall, across from his diplomas and medical

engineering awards, hung three framed newspaper clippings: Ember, at age nine, shaking hands with her grinning teammates at a kids' league soccer play-off; Ember at sixteen, arching her chest to break through the finish line ribbon at a national high-school all-star track meet; Ember at seventeen, dripping wet, triumphantly holding a high-school state championship swimming trophy. From the day he broke up her fight with the boy after the baseball game, he had never again set foot on Whaler Bay Island, but he had attended many of her athletic events elsewhere, even traveling out of state for the national competitions.

Over the past decade he had conceived a hundred ways to contact her, but always something had told him to wait. Wait until *she* was ready to learn the details of her identity. Then she would be willing to cooperate with him in research, to help him discover as much as he could about Neanderthals. But would she really come? And when? When?

Now she was here. Out the door and down the hall sat Ember, the living Neanderthal, the holy grail of his life's quest to learn more about human origins and evolution.

A trembling rose up from the core of his body and his hands began to shake. He closed his eyes and took a few deep breaths. It did nothing to smooth his mix of joy and panic. He shoved up from his chair and paced back and forth on the carpet.

The side wall of the office bore a giant logo of Micro-Radio Surgical Instruments Corporation, and the entire back wall was painted in oils: God reaching for Adam, as in Michelangelo's Sistine Chapel masterpiece, but the Almighty's hand wore a surgical glove fitted with a tiny radio-wave cauterizer at the index fingertip, as if to seal a wound on Adam's finger.

Yute did not waste his talent while waiting for Ember to grow up and find him. Over the past fifteen years he designed and patented a tiny radio-wave surgical instrument that mounted on the index fingertip over special gloves. A thin wire on the inside of the glove ran up the back of the hand to a small, lightweight power pack clipped to the surgeon's belt. More precise than laser scalpels, the micro-fine tip of the radio transmitter became an extension of the surgeon's fingertip, cutting or cauterizing wherever she pointed and touched. The tool made delicate procedures, such as reconnecting the tiny nerves and blood vessels of severed limbs, much easier and far more successful. A medical engineering journal ran a cover story on the device, and soon MRSI was a Seattle-based international company, and his patent royalties earned him a fortune.

Now he worked part-time as technical consultant with the firm, developing other special instruments for microsurgeries; and he shifted his academic role at Pacific College to that of visiting professor of paleoanthropology. He devoted most of his days to writing and research in paleoanthropology, and he made several extensive trips to visit Neanderthal sites and related museum exhibits around the world.

Yute had bought the small campus of the former Washington State Indian School, in Deer Park, and directed the remodeling of the main building into a museum. He intended to make the Museum of the

Neanderthals the finest scientific showplace in its field. But so much depended on Ember's cooperation.

Surely she's come to me to find out who she is, who her parents are. He ran his hand through his hair. *I've got to tell her in a way she can accept, I've got to make her understand that I'm as curious about her identity as she is, but to learn all there is to know about her—about* Homo sapiens neanderthalensis—*will take years of intensive study.*

He put his hands to the knot of his tie to straighten it, but it was already perfectly centered. He took a long gulp of air and then he walked down the hallway to meet his Neanderthal daughter.

Ember had spent the night in Bayside Park, and in the morning washed her face and armpits at a public rest room and changed into fresh clothes, a long-sleeved yellow T-shirt and blue sweatpants. Then two phone calls had led her to an address in downtown Seattle. Now she fidgeted on a black leather couch near the receptionist desk on the ground floor of a skyscraper office building, headquarters of Micro-Radio Surgical Instruments Corporation. A receptionist phoned Dr. Nahadeh and told Ember he would be down shortly.

She faced the elevator doors. *What's taking him so long?* She tried to keep herself hot and angry, so that she would not slip into cold fear. *This guy played God and manufactured me to his own specifications. I'd better be damn careful.*

"It's good to finally meet you again, face to face."

Ember jerked at the sound of a male voice.

"Sorry to startle you, I like to use the stairs."

A handsome Native man stood before her, his hand extended. Silver streaked his black hair like lightning in a storm cloud; his black eyes seemed nervous, but they shone when he smiled. Her mind went blank. Although she had seen him briefly, eight years ago, she wasn't prepared for the tall man who stood before her as if he had stepped from the pages of *Outside* magazine.

She stood and grasped his hand, uncertainly.

"Dr. Yute Nahadeh," he said in a bass voice.

"Ember Ozette," she said. His presence was charismatic; already she found herself slipping out of anger, into fear.

He gestured toward the elevators with a sweep of his arm. "This way, please," he said.

"We can take the stairs, if that's what you like," she said.

"My office is on the seventh floor," he said.

"Do you usually walk up?"

"Yes."

"Let's go."

He held open the door to the stairwell for her and led the way and they walked up seven flights. Neither of them slowed or breathed hard.

Ember noted that he didn't smoke. He wore a cologne that matched his underarm deodorant. He was a coffee drinker.

He opened the seventh-floor door for her and in a moment they were inside his office, and he motioned toward a set of deep chairs covered in forest-green leather.

As soon as they were seated he said, "I'd like to discuss with you anything you want to know about your origin and about your biological parents."

She was stunned. "You're willing to answer all my questions?"

"To the best of my ability."

She studied his skin color and Native American features. "You're not my father, of course."

He shook his head.

"Then Mike was right."

"Who?"

"A friend. He told me I was bioengineered by you, in a lab."

"Ember, I assure you, you were not bioengineered." He ran his hand through his hair. "I expect a lot of people on Whaler Bay believe that about you, but it's not true."

She did not believe him. Her eyes roved to the framed newspaper clippings on the wall above his desk.

"I see you've been keeping track over the years," she said. "Your little experiment."

"I've enjoyed watching you win," he said, and smiled. "You're a wonderful athlete."

She felt a rush of anger. "Is that what my birth was all about?" she said. "Sports?"

"Of course not."

"Then what do you want with me? Why did you create me? For what purpose?"

"Ember, I tell you again, truly—you are not the product of bioengineering."

"Yes, well, obviously, I don't trust you."

"I never met your father, but I do know your mother."

She sucked in her breath. "Who is she? Where is she? Is she alive?"

"She's . . . nearby."

"Where?"

"In Deer Park."

"Can I visit her?"

"I think so. But, well . . ." He sighed. "There is much to explain. We need to move slowly."

Her eyebrows gathered. "Why? What's wrong? Let's call her right now."

"Nothing is wrong. But you first need to face some facts about her, about yourself."

"You mean . . . she doesn't know about me, right?" She breathed out shakily. "I'm so glad. I always figured she didn't know about me—and that's good—I mean, what kind of a mom would not even bother to try to find her child, if she knew I was alive. Of course, that's what scares me—this is going to be so wrenching for her; first, she doesn't even know she has a daughter and then . . . I mean, she's an ordinary woman, and I look like this? What am I going to say? 'Hi, Mom! I'm the bioengineered daughter you never knew you had. Wanna see me lift a piano?' "

"You refuse to believe the truth. You were not bioengineered. I had nothing to do with making you."

"You modified the genes in the embryo that grew into me."

He shook his head. "Absolutely not. And your mother is no ordinary woman. She's your mother. She looks like you."

Ember's mouth fell open.

"Same skin color," he said, "same hair color, similar eyes, similar build."

Her heart leapt and she came to her feet out of the chair. "She's . . . *golden*?" she said in a choked whisper.

"Yes, golden." He stood and paced to the other side of the room, turned to her, clasped his hands in front of him as if in prayer, touching his fingertips to his lips.

"Ember, you're a very unusual human being," he began, carefully, rocking his prayer hands in rhythm with his words. "You're not like everyone else, not exactly. . . ."

She sighed in exasperation. *Tell me something I don't know!* She waited for more, but he hesitated, apparently at a loss for words.

"You said you never met my father," she said. "Was he just some anonymous sperm donor?"

"No. He and your mother conceived you in the natural way. His skin was golden, too, I'm sure. And I assume they were married in some fashion, according to their culture."

She frowned in confusion.

"Where's my mother? Take me to her now. I've got to see her."

He tapped his prayer hands against his tightly clamped lips. "You don't know how many times I've rehearsed our meeting—what you would ask, how I would answer. But . . . there's actually no easy way to tell you what you need to know."

She gulped. "Just spit it out, then."

He stepped closer and took her hand; his eyes met hers.

"Your mother is dead," he said, softly and clearly. "I found her, buried beneath a glacier on the arctic tundra. She had been dead twenty-five thousand years."

31

On the drive from Seattle to Deer Park, Ember's thoughts scattered in crazy confusion, like the raindrops racing across the windshield of the Mercedes gull-wing. Yute tried to get her to talk, but she did not dare, for she felt that her voice might lunge past her words into one long scream.

The car slowed and turned, entering a wrought-iron gate with a rusted metal sign: WASHINGTON STATE INDIAN SCHOOL. Two newer signs were affixed: PRIVATE, KEEP OUT.

In a moment she stood on shiny wet asphalt inside a gray cloud. The drizzle had died to a fine mist, but an occasional cold drop spattered her hair and face. Yute offered her his umbrella, but she only stared at him.

"What more?" she said. "What am I going to find out now?"

"Come with me."

He led her to a two-story brick building with a ceramic tile roof. Water gushed from a downspout at the building's corner and poured underground through a steel grate, gurgling loudly. She read in black enameled letters fastened to red brick: NEW CENTER FOR EARLY HUMAN RESEARCH.

Yute unlocked and swung open the door to his lab and a heavy blanket of odor enwrapped her: Lysol, formaldehyde, alcohol, chlorine, and dead flesh. The smell gagged her and she scanned the room for a receptacle in case she needed to vomit. A row of skeletons stood in chrome frames along the far wall. The left wall held an enormous oak bookcase beside a tall steel cabinet, honeycombed with many small drawers; nearby was a workstation with two computers and several file cabinets. The right half of the room was covered in pale blue ceramic tiles to her shoulder height, and the tiled floor sloped toward a central drain over which stood a black Formica lab table. The far right wall was dominated by the stainless steel case and door of a large walk-in freezer.

Her nausea passed and she plopped down on a stool beside the lab table. Yute walked over to the workstation and jotted something in a hardcover notebook.

"Ember!"

She looked up in time to see a coin spinning through the air toward her head. She caught it with her right hand. While the first coin was in midair, Yute tossed a second one. She caught it with her left hand. She looked at him blankly, not knowing what she was supposed to do or say.

"You're ambidextrous, aren't you?"

She nodded.

"I predicted you would be from the scratch marks on your mother's tooth enamel."

She frowned. "What are you talking about?"

"If you observe modern-day Inuits eating caribou meat, they grasp a large chunk in one hand, clamp their teeth on to a mouthful, and then slice off the rest with a knife. That habit leaves tiny scratches on their front teeth —normally in one direction only; that's how anthropologists inferred that Cro-Magnon humans were right handed."

He pantomimed holding a steak in his left hand, biting the end, and slicing the meat with his right hand, diagonally, from upper right to lower left.

"I examined your mother's incisors under a microscope and found hundreds of crisscrossing scratches in the enamel, meaning she sliced the meat she ate with either hand—she was ambidextrous."

Ember felt sick again, but managed to hold her nausea down. "What difference does it make?" she said, weakly. She had to repeat herself to be heard.

"More than you might expect," Yute said. "Neurologists have shown that right-handedness is linked to language and analytical ability, processed in the brain's left hemisphere. Ambidexterity shows that both your brain hemispheres are in remarkable balance, meaning you are equally gifted with intuition and critical—"

"Look, right now, my brain is sinking into a deep,

dark pit." Ember put her hands to her head. "I've been wanting all my life to find out who I am, but"—she closed her eyes and rubbed her temples—"I don't know if I can handle any more."

"I understand," he said. "Naturally, all this has been very upsetting for you. I'm sorry."

Ember eyed the skeletons against the wall.

"Is my mother . . . ?"

"No. She's not one of those specimens." He paused. "Would you like to see some color photos of her?"

Ember shook her head firmly and pressed her lips together.

"In time, then," he said. "You need more time."

"No, wait." She took a long breath. "I do want to see her. I've got to."

Yute stepped over to a file cabinet and in a moment handed her a heavy cardboard box that once held eight-by-twelve sheets of Kodak print paper. She rested the box on the lab table in front of her and gently placed her hands on it.

Her mother was buried inside.

She rehearsed how it was going to feel to see photos of her mother's desiccated body, skin stuck to bone, the features of her ancient face distorted in a gruesome mask of death. She bounced her knees up and down. Then she made her trembling hands lift the lid.

She gasped and jerked in her seat.

She saw the muscular back of a young woman lying prone on a stainless steel table; her shoulders were draped with many dark red ropes of tightly braided hair, and her skin looked soft, as if she were only asleep.

"She's golden," Ember whispered.

"Yes," Yute said. "At first I thought her color was an effect of refrigeration, but I found an unusual pigment in her skin."

"She's golden, like me." She swallowed hard and held her breath, struggling to hold back her sorrow. *Can't let myself fall apart in front of him.* A tear dropped onto the photograph, and she dried it with the long sleeve of her T-shirt. She tightened her chest and moved on.

The next photo, a frontal shot, revealed a curvaceously muscular physique that reminded her of her own. But it was the young woman's face that made her stand up from her seat. She studied the face closely, and her breath came fast. Then she quickly flipped through a dozen photos until she found a close-up portrait.

She stared at the broad golden face, framed with dark cornrow braids, and now it was unmistakably familiar, a face Ember recognized from a hundred childhood dreams.

U-Ma, the Shaman Mother of the blue ice cave.

"My God!" Ember clutched her heart. *U-Ma is my own mother!*

She remembered the little boy in her vision, who clung to U-Ma's leg and had to be tugged away.

My brother! Oh, I have a brother.

Then it hit her hard: *I had a brother—twenty-five thousand years ago.* And with that thought she could no longer contain her grief; it burst the floodgates of her heart and she felt that she would drown.

Sobbing, she asked, "Is—is—is this it? Nothing more of . . . my mom?"

"There's much more," Yute said. "I brought you here to show you my life's work. But I wanted you to adjust to all this gradually, starting with these photos."

She followed him, wiping at tears, down back stairs into a Staff Only corridor that led into the Museum of the Neanderthal. She heard the high-pitched whirring of a circular saw, and in a moment they entered a large room where a giant diorama exhibit was being built. The space was being converted into an Ice Age tundra scene.

Jutting from the left corner of the room a large cave mouth opened to the room's high ceiling. Inside the Fiberglas cave a small fire had been built of artificial logs fitted with gas jets. Lifelike mannequins of three golden-skinned women sat around the fire, heating slabs of meat on long sticks. One woman had a baby at her breast and two older children played with a wolf pup. A fourth woman scraped a hide spread on the stone floor, and an old man knelt and chipped away at a flint blade with a granite stone, flakes piling up between his knees. Outside, two boys walked toward the cave bent under bundles of firewood.

Painted on a concave wall to the right was a panoramic tundra landscape that gave an illusion of great depth. Knee-high grasses and clusters of flowers extended into the center of the room and seemed to stretch to the painting's far horizon, where snow-covered mountains spilled a dozen glaciers upon the plain. Several miles away a herd of woolly rhinos grazed. The tundra was in perpetual summer, and the afternoon sky looked warm, suffused with pinks and golds from theater floodlights hidden in the ceiling. A snowmelt stream unwinding from the distance in the painting trickled with real water along a mossy gouge just beyond the exhibit's railing. Nearby, a group of Neanderthal hunters waited in ambush on top of an outcropping of boulders, arms cocked above their heads, ready to thrust spears into a woolly mammoth as it lowered its trunk to drink from the stream. At its shoulder the beast stood twice as tall as Yute, and ten-foot-long upcurved tusks jutted from its jaw.

Two carpenters, their backs to Yute and Ember, squatted near a blueprint spread out on the floor beside a sawhorse. The younger of the two men wore his blond hair in a ponytail; the hair on his forearms was powdered with sawdust. The other man was as brown as chocolate and his shiny bald head reflected two spots of light, one pink, one gold. Yute walked over to the carpenters and told them to take a break. They nodded and glanced over at Ember. Their eyes darted from Ember to the women in the cave and back as they walked out the door.

Yute turned to her. "What do you think of it?" he said. "When completed in a few months this will be the world's finest exhibit of Neanderthal life. Not only the finest, but the only accurate one. All the others, even the one at the British Museum, are sad distortions."

Ember stood mute. Grief turned her body to lead. She sagged against the handrailing and stared at the scene from her mother's time—her *own* true time.

"Watch," Yute said, and turned a knob inside a wall panel. The gas logs erupted with blue-and-orange flames. "Hidden in the roof of the cave is all the necessary ventilation to meet state code," he said. "And watch this." He flipped a row of switches and the hunters came alive, yelling and jabbing their spears into the woolly mammoth's back. It raised its massive head and trunk, the great curving tusks gleaming like scimitars, and it trumpeted so loudly, the floor quaked under Ember's feet.

Any one of those hunters could represent my father. She squeezed the rail so tightly, her hands ached. *My family, my race, is extinct. No matter where I go on Earth, I walk alone.*

"This way," Yute said, nodding to their left. "I want to show you the centerpiece I have planned."

She pressed one hand over the pain in her gut and followed him.

They came to an area where a second diorama was being constructed—another cave scene—but this time the view was from inside a large cavern looking outward at a starry arctic night rippling with streamers of colored lights. In the foreground inside the cave sat three fire pits, each one the focus of activity. Around the fire on the left a golden-skinned man told stories in pantomime and sign language to a ring of wide-eyed boys; charcoal and ocher sketches of reindeer and bison and mammoths covered the smoke-blackened wall. Circling the central fire pit, several muscular men, spears raised, danced with a man dressed in a coarse reddish fur hide, his head crowned with the giant head of a cave bear.

But Ember's eyes swung to the fire pit on the right. A youthful golden woman sat cross-legged on the cave floor, while an older woman stood behind her, braiding her dark red hair into cornrows. The young woman seemed so lifelike, she looked as if she would turn her head if Ember spoke her name.

"U-Ma," she said in a hoarse whisper. *"Mom."*

"I hired a very skilled forensic sculptor from Holland to create the figure," Yute said. "Based on the photos, he built her out of wax, muscle layer by muscle layer, upon a resin skeleton cast from—"

Ember shot him a look that stopped him. "I want to see my mother's remains."

"Well, the red hair you see there is, in fact, her real hair."

"Let me see her bones."

"Her skeleton will be part of a separate, climate-controlled display," he said, "and I'm afraid it's not ready yet."

She grabbed his sleeve. "Take me to her bones, please—*now*—wherever they are. I don't care about your display, I need to see my mother."

Yute looked startled. "Okay, we'll go back to my lab."

She spun and strode out the door into the corridor. Yute caught up to her. "Look, I got carried away in there . . . and, uh . . . anyway, I know you're going through a lot with all of this. I'm sorry. Maybe we should have taken it slower."

"Eighteen years to learn the truth," she said, and wiped at her eyes. "That's slow enough."

Inside the lab room Yute and Ember put on sterile surgical gowns over their clothes, plus hoods, masks, and gloves.

"Brace yourself," Yute said as he opened a heavy

padlock on the steel handle of the walk-in freezer. "It's below zero in here."

He stepped in first. She hesitated, then followed. A sea of frigid air fogged her eyes and she blinked away the blurriness. Facing her, inside a tent of clear plastic, her mother's wired-together skeleton hung from a stainless steel frame against the back wall.

Ember bit her lip, breathing the cold air in and out. Then she stepped forward and unzipped the bag.

"Gently," Yute said. "Gently."

She ran her fingers along the cold, dry bones of her mother's skull; felt the solid jaw, the large white teeth, the high cheekbones—all like her own; the wide nasal cavity, through which her mother had once savored the fragrance of Ember's brother, as milk flowed warmly down in her breasts.

A sharp smell of chemical preservatives stabbed Ember's nose, and she zipped the plastic bag closed.

What was it her mother told the people in the ice cave? *Remember the aromas of this life. . . .*

She closed her eyes and let her breath settle inside her heart; down, down into a deep well of memory. She smelled the skin and hair and woodsmoke and furs and, below that, the essence of her people of the blue ice cave, and her mind roved among the tapestry of aromas until she located the threads of her mother's own scent. Sunk in memory, Ember inhaled deeply within her own heart-cave. *Mother, I remember you. You smell like love.*

Then she recalled U-Ma's final message. *"The ice womb of the Great Mother will preserve her children until they are reborn."*

I'm sorry, Mother. It's only a dream; an imprint left

in me of the world I came from. Your world. The children of the Great Mother are long gone.

"Long gone," she muttered, and turned her back to the skeleton.

"Pardon me?" Yute said.

"I'm not even supposed to be alive," she said, to no one. She held her hand in front of her face and flexed her fingers. "I'm a ghost, trapped in flesh. I don't belong in this world—not now. It's all wrong. I'd rather be a skeleton by my mother's side."

"Absolutely not," Ember said, hurrying down the stairs and out the door. "You can forget it."

"Just give me one year," Yute said, racing to keep up. "You owe me that much."

"I don't owe you jack."

"On the contrary." He grabbed her shoulder with a iron hand and spun her around to face him. "You owe me your very life."

She batted his hand away. "Look, let's get this straight," she said, and peered up at his broad face, into his black eyes. "You're the one who decided to play God. I didn't ask you to turn me into the last living Flintstone, and I don't thank you for it."

"But you saw the museum, the Tundra Woman exhibit is nearly completed, I just need more information."

"Her name is U-Ma, and she happens to be my mother."

"U-Ma?" He frowned.

"Never mind." She turned and strode off.

"Stop, listen." He was trailing at her heels again. "It's for science. I only seek knowledge, to understand. I was able to do extensive research on—on U-Ma . . . biopsies, X rays, CAT scans—but I could learn nothing of her mind."

"Her mind is extinct, that's all you need to know."

"No, no, I can conduct a series of psychological tests with you—IQ, personality inventories—"

"Have you got an inventory for loneliness? For sorrow? Because there's not enough of me left over to register on any other scales."

"All right, okay, eight months. I'll learn what I can in eight short months."

She walked faster.

"A half year, then, six months only, Ember, and I'll double my offer."

She didn't look back.

"You don't care about the money. Fine. What do you care about? What about knowledge? Self-knowledge, to discover yourself? To learn about your race?"

She stopped short and spun around and he nearly collided with her.

"So far today I've discovered that I'm a prehistoric cavewoman, that the people I've longed to find all my life have been dead since the Ice Age, and now all that's left of my family is my mother's skeleton. That leaves me with a homesickness in the pit of my soul that nothing in this life can cure. Got any more good news?"

He looked on the verge of tears. "How can I convince you that you are the greatest treasure of the scientific world?"

"The scientific world can kiss my fuzzy Neanderthal ass," she said, breathing hard. "You lab-coats are all alike—all brain, no heart. No gut feeling for the consequences of what you do. What do you think will happen to my life if you announce me to the world?"

"I . . . uh . . ."

"There'll be no end to the hype—Neanderthal jokes, Neanderthal burgers, Neanderthal hairdos—they'll want to put me on the talk shows next to the housewife who has sex with her Great Dane."

Yute shook his head vigorously. "What we learn together about you and your race will be published in the finest scientific journals."

"Yeah, like *National Enquirer*."

He sighed and held up his hands in surrender. "You win," he said. "I won't try any further to persuade you."

"Auf Wiedersehen, Dr. Frankenstein." She turned and hurried away.

"But there is one thing I wanted you to have that belonged to your mother."

Her pace slowed.

"A little flute, made from a bird bone. It should rightly belong to you now."

She turned around.

"It was hers?"

"Yes, I found it in her clothing. It's charming, it plays five sweet high notes, in the range of a piccolo. Come back to the lab and you can take it with you."

She took a deep breath and tried to calm her anger and anxiety. She wanted to go off somewhere by herself, anywhere, and scream her head off, fall apart in smithereens, and then try to figure out what to do next. But she envisioned her mother playing the flute to her brother and the image touched her.

"All right," she said. "Just the flute, no more brow-beating."

"Just the flute."

They walked back together and climbed the stairs to the lab. He walked over to a specimen cabinet. "I had an expert identify it as the thighbone of a swan," he said, with his back turned to her.

She smelled a powerfully acrid chemical odor—a preservative?

He turned to her and held out a small white flute, about eight inches long, with four finger holes. The rims of the holes were rubbed smooth from playing. *She was a musician*, Ember thought, and her hard anger began to melt again into grief. She held the flute to her nose and sniffed the finger holes, even while knowing it would be impossible to smell the oils in her mother's skin after so many centuries.

She only smelled the harsh chemical, much stronger now, and she glanced up. Yute stood behind her and clapped a handkerchief soaked in ether over her mouth and nose. She gasped in shock and inhaled the bitter anesthetic. Then she twisted her head violently and lunged forward, striking behind with her elbows, but his big hand clamped her face like an octopus. She crouched to throw him over her hip, but dizzily staggered to her knees. She squirmed and tried to squeeze her lungs shut, but finally sucked in another breath. Instantly her vision dimmed and she felt a sickening sensation that she was sinking through the floor as the lights went out.

32

EMBER SURVEYED THE main room of the one-bedroom cabin. The walls were made of bucked and hand-sawed douglas fir logs, chinked with gray mortar. Fragrant pine burned and snapped in a flagstone fireplace. Through the room's one window she saw a snowy mountain ridge rising beyond the crest of a steep wooded slope. The cabin appeared to be at or near the base of a deep gulch.

She wished she could recognize the glimpse of distant mountain. Was it Mount Rainier? If so, the youth camp for the deaf was not far.

On the way to the cabin, bound and blindfolded and bumping along in some kind of foldable cart, she had tried to orient herself by sense of smell, sniffing for special odors that might give her a clue to her whereabouts. But she had detected nothing unusual, just the nauseating trace of the anesthetic, the scent of rust and mildewed canvas from the cart, and the odor of Yute's sweat; top notes against the lush green base of the rain forest.

Closer to the cabin she had whiffed what seemed to her a sea of the sweet-rot smell of thousands of stumps being digested by fungi. Timber crews must have clear-cut some nearby hills, five, six summers ago. She figured Yute had driven his car to a trailhead and hiked in on an old log-skidding trail, or maybe a fire trail. As simple as it was, the cabin seemed too fancy for a timber crew—besides, the sap in the fir logs smelled relatively fresh; she was convinced the cabin was no older than a couple years.

Who else knows it's here? Wherever here *is.*

He had prepared another plate of food for her—a whole-grain peanut-butter-and-jelly sandwich, a Granny Smith apple, and some red flame grapes—but she had not touched a bite or said a word to him since her kidnapping, two days ago.

She reclined on a thick foam-rubber mattress that lay on the pine floorboards. A soft nylon climbing rope bound her wrists but left her hands free to handle objects. The same rope bound her ankles. During the day Yute was never far away. At night, while he slept, he secured the trailing end of the ankle rope to an eyebolt sunk into one of the flagstones of the hearth, and he simply tied a canvas bag over her hands, which rendered them useless for untying herself.

She studied the knots again. Merit-badge perfect.

Yute shoved the front door open with his boot and stepped up into the cabin with an armful of split firewood. He stacked it in a neat pile near the stone hearth and set another log on the blaze. He wore a raw wool turtleneck sweater and the heated air wafted to her the oily aroma of lanolin.

He stared straight ahead into the fire. "As a little boy in Swift Fork I helped my dad split firewood," he said. "He'd drive in the wedge, and then he'd steady the log and let me tap at it with my hammer." He pantomimed holding a hammer with both hands. "After a few taps he'd wave me away and bash it with a sledge, and the pieces would fly to the sides." He half smiled. "But he always led me to think that I'd done most of the work splitting those logs."

He looked at her. "Ever split firewood?"

She looked away. He returned his gaze to the flames and let out a long sigh. The moisture in the logs hissed and spit.

"Complex systems are inherently unpredictable. I read that years ago—Chaos Theory—it made perfect sense to me at the time. Yet somehow I missed the central fact: The most complex systems, and therefore, the least predictable, are people. Who can guess what we'll do, or why?"

He poked at a log with an iron rod and a swirl of sparks flew up the chimney.

"Ever since I was a boy, I've been hungry for learning—could never get enough. The sort of knowledge my father considered useless was the kind I craved. Every two months I waited with a pounding heart for the arrival of the bookmobile, like the other boys might wait to pounce on a snow hare. Then for a little while I was fed, and contented."

He didn't speak for a minute and Ember wondered what he had been getting at. She watched him from the corner of her eyes.

"The VISTA volunteers tried to convince my father that I had a special gift that was bigger than he and the tundra could handle." He glanced at her and she looked down. "Picture a fourteen-year-old Caiyuh boy in a small arctic village, begging his old-ways father to allow him to go live in Fairbanks so he could sit around all day at the university and study science.

"My father told me, 'A gift that drives you far from home is no gift.' But my mother persuaded him to let me go, finally, because she knew that I was miserable in Swift Fork. So off I went to college. Books and ideas to feed my appetite. But I was so homesick, I threw up for days. And while I was away that first term, my mother died giving birth to my sister."

Ember stole a glance at him. He gazed at her with dark, sad eyes, as if she were now the dancing fire.

"Ember, I know what it's like to feel different, to feel alone. If someone had come along in those days and said to me, 'Yute, it's obvious that you're very unusual, and I want to work with you to find out what makes you the way you are, why you're so unlike everyone else.' I would have jumped at the chance. And I made the mistake of thinking you would feel the same way."

He stood and ran his hand through his hair. "Complex systems . . . I didn't predict that Chena would want to keep you."

He turned and began to pace.

"I was devastated," he said, "but I decided the only thing to do was to wait for you to come to me—when you were hungry to know everything about yourself. So I waited, for years . . . *years*. At last, you came. But the next thing I knew, you walked away. I had missed your childhood, and this time I couldn't even gamble on you coming back. I had to stop you, or maybe lose you forever."

He turned to face her. "Ember, I'm sorry. I couldn't take that chance."

She narrowed her eyes and glared at him.

"I don't expect you to accept an apology," he said. "I was only thinking out loud, trying to explain my behavior to myself. I'd never have guessed that I would—would ever do something like this."

He turned and began to pace again.

"It's . . . I wish I could make you understand," he said. "For as long as I've been called to explore the sciences, I've been most drawn to evolution, and within that field, human evolution, and with human evolution, Neanderthals. It's as if my mind were a telescoping antenna, narrowing to a point, turning toward some great signal of truth about Neanderthals."

He brought his index fingers together in a point as he extended his arms.

"For years I told myself my ambition was to be the world's chief authority on Neanderthals," he said. "Recognition in my field . . . right . . . I nearly had myself convinced. But over the last two days I've come to admit that it's always been a private obsession. It's got nothing to do with my career, or the advancement of science. It's utterly personal."

He turned to face her and spoke with a quiet intensity. "Ember, I need to learn about Neanderthals—about you. It's my destiny, and I don't know why."

He looked down at her plate of untouched food. "So if you don't eat, eventually I'll have to intubate you," he said. "That means inserting a tube up one nostril and down your throat into your stomach, in order to feed you liquids. Please don't force me to."

She glowered and tried to match his steady gaze, but the fact was, she wasn't in the mood to have chicken broth piped up her nose. Besides, she felt weak with hunger. She reached out and greedily took a bite of the big green apple.

"I'm extremely allergic to many different foods," she said with her mouth full. It was a lie, a new strategy.

He raised his eyebrows. "Aha, she can talk."

"At the mildest I break out in hives, but at the worst my windpipe closes off. I've been rushed to the emergency room a couple dozen times, just because of a cookie or part of a sandwich I ate."

"That so?"

"One time I even stopped breathing and had to be resuscitated."

"You don't say."

"I am saying—you don't have the foods I need here."

"Tell me exactly what you eat at home, and I'll be able to get any of those foods when I go into town."

"You'd have to be a dietician to shop for what I need." She tried to remember every food allergy she had heard about. "Gluten-free, wheat-free bread. I can't tolerate food additives or artificial flavorings or colorings of any kind; absolutely no MSG—that's what almost killed me once. I need pure water, without fluoride in it. And toothpaste without fluoride. And, uh . . ."

"Make a list, I can get you everything you need at the health-food store where I shop."

"What about clothes? I can't wear the same underwear for however long I'm supposed to be your prisoner."

"I brought in your backpack full of clothes," he said. "I'll get it." He turned to walk into the bedroom.

Her mind clicked and buzzed like a pinball machine. She had a plan.

"You said before that if I cooperated, you would help in every way to make my stay here more comfortable."

He paused. "*If* you cooperate."

"Well, I have this very strong physical and emotional need for exercise. Daily exercise," she said. "I'm going nuts already from being unable to move about freely."

"I can't let you go outside."

"Just to ride my bike around. I won't try to run away, I promise." She cupped her hands over her mouth and then cupped her hands over her heart. "By the Heart Breath of the Earth Mother, I promise not to run away. If you know anything at all about Quanoot-cha, you know that's an unbreakable vow for a Quanoot."

"But . . . you're not Quanoot." He tilted his head. "Is that the trick you're pulling?"

"I was raised a Quanoot. I sympathize with their tradition, it's the only tradition I've ever lived."

"Even so, you're not a Quanoot."

"Then on my mother's bones, on my parents' blood pumping through my veins—I won't try to run away."

"Even so, you still might be spotted by someone. I'm sorry, you'll have to be content with isometrics or some kind of exercise you can devise indoors."

He spun to go.

"Okay, indoor exercise."

He turned back.

"Buy me a set of rollers for stationary cycling."

"An exercise bike?"

"No, I hate those goofy things, they don't feel right. Bring my mountain bike to me. That's the whole point of the device, it trains you and gets you in shape for real riding on your own bike."

He put his hand to his face and stroked in a circle around his mouth.

"And if I buy you the rollers . . . you'll cooperate with a battery of psychological exams?"

"You'll learn all you need to know about the way my mind works."

"And a blood series, biopsies . . ." He rubbed faster. "The tests will take a few months to complete, but if you work with me, if you cooperate fully—"

"Bring me my bike and a Shimano indoor track, and maybe I'll even make you breakfast each morning."

His face softened and she could see his shoulders relax from across the room. He broke into a grin.

"Ember, you've got yourself a deal."

33

EMBER LAY AWAKE on her back on the foam mattress, working out the details of her escape plan. Orange tentacles of firelight flicked over the grain and knotholes in the rafters. She was alone in the cabin, Yute had left for town during the night.

A part of her welcomed her predicament; it gave her an immediate clear-cut goal to focus on, and allowed her to shove aside the deeper long-term questions of what the hell to do about her life, her *Neanderthal*-ness. How would Mom and Dad and Kaigani feel about her now? And Mike? And most troubling, how did she feel about herself?

She shook her head roughly.

Not the time or place for an identity crisis.

How will he react if things go wrong with my getaway? Surely, I'm too precious a specimen to damage or destroy—though I'd rather be dead than be paraded before the world as a freak from a museum.

She rehearsed her escape again and again, playing out variations in her mind. Near dawn, long after the fire dimmed and died, she was confident enough that her plan would succeed that she could finally let herself drift off to sleep.

Footsteps coming up the path. She sat up with a jolt, her heart thumping.

"I'm going to do it," she whispered, "no matter what."

Yute opened the door onto a gray overcast morning. A foldable canvas wagon stood outside, loaded with several grocery bags and a couple dozen cans and jars, a box of apples, and what appeared to be a half-gallon jar of peanut butter.

Yuck. She could smell peanut butter on people's breath from the next county. All the more reason to get away from him.

The cabin was not equipped with a stove, but it had a small gas-powered refrigerator, and Yute placed vegetables and fruits inside it, dried fruits, cheeses, and jars of organic fruit juices.

"Any suspicious chipmunks spot you coming up here?" she said.

"This cabin is on private property, nearly surrounded by national forest land. We're rather secure from wandering eyes."

"I feel better already. Did you get the bike?"

He put the last of the groceries away. Then he kneeled in front of the glowing embers, piled on kindling and logs, then puffed at the bed with a leather bellows. Flames rushed up with a *wooomph*, reflecting hot yellow tones in his black eyes.

Fear leapt up in her throat, as sudden as the fire.

I need the bike.

"Well?" she said, trying to keep her voice from shaking.

"I thought more about the bike," he said, poking the fire with an iron rod. "I decided it wasn't such a good idea."

"Damn." She tossed her long tresses like a whip. "I already promised you I wouldn't try to run away." She glanced around the tiny room, a shrinking box of logs. Her mouth went dry and her palms grew clammy. Her escape plan seemed hopeless now.

"What do you want from me?" She groaned. "How can I take psychological exams, when I'm going crazy from lack of exercise?"

She kicked her legs, bound at the ankles and tied to the eyebolt; they snagged in midair with a jerk. "I got better workouts as a fetus."

He stood and faced her, his hands on his hips. She had to tilt her head up to meet his gaze.

"The fact is, against my better judgment, I did bring your bike."

She let out a sigh and her head swam with relief.

"But before I bring it in and set you loose, let me warn you: I have a handgun with me, and I won't hesitate to use it if I have to."

"You'd shoot a scientific treasure?" Ember said, as calmly as she could manage.

"Not in the head or chest," he said. "I'm a good marksman, and I have a doctor's kit on hand. I could clean and repair a minor gunshot wound."

"Gosh, I'm touched, Doctor. You really do care."

"Look, Ember, I don't blame you for hating me. But sometimes one has to do things toward an ultimate good—even when it goes against an individual's will."

"Hope this doesn't sound ungrateful, but how is being kidnapped and roped to the floor going to lead to an ultimate good?"

"Yes, well . . . it's . . ." He broke off from her gaze. "There's much more at stake here than your comfort or even your freedom."

"Try me."

He sat down cross-legged on the floor near her. "You are a living representative of a distinct human race that died out hundreds of centuries before writing was invented, let alone cameras, or any of the marvelous archival tools we have now."

He held up his hands in front of his chest. "You, just as you are, without any special effort, embody more knowledge about human evolution and physical anthropology than all the volumes that have ever been written on the subjects. *That*, Ember, is what is more precious than your personal feelings."

"Information is more important than people?"

"Absolutely. The advancement of understanding—"

"You're lying to yourself again. You told me only yesterday that you realized this is your own personal obsession. It's not about the advancement of understanding, it's about Dr. Nahadeh and his lifelong fixation."

He nodded and then ran his hand through his hair. "There still may be a way to redeem myself, to make my actions count for something positive. Every great scientist, artist—every great *person*—has been driven, has had to submit to his own calling, no matter how mysterious or unsettling—"

"Or hurtful to others . . . ?" she asked.

He stood and laid his hands on the mantel of the fireplace, then lowered his forehead to press against the gray slate. "I'm sorry for the hurt I've caused you," he said with his eyes squeezed shut. "My life also has been threaded through with pain. But as I see it, you and I are players in a greater drama—a bigger destiny—that takes precedence over our needs as individuals. So it doesn't matter so much about me or you. Every advance in scientific knowledge has come about through personal sacrifices." He looked at her. "Were it not so, where would humankind be?"

"Living closer to the Earth?" she said.

"We'd still be lurking in caves, unaware of the reaches of the universe, or the microcosms within our own bodies; helpless and afraid of the night, like perpetual children; unable to live above the navel, to stand higher than the beasts."

His words washed over her like a foul wave. Her face burning with shame, she hung her head, sickened by what she was, the daughter of cavepeople, a solitary beast in a world of humans. She swallowed hard and bit her lip, not wanting him to see her cry; she knotted her chest until it cut off her breath, but it didn't stop her tears of self-hate.

"No, that's not . . . I—I didn't intend to insult you," he said. "I'm not saying that you, personally, are less than . . ."

She cupped one hand over her eyes and waved his words away with the other hand. Her breathing sputtered in quiet, high-pitched sobs.

"Actually, you Neanderthals were a very loving and compassionate race. I'll tell you about some striking evidence of that, if you'd like."

She shook her head without looking up. In a moment he turned to retreat into the bedroom.

"Wait," she said, and when he turned, nodded. "Please."

He stood in the doorway. "At a place called Shanidar Cave in Iraq," he said, "the bones of a man about forty-five years old were uncovered—that's an old man in terms of the average life span in prehistoric times. What's remarkable is that this man had been badly injured years before. He had a crippled right leg and withered right upper arm—the lower arm was torn off. The right side of his skull was crushed, compressing the eye socket, so it was plain that he was sightless in that eye. And he also showed signs of severe arthritis on his injured side.

"So. Here was a man who hobbled around in pain and couldn't possibly have hunted or even gathered plant foods for himself. Yet his comrades in the cave not only provided for him for decades, but when they buried him, they heaped his body with mounds of flowers—the pollens and seeds were still present."

Abruptly, Ember pictured herself laying armloads of bright orange poppies on a golden-skinned body. She could not make out the face of the deceased, but the rest of the scene was so vivid that the sweet perfume of the poppies overpowered her senses, and for a moment she forgot about the cabin and Yute.

Yute did not speak for a long while.

"You're warm enough without a fire?" he asked at last.

She nodded.

"Then try to get some rest," he said. "Tomorrow you can exercise on your bike." He stepped inside the bedroom and was about to shut the door. "Ember, everything's going to be all right," he said. "You and I . . . we're woven together somehow . . . and . . . well . . . just get some rest. We can talk more in the morning."

Ember threw herself on the mat, buried her face in the crook of her arm, and closed her eyes to the world. She wished she could return to the warm, dark cave of her mother's womb and dissolve in the sleep of time.

U-Ma sat cross-legged on a mossy rock shelf near the mouth of a large cave. She played a bird-bone flute while a blond infant slept peacefully in her lap. Dusk was settling over the summer tundra and the cloudless sky glowed red and gold behind the snowy mountains, blending upward through blue into deep purple. The ruddy light turned the blond fuzz on her bare torso into golden velvet.

Across from her a young man built a cone-shaped

pile of sticks over a core of shredded dry grass. Then he struck a flint against a flat rock, shooting sparks into the grass, leaned his face close, and puffed on the smoldering mound until it burst into flames. When the kindling burned steadily he stacked several limbs on top. Finally, he sat and smiled, swaying to the music, sometimes singing along, without words, in a high tremolo voice. His neck and shoulders and chest were bisonlike, and he was furred with blond woolly hair that simply grew denser over his cheeks and scalp.

U-Ma set down her flute and reached out with her fingertips as if to pluck the evening star from above the far peaks. The young man laughed, and cupped his hands as if to capture and bring down the quarter moon. They made a show of exchanging gifts, the sparkling diamond and the bright crescent. Their eyes embraced. He crouched on all fours and stalked toward her like a cave lion, his breath purring in his chest with a bass rumble. She giggled and shook her dark red braids; her cheeks and her breasts blushed with heat. She gently set the baby on his belly on a thick sheep fur. Then she and her mate made another kind of music, with their whole bodies.

Ember awoke on the floor of the small cabin, still drifting in the wide open spaces of the tundra. When she opened her eyes, the log walls rushed in on her and crushed her mood in an instant.

Then she recalled her dream, and knew she had seen her own father in the heart-shared realm of never-lost emotion.

34

It was midafternoon when Yute emerged from his room. Without a word he stepped outside and rolled in Ember's mountain bike, painted with prismatic metallic flakes that gleamed in the sunlight like scales on a rainbow trout. Yute leaned out the door and pulled in a rectangular white cardboard box with the Shimano logo printed on the top and sides.

Ember held up her wrists eagerly, and Yute untied them and her ankles. She rushed over to the bike and gave it a quick inspection. Perfect.

She popped the staples on the box and assembled the floor stand: a rectangular steel base with two pairs of hard rubber roller pins, front and back. On the rollers she balanced the front and rear wheels of the bike, made a few adjustments, and went through the motion of securing the bike with four steel braces that attached to the lever nuts of the wheels. But she did not tighten the nuts, leaving the bike easy to slip free.

Yute handed her a shopping bag that held a pair of padded biking shorts and a matching jersey, emerald-green, with red stripes.

"Gloves?" she said.

He gave her a smaller bag. "Everything on your list."

She took out a pair of half-finger gloves with fish-net nylon backs and padded leather palms—men's large. Another box held a pair of men's size 11-EEE bicycle shoes, shaped like track shoes, but built with a rigid sole and toe box to deliver more force to the pedals.

"Christmas gets closer to Thanksgiving every year," she said. "Thank you."

She held the jersey to her torso. "I'll need to change. . . ."

"Sure," he said, and walked into the bedroom.

As soon as the door closed, she hurriedly changed into the form-fitting biking clothes, then retrieved four twenty-dollar bills from her sweatpants pocket, folded them into a tight rectangle, and tucked them into the key pouch inside her biking shorts. She pulled on the padded gloves, then quietly lifted the bike off its stand, flipped the lever nuts tight, and rolled it toward the front door. She eased the door open gingerly, praying the hinges would not squeak.

The door swung open soundlessly, but her heart sank.

Through the side window she had seen towering evergreens climbing the steep slope, and assumed the cabin was nestled in a forest clearing at the base of a gulch; she believed that after making it past the clearing, she would be safe, a nearly impossible target weaving downhill among endless trees. But downhill from where she stood, she faced only a rolling sea of stumps. The surrounding hills and ridges looked naked and raw.

Clear cut.

She took a breath. *Here I go, anyway.* She rolled the bike out the door.

Yute called from the bedroom. "Ember, I just remembered, I bought you the sport bra. Want me to hand it to you?"

She froze and screwed her eyes shut. Damn. She leaned her head toward the open cabin door and tried to project her voice. "No, thanks."

"Ember?" Yute stuck his head out of the bedroom door and saw her.

She took three running steps and threw her right leg over the saddle of the bike, clipped her shoes in the toe locks, and then stood in the pedals and pumped with all her strength.

"You promised!" Yute yelled from the doorway.

She shot a glance back. "I'm not running," she yelled, "I'm riding!"

He ducked back inside.

Go! Go! Go! She strained at the pedals, riding up a hump in the floor of the gulch; the ground was mossy and soft, stumps were everywhere, and the bike seemed to crawl.

"Stop!" he shouted.

She heard a sharp clap and splinters flew off a stump a few feet to her left.

"That's a warning!"

"Shoot me, you bastard, and my dad'll kill you!" she screamed over her shoulder.

Yute sprinted after her, closing the gap.

Another loud clap and a clump of dirt and moss exploded next to her front wheel. She involuntarily jerked the wheel sideways and almost hit a stump. She didn't look back, but hunkered over the handlebars and pumped her legs like pistons in a steam engine, accelerating up the rise.

Blam. The air beside her head imploded with a pop, like the sound made by puncturing a vacuum seal, and she realized a bullet had whizzed by within inches.

Good marksman, my ass, unless you're trying to kill me.

She pressed on, harder. The bike topped the small crest and the far side dropped off steeply. Now the trick was to dive like a kamikaze, while missing the scattered stumps and boulders. She slid backward off the saddle and rode with her center of gravity over the rear wheel, to prevent cartwheeling. A limb blocked her path and she bunny-hopped it, both wheels off the ground at once.

A deep stump hole loomed ahead. She hit both brakes, planted her left foot, and jerked the bike sideways. *Bam.* A fiery hammer slammed into her left shoulder in the instant she swerved. She screamed and the bike veered wildly until she wrestled back control. Stumps rushed past on either side and she didn't dare glance behind her.

"Kill me, then!" she yelled, looking straight ahead. "That's what it'll take!"

"Ember!" Yute bellowed. "Ember!"

The flesh of her shoulder burned as if branded, but she couldn't take her eyes off the slope. It steepened and dropped to a long ridge, with plunging ravines on either side. She was forced to steer the beeline along the knife edge of the ridge, a clear target below Yute. A half mile ahead the rain forest began again, densely covering the mountainous terrain, and she raced toward the wall of green as if it were Eden.

How many bullets has he fired? That doesn't help me, I don't how many bullets are in his gun, and maybe he's got extra.

She kept riding, but cringed with the sensation that her back was one big fluorescent bull's-eye.

A dozen yards ahead an ancient pine had broken halfway up, and keeled over to form a narrow A-frame across the ridge. It was the sole tree since her flight began, and she was about to ram headlong into it. She aimed for the opening and at the last second tucked so low, her chest mashed into the top tube. She punched through the doorway, sending pine cones skittering down the drop-offs on both sides.

"Threaded the needle!" she shouted.

Yute cried out from the high slope behind her, "Ember!"

On the far side of the tree a narrow ravine sliced downward from the ridge, and hidden in its deep cleft she spotted an old timber flume. She squeezed the handbrakes and skidded sideways to a stop.

Now she knew her whereabouts.

On a family trip as a schoolgirl she had watched the Colgate Flume in action—timber plunging four thousand feet along an eight-mile waterslide—down, down to the Skookumchuck River, where the logs floated to the Colgate Lumber Company sawmill. It was the longest flume north of Oregon, but it had become obsolete years ago when crews started hauling out logs from the mountains with giant Skycrane helicopters.

She glanced at her shoulder. The bullet appeared to have passed cleanly through the thick muscle, but the flesh sizzled with pain.

"Just hold on," Yute shouted, "I'm coming down to help you. Oh, Ember! It was an accident. I only meant to fire warning shots."

He scrambled down the slope that led to the ridge where she straddled her bike. Ember glanced at the distant evergreens, which she now knew marked the edge of the Snoqualmie National Forest, then glanced back at Yute.

No way I can make it to the trees before he grabs me.

Then she stared again at the weather-beaten wooden trough that disappeared around a bend in the ravine. It was a feeder flume, one of many that once delivered stream water and small timber to the main flume. The feeder was built over a streambed and its water supply was a spring that trickled out of solid granite just below where she stood. She saw debris from a log dam that had once raised the water to the mouth of the flume; now the boards looked as dry as the shed skin of a snake.

This feeder will shoot me into the main flume, which will dump me in the river, and if I don't break my neck first—or at the end—I can climb up to the highway there and flag down a car. On the other hand, it's old, untreated lumber, probably rotten in places, and over short runs it's as steep as a playground slide.

An all-downhill thrill ride to freedom. Or mangled death.

A crimson bloom spread from a neat hole in her jersey and now her shoulder wound began to throb with each thump of her heart. A pine needle was embedded in her forearm and she yanked it out. Yute jogged toward her on the ridge, from the other side of the fallen pine.

"It was an accident, Ember," he said, puffing hard. "You've got to believe me."

He was a hundred feet from the tree, and it blocked his vision.

She hopped off her bike and quickly lowered it to the streambed, then slid on her butt down the rock face, into the ravine. Yute saw her, but she still had a few seconds. She scrambled onto the flume, reached down and grabbed up the bike, straddled the seat, and gazed down the long, swooping curve.

Her heart ba-boom-ba-boomed in her throat, and her shoulder kept time like a drum.

I can't. Can't do it.

Yute came at a dead run. She gritted her teeth.

I just can't.

She peered up at the sky, at her father's crescent moon serenely watching. She sucked in a breath down to the soles of her feet.

Got to.

Yute jumped into the rocky trench behind her. She shoved off and rolled over the lip of the chute. The bike nearly dropped out from under her. Her gut recoiled like a spring.

There was not the slightest possibility of turning back.

35

Ember plummeted down the chute and the ravine blurred at the edges of her vision.

The sides of the flume were five feet tall, angled inward like a V, with a narrow floor at the bottom, and the shape worked in her favor, allowing her to climb the outside wall as she shot into the curve, like a bicycle sprinter banking around a velodrome. She squeezed both brakes evenly, anchoring her center of gravity over the rear wheel, careful not to zoom over the top. The first bend turned into an S-curve and she dropped through the center of the trough and zoomed up the opposite wall.

The flume leveled off to a moderate pitch and followed the meandering streambed in the crotch of the ravine. Then she came to another breakneck plunge, and another, and then a long, steep ramp as the stream below turned into a cascade, tumbling down a dozen rocky steps.

Then the ravine opened into a wide gulch where the smaller stream fed white waters that gushed over rocks, and she saw the main flume ahead, angling down from far up the mountain. The feeder curved to run nearly parallel with the main flume, then the two blended into one and she was now on the flume to the river, coasting above the rapids that dropped through the forest.

Evergreens whipped past on both sides and their fragrance was the glorious smell of freedom; in spite of the pain from her wound she felt exalted.

Then the mountain broke in half and fell away from her.

She gasped. The stream shot over the edge of a cliff and mist from the waterfall sprayed her face. The flume crossed a deep canyon, atop two-hundred-foot trestles. The beauty was breathtaking, and Ember began to wonder if she had invented a new sport.

Abruptly, she saw a break in the floor of the trough. She jammed the handbrakes and dragged her right foot against the wall. The bike skidded toward the gap. She grabbed the top edge of the wall and jerked to a stop just as the front wheel dropped in. Her left shoe clip was locked in the pedal and she felt the weight of the bike sag forward. Below, the rapids splashed over jutting rocks. She walked her hands backward, her shoulder wound protesting, and towed the bike back from the splintered edge of the hole.

She dismounted and laid the bike on its side, then eased herself down to sit on the floor of the flume, her back propped against the wall. Her shoulder stung and throbbed, but at least it was not bleeding much, only seeping.

The sun was three fingers above the horizon. In a half hour it would be too dark to spot other holes in time to stop. The gap was as wide as two bike lengths; the stream she had jumped with Mike was wider than that, and she had almost made it. Of course, when she'd landed short of the far bank, she had only busted her lip; to miss here would flip her backward to her death—or worse—on the boulders below.

What do I do?

If Yute knows where this flume leads—and I have to assume he does—he may try to beat me to the river in his car and recapture me. But the flume will get me there much faster than his winding mountain roads, as long as I keep moving.

Jump the hole.

Or, I can turn around and walk back to the other side, probably climb down to the ground—even with a bad shoulder. But where will that leave me? Stumbling through the boondocks all night, with Yute hunting for me, or waiting to pounce on me at the river?

Jump the hole. It's the only way.

She pulled herself to her feet with her right arm and walked to the edge of the hole and peered down, trying not to focus on the jagged boulders at the bottom. Half a dozen braces had popped loose beneath the flume, causing a ten-foot span to collapse. The floorboards at the near edge were rotted, sagging into the hole; the far side looked as weak.

Not good.

I'll have to get airborne two feet back from the near edge and land two feet beyond the far edge, which makes it wider than the stream I fell short on. Gotta rethink this little stunt.

"Stunt," she said, and snapped her fingers at the image of a motorcycle stuntman launching from a ramp.

How can I make a ramp?

She remembered a wobbly floorboard near the canyon wall and hurried back to it. The wood was soft and rotted around the rusty nails, and with some straining she managed to pry up the board from one loose end, until it popped free. It was about fourteen feet long, two inches thick, and ten inches wide.

Narrow for a ramp, but it'll have to do. Now I need something to support it.

She carried the plank to the hole. Then she lay on her belly, grabbed a four-inch-by-four-inch strut that dangled by one nail, and wriggled it until it twisted free; the weight fell into her hand and she dropped the strut.

"Damn!"

The strut slowly flipped end over end as it fell. It struck a sharp rock and splintered in two with a loud snap and the sound bounced around the canyon. The frothy water swept the chunks away.

She worked loose another dangling strut. This time, she held on. She stood and wedged it sideways between the flume walls to form a brace for the ramp. Then she propped the end of the floorboard on top of the strut, making a ramp with a three-foot height at takeoff. She walked up the ramp, bouncing slightly, to test it.

Strong enough, but too springy. It'll kill my forward momentum, like hitting the brakes while shooting up the ramp to make the jump. Need a shorter, stiffer ramp.

She looked for short floorboards that were loose at the ends; but the only loose ones she found were long; the short ones were nailed fast. She hurried back to the bike and grabbed from the underseat pouch a tire-changing tool—a small L-shaped steel lever with a beveled edge, used for popping the stiff lip of a rubber tire on or off the wheel rim. In ten minutes she pried free a six-foot-long board.

She set one end of the short board on the support strut and stood on the ramp. Much stiffer. She gazed across to her goal, and blew her breath out through pursed lips.

She dumped the long board over the side of the flume, then walked uphill with her bike, half the length of a football field. She shook out her leg muscles.

She straddled the seat, closed her eyes, and pictured herself as human-powered aircraft. Then she looked at her runway, her takeoff spot, her flight path across the English Channel, her victorious team waiting with champagne on the far side.

She set her jaw and shoved off hard, standing in the pedals, huffing, picking up speed; then she tucked down and put her gut and butt and back into it, spinning the cranks like twin props, racing toward her takeoff mark—twenty feet to go.

The hole seemed to expand and gape like a ragged wound.

She panicked.

I'm not gonna make it!

She squeezed the brakes and the tires locked and stuttered along the floor and the bike banged hard into the right wall and ricocheted straight up the ramp. She threw all her weight behind her, yanked up on the handlebars, stood the bike on its rear wheel; it flipped backward and crashed down beside her at the ramp's edge. She jammed her legs against the flume walls and grabbed for the sliding bike. It tilted into the hole and the weight jerked her arm and she screamed and let the bike drop.

She held her breath.

It seemed to take half a minute before she heard a tire explode as her mountain bike smashed into scrap on the granite.

36

EMBER SCOOTED DOWN the ramp and rested on her back on the floor of the flume, panting and trembling. Where her right forearm had rammed the wall, a patch of raw skin oozed blood, and a deeper scrape on her right hip bled through a rip in her biking shorts. A splinter pinched between her shoulder blades, but she could not reach it; she managed to pull out several others.

Then she leapt up, kicked the wall, and slugged the air with her fists.

"Yeow!" She clutched her wounded shoulder and sucked in her breath through clenched teeth.

"Damn." She stamped the floor and spit every curse word she knew—at Yute, at the hole, at herself for chickening out. Finally, she stepped back toward the edge and peered at the wreckage. The bike frame had jackknifed like a folding bike, so that the wheels overlapped.

Truth is, if I hadn't bailed out, I'd probably be splattered all over those boulders.

So now what?

She began pacing up and down in a tight circuit, uncoiling her hair in front of her face and letting it spring back.

She was not scared of spending the night alone in the woods—she had camped by herself, made her own shelters, even hunted and foraged, since she was eleven or twelve—but now she was in no position to enjoy the wild canyon.

If I climb down near here, I'll be without medical help—besides, it won't keep me safe from Yute—he might bike up the flume hunting for me. I'd still have to make it out of these woods, and I don't know how long my strength will hold up.

If I stay on the flume, it'll take me straight to the river, but Yute might be there, waiting in ambush.

The shadows of the canyon deepened and Venus rose over the dense green canopy of the surrounding slopes. Over the white noise of the waterfall a screech owl called to her left, answered by a second owl, behind her, and another, in front.

Okay. Stay on the flume. Get to the river. Outsmart Yute—somehow.

She looked up the flume at the canyon's vertical rock wall. No way she could climb down that, ford the rapids, and climb the far cliff, to get back on the flume. Crossing the gap was her only option.

What if I work some more of these boards loose and place them across the gap as a bridge?

No. Even if I found boards that were long enough, they're too thin to support my weight over that distance without bracing from below.

She hung her head over the side to study the trestle.

I'll have to climb down the braces, cross below the gap, then climb back up the other side.

She tested her wounded left shoulder, gingerly lifting that arm above her head. It felt as if she were using the muscle to grind shards of glass. She knelt and hung from the wall by both arms, then slowly shifted the load to her left arm. Tears sprang to her eyes.

All right, so it's not going to feel like soaking in a bubble bath.

"I can do it," she said.

She stood and grabbed the top of the wall with her right hand and, with a sideways jump, like mounting a horse, swung her right leg up and over the wall; she straddled the board, lying on her belly, then lowered herself over the side, and felt with her toes for the four-inch-by-four-inch girder.

Now she stood on the side of the trestle, two hundred feet above the rapids, panting and blinking at tears. After she'd caught her breath, she shuffled down a diagonal brace, lowering herself to the next level. In this manner—puffing like a woman in labor to push through her pain—she descended twenty-five feet below the flume.

Then she began shuffling sideways, walking her hands above. Twice she found loose braces, and took a longer route down and around. It was twenty minutes before she looked up and saw the gap directly overhead. Sweat ran down her forehead into her eyes and mouth.

She paused to rest, and admitted, finally, that she had an irresistible urge to pee.

"What next?"

No way to wriggle out of skintight biking shorts while balancing on narrow beams in the sky; she spread her legs wide and emptied her bladder; a trickling stream fell far below to the rapids. *At least I don't have to crap.* She giggled at her predicament, then she laughed out loud and her shoulder stung with the shaking of laughter that turned to sobs.

"Time's up," she said, sniffling. *Survive first, feel sorry for yourself later.*

She moved onward, section by section of X-braced box frames. A rotten beam snapped under her feet, and though her shoulder wound seared like lava, she hung on by her arms and scooted, hand-over-hand, to the next footing. As her soles touched down, she allowed herself the luxury of screaming in pain, like a steam whistle.

At last, she stood under the far side of the hole, and hung her head, exhausted. Now the outward-leaning walls of the flume looked impossibly far above.

What the hell was I thinking? How can I climb that?

"Because you have to."

She climbed.

It was night when she reached the top. She grasped the outer edge of the flume, stood on tiptoe, and kicked up with her right leg. Her foot banged the side and bounced off. After three tries she had not straddled the wall.

Do it now, or die—you've got only one kick left in you.

Hissing through her mouth and nose, she stood on tiptoe and kicked up her leg with all her strength. Her right foot just caught the tip of the wall and she hauled herself up by the muscles of her inner thigh. She swung her legs over and flopped down on the floor, too tired for tears of joy or pain.

She rested on her back, dizzy and weak; knowing she needed to press on, but too drained to budge. She strained to hold her eyes open, but they rolled upward and she passed out.

Hooting owls warned of an intruder in their territory. Ember opened her eyes with a start. The quarter moon now floated high above in a milk of stars.

She jumped up. A mild breeze wafted toward her from where the flume disappeared into the dark woods ahead. She tilted her head slightly and sniffed the air, nostrils flaring.

Yute's cologne, mixed with sweat and gunpowder. He was close, coming her way. He must have made it to the river and then headed up the flume when she didn't show up.

Ember crouched low. She couldn't see or hear him. She threw a leg over the wall and lowered herself over the side, suppressing a groan as the movement wrenched her stiff, blood-crusted shoulder. Within seconds she felt the vibration of someone coming up the flume.

If he spotted me, I'm frozen here, like a deer in his headlights. She glanced down at the rocks. *I swear I'll let go, I'll just let go.*

She closed her eyes and held her breath, listening to his approaching footsteps—he was jogging.

He passed by.

She breathed again. He headed toward the hole—if only he would stumble and fall through.

"Oh, no! Oh, no!" Yute screamed, and she knew he had found the hole and the ramp. A flashlight beam poked down to the wreckage.

"Ember!" he called below. "Ember, are you alive? Can you hear me? Where are you? I don't see you! Hold on, I'm coming, I've got my medical kit—please—hold on!"

His footsteps raced down the flume toward her, then abruptly stopped, almost directly above.

Does he hear me? She breathed softly through her open mouth, making no sound.

Yute clambered over the far wall of the flume. There was nothing she could do but keep as still as a wooden brace. He appeared on the other side, nearly opposite her and only a dozen feet away, climbing down quickly, and she could easily see his salt-and-pepper hair in the moonlight. The flashlight dangled from his belt loop and danced wildly, whipping a swath of light across her body. All he had to do was look over and spy her, and it would be finished. But he continued to look down as he descended and in five minutes he was at the bottom.

"Em-ber!"

He swept the flashlight beam in slow arcs near the twisted bike.

"Em-ber! I don't have a gun! Please. It was an accident. I'll let you go, I promise."

Ember eyed the overhanging wall and knew she didn't have the reserve to pull herself over it again.

"Please, Ember. I was wrong. I'm only here to help you."

She shuffled sideways, then came to a plank cat-walk that ran along the underside of the flume all the way to the cliff. She stepped onto it and walked in a crouch.

At the cliff she wedged herself between the flume and the granite face and managed to scurry up and slip over the top of the wall. Her weak shoulder gave way and she landed off-balance with a thud; pain bells clanged in her brain, but she stifled her outcry with a hand clapped over her mouth.

The flashlight beam swung up from below and played over the flume where she hid, cursing her luck.

"Ember!" Yute shouted. "Is that you? Are you up there?"

She sat up, untied a shoe, and tugged it off. Then she crouched facing up the flume, with her arm cocked, and waited for the beam of the flashlight to slide away. She quickly stood and hurled the stiff-soled shoe toward the far side of the rapids. It rattled on the rocks.

The light dived to the canyon again, and Yute re-sumed calling for her near the rushing water.

She pulled off her other shoe and ran barefoot

toward the river as fast as she could go. From the north the Drinking Gourd tilted down, pouring out liquid night. She gazed at it and realized her body and soul had never been more thirsty.

37

EMBER AWOKE ON an exam table. A clear fluid dripped into her arm from a bottle on an IV stand. The fabric walls of the small room reached only partway to the ceiling, and a green plastic curtain hung in the door frame. In the busy hallway outside a drunk hollered and cursed; a male voice told him firmly to calm down.

Ember remembered dragging herself from the riverbank up onto Highway 5, leaning against a speed limit sign to flag down a truck. The last thing she could picture was the alarm on the driver's face when he saw her bloody shoulder.

Never got to thank him.

A short, thin man in blue surgeon's pajamas

stepped into the room. His head was bald and knobby; a black Vandyke beard sharpened his narrow face into a point at the chin.

"G'morning," he said. "You're in the trauma center at Harbor View Hospital. My name's Sam, I'm a physician's assistant."

He propped a pillow under her head and tilted the head of the bed upright like a lounge chair. His skin smelled like cigarettes and coffee.

"What time is it?"

He glanced at his watch. "Almost two A.M."

"A truck driver brought me here?"

He shrugged. "They'll know at the front desk."

"I just wanted to thank him."

"They probably took his name and stuff." He held a pair of scissors. "Let me see that shoulder." He cut away the blood-caked sleeve of the jersey.

"What's your name?"

She said the first name that came to mind. "Kim Ocheba."

"Who shot you, Kim?"

"Deer hunter, I think."

"Geez. Those guys are a menace."

He asked a few questions about drug allergies, jotted notes on a chart, and stuck it at the foot of the exam table.

"Back in a flash, Kim." He left the room and returned in a moment with two hypodermic syringes. "This one's for the pain," he said, and injected the contents of one syringe into a port on the IV tube. "And this is to prevent infection." He emptied the second syringe. "Give that a few minutes, then I'll be back. Okay?"

She nodded. The narcotic quickly dulled her senses, blunting the thorny edge of the hurt. Her head sank back with relief and she drifted near sleep, in a soft-focus euphoria. She woke as the physician's assistant wiped a cold alcohol pad on her skin around both sides of the wound.

"What were you doing out in the boondocks, Kim?" He drew an amber liquid into a syringe from a small glass bottle.

"Mountain biking."

"Did you see the guy who shot you?"

"Just a kid, I only caught a glimpse of him."

"Damn, didn't he see afterward you weren't a deer?"

"Maybe he saw what he did and ran."

"Nice guy." He squirted a thin spray from the hypodermic. "All right, Kim, I need to inject a local anesthetic, and it's gonna pinch like hell, but it'll be over real quick, just hang on."

He grasped her shoulder firmly. She winced as the needle stabbed the raw flesh in four spots, front and back. Then the pain cooled to numbness, and she didn't fidget as he briskly scrubbed the wound with Phisohex soap sponges held in tongs. He rinsed the site with hydrogen peroxide followed by saline.

"Ever compete?"

"What?"

"How long you been pumping iron? Ever compete?"

She shook her head.

"Really? You should, I'm telling ya, you'd be a champ."

She snorted. "Too ugly."

"Sheesh. That's not a nice way to talk about yourself. Even I don't go around admitting I'm ugly."

He tossed out a bloody sponge and picked up a fresh one in the tongs. He dipped the sponge in and out of the bullet hole and orange soap and bright red blood ran out, which he sopped up with surgical sponges.

"Exotic is in, Kim. Big time. Why do you think the fashion mags go hunting all over the world for more and more unusual-looking models?"

She frowned. "I'm exotic, all right. . . ."

He rinsed the wound with hydrogen peroxide from a large plastic syringe. He switched to saline and irrigated the bullet hole from both sides. Ember watched, fascinated, as saltwater flushed into the back of her shoulder ran out the front.

"Wound looks real clean," he said, and snapped off the latex gloves. "Gotta run. Believe it or not, we got two other gunshots in here right now, and they're half your age."

He leaned toward an intercom and pressed a button. "Room Six ready, Doc." He turned back to her. "A surgeon will be in shortly to take a look."

"Thanks, Sam," Ember said.

He glanced back as he parted the curtain door. "Stay out of the woods during deer season, eh?"

In a few minutes a woman in a white lab coat over green surgeon's pajamas entered, with X rays in her hand. Silver bell earrings and a silver necklace accentuated her prematurely silver hair, which hung in straight bangs over bright blue eyes and skin so fair that tiny blue veins showed in her forehead as she bent forward to introduce herself. Her name was embroidered above her pocket: Olivia Francis, M.D. She wore no perfume and her skin smelled like warm bread, with balsam shampoo in her hair.

The surgeon checked the IV bag. "Has the pain eased up?"

Ember nodded. "Much better."

The doctor picked up the chart at the foot of the exam table and glanced at it, then stuck the X rays on a light box and peered closely. Finally, she pulled up a rolling steel stool to examine Ember's shoulder.

"If you want this scar to look beautiful, Kim, we'll need to call in a cosmetic surgeon."

"I don't need it to look beautiful."

The surgeon nodded and her silver bells tinkled. "I'll do a good job. I'm just going to trim away this little bit of ragged skin." She snipped around the rim of the exit wound with a curved pair of shiny scissors.

To Ember the little treatment room reeked of dried pee and sweat and blood.

"Sorry . . ." she said.

"For what?" The doctor paused and met her eyes.

"For the way I smell."

The doctor made a little hiss and went back to her work. "Doesn't bother me. That you're a young woman with a bullet wound—that bothers me a lot."

"It was a hunting accident."

"So I hear."

Although they were a deeper shade of blue, the doctor's eyes reminded Ember of her old friend Dr.

Jackson, the speech therapist. *Kindness.* That was it. Her eyes were backlit with mercy.

"Dr. Francis, anyone ever call you Saint Francis?"

"Ha. If you knew me, you'd know I'm no saint. Ask my kids when they get grounded."

"If people like you aren't saints, there's no hope for the rest of us."

"Hmm?"

"Nuthin'." Ember closed her eyes, feeling groggy.

"Kim is my daughter's name," the doctor said as she wrapped a sterile gauze bandage around the shoulder and under the arm. "She's a couple years younger than you."

Ember nodded sleepily. She liked the doctor's touch, gentle and confident.

"Who did this to you, really, Kim?"

"Some kid was hunting—"

"Boyfriend?"

"No, a kid was hunting—"

"Drug deal?"

"I've never done drugs, till just now," she said. "My head feels like a fog is rolling in."

"Did a trick do this to you?"

"A trick?"

"A customer. Did a customer shoot you?"

Ember opened her eyes. "You think I'm a prostitute?"

"I think you're a runaway who got herself into a bad jam. Do you want to press charges?"

Ember shook her head.

"I'll help you fill out the paperwork."

"No, he can't hurt me now," Ember said. "I'll be

all right. I just . . . I want to be left alone." She closed her eyes again.

The doctor sighed. "Have it your way, but I'd sure hate to see you back in here in a few weeks with a tag on your toe."

"No, I'm safe. He doesn't know where I am."

The doctor secured the bandage with two butterfly clips. "You're very lucky—if a gunshot victim can be called lucky. The bullet passed through the muscle and missed everything vital. I left the wound open so it will drain properly. It will heal from the inside out, should close up in three or four weeks."

She patted Ember's cheek. "Kim, look here."

Ember opened her eyes. The doctor held up a fat white tube of medicine.

"Antibiotic cream. Smear on a big dab each time you change the bandages." She held up a large box of bandages. "Change the dressing twice a day. I'm going to write you a prescription for painkillers. Go easy on them, okay?"

"Okay."

"Don't sell them to anybody, okay?"

Ember nodded, unable to keep her eyes open.

The doctor stepped toward the door and switched off the light.

"You can stay in here and sleep for a few hours. My shift's over at seven, I'll give you a ride to the homeless shelter. You going to be all right?"

Ember tried to say, *Yes, thank you so much*, but the words came out slurred as the fog rolled over her, carrying the fishy smell of low tide. She sighed once and deeply slept.

A powdery snowfall. Ember sniffed the cold, dense air and smelled greasy smoke—fur and flesh and animal fat burning. Her stomach churned. She sensed that she stood near the cave of blue ice, but everything looked wrong. Cranes, bulldozers, heavy equipment, crowded near a square pit with vertical white walls. A diesel electric generator chug-chug-chugged nearby. Then she became oriented and realized she was standing atop a glacier, several hundred feet above the cave.

Barefoot, she wore only her biking shorts and jersey. Her toes were numb from the cold. Goose bumps made her body hair bush out like blond fur. A frost mustache coated her upper lip and with each white puff of breath new ice crystals formed, making tiny tinkling sounds.

An elevator like a steel mesh cage glided upward on a cable and braked to a stop at a wooden platform. Two men stepped out. Each wore insulated boots and a puffy orange jumpsuit; fur-lined hoods framed round dark faces with high cheekbones and almond eyes. Muffled echoes of voices and the noise of machinery rose from below. Someone barked orders.

What were they doing here?

Her chest tightened as she moved toward the deep shaft and stepped aboard the elevator. The steel mesh car sank past the frozen walls. A metallic sound, like steel striking rock, became steadily louder.

Chink, chink, chink, chink.

She entered the cave. The ceiling and walls were rigged with electric worklights in metal cages. She came to the cavern where the animals were penned. A large musk ox lay on its side, its mouth sagging open, and workmen in orange jumpsuits hammered and chiseled at its jawbone, breaking the teeth loose. She floated closer, a grimace on her face, and saw that the teeth were solid gold, like nuggets. The workers tossed them into a plastic bucket filled nearly to the brim.

A two-stroke engine whined loudly and the sound spun her around. A workman with a chain saw cut through the curving tusk of a huge woolly mammoth. The other tusk rested on the floor, gleaming gold in the incandescent light.

Next she hovered above a crew in the cavern where her people had rested for thousands of years. Chink, chink. *Chisels chopped the golden teeth out of the jaws of men and women and children.*

"Stop!" she screamed. "You can't do that!"

Gold teeth plunked into plastic buckets. Bodies were dragged away on sleds. She followed. Two workmen grabbed a small body by the arms and legs and heaved it onto the peak of a burning pile of people and animals. The body bounced and rolled partway down and its head flopped to face her. A blond boy, green eyes, his mouth a ragged wreck.

Workers splashed on more kerosene. Yellow-orange flames hissed and sizzled. A fat black worm of smoke ate its way upward into the dead sky. Falling snowflakes bounced and danced in the rising column of heat. Wind moaned down the throat of the shaft.

Ember woke in a panic and screamed.

A nurse slid around the corner, punched past the

curtain into the room, and flipped on the light. Dr. Francis was right behind.

"What is it?" Dr. Francis said.

Ember shook her head. She held her breath, afraid the air would stink like burning flesh.

Dr. Francis sat down on the exam table next to her and put her arms around her.

"Kim, take a deep breath."

The air filled her lungs, bearing the faint aroma of warm bread. She pressed her face against the doctor's shoulder and inhaled deeply with her eyes closed.

"Nightmare?"

Ember nodded. Her skin felt clammy. A terrible urgency seized her.

Hurry.

There was something she was supposed to do.

Hurry.

She had no idea of the nature of the crisis—only that it was as central to her life as her pumping heart.

38

THE SHOWER STEAMED and Ember scrubbed with peppermint-oil soap and shampooed her hair twice. The wet heat felt good on her injured shoulder and she peeled off the bandage and let the water splash on the reddened, puckered skin of the bullet hole; wincing and dancing in the spray.

Wrapped in a towel, she stepped out of the fogged-up shower room into the women's dorm of the homeless shelter and fished through three cardboard boxes of donated clothes, coming up with a pair of women's black denim jeans, a red T-shirt, and a men's blue denim work-shirt. In a fourth box she found a pair of men's steel-toed workboots wide enough for her feet. She sat on the edge of a lower bunk bed and applied the antibiotic ointment and a fresh bandage, then eased her left arm into the shirts and tugged on the jeans. The well-worn clothes fit comfortably.

At the building's front door she passed beneath a sign: GREATER SEATTLE COUNCIL OF CHURCHES HOMELESS SHELTER. Outside, a Christmas tree stood on the small front lawn. The grass was rubbed bare along footpaths where people cut corners from the parking lot to the front door. Across the street a dingy bar squeezed shoulder to shoulder between two run-down warehouses. She smelled gas fumes and burnt oil and heard from several directions the swish and gush of expressway traffic.

A young couple ambled by, hand in hand. The woman wore a gold chain earring that pierced her earlobe and hung slack across her cheek, ending in a stud that pierced her nose. Her boyfriend had six or eight loops climbing the outside of his ear, and a small gold cylinder stuck through the base of his nostrils.

People go to extremes to be different, Ember thought. *But they want to be different as a group. No one really wants to be one of a kind, to stand out all alone.*

She walked to the sidewalk and stopped, not knowing where to go, what to do. For the past few days the need to escape from Yute had energized and focused her body and mind. Now the crisis was over, the adrenaline gone, and she felt depressed and scattered. She stared at the Christmas-tree lights until they turned into blobs of pastel colors and swam in her vision.

The nightmare at the hospital deepened an emotional pressure that had built in her from kindergarten age, when the dreams began. Each episode brought the same insistence to do something, yet no clue to what she was supposed to do. Now the need for action clanged in her like a fire alarm. She could not ignore the urgency, but she felt as blind as ever to what was required of her. She shuddered, resisting the impulse to run and run.

Run to where?

Like a compass arrow she turned her body to the north, and strolled up the sidewalk. She thought of what Yute told her about the discovery of her mother in the Kantishna Hills near Denali National Park. The blue ice cave must be nearby, the golden people still entombed. But what could she accomplish there that would make any difference?

She strode faster. Just walking northward made her feel a little better. She intuited that if she made it to the Kantishna Hills, she would somehow be guided to act.

I have to return to my native place. That's where I'll learn the meaning of my dreams, and know what to do.

From her jean's pocket she pulled out a wad of eight bills. One hundred and sixty dollars. Might be enough for a one-way bus ticket to Fairbanks; she could hitchhike from there.

I can tell the Indians at Swift Fork Village that I'm Quanoot. If they're like the Indians I know, they'll welcome me to stay with them a few days, even if I'm broke.

"But it would be better to have more money," she said aloud.

Across the way about fifty street people stood in a line in front of a drab green building. At first Ember thought it was a soup kitchen for the homeless. Then she saw the sign over the doorway, PLASCO PLASMA COLLECTION

UNIT NO. 4, and in smaller letters below: DONORS WANTED: INSTANT CASH FOR PLASMA.

She took a spot at the end of the line near a thin man with scraggly gray hair and deeply etched wrinkles around his mouth and eyes. He wore a heavy V-neck sweater over a T-shirt. The skin at his throat showed tattoos disappearing under the T-shirt collar; dark ink patches on his knuckles blotted out earlier tattoos.

"How much do they pay?" she asked.

"Forty bucks your first time, thirty a pop after that," he said with a heavy southern accent. His breath reeked of soured wine.

"How often—"

"Every three weeks, but most of us sneak back once a week or so. They hardly ever check—they want the stuff in your veins. But you better get here earlier from now on. I slept late, and now look at this line. We'll be out here for hours."

"Is there an interstate bus station near here?"

"Greyhound." He pointed up the street with his chin. "Five or six blocks."

A crescendo of cymbals, drums, and chanting rolled up the sidewalk, echoing off the warehouses. Ember turned to see an approaching group of men, women, and children dressed in orange robes or pajamas, singing loudly in a foreign language. They danced and twirled, faces upturned and arms raised to the overcast sky. Some of the people waiting in line yelled taunts at the celebrators, who danced on by, oblivious to the mockery.

Ember couldn't help but smile, amazed to see people in costumes, singing, drumming, and dancing in the street; it made her think of the Salmon Moon festival on

Whaler Bay. For a crazy instant she felt like joining them, shouting and spinning, as the drums and cymbals and songs faded into the concrete and asphalt.

"Never seen Krishnas before?" the man said.

She shook her head. "Looks like fun. What are they singing?"

"Krishna, Krishna—he's a blue-skinned god, plays a flute."

"What?"

"I kid you not. Where you from?"

"Around."

"Uh-huh. Well, let me tell you, those wackos serve the best free meals in town. You got a choice: Salvation Army—listening to a Bible sermon, then eating Beanee Weenees; or the Krishna Temple—listening to a Krishna rap, then eating hot, fancy vegetarian food, much as you want. For my money—my lack of money—I eat at the Hairy Krishnas every night. Just up the street on the right."

"Thanks for the tip," Ember said

It was afternoon, and Ember's shoulder was throbbing, before it was her turn to go inside. The interior walls were the same green cinder block as the exterior. The place stank like dirty feet. An obese woman in a nurse's white pantsuit sat Ember down in a blue vinyl lounge chair patched with duct tape.

The woman poked Ember's right index finger and squeezed several bright red drops of blood into a glass pipette. The bag of skin under the woman's chin wobbled as she worked, and Ember thought of a pelican gulping a fish.

After a moment the nurse returned with a short,

very dark man in a white lab coat, both of them frowning. Without saying a word, he poked another of Ember's fingers and left with the woman.

Ember waited, fidgeting on the lounge chair. During the day the pressure to head north had grown so compelling that she had needed to pace near her spot in line to control her agitation. She felt the way a swan must feel when the sun brings longer, warmer days after the winter solstice.

Fly north. Fly home.

In ten minutes they were back.

"You are Kim Ocheba?" the man said, in a thick East Indian accent.

"Yes."

"Kim, what is your blood type?"

"Don't know, that's what I checked on the form."

"No one's ever made any remarks about your blood type before?"

"Who are you?" Ember asked.

"Dr. Dhanesh, the owner," he said, extending his hand. His skin was cool, his handshake limp. "Twenty-eight years in this business, I've never seen blood like yours. Doesn't fit any known blood type. It's quite bizarre."

Ember stood to go.

"Wait. I'd like to study your blood. This could be very profitable."

"I don't want to be studied," she said, moving toward the door.

"Just wait." He crossed in front of her and held up his palms. "There might be much money in it—for you too."

"No, thanks." She sidestepped to slip around him.

He grabbed her wrist. "One pint, I'll pay you two hundred dollars."

Ember lifted and twisted her wrist outward, popping his grip loose, then dived out the door. She hurried down the sidewalk in the direction of the Greyhound bus station.

My blood doesn't fit any categories, any more than I do. I don't belong here. I'm going back to the tundra even if I have to hitchhike.

She approached a windowless warehouse bar with a small neon sign over the door. The Cave. A gaudy mural, big as a billboard, covered the aluminum siding: an apelike caveman gripped a club and dragged a topless woman by her hair toward a cavern; the captive woman grinned and winked. A repeating motif of bison and horses, made to resemble cave paintings, framed the mural.

Ember winced. *This is just a little taste of how people view the world I came from. What will everyone say about me when the whole planet learns I exist? What will I do with my life then? Join a circus freak show?*

She stopped and stared at the caveman in the mural: a thick mop of hair hung over his low forehead and his woolly eyebrows merged across a bulging browline. Her fingers touched her own eyebrows and browline.

SEE EMBER, THE LIVING CAVEWOMAN—**NOT FULLY HUMAN!**

By a muscular effort she had kept her spirits up, but now her strength of will collapsed. Everything good in her life seemed to have been sucked away on a dark undertow.

She sank to the sidewalk, weak and dizzy. The mural blurred and then resolved itself into a new scene, moving now, like a cinema on a big screen: workers in hooded orange jumpsuits milled about an icy plateau near a deep vertical shaft; black smoke rose into cold, still air, heavy with the stench of burning skin and fur and fat.

She cried out and clamped her eyes shut. When she peeked, the warehouse wall was a painted mural again. The neon sign—THE CAVE—glowed and vibrated in the dusk, and she sighed with relief.

Then a sense of great danger shot through her nerves, and she leapt up in a fighting stance. Her eyes darted up and down the sidewalk. No one there. She held her breath and listened. Strands of chanting and beating drums drifted from the Hare Krishna Temple on the next block.

It took her a moment to realize the danger was not to herself; it was tied to her vision. The calling to prevent a great tragedy became a physical force in her. Her skin grew hot, and she sprinted all the way to the bus station.

39

THE DRIZZLE STOPPED and dusk turned the scudding clouds over Deer Park into long, pale wisps. Mike and Kaigani cruised in his Jeep Wrangler alongside the iron fence of the old Washington State Indian School. Twelve-foot-tall lance-shaped black posts met at arched wrought-iron gates.

Mike frowned. "Damn," he said. "Might as well have a moat."

Kaigani read his lips and nodded, making the hand sign for *bad luck*.

"Time to rethink our game plan." He pulled the Jeep to the curb and parked near the gates with the metal signs PRIVATE, KEEP OUT. "We'll have to get ourselves inside his office on some ruse," he said, "rather than try to break in."

Kaigani's eyes scanned the campus. White clapboard buildings—the former dorms?—clustered around a two-story redbrick classroom building on the crest of a grassy hill. There were several lights shining from windows of the former school building, and as she watched, the bulbs of a dozen scattered light-poles flickered, then shone brightly. Automatic switch? Or a night watchman in one of the buildings up there? Most likely the brick building held Dr. Nahadeh's office, but who knows. And how would they locate the notes or documents they needed in order to learn about Ember's origins?

"Good grief, I feel like a spy," she said aloud.

"Yeah, amateur spy," Mike said. "Wish we knew what we were doing."

She thought about what they had learned from talking to the workers at the building in Seattle where Dr. Nahadeh kept his business office.

"What keeps bothering me," Kaignai said, "is that she left her bike downtown. Where would she go without her bike? How would she get there?"

"That's if the parking garage guy knew what he was talking about."

"I think he did. He described her bike—"

"Except it's not white," he said, "and it's not there anymore."

"Those metallic flakes look kind of white . . . he said it was there until a couple days ago."

"If it was her bike, I'm hoping Ember came back and got it," Mike said, "and she's safe, riding around somewhere." He glanced in the rearview mirror as a police car swished by on the wet asphalt street. "But I doubt it. The receptionist saw her leave with Nahadeh Tuesday morning. I think she's still with him."

Kaigani shuddered. "I get a feeling . . . a scary feeling. . . . Ember has been here, and she's in trouble, Mike."

Mike looked at her and his brow furrowed. Suddenly he banged the steering wheel with his palm. "I blew it," he said. "I was so damn sure she was bioengineered. That really hurt her. I shouldn't have been so smug."

Kaigani took his hand. "Yeah, well, I didn't help matters by getting jealous of you two."

"That was my fault too," he said, and covered her hand with his. "Let's just say I was confused for a while. But that's over. I realize that Ember belongs to something way beyond me. Beyond you and me. She belongs to her destiny." He squeezed her hand. "And you, beautiful"—he smiled and leaned toward her—"I've been half intoxicated by you since the day I saw you on the trail. You don't need to be jealous of anyone ever again. I promise you that, Kaigani."

Kaigani returned his smile warmly, and a subtle knot melted away under her breastbone. The hurt was gone. She held his gaze till his lips were a few inches from hers and their eyes softly closed and they rested their souls in a long kiss. He cradled her face tenderly in his strong hands while their lips brushed and pressed together; then their mouths opened and their tongues met. An image came to her of dolphin lovers swimming together in a warm sea. The embrace sent a surge of feeling deep into her heart and on down through her belly, until the force came to its home between her thighs so tangibly that it seemed that Mike had reached down and touched her there.

Mike pulled back and looked at her with his large hazel eyes, his face grown softer than she had ever seen it.

"Wow," he said, and took a deep breath. "You—you're amazing." He smiled. "We better hold back—"

"I know," she said, and put her hand over her thumping heart. "I know." She smiled and took his hand again.

Mike sat up straight. "For now, I think, the best way to help Ember is to sit right here and watch and wait for an opportunity to show itself." He glanced at his diving watch. "Almost six. If there's a security guard up there, there might be a shift change coming up, maybe we could talk our way inside."

They sat in the cloth bucket seats as darkness engulfed the Jeep and sprinkles of rain began to patter the canvas top and the windshield. Since their drawn-out kiss Mike and Kaigani had not stopped holding hands.

"You never finished telling me what you turned up on the Internet," she said.

"Oh. Great stuff. Not only did the names and details from two centuries ago check out, but then I found a British report from colonial India of a yogi who was more than two hundred years old. So I think, if some dude managed to live that long in India, why not Old Man, right here?"

"Old Man is real?" She marveled at the

thought, remembering tales about the shaman from her girlhood.

"I'm beginning to believe it. He really got to me, really did."

"And the O-kwo-ke?"

"Well the part that boggled me was this: How could Ember remember something that took place before she was born? So I browsed the latest research papers on the brain and consciousness and memory, and believe me, it's getting so you need a program to tell the neuroscientists from the mystics."

He shifted in his seat and faced her more squarely, and used hand signs along with his speech. A melon-colored streetlight cast shadows below the level of the dashboard, but it lit the elongated features of Mike's face, and she could clearly read his lips.

"Scientists have tried for years to pin down memory somewhere in the brain," he said. "Where, exactly, is this capacity to learn—to store and recall data—located? They never did find it, they finally gave up. Turns out, memory is not localized, it's distributed throughout the brain. You can't draw a circle around it, it's diffuse.

"Say a part of your brain gets injured; it may make your memory hazy in general, but it won't cause specific memory gaps—you won't forget half your friends, or half of a novel you read. You follow me?"

"I think so," she said. "Go on."

"Well, that led to the theory that memory is holographic in nature. You know about holograms?"

"Not really."

"See, every piece of a holographic film image contains all the information of the whole. If you cut in half a holographic film of a beachball, and beam a laser through the half, you still get a three-dimensional image of the whole beachball. You can even cut the half-film into fragments, shine a laser through any of them, and you'll see the whole beachball. As the pieces get smaller, no gaps in the image appear, instead, the *whole* image fades away."

Kaigani repeated part of what he had said to make sure she understood.

"Right," Mike said, nodding. "That's right."

"And they're saying memory works like that," Kaigani said.

"Exactly," he said. "Then you have the fact that people can remember things they experienced while in coma, under anesthesia, in the womb—stuff like that. So memory is apparently not based in the brain, but only related to it. The current model is that the brain is a tuning device, like a TV set, and memory storage is outside the brain and body—it's nonphysical, pure information, recorded as a holographic field."

The idea formed a sudden picture in Kaigani's mind and she grew excited. "You know, when Grandpa Ozette was in a coma," she said, "I talked to his spirit. I didn't pretend he was going to sit up and answer me, I knew his brain was dead, but his essence was there. I felt it."

"The receiver was broken beyond repair," Mike said, "but the signal was still present."

"So what you're saying . . . you think that Ember can tune in memories of ancient events?"

"It would explain how her dreams matched Old Man's story," Mike said. "Look, you've heard of Carl Jung, right?"

She nodded. "In high school."

"His theory of racial memory?"

She shook her head. "I'm not sure."

"Jung believed there's a collective unconscious —I just reread some of his work on it—it's a universal memory field, in which all information is pooled in one holographic record. Not that Jung knew about holograms—he died before they were invented—but that's exactly the model he described. He believed we have access to the collective experiences of the human race over the eons."

"I remember," she said, "—my class talked about that, fits right in with Quanoot-cha: We each embody the life journeys of all our ancestors—not just a genetic heritage, a spirit heritage."

"It makes sense," he said. "If each of us is an integral part of one great holo-mind, then we each encode the information of the whole."

She brightened. "And maybe Ember's ability to tap that information is much stronger than for most of us."

"Sure looks that way."

"Oh, Mike, that could explain everything. I wish she'd heard this from you."

He sighed. "Me too—instead of what I told her."

His eyes grew wet and he looked away. His long fingers traced the outline of his auburn mustache and slid down over his bearded jawline, then back to his mustache to repeat the circuit.

"I'm still baffled by her looks," he said, after a time. "Where did she get her skin color? That's what made me think of bioengineering in the first place."

"The people in her visions are golden and muscular," Kaigani said. "She's not one of us, Mike. She's one of them."

"Yeah, but who are they? Where are they?"

She glanced up at the buildings on the knoll. "We've got to find out what Nahadeh knows."

He grabbed her arm. "Hey, look."

A white van backed out of a garage near the largest of the brick buildings.

"Here's our chance," Mike said, and started the Jeep's engine. "Let's go."

The van headed their way.

"Kaigani, tell him—tell him . . . you're the daughter of a woman who used to be a student here at the Indian School, right? And you just want to have a quick look, to see all the things your mom told you about. While he's ogling you and trying to cope with your deafness—you know, talking extra loud and slow—I'll excuse myself to go to the bathroom, see if I can get into the lab, snoop around, find out as much as I can in a few minutes."

The iron gates squeaked as they swung outward on electric motors. Mike drove alongside the van, smiled and waved at the driver. The other driver gestured for Mike to stop, then cranked down his window.

"Who are you?" he said to Mike.

"Did the next shift start?"

"Yeah. Doug's on duty now."

"Great. Brought his thermos." Mike smiled and

held up a polished steel thermos and, without waiting for a response, stepped on the gas and rolled through the open gate. The van stayed where it was for a moment, then drove away.

The gates closed behind.

40

Nika Nahadeh cranked the throttle handle on the snowmobile, gunning it along the hard-packed snow of the mine road. In the beam of the headlights wet snowflakes fell in clumps the size of quarters and the wiper smeared them in watery streaks. A below-freezing wind whistled over the edges of the plastic windshield. Over her National Park Service ranger's uniform she wore a traditional Caiyuh hooded parka of musk-ox hide, sewn with the long, shaggy wool on the inside.

The man who had phoned from the mine said it was an emergency, but gave no details. Maybe someone had found a bear killed by a poacher. These days, Chinese and Korean smugglers were paying big bucks for bear gallbladders, which they dried and ground and pressed into tablets, and sold as a cure-all for everything from impotence to cancer. Earlier this winter two grizzlies had been killed, tracked to their dens where they hibernated and shot through the head. Only local Indian trackers would have had the skill to find the caves and the guts to crawl in after the bears, but she had found no leads to the culprits.

Her father said that if he caught a Caiyuh killing a grizzly, "I'll have to be held back from cutting out *his* gallbladder."

Probably another dead bear. Only about a thousand grizzlies were left in the wild, but as much as she cared about them, she hoped that's what the emergency was about.

A snowshoe hare hopped out of a snowbank into the white roadway, spun, and leapt back the way it had come. She backed off on the throttle. Driving too fast wasn't going to change anything, and if she hit an elk or moose out here . . .

She wiped at her frosty goggles with a fiber-filled nylon mitten. It didn't make sense to get a call in the middle of the night—frozen bears can wait till morning. And a grizzly wouldn't be hibernating anywhere near the mine; the place was noisy and lit up like an airport. The man on the phone had seemed upset, gulping his air, telling her to hurry. "We need you here, now."

Why had he been so vague?

Her stomach ached and her mouth felt dry. Hell, no, it wasn't a dead bear.

Oh, Father, what did you do now?

The snowmobile roared toward the ghost of Swift

Fork Village. The abandoned cabins sat in shadowy silence beside the dark river ice. Only her father and two old women still lived in the village. The rest of the elderly Indians had been removed to a government housing project in Fairbanks. The younger families lived in CANARD dormitories next to the gold mine.

Nika strained to see smoke rising from her father's cabin, but smoke curled only from the cabin of the old sisters. Her heart sank.

Her father was at the mine.

He and his supporters had passionately fought the proposed mining project and managed to delay its start-up for more than a decade. But the day had arrived when a rack of dynamite blasted the first wound in the hills above the tundra. Defeated, the Indians gave up their united drive to preserve their old way of life and began to scramble over each other, trying to grab a foothold on the new ground, to keep from sinking.

"We were like a dog team that fell through the ice," a friend of hers confessed, zipping up his CANARD jumpsuit to report for work. "We survived, but not as a tribe—we're not Caiyuh no more."

Her father wouldn't give up. CANARD had been digging gold for six years now, and he was still bent on shutting down the mine. Last winter he'd been nabbed for industrial sabotage: pouring sugar into the fuel tanks of diesel-powered electric generators.

"You say I've turned bitter," he told her, late one night in the cabin where she and Yute had been born and raised. "But anger is the only way I can live with my sorrow at what they've stolen." Tears made his black eyes shine in the kerosene lantern glow. "Your children, Nika, will never hunt in the foothills as we did, as our ancestors did. And will they learn the skills for living in the natural world? What about our beautiful songs? Our language? The wonderful stories? Take a look at the generation around you, daughter, at the little ones growing up in the dormitories. All of our culture is falling away—sucked down that mine shaft." He pounded his chest with a big, callused hand. "No, I must be true to my anger. Anger is my ally. If I didn't have it to shield me, my grief would kill me."

When she visited him last, a week ago, he said, "Sometimes it's better to fight a hopeless battle than to lie down and be trampled."

Those words haunted her now. That same visit he seemed to make a point of telling her how much he loved her; he said it more than once, with much sweetness in his round, wrinkled face. He gave her heirlooms that had been in the family for generations; a hunting knife that had belonged to his grandfather, his mother's wedding robe. He even gave her his bow, and many arrows.

She cursed herself. *Am I so blind? Or did I deny everything before my eyes? Why didn't I read the signs?*

The snowmobile slid across dense-packed snow covering the gravel roadway that crossed the tundra. Trucks rumbled along this route during the day, carrying food and equipment to the mining settlement; armored trucks brought back gold, processed from ore.

A low ceiling of clouds dumped a heavy snowfall; now the flakes clumped as big as half-dollars. About fifteen miles from the mine she stopped to scrape the windshield. A silvery-blue "dawn" glowed in the foothills from the banks of mercury-vapor lamps atop the mine's light towers.

A half hour later Nika arrived at a sliding gate in a tall chain-link fence. A metal sign in the shape of a flying duck announced:

KANTISHNA HILLS MINE
Central Alaska Native American Resource Developers, Inc.
(CANARD)
A Division of Matsuyo, International
WARNING: PRIVATE—NO TRESPASSING—ENFORCED BY
ARMED PATROLS
Visitors MUST Register with Guard Before Entering Gate.

Two guards in neon-orange jumpsuits dashed out of a heated aluminum hut. Each wore an automatic weapon slung over his shoulder. One guard hurriedly checked her ID, and signaled the other, who switched on the motorized gate. It rolled open slowly on small rubber tires. They waved her through.

Once inside, two more guards and a third man in a bright blue jumpsuit met her and quickly escorted her from the snowmobile to a Sno-Cat personnel carrier. A driver was seated, the engine was running, and the caterpillar treads lurched forward before the door was closed. It wasn't until the man in the blue suit pulled back his hood that she recognized him: Chief Willy.

"Ms. Nahadeh, uh, I've got terrible news. . . ."

She gulped. "My father?"

"He was trespassing again, and I'm afraid this time there's been—"

"Is he alive?"

"Just barely. He's been shot."

Her heart caught.

"Our doctor and paramedics are with him, but . . . well, quite honestly, they don't expect him to make it. I'm deeply sorry."

"What about your helicopter, the hospital in Fairbanks?"

"Can't fly in this weather. Besides, they can't move him, he has a spinal injury. They've managed to build a windbreak around him."

The transport slowed and she pressed her face to the Plexiglas window, staring at a dome-shaped white nylon canopy with a large red cross on its side. Before the vehicle stopped she flung the door open and leapt out. She skidded and fell on all fours and scrambled to her feet, sprinting. She pushed a huddle of orange-suited workers out of the way to get inside the shelter.

The tentlike space had no floor. A ceramic heater warmed the air, trapping an ice fog under the canopy.

Her father was flat on his back on the snow, with several arctic sleeping bags zipped open and draped over his body. His eyes were closed and his body jerked and shook in rippling spasms. Two holes in his upper chest made sucking, gurgling noises. A tube stuck out from a slot in his throat and a paramedic pumped an oxygen bag rhythmically, inflating his lungs.

Nika gasped.

A man wearing a stethoscope turned to her. "You the daughter?"

She nodded, kneeling beside her father.

"He's been holding on for you for nearly two hours. It's amazing, he's a very, very strong man."

She brushed the strands of gray hair from his forehead with her fingertips, and spoke near his ear.

"Father?"

She lifted a heavy limp hand and held it in her lap, squeezing.

"I'm with you, Father."

Immediately, his body relaxed and the shaking stopped.

His eyelids fluttered and opened. She leaned over him and met his gaze, saw the familiar tenderness, the light. She drank it in.

"I love you, Father," she whispered hoarsely. "I'm grateful I'm your daughter—so grateful! Thank you."

He offered the smallest hint of a smile. His big hand gave a faint squeeze. Then his gaze lost all focus. From the moment his body had relaxed, he did not take another breath.

She jumped up. "Take down the canopy, hurry!" she shouted.

The medical team only stared at her, blankly.

The doctor stepped forward and put his arm around her shoulders to comfort her. She shrugged off his arm, dove to the outer edge of the rod-braced dome, and yanked up one side. Stakes popped loose. Wind and snow gusted in.

"What the hell are you doing?" the doctor shouted.

"My father is Caiyuh—he wants to die in the open."

"What?"

She dodged two men and dashed to the other side of the canopy.

"Stop!" someone yelled.

She yanked up the stakes. The wind caught the dome like a parachute and it rolled and bounced away across the field of snow. Several workers chased behind.

Nika was only dimly aware of the commotion and cursing around her. She knelt beside her father as clumped flakes of snow spattered his face, some of them falling into his open eyes.

"See? You're outside, Father." Teardrops rolled off her chin. "No ceiling, no walls—open to the Earth and Sky."

She sang the Caiyuh song of farewell. It was meant to be sung by several voices, in which one singer asks about the loved one and the other singers answer with stories of the person's life. She sang all the parts, taking care to honor the bad memories along with the good.

"From the peak of Denali, high above the eagle's path," Nika sang in her guttural tongue and slapped her thighs like a drum, "Mother Spirit sees in all directions, Her eyes as bright as sun on snow. Look there! She finds Her son, John Nahadeh, 'Magic River,' and She remembers well his life and words and deeds. Now She rolls down Her thunder-voice as witness: 'Here I see the greatest caribou hunter, the bravest heart, the best father under the sky.' Now She sends down Her Spirit like a willow basket and lifts him up and carries him home to sleep inside Her, tucked under Her beating heart-drum, until he is born again.

"Farewell, John Magic River . . ." Nika now chanted in a whisper, "Father . . . farewell."

When she finished, she saw that the others had gathered in the personnel carrier to keep warm and that a second vehicle had arrived. Then she saw that her tears had frozen where they splashed on her father's face.

Chief Willy climbed out of one Sno-Cat and draped a heavy quilted blanket over her shoulders. His eyelids looked puffy and his black walrus mustache seemed to droop with sadness.

"Where can we take him?" she asked.

"We don't have a morgue," he said. "We can keep the body overnight in an outdoor locker. Tomorrow, we'll make arrangements for one of our vehicles to transport it wherever you like."

She nodded. The Caiyuh, like other arctic tribes, had no tradition for burying their dead; it was too tough to dig through the rock-hard earth in winter. Besides, burying the dead was a waste of food for the wolf tribe in a hungry whited-out world.

A vivid memory came to mind. Once, walking past a scrap metal yard in Fairbanks, she and her father paused to watch a big compactor crush old, rusted cars between its jaws; the metal groaned and snapped, squeezed into cubes. Then a crane with a big electromagnet stacked the cubes onto flatcar trains bound for mills that reprocess scrap into new steel. Her father liked watching. He tied it to their people's vision of eternally recycled lives: old caribou to the wolves, to the wolf droppings, to the soil, to the hawthorne berries, to the young caribou—a self-cleaning engine that runs for millions of years on earth, rain, wind, and sun.

Tomorrow, she would carry her father's body on the snowmobile to one of his favorite spots, in the hills above the lake of swans. There she would leave him—after calling the wolves to feast on their old friend.

Chief Willy turned and signaled to the second Sno-Cat. Three men jumped out and wrapped her father's body in a sheet of clear plastic and carried it to the transport. Frozen puddles of blood blotched the snow where his body had sprawled.

"Come, get in," Chief Willy said. "It's way below zero."

She only stared numbly at the dent left in the snow. Half her world had broken off and dropped into black space. The crater left behind seemed bigger than her life could fill.

Chief Willy gently turned her toward the transport. As she turned to go, she saw for the first time that her father had scrawled a pattern in the snow with a bloody finger: a shape like the letter *V*, made of red dots.

"It's over," Chief Willy said. He placed his arm around her shoulders and tugged lightly. She walked with him to the Sno-Cat.

"I've arranged for you to use a bedroom in the women's dorm tonight," he said. "I apologize, but we don't have a guest room vacant."

She nodded.

Chief Willy and her father were friends years ago. Even though they fought bitterly over the mine project, her father respected what Chief Willy was trying to do for his tribe. "I won't badmouth him," he had said. "He's a good man—even though he thinks sinking a shaft to hell will buy his people a piece of heaven."

She rested her head on Chief Willy's shoulder, for no other reason than that he had once been her father's friend. He squeezed her hand and sighed.

She would need to learn the details of what had happened, but not now, she wasn't ready to hear them. Her father had been arrested for trespassing three or four times, slapped with restraining orders, and convicted of wrecking mine equipment. Chief Willy had warned him of the danger of sneaking around the heavily guarded property, and she also had pleaded with him to be sensible. Sabotaging the most productive gold mine in history—what had he expected them to do? But he was driven by his struggle to outrun his grief.

Still, why did they need to shoot him? He was in an open field, nowhere near the mine shaft or any equipment. She was no expert on bullet wounds, but it looked as if he'd been shot in the back. Gunned down for trespassing? Beneath her pain, rage kindled in the pit of her belly.

"Ms. Nahadeh," Chief Willy began, barely loud enough to be heard above the engine's rumble and the whine and crunch of the treads on snow. "May I call you Nika?"

"My father was your friend," she said softly.

"I remember when we were young, our long talks into the night. We both wanted what was best for our tribes. He stood for the Old Ways, I believed in adapting to the new."

"Guess you won."

"Nika, it's important that we lay this trouble to rest here, tonight, and not allow this incident to become a greater tragedy than it already is."

She raised her head. "What do you mean?"

"Your father, he was always sort of a hero, even to me. Larger than life. I just don't want to see his death turned into a martyrdom for a cause that's hopeless."

She pulled her hand away from his. "I wouldn't worry—no one else seems to give a damn."

"More than a thousand Indians are employed here, and several hundred of them are Caiyuh—"

"And millions of fish are being poisoned from the acid runoff. Have you seen Moose Creek? The water has an orange tint. And if there are any fish left in Lake Kantishna . . ."

"I feel real bad about that. At the end of Phase Three, CANARD will invest millions to restore those habitats."

"You can't restore what's dead. These hills were a breeding ground for elk and moose and caribou. Now that all your blasting has scared them away, you think they'll just wander back someday?"

"Talk to the workers, see how they feel about the mine. A decade ago they were all well below the poverty level—"

"And now they've got all the happiness money can buy. Who needs trout or caribou—or a culture?"

"Nika, I'm very sorry about your father, my old friend. But it's over . . . it's over."

She badly wanted to sleep, to blank out everything for a while. She laid her head back on the seat until the Sno-Cat came to a stop in front of the women's dorm. Chief Willy walked her to the elevator and to her room on the third floor.

Once inside, she peeled off her parka and boots and sank into the bunk, still wearing her ranger uniform.

Lucid images played on the inside of her eyelids. The best father under the sky was dead.

She would phone Yute in the morning. Thinking of her brother brought on a familiar mixture of love and regret. How much stronger those feelings must have been for her father; the sadness pooled in his eyes whenever they spoke of Yute.

Nika was too exhausted for more tears, but she could not sleep. She opened her eyes and stared at the plaster swirls on the ceiling.

V? What starts with a V? It made no sense. Somehow it had been important enough to scrawl in the snow after being shot.

Maybe it wasn't a *V*. . . . An arrow, pointing? To what? He'd been in the middle of an open field near the vertical shaft. An arrow. But why bother to draw it with dots?

At last, sleep began to wash over her, melting her thoughts. She gratefully closed her eyes.

Then she bolted upright.

It was not the letter *V*, but a V of flying swans.

She tugged out the gold amulet from inside her shirt, whipped the leather cord over her head, and stared at the side with the flying swans. Stick-figure birds scratched into the metal formed an inverted V, pointing north. She flipped the amulet over and looked long and hard at the side that showed a map of the connected caverns, which she had once mistaken for the mouth and nose and eye sockets of a demon's face. She rubbed her fingers over the tiny stick-figure etchings of animals and people.

Her heart skipped a beat. *The caves are here. Prehistoric people and animals, here at the mine.* If word got out, scientists would race here, drooling, like huskies toward a pile of salmon. News teams from around the world would be camping out at CANARD's front gate. The research would interfere with the mine's operation, probably even shut it down for months. CANARD would lose thousands of dollars a day—all told, maybe millions.

Father found out, that's why they killed him.

She got up and threw her parka on, then yanked it off and rummaged through a closet, found an orange jumpsuit, and put it on instead. The name on the ID badge was Yanu Nushagak. The color photo showed a dark, round face like her own. She checked her looks in a full-length mirror and drew the strings on the fur-lined hood tighter to hide her face as much as possible.

A tiny red light blinked on the left thigh of the jumpsuit. She unzipped a small holster and found a suit-heater unit inside. The dead-battery flasher was bound to get her noticed.

She scanned the room and saw a battery pack plugged into a wall outlet, its charge indicator light shining steadily. She exchanged the old pack for the fresh one. Then she stepped into the hall and moved swiftly and quietly down the stairs. A frigid sea swallowed her as she dived into the arctic night.

You were wrong, Chief Willy. It's not over.

41

THE SNOWFALL HAD stopped. The open field sparkled silver-blue in the glare of the mercury-vapor lamps. Nika's boots squeaked and crunched across the frozen crust; the noise seemed loud as gunshots. She glanced around. No guards in sight.

She felt the amulet against her skin, recalled the day her father found it at the grave of the ancient woman, a few miles southwest of where she now walked.

On her father's advice she had taken the amulet to Frances Dream-Singer. The blind woman had shuddered as she ran her trembling old fingers over the etchings. Then Frances told her the legend of the Heart-Talkers and He-Who-Returns, and declared that the amulet had belonged to the people of the story.

"Swans fly south, return north," old Frances had said. "Expect He-Who-Returns to arrive from the south."

"Expect him?"

"You will meet him."

That was nearly twenty years ago. So much had happened since, she had all but forgotten the old woman's prophecy.

Nika came to the fence that surrounded the deep vertical shaft. Still no sign of any guards. The gate leading to the elevator platform was locked. She heard machines operating below, and occasional voices.

"So now what?" she whispered.

A metal sign on the gate showed a diagram of the underground tunnels, and announced: CANARD KANTISHNA HILLS MINE, PHASE TWO, SHAFTS 24–36.

She studied the map. The man-made shafts crisscrossed in straight lines that linked a vast system of natural caverns. In the maze of mine shafts and subterranean cavities, she failed at first to recognize it. But, suddenly, it stood out: the face, the demon mask—at the lower left of the network. A dashed line in red showed a more narrow shaft, number 27, slicing toward the resting place of the First People.

Footsteps behind her. A male voice said, "Put your hands up and turn around, real slow."

She turned around. An automatic rifle pointed at her chest. The guard's helmet lamp lit up the ID badge on Nika's jumpsuit. He peered from it to her face. Nika smiled crookedly, like the woman in the photo. He rested the rifle barrel in the bend of his elbow and passed a handheld computer scanner over the bar code on the badge.

"Yanu Nushagak," he read aloud from the tiny screen. "You on night shift now?"

Nika nodded.

"How long?"

"Couple weeks."

"Why didn't you get your badge recoded?"

"New boyfriend."

"What's that got to do with it?"

"He keeps me too busy."

"Ha." The guard grinned and shouldered his weapon. "What the hell you doing up on the surface, Yanu?"

"Had to go back to my room to get some stuff."

"Room number?"

"Uh . . . C-21."

"Stuff?"

"Forgot to take my medication."

"Why couldn't it wait?"

"Dilantin—for seizures."

He tapped a few keys, studied the screen.

"Says here you got an allergy to penicillin, not a thing about epilepsy."

She frowned. "That's odd. It was only diagnosed a couple months ago, but still, you'd think it would have gotten into the computer by now."

His staring eyes behind the goggles did not blink. "Look, the rule is, never go back to your room unescorted. You know better than that. I'm gonna have to report it, and security is gonna have to tear your room apart looking for pilfered gold."

She read the name on his ID badge. "Sorry, Scott," she said, and smiled Yanu's crooked smile again.

He shone his helmet lamp straight into her eyes and she squinted.

"You're not wearing your contacts tonight?"

"No, I goofed and cooked them to death. I'm waiting on a new pair."

"That's real strange," he said, reaching back and grabbing his rifle, lowering it at her chest. "Yanu doesn't wear contacts. Let me see your whole face."

Nika sighed and pulled the hood off her head. "Damn. Didn't think going for my pills would turn into such a big deal."

"Well . . . I admit you could be her sister," he said, studying the photo again. "But you aren't the woman in this photo. Better come with me."

"They had me on steroids at first, I gained a bunch of weight and then lost it again."

"Uh-huh." He motioned with the rifle barrel. "You walk in front. We're going over to the security station."

"Steroids do funny things to your looks."

"Move it."

She walked in front of him. They trudged through knee-deep drifts, heading toward the security station at the front gate. The image of blood-splotched snow flashed before her eyes. Was this how Father got shot in the back? She slowed to a shuffle.

"I feel really weird," she moaned.

"Keep moving."

"Wait, really, I feel sick, gotta rest."

"It's not far."

"Whoa . . . *ugh* . . ."

Her neck jerked violently and her legs buckled. She sank to her knees, let out a loud grunt, and toppled facedown in the snow without breaking her fall with her hands. Her body convulsed from head to toe, flopping spastically against the white.

"Oh, geez," the guard said, and turned her over with his boot, still pointing his rifle at her. Her eyes rolled up in their sockets and her tongue lolled around her slack mouth. He shouldered his rifle, bent near her face, snapped off her plastic ID badge, and wedged it in her mouth like a tongue depressor.

She turned her body toward him and snap-kicked into his groin with all her strength and he bellowed and staggered forward. She grabbed his rifle and rolled to the left, yanking it off his shoulder and coming up onto her feet in one motion. He knelt in the snow, clutching his groin with both hands, rocking and groaning.

"Toss me your radio," she said.

"It's on my belt," he whined, hoarsely.

"I can see that. Toss it at my feet."

He unhooked the walkie-talkie and tossed it in the snow. Without taking her eyes off him, she stooped and picked it up, then hooked it onto a waist clip.

"Where'd you get the company uniform?" he asked. "You one of the saboteurs?"

"My turn to ask the questions," she said. "What do you know about Shaft Twenty-seven?"

"Nothing. They all look the same to me. Be lost in a heartbeat if I ever went down alone."

"Have you heard rumors, wild stories, about Shaft Twenty-seven?"

He shook his head. "Why do you care about that tunnel?"

"When's the last time Chief Willy personally inspected the mine?"

"Can't remember him ever setting foot in it. Heard he's claustrophobic. He's just sort of a goodwill ambassador around here, keeps the Indians and the whites from each other's throats. He's no miner."

Maybe Chief Willy doesn't know, she thought. *If he never tours the mine, it would be easy to hide the discovery from him. What would he say if he did know? Could an Indian be so cold about destroying native ancestors, even if they weren't his own? Surely his tribe also knows the tales of the First People—those old myths are universal.*

"So who's in charge of the mining operation?"

"Mr. Kaiser. He's the big boss, he *is* CANARD."

"Do you have any special orders about Shaft Twenty-seven?"

He eased himself down onto his butt with a groan and sat facing her. She pointed the rifle at his chest.

"Take it easy." He held up his hands. "Shaft Twenty-seven . . . it's one of the tunnels on the map with a dashed line, right?"

"Right."

"That means there is no Shaft Twenty-seven. It's under construction and it's not finished. All they have now is a scooter hole."

She knitted her eyebrows.

"A narrow tunnel," he said, "just big enough to drive an electric scooter through."

"So they made it back to the cavern?"

"Guess so."

"And you haven't heard anything unusual from anyone? No strange reports?"

He shrugged. "The ghosts?"

"There's talk about ghosts?"

"Only the Indians. I'm from Denver, I believe in Burger King and McDonald's, I'm just up here to earn some bucks for college."

"They found the bodies?"

"*Bodies?* Lady, nobody's found nuthin'. Some of the Indian workers say they feel old spirits hovering around the shafts, that's all. C'mon, what's this all about?"

"When will they finish Shaft Twenty-seven?"

"Dunno. First they gotta do a meltdown."

Her heart pounded faster. "What's that?"

He shifted his position and winced. "Hooo, you just gave blue balls a new meaning. . . ."

"Scott, look, I'm not a saboteur, I'm not here to wreck anything or hurt anybody—"

"Well, you're doing a lousy job not hurting anybody."

"What's a meltdown?"

"The caverns are filled with blue ice. The augers can cut through it, but it's got a nasty habit of shattering in big panes and coming down on people's heads. So first they stick a gas nozzle into the cavern, keep it burning, like heating up an oven. Melts the ice down to the rock. They pump out the water, then they finish carving out the shaft."

Nika's heart lurched in her chest.

"Can you reach Chief Willy on the radio at this hour?"

He nodded. "The head honchos keep radios in their quarters."

She unclipped the radio and set it down, then stepped back. "Get up." she said. "Call Chief Willy. Tell him I want to meet him in private, right away."

"Aw, shit," he said, standing. "There goes my job."

She raised the rifle, nestled the butt of the stock against her shoulder, drew a bead on his breastbone.

"Okay, okay, I'm calling, I'm calling. . . ."

"If you contact anybody other than Chief Willy, you'll be dead before the radio hits the snow."

Her mind raced. *Either Chief Willy doesn't know about the First People in the cavern, or he knows but doesn't care. If he hasn't been told, then he probably had nothing to do with killing my father. He said it was a tragedy—he seemed genuinely sad.*

Everything depended on Chief Willy being on her side.

42

NIKA AND THE guard tramped toward a white double-wide mobile home, with CANARD painted on the side in big, boxy black letters. The guard walked in front, limping slightly.

"Stop and turn around," she said. "Give me all your ammo."

He hesitated.

"The clips in your waist pockets. Move."

He gulped. "What are you gonna do, storm the place?" He reached for the clips.

"Trust me, I'm no murderer."

He handed over two extra clips.

She stuffed the ammo into her waist pockets, then

popped the clip out of the rifle, dumped the bullets into a thigh pocket, and shoved the empty clip back in place with a click.

"Here, take your rifle, now I'm your prisoner—maybe you won't lose your job. If Chief Willy doesn't believe me or doesn't care, it's all over anyway."

He met her eyes for an instant as he took the weapon. "Thanks."

Chief Willy answered the door to the CANARD operations office. Only a small desk lamp lit the room.

Nika stepped in first, followed by the guard. The overhead lights came on. Two more guards aimed rifles at her, standing on each side of a heavyset man seated in a highback executive chair.

Her heart sank.

The seated man looked at Scott. "Get back to your patrol."

"Uh . . . yes sir," Scott said, and turned and left.

"Sorry it had to be this way, Nika," Chief Willy said.

"This your idea of a private meeting?" she said.

"Chief Willy didn't betray you," said the seated man. "My security staff monitors all transmissions. I like to keep tabs on what's going on around my mine."

He stood and extended a meaty hand, a gold-and-turquoise watchband on his wrist. Thin gray-blond hair swept up and across his scalp from one ear to the other to hide his bald crown. Watery pale-blue eyes stood out in a reddened, windburned face. He wore a white rodeo shirt and a black leather bolo tie with gold tips.

"Rex Kaiser," he said.

Nika only glared at him.

He chuckled and sat down, leaned back in the tall chair, and tucked his hands behind his head.

"Your father was hellbent on shutting down my mine, Ms. Nahadeh. Now he's dead. Next thing I know, you're snooping around where you don't belong. What is it with you people? Can't accept defeat?"

"Sometimes it's better to fight a hopeless battle than to lie down and be trampled."

He leaned forward and grabbed the edge of his desk.

"Who's trampling whom? I employ two hundred and fifty-six Caiyuh Indians here. For six years they've had a decent, steady income. They're not on your side. They don't want to see this project sabotaged."

"I'm not a saboteur. Maybe my father was, I don't know. I only know he was shot in the back in an open field."

"Perfectly justified, under the circumstances. He was armed and running toward the dorms. Refused to halt. And he was a known threat."

"Armed with what? A hide scraper?"

"A nine-millimeter semiautomatic pistol we kept as evidence."

"My father never fired a semiautomatic weapon in his life, or a pistol, for that matter."

"His fingerprints tell a different story."

"Fingerprints? Even a Caiyuh doesn't go around in the middle of winter without mittens."

Rex started to say something more, but Nika held up her hand.

"Never mind. The law ordered him to stay away, and I'm sure you'll find a way to come out smelling clean." She looked at Chief Willy. "Sir, I'm not here to talk about my father."

"Just what are you up to, Nika?" Chief Willy said. His moon-round face looked tired.

"I'm here to tell you about the prehistoric people down inside the caverns."

Chief Willy's eyebrows shot up and he glanced at Rex, whose jaw muscles twitched.

"Aha. See, he knows, Chief Willy. He knows."

"Utter bullshit," Rex said. "How can we, as adults, seriously discuss this crap about ghosts?"

"You know I'm not talking about ghosts," Nika said. She met Chief Willy's eyes.

"About twenty years ago my father and I found a prehistoric man buried under the edge of the glacier not far from here."

Chief Willy nodded. "A team from *National Geographic* stayed in our village for six weeks."

"I have good reasons to believe a prehistoric woman was uncovered nearby, a couple years later, by my brother Yute."

"Yeah, big deal, so what?" Rex said.

"Chief Willy, do the Chilkakot have stories about the First People?"

He nodded. "I heard them as a boy from my grandmother."

"Remember the part about the Heart-Talkers hibernating in a cave until spring arrives in a new world?"

"We call them the Listeners—I know the story. He-Who-Comes-Back will restore the Listeners to life."

"Swans fly south, return north," she said.

"We say geese. The snow geese fly away, then come back to start a new generation."

Rex snorted. "Myths . . . campfire tales."

Chief Willy bristled and shot him a sharp look.

"No offense," Rex said, "but you know what I mean. That stuff is for anthropologists, college journals. We're running a mine here."

Nika unzipped the top of her jumpsuit and pulled out the amulet, slipped it over her head, and handed it to Chief Willy.

"What do you see?" she asked.

"A V of flying birds." He bounced the metal disk in his hand, feeling its weight. "Solid gold? Where did you get it?"

She stepped around the table and pointed to the map of the mine.

"Look here, at the caverns entered by Shaft Twenty-seven—this whole area looks a little bit like a mask, right? A demon's face?"

"So what if it looks like the head of John the Baptist?" Rex said.

"Turn the amulet over," she said.

Chief Willy stared at the map on the back side of the gold disk and glanced up at the large map on the wall. His eyes grew big. "Nika, where did you get this?"

"My father found it in a small grave where the prehistoric woman was buried. It's a map. The figures on it are people and animals—"

"Yes, I can see that. . . ."

"They're here, Chief Willy. The First People—the

Listeners—are here, in the cavern at the end of Shaft Twenty-seven."

He pointed to the wall map. "But there's already a scooter hole extending all the way into the cavern. No one has found anything."

"You mean, no one has told you anything."

"I assure you, nothing of the kind has been discovered," Rex said. "Chief, you can tour the cavern yourself, anytime you like."

Chief Willy grimaced.

"I'll take you up on that tour," Nika said. "In fact, I want to go right now, this minute."

Chief Willy looked at Rex and nodded. "We'll arrange it, right away."

"Like hell we will," Rex said. "We can't risk the liability of a nonemployee getting hurt down there."

"I'll sign a stack of releases," Nika said.

"That should work," Chief Willy said.

"Hold on," Rex said. "Be reasonable—it's four-thirty A.M. These things take a little time to set up."

"Time enough to hide all those bodies?" she said.

Rex slammed his fist on the desk. "This is all ridiculous crap."

"Then let's look," Nika said. "Now."

"Why can't she go now, Mr. Kaiser?" Chief Willy said. "Holding this amulet in my hand . . . I get a funny feeling . . . how can we say there's nothing to it? Let's send some men down with her to explore that cavern."

"It's a hoax," Rex said. "Who says that piece is prehistoric?"

"I'll make a deal with you," Nika said. "I'll let you carbon-date the amulet; you let me see inside the cavern."

Rex sniggered. "You can't carbon-date gold, there's no carbon in it. I think that shows how much you know about these things."

"That's beside the point," Chief Willy said. "I want to let her inspect the cavern."

Rex shifted uncomfortably. "Out of the question."

"Now, wait a minute," Chief Willy said. "This is an Indian affair, and that's my responsibility. I say she gets to see it, as soon as possible. If there's nothing to it, the sooner we clear the air, the better."

"And . . . uh . . . what would be your position otherwise?"

"If that cavern is the resting place of the First People, we need to shut down temporarily, call in the scientists—do whatever is neccesary to preserve the historical treasures. Children in every arctic tribe have grown up with that myth, it's part of our culture."

Rex rested his chin on his folded hands. He worked the muscles in his jaw and his eyes played around the room.

"All right, Ms. Nahadeh, I'll see to it that you get a tour of the cavern within the half hour. It'll take you that long to get the proper gear on. Good enough for you?"

"Fine," she said.

"Meanwhile, you bet I'll gather that stack of releases for you to sign." He picked up a radiophone and turned to the guard who stood on his right. "Rocky, I'm gonna wake up central supply. You drive her over and see to it she gets outfitted."

"Yes, sir."

Nika followed the guard to the door and glanced back as she stepped out. Chief Willy stared at the amulet in his hand and his aged-bronze face was bright with wonder.

43

THE SMALL YELLOW air-tank on Nika's back clanged against the steel mesh cage of the elevator as it started down, and she grabbed the handrail to steady herself. Surface air pumps ventilated all the shafts; only miners going into unexplored territory wore the emergency tanks.

Nika felt as bulky as a badger. Beneath her electric-heated, fiber-filled jumpsuit, she now wore a body stocking made of a silklike synthetic designed to wick away moisture; plus steel-toed neoprene boots with tiny ice-gripping studs on the soles; neoprene gloves; a thick cotton ski mask; goggles; and a white Fiberglas helmet with a halogen spotlight on top.

The elevator braked and stopped at the floor of the vertical shaft, 150 feet straight down through the glacier. Before her an open mine shaft dropped off like a ramp through the solid rock; electric lights in caged reflector wall-mounts trailed off and converged in the distance.

Rocky led the way. Inside the shaft, without visual clues to the level horizon, only gravity told Nika she was heading downhill at an ever-steeper angle. Her breath made white vapor puffs that broke up in the breeze from the humming surface fans. The ramp leveled out in a large natural cavern buttressed by prefab concrete beams. Stalagmites thrust up from the floor toward stalactites hanging from the ceiling. Open shafts radiated from the cavern in a dozen directions.

"Grand Central Station," Rocky said.

"It's huge."

"Yep."

"Just beautiful."

He led her across the massive room to the far left corner. An unlit tunnel, two and a half feet in diameter, disappeared into blackness in the rock wall.

"The Cannon Barrel," he said.

"Yeah, I see. No lights?"

He reached over and switched on her headlamp. "The scooters have a headlight. From here you ride to Twenty-seven-A."

"What about you?"

"Right behind you—we'll form a train. Tunnel's only wide enough for single file."

From a storage corral he rolled out a low-profile electric go-cart with six small rubber tires along each side. He showed her how to recline on the scooter, her head resting on a pad, her feet on the accelerator and brake.

"Here, take off your air tank. It goes in these clips."

"What's the white tank?"

"Extra air. Stays with the scooters."

"I'm feeling safer by the minute."

She climbed aboard and lay back. He slid a metal mesh canopy forward on tracks till it clicked in place to cover her from head to toe.

"What's the cage for?"

"So if the ceiling caves in, it won't squash you. Maybe."

She gulped. "Had to ask."

"That releases the canopy," he said, pointing to a handle above her head. "Watch your hands when you slide it back, it's spring loaded."

He switched on the scooter's headlamp and rolled the vehicle over to the ramp that led up inside the narrow tunnel.

"Okay, give it a little juice," he said.

She tapped the accelerator. The scooter bucked forward a couple feet and rolled back. She held her foot down halfway; the scooter hesitated, then shot up the ramp into the tunnel. "Whoa." She mashed the brake. Her gaze followed the headlight beam slicing through the long tube of blackness.

Rocky chuckled. "They're pretty fast. We drag-race them in the caverns."

"Feels weird, no steering wheel."

"Just think of yourself as a human cannonball."

"I'd rather not."

"Meet you in the cavern—it's six hundred yards."

"It's a little spooky." Her heart beat fast. "I'll wait for you."

"Fine."

In a moment the light beam from his scooter cast a bouncing silhouette of her scooter on the curved ceiling.

"Go," he said.

She pressed the accelerator and surged forward; the electric motor whined. A couple minutes later the scarred granite walls and ceiling vanished, and she gasped as the scooter dropped out from under her and rolled down the ramp. She hit the brake and skidded several feet on slippery ice, banging into the solid rubber bumper of another scooter. The headlight beam reflected from the far wall of the cavern as a ball of bright blue light.

She tugged the canopy release and with a pop the cage sprang back several inches; a shove sent it sliding over her head and it clicked in the open position. Nika stepped out and aimed her headlamp around the lofty room.

Her jaw dropped. Nothing could have prepared her for what she saw. A quivering began deep in her muscles and spread outward over her skin; her hair stood on end.

A moment later she realized that her mouth still hung slack. *"Aiyoo wa Denali!"* she finally whispered.

She stood in a fifty-foot-tall domed mausoleum of blue ice. The smooth walls glowed in her headlamp like mirrors. Bodies were everywhere, maybe hundreds; and all of them looked alive.

When she and her father had found Tundra Man,

the corpse was totally dehydrated; the skin looked like parchment stretched over muscles made of baked clay. But these bodies were not dried-up mummies.

To her right, reclined on a woolly hide atop a low bunk carved from the ice, a small boy seemed to doze at his mother's breast, his mouth still attached. A hairy man embraced both of them with hugely muscular arms. Other ice shelves held many couples and family groups nestled in each other's arms; all apparently only resting in a dreamless slumber.

"O, you Heart-Talkers, I am Nika Nahadeh, daughter of the Caiyuh." Her voice trembled. "I have heard of you since I was a girl, but I did not know how real you are."

She paused to catch her breath, and noticed she was breathing rapidly and shallowly. She placed her hand over her diaphragm. Slow, deep breaths. Slow, deep breaths.

"Frances Dream-Singer did not tell me you were golden. The Caiyuh tales about the goldens, the good witches that can hear your deepest feelings . . . I did not realize until now that those stories are also true. The First People, the goldens, you are one and the same."

She laughed, awestruck. "If even the goldens are real, is there any story from my girlhood that isn't real? Is the world really magic?"

She wanted to touch the nursing mother, but her heart fluttered at the thought. She stepped to the bunk where the family snuggled. Her breath puffed fast in little clouds. She slowly reached out her hand. Then drew it back.

Again, she slowed and deepened her breathing.

After a pause she removed her neoprene glove. She touched the cold, soft golden skin of the mother.

The woman's breast jiggled.

Nika gasped and yanked her hand back; her heart drummed like stampeding hooves. Her headlamp swam around the room. *Where's Rocky?*

"Rocky!" she yelled. "Rocky!"

She heard the loud staccato racheting of an electric drill tightening a nut. *Brttttttt-ttttt-ttttt.* She dashed up the ramp to the scooter tunnel. It was blocked by a heavy metal plate.

"Hey, what the fuck you doing?"

Brtt-ttt-ttttt-ttt-ttt.

She raced back to the scooter. Grabbed the air tank. Ran up the ramp. Battered the metal plate with the steel tank. The clanging echoed off the blue ice. The air tank left yellow paint scuffs on the metal plate, but the plate did not dent or budge.

"Rocky, let me out!"

Brtt-tttt-ttt-tttt-ttttt.

"Bastard! I'll kill you." Her headlamp whipped around the room.

Brrt-brrrt-ttt-tt-ttttt.

She sprinted down to the scooter. Dragged the tail end around until it faced the ramp. Rolled it back another twenty feet. Jumped in and stamped the accelerator pedal to the floor. The engine whined, screamed. The scooter hurtled up the ramp. Nika held on. The scooter rammed into the metal plate. The canopy slammed forward over her head.

The front of the scooter was crumpled, the plate was not dented.

"Ow, you stupid bitch," Rocky moaned from the other side of the plate. "I think you just broke my fuckin' thumb."

"Who put you up to this?"

"Who writes the checks around here?"

"Tell him he won't get away with it."

"Sure he will."

"No one's going to be just a little curious why this scooter hole is blocked with a goddamn metal plate?"

"That's standard operating procedure."

Her breath froze in her lungs.

"See, when you do a meltdown," he said, "it generates a wicked hot fireball. You gotta make sure the inferno stays in the cavern."

She staggered backward.

"The valve in the center is where we stick the nozzle of the flame thrower. We ignite it, burn it six, eight hours—the blaze will turn you and all those dead freaks into ashes. Not a short hair will be left."

"Chief Willy knows I'm down here."

He laughed.

She heard his scooter canopy slide forward and latch with a click, then the whine of the engine receding down the tunnel.

"Chief Willy knows I'm down here!" she screamed, and screwed her eyes shut against the nightmare. Her shoulders slumped and her knees wobbled; she felt that she would sag to the floor, but she drew in her breath and stood up straight again.

"I'm John Nahadeh's daughter," she said aloud, and opened her eyes.

She made herself turn around to face the icy tomb.

She stepped down the ramp, her helmet lamp playing over the crowd of ancient bodies.

Alone in the lodge of the dead.

"O, Listeners, hear me," she said, shakily. "I am Nika, daughter of John and Late-Snow of the Caiyuh tribe of Swift Fork. I am a silly woman who is afraid of your magic. You are dead for thousands of years, but you only seem to hibernate. I—I came as your sister, to save you from being destroyed, but . . . now I'm in danger too."

She sat down next to the nursing mother and gently placed her hand on the baby's soft, fuzzy back. She relaxed her chest and in a few moments her breathing grew calm and even.

"Forgive me for being afraid," she said quietly. "I seek peace among you now. Teach me to sleep as serenely as this baby. Help me to be easy when my turn comes to die."

A noise.

Her hair bristled. She had the creepy feeling that one of the corpses was going to move. She clenched her teeth and turned her head toward a far shelf on her left.

A body very slowly sat up. It wobbled, supported itself.

It croaked her name.

44

EMBER SAT ALONE near the front of the Alaskon Express bus, legs tucked by her side, head resting on the icy window glass. Clumped snowflakes tumbled in the headlight beams and the wipers squeaked, swishing a smudged arc on the broad windshield. Beyond her reflection in the glass, morning traffic splashed through the slushy streets of downtown Fairbanks. The arctic city leaned away from the winter sun, hours still from the light of dawn.

Ember rubbed the back of her neck and forced a yawn to stretch her tight jaw. The constant pressure of her emotions had kept her awake and restless during the two-day bus trip from Seattle. The closer she came to her mother's land, the more she felt linked to the force that was drawing her to her destiny.

Now I'm nearly home. Today is the day.

She opened the bandage box and used the last gauze bandage to change the dressing on the bullet wound in her shoulder. Then she slowly stretched that arm above her head. It was stiff and sore, but she pushed through the pain. She might need to use the arm soon, she thought, and with the thought a sense of emergency rushed through her body on a wave of heat. Her heart beat faster and she crouched in her seat, ready to bolt.

What's happening?

A white panel truck passed the bus in the right lane. The logo on the driver's door read CANARD, INC. above a graphic of a flying V of ducks, and the words KANTISHNA HILLS MINING PROJECT.

Before her thinking mind had time to react, Ember jumped up and dove toward the front door of the bus. The bus driver took his foot off the gas and shouted at her.

"Miss, what are you doing? Get back to your seat."

"Sir, I need to get off right here."

"No, no. I can't do that. I can let you off only at the terminal. We're almost there. Get back to your seat. Please. Come on, I'm not kidding. Get back there now."

The bus slowed and came to a stop at a traffic signal alongside the CANARD truck.

"I'm getting out," Ember shouted, and pushed the door. It swung partway open and stopped, the hydraulic arm still retracted.

She shot a backward glance at the driver. "Let me out, hurry."

"Dammit, get back to your seat. We're only blocks from the station. Don't get me in trouble."

"Sorry. I gotta get off," Ember said, and bent low and shoved the door hard with her whole body. The metal arm bent and sprung free and she lurched out onto the wet asphalt and nearly sprawled on her face. She scrambled up just as the light turned green. Horns honked. The truck pulled ahead with a lumbering acceleration.

"Wait!" Ember shouted. "Wait!" And she sprinted after the truck, waving her arms.

The truck didn't slow. With a lunge she leapt onto the wide bumper and grabbed the rear door handle. She looked up at the driver's face in the hemispheric rear mirror at the same time he spotted her. His eyes grew huge and he cursed as he pulled over to the curb and parked in the mercury light of a streetlamp.

Ember hopped down from the bumper as the truck driver came running back. He wore a bulky orange jumpsuit, the kind she saw in her visions. His face was round and dark, with slanted eyes and a wispy black beard that thickened at the chin.

"You all right?" he said.

"Yeah," she said, "I'm okay." She rubbed her injured shoulder.

"What the hell? What were you doing? How'd you get back here?"

"I need to go where you're going."

"What are you talking about?"

"To the mines, I need to get to the mines."

"You're hanging on to my bumper in downtown

traffic so you can ask me for a ride to the mines? You nuts?"

"Give me a ride and I'll give what you want."

"What I want? I don't want nothing from you. You're crazy."

Ember unbuttoned her blue flannel shirt halfway and spread it open it to reveal a red tank top underneath. Her breasts stood out against the thin cotton.

The driver gawked. "You are crazy. That's it. You're crazy for real. But you're wild; I like that."

"Will you take me there?"

He tugged on the whiskers at his chin. "They take trespassing real serious at the mines," he said, "like you starved your best sled dog or something."

She met his eyes and said, "I'm the strongest and the warmest woman you could ever be with."

He laughed nervously. "Okay, I'm thinking. You want to sneak inside the gate? See a boyfriend or something? You don't even have warm clothes. Don't you even have a coat?"

"I'm not cold."

"I think I can get you into the gate if you'll hide in the back, inside a shipping carton. Yeah, that should work."

"Let's go, then," she said. "I have to get there right away. We've got to move."

"Wait, I still haven't decided if I'm in this game," he said.

She hurried to the passenger side of the truck and banged on the door. The door was locked, but in a moment he opened it for her from the inside.

The CANARD truck drove south along the Anchorage–Fairbanks Highway, skirting the frozen edge of the tundra. The snowfall stopped, but midmorning was dark as night. The driver hunched over the steering wheel, the green glow of the dashboard lights on his face.

Ember wore only her tank top and jeans. Her skin was damp with sweat. The driver glanced at her and then turned off the truck's heater. He studied her for a moment.

"You feel all right?"

She nodded. "I'm okay."

"Got a fever?"

"I'm just . . ." She gulped and shrugged her shoulders. "I feel hot."

"Something's going on. Look at you, your whole body is flushed."

He reached over and flipped down the sunshade on her side so she could see her face in the mirror. A pink glow shone through her golden skin like a sunburn. Sweat beaded her forehead and upper lip and ran down her temples.

She touched her flushed cheeks. The power in her had been growing more intense by the hour. When she closed her eyes she saw fiery light. From deep in her marrow she felt the brightness emanate. Even her teeth felt as if they were glowing with heat.

One part of her was scared, she admitted. But another part had never felt more powerful, and that part was taking over, bodily. She relaxed her resistance and gave herself to the fiery presence, and as she did so, her fear faded and the energy expanded. But along with the steady infilling of power, her sense of urgency had also become physical. She felt that she could fling open the door, leap out, and run a hundred miles through the waist-deep snow before spending the force that now surged through her body in waves.

Ember looked at the driver. "Can you drive any faster?"

"You mean with a snowmobile? Not with this truck, not on these roads." He frowned. "What's your hurry? Who's waiting for you there?"

"I don't know."

He straightened up and reached over and placed his palm on her forehead, then flinched at the touch. "Damn, you're hot as a heating pad. Not good." He slowed the truck. "I need to turn us around and get you back to Fairbanks, to a hospital."

"No, don't." She grabbed his arm. "I'm not sick. It's an energy—it flows through me."

A current of force passed through her hand into his flesh. He drew back his arm and looked at her with widening eyes.

"Who are you?" he whispered.

"Someone who needs your help," she said, "to get home."

He gulped. "Aiyoo. You're not human. I thought you looked odd. You're a spirit. Hanging on my bumper! One of the spirits the old folks talk about."

"Yes. I'm a golden. I'm going back to where I began."

He yelped a string of words in a guttural tongue,

gritted his teeth, and tightened his grip on the steering wheel. He stared straight ahead, avoiding her eyes. And he drove faster.

Ahead, a green metal highway sign read: CANARD KANTISHNA HILLS MINE 20 MILES. The driver braked and turned, skidding slightly. Hard-packed snow covered the gravel road to the mine. The truck pulled ahead, all four wheels gaining traction. The gravel crunched beneath the snow. A pink smudge of light appeared on the eastern horizon, thumbprint of the dawn.

Almost there.

She breathed in and out slowly, feeling that her heart was like the rising sun, the center of a bright sphere of energy. Her breathing was deep and ablaze. She closed her eyes and began to lose herself in the heartfire and its golden light.

"You're turning the cab into an oven," the driver said, and cracked open his window to the cold air.

The heavy fragrance of snow and earth stirred a strange and deep nostalgia in Ember. Something loosened in her heart. The emotion became overwhelming and she fell into a swoon.

Springtime. Snow melt.

Flowers painted swaths of rich color across the rolling tundra. Ember stood, clothed in hides, with other goldens on a hillside. In a grave made of stones piled in a ring, a body lay on top of the mossy earth, blanketed with orange poppies. Ember leaned forward to see the person.

It was herself.

Then suddenly she was floating high above, watching people toss orange poppy flowers down on her body.

She sensed a presence behind her and turned around

to see a radiant figure. His body suffused a soft light like the new sun at dawn. He was golden-skinned, furry, and very muscular, with blond hair and beard; at least for the moment, for he was in flux.

"Father?" Ember asked.

But the figure resolved into a new dawn-lit form, light into light. Ember was now in the presence of a young golden woman with red hair and green eyes, who smiled at her lovingly.

"U-ma! Mother!"

Her mother's shape melted and turned into a pretty Indian woman with shiny black hair.

"Mom! Oh, Chena," Ember whispered. "You are my mother too."

Chena shifted and evolved into Ember's own form, as if Ember now faced a mirror. Ember shut her eyes to block the vision of herself, but she saw the nude golden woman in her inner sight as clearly as when her eyes were open.

Her own image smiled kindly at her, and Ember was deeply surprised at her loveliness, from her thick red hair to her sinewy feet—as beautiful as any human being she had ever seen. A laugh sprang from her as she realized that she loved herself. And not because she had struggled so hard to accept herself, but because all self-concern had suddenly burned away, clear through to her living essence, where she already existed as love. For here, at heart, the gift was given, not earned. She was forever beautiful. And this revelation was not a private victory—it was the truth at the origin of all things: Beauty was their mother, the giver of life. Again she laughed at the obviousness of it.

Instantly, the vision of her own form vanished. Now Ember stood starkly alone, with no images outside or in.

Then—at her very soul—she, too, dissolved.

She felt as if she had been holding in her breath all her life, and had suddenly released it. Heart and breath, unbounded, filled all of space and time. Her heart was bright and her breath was the same light. She was not truly fitted into any shape or form, but bright without limit, beyond measure, undefined.

Then light breathed in, and the personality named "Ember" reappeared.

Ember opened her eyes and found herself staring through the truck windshield at the snowy road that shot straight ahead across the tundra.

The driver shot a glance at her. "You sure you're okay?" he asked. "Can a spirit get a fever?" He cautiously touched a finger to Ember's shoulder, as if he were scared that sparks would fly. Then he yanked his hand away and examined his finger, looked back at her with a furrowed brow.

"I'm all right," she said. "Just hurry."

A frozen river came into view on the right, snaking through the dwarf evergreens, under the new yellow sun. The road began to hug the riverbank. In another few minutes Swift Fork Village appeared. A huddle of wooden cabins lined the steep bank, most of them nearly buried under drifts of snow up to the rooftops. One cabin had collapsed under the weight, and several others tottered.

Ember sat up straighter. "Wait, stop here," she said.

The driver slowed the truck. "Just a ghost town."

"No, there are people. . . ." She pointed to thin lines of smoke rising from the chimneys of two cabins. Images flashed within her intuition. "There's someone here who knows about the goldens."

"Somebody's got a brand-new snowmobile," he said. A bright red snowmobile with an enclosed canopy was parked at the closer of the two cabins.

Ember leapt out of the cab before the truck stopped rolling. He parked the truck at the side of the road. She ran along a footpath that cut a narrow canyon through the snowdrifts to the first cabin. Ember knocked on the wooden plank door. After a short pause she pounded.

"Maybe they're out collecting firewood," the driver said, coming up behind her. "C'mon, let's try the other one." He turned to walk toward the far cabin.

"This is the right cabin," she said. "A girl who lived here—a woman now—she knows about my people. She—she's in danger. Right now."

She closed her eyes, and like film in a developer, ghostly images resolved into sharp focus in her mind. The cavern of blue ice. The woman was there, with the goldens. She would be incinerated with them in the coming inferno.

Suddenly Ember sniffed a familiar scent, and recognized it even before she turned around. A tall Indian man in a bright red quilted snowmobile suit appeared from behind the corner of the far cabin, his arms loaded with split logs.

Yute.

Ember and Yute both froze.

Then Ember bolted, tugging the truck driver by the hand. "Back to the truck, hurry," she said.

Yute dumped his firewood and started toward them, empty hands held high.

"Ember, wait!" he shouted. "Don't run away. I'm not after you, not like before. I just want to talk."

Ember threw open the passenger door of the truck and jumped in.

"Ember, please," Yute said, striding toward her. "I knew we'd meet here. Don't you see? We're tied together. You must feel it too."

The driver cranked the truck's engine and Yute broke into a run toward Ember's door.

"Go, go!" she yelled at the driver.

He threw the truck into gear and the snow tires spit snow and gravel as it sped away. Yute chased behind it a hundred feet before giving up. In a side-view mirror Ember watched him shrink in a cloud of settling snow as the truck raced across the tundra. The driver kept his right foot heavy on the gas pedal all the way to the Kantishna Hills.

45

In the blue ice cave one body sat up, shakily.

"Nika?" it croaked.

She stumbled backward, muffling a scream. *Please lie back down and go to sleep!*

"Nika, is that you? It's dark, I can't see you."

"Go back to sleep," she said in a squeaky voice. "You're supposed to be dead."

She tripped over the front end of a scooter and sat down hard on the ice, trembling.

"Nika, don't be afraid, it's Chief Willy."

She moaned with relief. "Chief Willy, you scared the piss out of me."

"My fault, I should have realized . . . it's so spooky down here."

She walked over to where he sat. He held his hand over a lump on his head; his hair was matted with blood. Her headlamp shone into his eyes; his pupils shrank to pinholes.

"No brain damage, I guess," she said. "You all right?"

He breathed rapidly. "I'll live. But I—I hate being trapped."

"Let's get some light in here."

She walked over to three scooters and flipped on their headlights. The spacious cavern lit up with a blue glow. Bodies rested everywhere on tiers of ice, as if the place were a warehouse for mannequins.

"Would it help to wear my headlamp?" she asked.

"Maybe. Yes."

"Here." She took off her helmet and handed it to him.

"Thank you."

He put on the white Fiberglas helmet and shone its halogen light all around the room. Gradually, his shoulders dropped and his breathing slowed.

"I feel a little better now," he said. "Thanks."

Nika studied the still figures closest to her and shivered, though she sweated slightly in her heated suit. She unzipped the collar to her breastbone, pulled off her ski mask, and shook loose her hip-length black tresses.

"You warm enough?" she asked. "Must be twenty degrees in here, tops."

"I'm okay for now, but I don't know how long this battery pack will hold out—it's not fresh."

"Why are they doing this to us?"

"Greed." He spit the word. "Two days ago, under this ice, they struck the mother lode. The other shafts yield gold-laced sulfur, but in this cavern and the next they've chiseled out nuggets the size of quail eggs—solid gold."

She sat down next to him. "And we got in the way of their jackpot."

"I only found out about it right before one of the guards clubbed me with his flashlight."

"Can they really get away with it?"

"Maybe. I've seen meltdowns before. There's nothing left but gritty black water in the pump-out."

"Makes me feel just great." She clapped her hands together and a sprinkle of ice flew off her orange gloves. The echo bounced around the cavern.

"I think they've been suspicious of me for a while," he said.

"What do you mean?"

"About two months ago Kaiser started pulling the Indians from the guard units and placing them in low-security jobs. Now the guards are all Anglos."

"What are you telling me? What were the Indians up to?"

"CANARD reneged on almost every promise it made to me and my tribe. And since I had a hunch something like that might happen, I made sure several of my own men were always on duty guarding the mine against saboteurs."

Nika's eyes grew wide. "Your own people were doing the sabotage?"

He nodded. "Every time the corporation needed a

shove in the right direction. When Kaiser decided not to build the medical clinic in my village, we monkey-wrenched the shaft ventilation fans. When he decided not to restore Bluegill Lake, we poured sugar in the electric generators. The terrorists left ultimatums and Kaiser quickly changed his tune."

"But my father almost went to prison for pouring sugar in those generators."

"I persuaded Kaiser to drop the sabotage charges and only press charges against trespassing, go for the restraining order. I argued that many local Indians and sympathetic people around the world would see your father as a martyr."

"Did my father ruin the generators or not?"

"No, he was only trespassing, searching for these caverns. He took the sabotage rap to draw attention away from the insiders."

"Then you already knew about these caverns."

"I only knew your father believed they existed. I told him if he could find the First People, then, yes, we would halt the mining, at least for a while."

"But when someone found out that he knew . . ."

He touched her arm. "I'm sorry, Nika. He must have sneaked down into this cavern and then been caught."

"No, I don't think he came down here," she said, looking around in the blue glow. "He didn't need to. He recognized the map near the elevator, just like I did."

"But then how would anyone realize that he knew?"

"Because my father could never hold in his joy. He could hide every other emotion. He could be in pain, you'd never know it . . . a sled dog bit his little finger off, I didn't find out till we got home, hours later. But when he was really happy everybody in the village knew."

"I remember him, just like that, when we were young. If he was talking about something sad, his face was stone, his voice didn't quaver. But if he was telling about his little daughter—you—or about hunting with his father, his eyes glowed like seal-oil lamps."

"And when he realized he'd found the caverns . . . I can just see him, shouting out his victory song. He never guessed that Kaiser and his goons couldn't care less about the First People. He wouldn't be able to imagine that."

She followed the beam of the helmet lamp as it played over the rows of golden bodies.

"Chief Willy, I touched a woman over there. She's cold as ice, but her flesh is just as soft as mine. What kind of magic is that? Are they really only asleep?"

"They don't breathe—they're dead all right. I don't know why they aren't frozen stiff as winter meat."

Nika's fingers reached by habit to touch the amulet, beneath her body stocking. It was gone. "The amulet. Do you still have it?"

He patted his breast pocket. "Damn. Kaiser's got it now."

Nika felt a sharp sense of loss. "My father gave it to me; I've worn it since I was fifteen."

"Kaiser will melt it down—get rid of the evidence, keep the gold."

"That's what he plans to do with us," she said, and a bolt of defiance shot through her body. She leapt up.

"Got an idea."

From a pleated thigh pocket she pulled out a handful of high-caliber rifle bullets.

"Where'd you get those?" he said.

"The guard who brought me to Kaiser. Scott. I thought he seemed okay and I felt sorry for him, so I unloaded his rifle and handed it back to him."

Chief Willy raised his eyebrows. "You'd already disarmed him?"

"Yeah. But then I didn't want him to lose his job . . . stupid, I guess. Anyway, if I can make these bullets fire, will somebody hear us?"

He shrugged. "You mean, someone who cares that we're in here."

"We can't just do nothing," she said. "I've got to try." She hurried up the ramp and wedged a bullet into the small hole in the center of the iris-shaped valve of the fire seal. She looked around for a rock to strike the end of the casing. Only ice. Finally, she slipped off one neoprene boot and hammered the bullet with the boot's steel toe.

On the fourth strike the bullet fired into the scooter hole with a terrific bang that reverberated inside the natural megaphone for half a minute.

"Aiyoo!" Nika said, taking her hands from her ears. "Somebody ought to hear that."

"Unless they've already given the order to clear the area for the meltdown procedure."

She took a deep breath and put her mouth to the hole in the metal seal, yelled from the bottom of her lungs.

"Help! We're in here! Help! Let us out!"

She held her breath and listened. Only her pulse thrummed in her ears. Again, she yelled for help. Deep silence. Then she picked up the faint rumbling of machinery. She fired another bullet. No response. Two more bullets. The machinery seemed to be coming closer.

She gave up and turned back to Chief Willy.

"How long does it take to set up the equipment for a meltdown?"

"Normally about an hour. But this morning they're going to find out that an ecoterrorist has ripped holes in the hose that carries the propane."

"Really?" She felt a spark of hope.

"It's the last thing my men did before they were taken off guard duty. Kaiser was starting to act wishy-washy about the scholarship fund he promised for the families of Indian miners."

"How long to fix the hose?"

"I don't think it can be repaired. They'll have to send for a new one from the sister mine at Terra Cotta."

"How long?"

"Couple, three days by truck. Half a day by helicopter."

"Did you see the ring around the moon last night after the snowfall stopped? With any luck it's snowing flakes as fat as river snails up there. Chopper can't fly."

"Then we've got three more days trapped down here," he said, and shuddered. "Is it really such good luck?"

"Chief Willy, when I was a girl my father took me to Slow Fork Village to see Frances Dream-Singer. She told me about the amulet and the Heart-Talkers. She said that He-Who-Returns will come, that he and I will meet."

"I hope he comes very soon, Nika. Otherwise, I'll freeze solid before I burn."

He pointed to the flashing low-battery warning light on his jumpsuit heater unit.

She groaned. "What next?"

The whine of an electric motor resounded in the scooter hole.

"Someone heard us!" she shouted. She screwed her eye to the hole and tried to peek. A headlight approached. A scraping sound echoed through the tunnel; the scooter was dragging something heavy.

Chief Willy went to her side. She filled her lungs and yelled, "Help! We're trapped in here! Let us out!"

The headlights stopped ten feet back.

"Save your breath, it ain't the cavalry—it's Rocky." His voice was amplified as if he were talking down a well. "Gotta hook up the hose for the meltdown."

"It won't work, it's full of holes," she said.

"Wrong. The old hose is full of holes. We found that hatchet job two weeks ago."

Rocky crawled toward the steel plate, dragging the metal-reinforced hose behind.

"This is a new hose, all the way from Montana. Tell Chief Willy he owes Kaiser thirty-five grand, plus shipping."

"Tell Kaiser to hop on a long icicle," Chief Willy said.

Rocky jerked at the heavy three-inch-wide hose. Its end was capped with a brass clamp coupling from which poked a slender high-pressure nozzle. He looked up at the valve hole, and winked.

"Won't be long now. You two are gonna be a cloud of Indian vapor."

Nika jammed a bullet in the hole. Whacked it with her steel-toed boot.

Bang.

Rocky cried out.

She peeked through the valve hole. The bullet's impact had bowled him backward, knees pinned under, helmet lamp shining straight up. The circle of light on the ceiling did not waver.

She glanced back at Chief Willy in shock. "Oh, God, I think I killed him."

Chief Willy knelt and peered through the hole. Then he looked up at Nika and a grin spread over his face.

Nika's stomach squirmed. She felt bewildered, not knowing how to react.

Chief Willy stood and slapped her on the back.

"Self-defense. He was trying to murder us. But we're gonna fight back as best we can until the bitter end."

He gave a war whoop and his earlier fear seemed to have left him.

"You were right, Nika. It's better to fight a hopeless battle than to lie down and be trampled."

46

NIKA PEERED THROUGH the valve hole in the center of the metal firewall. Rocky did not budge. The headlight of his scooter lit him in a stark white flood. One eyecup of his goggles had darkened, filled with blood. She stared a long while at his chest until she was certain that he was not breathing.

She exhaled heavily and stood up.

"I should have warned him first," she said.

"I keep telling you, he was a murderer, trying to kill us," Chief Willy said.

"Now *I'm* the murderer."

"It's a lot easier to get over feeling guilty than to get over being burned alive."

A crackling voice spit from a radio clipped to Rocky's utility belt.

"Rocky. You having lunch down there? What the hell's taking so long?"

"Here we go," Chief Willy said.

"Rocky . . . come in. Rocky . . . Rocky . . . talk back."

"They'll send more men down," Nika said.

"Let them," Chief Willy said.

"Rocky . . . Rocky . . . goddammit, hit the talk button. Got your radio turned off? What the hell's the matter with you?"

"How many bullets you got?"

Nika counted the bullets in her thigh pocket.

"Fifteen."

"Good."

"Rocky, this is Nick. Hit the talk button, asshole."

"How long can we hold them off?" Nika said.

"However long it takes to clear all those bodies out of the tunnel."

"Okay. I'm coming down. But if I get all the way down there and find out your radio is turned off, I'm gonna kick your ass."

Nika's heart skipped a beat. Chief Willy grabbed her shoulders and squeezed.

"Just like Custer's Last Stand," he said.

"The Indians won that one."

"Exactly what I mean."

Ten minutes later an electric engine whined at the end of the scooter hole, heading their way. Nika put her hand to her chest and felt her heart thumping beneath the bodysuit.

She watched. The scooter approached fast. The headlight hit Rocky's scooter, shooting angular shadows onto the curved rock walls. The scooter braked sharply.

"Man! What the fuck?" the driver shouted.

A pop, and the canopy slid back and latched. A big man wriggled out in a tight forward tuck and crawled on his hands and knees toward Rocky's scooter. He craned his neck to look over the scooter at the body.

"Holy shit!" The man shot a glance of alarm at the firewall.

"Tell your boss we've got a gun," Nika said. "We'll kill anyone who comes down here. You've got five seconds to get back in your scooter and scram."

The man scurried backward and flopped into the supine seat of his scooter. The tires spun. He shot down the tunnel in reverse.

Chief Willy threw up his hands. "Why'd you tell him that? Now they'll figure out some way to get past our defense."

"Well . . . I—couldn't just shoot him."

"*I* could have shot him," Chief Willy said, then he managed a smile.

They waited. The white puffs of their breaths punctuated the silence. Chief Willy rubbed and teased at his black mustache. He saw that Nika noticed that his hands shook and he tucked them under his armpits.

"You cold?" she asked.

He shivered. "A little."

She pointed to his battery pack. The blinking warning light had gone out. Dead batteries.

"I know." He met her eyes and smiled sadly.

"Some say the world will end in ice, some say in fire. Our world will end in both."

"Here, take my battery pack," she said, and unzipped the small holster and unplugged the black metal cartridge.

He brought up his hands. "Don't."

She held the battery pack out to him. "We can take turns with it."

"You're more than generous, Nika, but no, I refuse." He took the pack and plugged it back into her heating unit. "The batteries will run down fast reheating both suits if they're allowed to cool."

She sighed and gazed around the cavern at the golden bodies in the reflected glow of the scooter headlights.

"Everything I've heard about the goldens seems true," she said. "They're magic. Frances Dream-Singer said I would meet He-Who-Returns. . . ."

"Perhaps. Perhaps."

He hugged himself, shivering.

"Please, Chief Willy, we'll take turns with the battery pack. I've got on an extra layer—a body stocking."

He shook his head. By the time they heard noise in the tunnel, his teeth were chattering.

Nika crouched and peeked. The headlight vibrated as a scooter sped toward her. The scooter stopped behind Rocky's scooter. The driver wore a bulky yellow suit with a large enclosed helmet.

"Looks like he's wearing some sort of . . . almost a spacesuit."

"A bomb squad suit," Chief Willy said. "Now he's bulletproof from head to toe."

"What about the faceplate?"

"Stronger than steel."

The man hooked a cable to Rocky's scooter, then backed his own scooter down the tunnel, towing the other vehicle. The headlights receded until they were distant bright spots, then tilted up and were gone. After a moment a wavering headlight appeared again.

The scooter braked sharply close to the body, where the tunnel widened. The canopy was already latched open. The man in the protective suit scooted off the vehicle feet-first, then squatted and stiffly waddled to the body. He reached out a fat-gloved hand and lifted Rocky's goggles. Blood slopped out.

He looked up at Nika and glared. Only his eyes and the bridge of his nose were visible in a narrow slit.

"Now it's your turn," he shouted. His muffled voice seemed to come from inside a submerged steel drum. "Kaiser decided burning you to cinders isn't good enough. Cinders is still evidence."

He shuffled back to the scooter and returned with a small black box. He dragged the hose to the firewall and began affixing the box to the base of the nozzle. "It's a timer. We're gonna fill up the cave with propane and then blow it to smithereens—industrial accident."

Nika backed her eye away as he shoved the gas nozzle through. It protruded a half inch through the hole. The couplings clicked into place.

Nika grabbed up the steel air tank from the cave floor. She raised the tank above her head and, bending her legs slightly, brought its flat base down on the nozzle with all her strength. The air tank glanced off the nozzle with a *clong* that echoed around the blue ice walls. She stared. The nozzle was undamaged.

Chief Willy looked down at his feet. His shivering had grown calmer. He knelt on the ice.

"Come sit near me, my beautiful friend," he said, so softly she could barely hear him. "When I was a boy, I used to braid my mother's long black hair, and she would sing Chilkakot songs to me. Sometimes she would tell me tales about the First People. . . ."

His old black eyes met hers.

"If you would let me, I would love to braid your hair."

Nika swallowed past a hard lump in her throat. "If you'll share my battery pack, I'll let you braid my hair." He smiled at her and she transferred the unit from her suit to his, then sat cross-legged on the ice in front of him. Chief Willy's wrinkled hands began to tug at her hair, combing it with his fingers and braiding it.

She clasped her hands over her chest, where her gold amulet once hung, and closed her eyes in heart surrender.

He-Who-Returns, come soon.

47

THE LONG CHAIN-LINK fence of the CANARD mining operations compound came into view, partway up a wooded slope, a half-mile ahead. Ember ducked into the back of the truck and hid inside a large plastic chest half-filled with cardboard mail cartons.

The driver and a gate guard exchanged muffled words, then Ember felt the truck pull forward. After a moment she returned to her seat in the front. Near the western edge of the fence she spotted the tall arm of a red crane, the machine she had envisioned in her nightmare.

She tapped the driver's shoulder and pointed. "There, to the right," she said. "See the snowmobile trail? Follow it, hurry. Head for that crane. That's where they are."

"Where who are?"

"Golden people, just like me," Ember said.

He shot her a worried look and abruptly stopped the truck.

"No way," he said. "Sorry. You're on your own from here. This is too spooky for me."

"But there's no time!" she said.

"I can't," he said, "I'm too scared." He turned the engine off and yanked the keys out of the ignition.

Ember was already out the door, running as her feet hit the snow. She raced toward the crane in a breathless sprint, pumping her legs until the muscles burned. Ahead, a crew of orange-suited workers milled about a big tanker truck. The words PROPANE—FLAMMABLE covered the side of the mirror-polished stainless steel tank. A fat hose led from a brass coupling on the top of the tank and disappeared over the edge of a deep vertical shaft in the glacier.

"Shut off the gas!" Ember yelled as she ran toward the tanker. "A woman is trapped down in the cavern."

Two workers monitoring the pump rushed to shut it off. One of them shouted, "We've been burning for twenty minutes. Who the hell's down there?"

"A Caiyuh woman from Swift Fork," Ember said. "And another . . . a man . . . an old man. I don't know their names."

A group of Indian workers looked at each other with horror and spoke rapidly in their own language.

"How do you know they're in the cavern?" several of them shouted.

"I know through spirit-knowledge."

A burly man in a blue jumpsuit shoved his way past a semicircle of workers gathered near Ember.

"I'm Rex Kaiser," he said, "I run this mine. Who the fuck are you?"

"There's a woman and a man, still alive, down in the cavern," Ember said, "Along with the bodies of many goldens—Neanderthals, like me."

"Neanderthals?" Kaiser frowned. "What've you been smoking? Nothing's down there but tons of ice. We're melting it to the bare rock."

Ember stepped closer to face him. "You're a liar and a murderer," she said. "Look at me. I know my people are down there, and I know they aren't yet destroyed."

Kaiser reeled back.

"I . . . I don't know what you're talking about."

She scrambled onto the hood of a Sno-Cat.

"Native people, look closely at me," she called out in a loud voice. "Have you heard the legends of the goldens when you were children? See who I am. I am of the First People. Others like me are down in the cavern. They've lain there, undisturbed, for two hundred and fifty centuries. Now you must help me bring them up into the light of day."

Three Indian men and a woman hurried closer to Ember and a look of wonder spread across their faces as they saw her features. The woman reached out and touched Ember's hand, then drew her own hand back in awe at the heat flowing from Ember's fingers; the woman's mouth fell open, then she clapped her hand to her mouth and burst into tears. More Indian workers gathered in a huddle in front of the Sno-Cat.

"You're golden," the woman said, between sobs. "My grandmother told me about you . . . but . . . those folk tales . . . you're real. . . ."

"Yes, and the goldens are really here," Ember said. "They're in an ice-filled cavern with a Caiyuh woman, and someone else, too . . . a native man . . . a chief . . . is with her."

"Chief Willy?" A worker said, and shook his head, wearing a dazed look. "We shot flame into that cavern for twenty minutes," he said. "There won't be no one left alive."

"No," Ember said. "That can't be true. I still feel them. They're still alive."

"What the hell's going on here, Mr. Kaiser?" a dark-skinned Indian demanded. Other workers added their angry voices to his.

Kaiser turned slightly and gave an almost imperceptible nod to one of his guards; the man quietly walked away.

Kaiser faced the workers. "I tell you, we did a thorough inspection of the cavern—nothing down there but slabs of ice."

"We better not find the slightest clue that you're lying, or we'll tear this mine apart."

Abruptly, an air horn alarm blared a shrill repeating wail from the direction of the vertical shaft. The two men standing at the pump quickly checked the dials and shot glances of alarm and confusion to each other.

Ember jumped down from the Sno-Cat. "What's that?" she shouted over the noise.

An Indian woman tugged at Ember's arm. "Come on, hurry! That's the clear-the-area alarm. Something went wrong with the meltdown."

"What went wrong?" Ember yelled.

The woman shook her head. "Don't know—the whole thing could blow any second."

Ember shook loose from the woman's grip. The woman fled at a run with the other workers and guards and Kaiser. Some of them ran in a crouch, keeping their hands around their heads.

Ember grabbed a worker as he dashed by.

"What's happening?" she yelled.

"It's gonna blow. Lemme go."

She gripped the belt on his jumpsuit. "What's happening down in the cavern?"

"It's like an oven filled with gas, one spark, and boom! and the blast could make it all the way back to the tanker truck!" He strained against her.

"Gas built up in the cavern because it wasn't burning?"

"Yeah, yeah, that's right," he said. "Now let go!"

She released him and he sprawled forward, scrambled to his feet, and ran. She ran in the opposite direction, toward the elevator gate at the deep vertical shaft.

The trick is to get down there and let the gas out of the cavern without sparking it off.

Just as she reached the elevator, the wailing siren shut up. The elevator car sat at the bottom of the shaft, a long way down. Ember punched the up button, but the car did not budge.

Damn. She slammed the button with the heel of her palm. *Must be an emergency electrical shutoff. Can't use the elevator.* She peered over the edge of the shaft that sliced into the glacier. *How do I get down?*

She studied the metal sign with the map of the shafts and caverns. Two oval caverns seemed to form the eye sockets of a face, with a big central cavern as the mouth. Her heart pounded faster. Ancient memories opened and opened in her mind like Chinese boxes.

So close now.

Ember glanced at a refrigerator-sized aluminum tool locker on one side of the elevator dock. She threw it open. Inside were a half-dozen yellow air-tanks, two fire extinguishers, and several large coils of rope. And some kind of short, stubby rifle. Ember thought the rifle was made for firing flares, until she saw, next to it, a folding grappling hook on a steel shaft.

Her heart leapt. *A way down. The rifle's made for shooting the hook up over a ledge, in order to climb from below, but what if I aim it directly at the ice wall in front of me? It might bury itself deep enough to hold my weight.*

She lifted out the tools and loaded the grappling hook into the barrel of the rifle. The folding end of the hook projected as a conical point from the two-inch-wide barrel. Beneath the barrel, in front of the trigger, an eight-inch spool of woven nylon cord hung on a metal axle. The tough cord ran through two nickel-sized eyelets welded to the barrel, and she clipped one end of the cord to the grappling hook shaft, near its tip.

She climbed over the wire mesh elevator gate with the rifle. She grasped an overhead girder with one hand and shuffled her feet, careful not to slip on the ice-coated metal. She scooted to a flat rib on the far side of the elevator frame. She clung tightly with her right arm, cradled the grappling hook rifle in the crook of her left arm. Aimed at the sheer wall of ice. Bent her knees. Squeezed the trigger.

Bam. A high-pitched whine, and a spray of ice chunks stung her body.

The kick from the powder charge nearly knocked her backward off the platform. When she regained her footing and looked up, the hook was buried to the middle of its shaft. She grabbed the nylon cord with both hands and gave a sharp tug. Solidly anchored.

She quickly unwound the cord from the spool, letting the slack drop down the wall; the played-out cord formed a long U. Was the bottom of the loop halfway down?

Next she shuffled along the girder toward the crater in the ice from which the cord dangled. Then she lowered the rifle itself down the wall until the cord reached its full length. The rifle hugged the vertical face, about twenty-five feet from the bottom.

Doesn't reach all the way down. Can I drop that far?

"Piece of cake," she said aloud, and heard her voice quaver. She opened and closed her fingers a few times, then gripped the cord in her bare hands.

You can do it. Just stare straight ahead at the wall.

She stepped off the girder. Hand under hand she lowered herself down, feet wrapped around the rope as a brake. Halfway down the ice wall her hands began to blister and burn.

Don't let go. Don't look down.

Finally her feet touched the dangling rifle and she lowered herself to the end of the cord and glanced down. The hard-packed snow resembled concrete.

Keeping her knees together, slightly bent, she faced forward and, without looking down, let herself drop.

Stars flashed in her brain when she hit and her breath exploded in a loud *"Oof!"* Her legs stayed together and absorbed the shock as she rolled down the outside of her right leg to her hip and let the momentum carry her onto her back and over, in a backward somersault.

She sat up slowly, stunned, and pressed her blistered palms against the cold snow. A drop of red splatted the white; the impact had jarred open the wound in her shoulder. She took a few deep breaths and then hopped up and ran into the passageway that led down to the mouth of the ancient face.

48

A HUNDRED FEET into the passageway the darkness became total. Ember could not see her hand when she touched her nose. She dragged her right foot along the gas hose, moving quickly in a kind of skipping gait. After a moment a subtle shift in air pressure and drafts told her she had entered a large cavern: the mouth.

She followed the hose, edging along more slowly, hands feeling ahead through the blackness. The cavern floor was toothy with rock formations and her hands saved her from colliding with stalagmites. The hose led upward and Ember felt the entrance of the scooter hole. She crawled inside and scurried along, hunched over on all fours. Her heavy breathing made hollow sounds in the rock tube.

Ahead, a tiny red light stood out sharply in the black void. The tunnel widened and she could stand up nearly straight. The hose lifted from the curved tunnel floor and ended at what felt like a metal plate in a solid wall.

"Hey, in there, I'm here to help," she yelled. "Can you hear me?" Her loud voice in the granite megaphone hurt her ears. She yelled a second time before she heard footsteps from the other side.

"We're here!" Nika shouted. "Me and Chief Willy. You gotta smash the timer."

Ember felt the bolts that circled the round plate.

"How do I get you out?"

"No, smash the timer first, it's set to ignite the propane any second."

"Where is it?"

"Near the end of the hose. Hurry."

Ember touched the red light. It was part of some kind of box. Her fingers wrapped around what felt like batteries. She fumbled in the dark and unclipped the batteries. Then with her right foot she crushed the box to junk and kicked it twice more, until it tore loose from the hose.

"I smashed it."

"Oh, thank God."

Ember thought she heard the sound of a scuba-type respirator.

"You've got an air tank?"

A pause.

"Yeah—this place is filled with propane, we'll all have to buddy-breathe as soon as you get the plate off."

"How do I do that?"

"Feel around for a drill, on the tunnel floor somewhere."

Ember groped the cold rock for a drill. She smelled blood and her fingers touched patches of sticky frost.

"A big drill," Nika said. "I pray it's there. Can you find it?"

Ember's hands came upon a heavy portable drill with a socket wrench attachment.

"Got it," she said.

Rrrr-tat-t-t-t-t-tat. The first nut came loose and a curved sliver of light escaped around the edge of the metal plate. Another nut spun loose. She smelled propane. One more nut, and vapors began to seep into the tunnel, filling the space where she was kneeling. It was getting hard to breathe.

Two more nuts spun off, and light rays from inside the cavern lit a thick cloud of gas in the tunnel. Her lungs began to burn for need of fresh air.

She held her breath. One last nut.

The drill spun the last nut free. She inhaled the propane and slumped forward, dizzy, graying out. Nika rolled the metal plate to one side, and hurried through, shoving a rubber mouthpiece into Ember's mouth. Ember hungrily sucked in the compressed air.

Nika's silhouette crouched near her in the gloom. After a moment Nika patted her on the shoulder. "My turn."

Ember sat up and passed the mouthpiece to Nika, who took a few deep breaths from the air tank. Suddenly the surface fans came on and began to pump in outside air, driving out the propane.

"By now some people are wondering why this place didn't go boom," Nika said, handing back the mouthpiece. "Chief Willy's inside, he's unconscious." She stepped back into the cavern.

Ember inhaled from the air tank and followed Nika through the port.

Scooter headlights reflected from the ice walls and bathed the cavern in a bluish glow. Ember glimpsed rows of golden bodies and instinctively looked away, to focus on Nika kneeling beside a supine figure in a blue jumpsuit. Chief Willy lay sprawled on the floor with a respirator in his mouth and a scooter air tank propped in the crook of one arm. With an effort that made her tremble, Ember shoved aside her feelings, to deal with the emergency at hand; the full impact of her homecoming would have to wait.

"I need your help," Nika said. "Gotta move him outdoors. He's hypothermic, I'm scared it might be too late."

Ember hurried to Nika's side, handed her the respirator, and in the bright blue light saw Nika's face clearly for the first time. Ember put her hand to her mouth.

"What is it?" Nika said.

At once the whole situation became clear to Ember, as if a complete symphony were contained in the first violin note.

"You're his sister," Ember whispered, awestruck.

"You know Yute?" she said. "I'm Nika."

Nika took a few puffs of air from the respirator,

then tried inhaling without it. "It's okay," she said, "I think we can breathe this junk now. Let's get him into a scooter, I'll tow it behind mine."

Ember and Nika dragged Chief Willy to a scooter, shoved him inside, and closed the cage. Nika lined up her scooter with his, and Ember linked the two with a tow cable at the back of the first scooter. Nika lay down in her vehicle.

"Meet you up in the sunlight," she said, and towed Chief Willy's scooter behind hers, up the ramp and into the tunnel.

Ember only nodded, unable to speak. All around her were the golden bodies of her people. Sorrow and love ran together in her heart like wine and honey. Tears streamed down her face into her mouth.

She tried to sort her great joy from her immense grief, the relief from the horror. But she could not, and her feelings spilled over in quaking sobs, a hundred sentiments at once. Her soul was intimately connected to the goldens and also to Nika, who had helped save them, and through Nika, to Yute, and to Yute's father and mother and his birthplace and his whole life. All of their destinies seemed to her now to be as interwoven as long strips of bark in a cedar basket.

Ember began to wander the huge room. Some of the golden people she recognized from her dreams and visions.

Her eyes came to rest on a toddler, apparently only sleeping, nestled on the bare breasts of a red-haired woman. A jolt of emotion rocked her body.

"Rayne!" she whispered, and clutched her chest.

My brother.

49

EMBER SCOOPED THE little body up and hugged it close; the skin was icy, but soft. She sank deep into her feelings, beyond tears.

She carried Rayne to the third scooter and lay down on her back, draping the limp body across her torso. The scooter shot up the ramp into the tunnel, tires straddling the gas hose; it sped toward the lighted cavern on the far end.

Ember zoomed in a beeline between stalagmites into the exit shaft at the far side of the cavern. Soon daylight filled the passageway near the entrance and the scooter burst outdoors.

Nika ran back to Ember's scooter.

"Chief Willy's not breathing, he's cold to the bone. I gave him CPR, but he didn't respond. I don't know what to do."

Ember slid out of her scooter, leaving Rayne lying prone in the seat. Chief Willy lay on his back in a scooter with an open cage; one of his arms had flopped to the snowy ground.

Ember knelt and placed one hand on his heart and the other on his abdomen. Then she breathed deeply into the living fire—letting it shine from her own belly and heart and radiate through her arms and hands. Within seconds she could feel her nervous system link with his. With each of her breaths he grew brighter and warmer, energized from the inside.

Then Chief Willy took a big breath along with Ember, they exhaled together in a heavy sigh.

"How are you doing that?" Nika said. "He's coming around."

Ember experienced herself as a bright sphere of force that surrounded and pervaded her own body and his body. She closed her eyes and saw his bones and blood vessels, nerves, organs—and the light that sustained them.

The light brightened steadily and Chief Willy opened his eyes. Ember held them in her gaze, and his face gradually took on an aura of her glow. "Thank you," he said in a bare whisper.

"*Aiyoo wa Denali*," Nika said, and rubbed Chief Willy's hands in hers. She turned to Ember. "Who are you? Where did you come from? Where do the goldens live now?"

Ember shook her head. "I'm the only living one. My name is Ember Ozette, I came from here."

Nika's eyebrows knitted.

"It's a long story," Ember said. She walked over slowly and knelt beside Rayne.

"He's my brother," she said, more to herself than to the others. She rolled him over and peered into his little boy's face.

Sunlight poked through the square of sky that marked the lip of the vertical shaft. The golden light fell upon her hands as she laid them on Rayne.

"Is that a sign?" She turned her face to the sun. "Is this what I'm meant to do?"

She closed her eyes. *If the life force is only strong enough, bright enough . . . maybe . . . maybe . . .* please. . . .

Ember shook with the intensity of her feeling. With each inhalation she drew the life force from a bottomless well and poured this power into Rayne, flooding the limp body with all her love.

But she could find no spark to breathe upon and make brighter. She inhaled deeper, rocking and moaning with the outpouring of her soul. But no channel stood open for the light to infill. She could not link with what simply was not there.

When she finally opened her eyes, the snow had melted and puddled in a circle around her knees. But the little body remained as vacant as a tossed-off parka.

Ember raised herself shakily, supporting her weight with her hands on the scooter. She took a few wobbly steps and flung herself full-length in the snow and beat the ground with her fists.

Nika and Chief Willy tried to comfort her, stroking her hair and rubbing her back.

"I've come so far for this? A mass suicide?" Her voice choked. "My dreams and visions—it's all been a lie. My people are dead and there is no new life for them . . . and—and when I die, there will be no more goldens, forever."

A snowmobile engine revved loudly near the lip of the vertical shaft.

"No!" a deep male voice shouted. "Stop!"

A loud gunshot. The snow burst up in a plume beside them.

Nika threw her body over Ember to protect her.

"Bastards are back to finish us off."

50

MORE SHOTS RANG out. The snowmobile roared closer. A man screamed and a figure in a blue jumpsuit plummeted backward off the edge. Legs pumped wildly, as if to scramble to solid ground. The body thudded in a heap, still clutching a rifle. Then a red snowmobile appeared, without a driver, skidding along the ledge.

"Move!" Nika yelled.

All three dove toward the far side of the vertical shaft.

The snowmobile hugged the brink for an instant, tottered, and toppled over. It bounced and cartwheeled and exploded in an orange fireball. Bits and chunks of burning debris rained down and sizzled in the snow.

The booming echoes died and the drone of dozens of snowmobiles could be heard approaching from above.

Chief Willy grimaced. "What now?"

"Hurry, back into the mine," Nika said. "We're sitting ducks out here."

Ember grabbed her arm. "No, it's okay, they're friends. Trust me—I can feel them."

A wake of wreckage smoldered beside the crumpled body in the blue jumpsuit. The dead man's neck twisted nearly backward over his shoulders, like an owl's.

"Kaiser," Nika said.

Chief Willy nodded. "Custer."

The other snowmobiles arrived above. In the next moment workers in orange jumpsuits were peering over the lip, calling down to the trio.

"My friends," Chief Willy said, and sighed with relief.

"And mine," Ember said, and stared in amazement as a tall auburn-haired man shouldered his way through the fringe.

"Ember, you all right?" Mike shouted with cupped hands. Kaigani joined him on the ledge.

Ember gave them the thumbs-up sign, but could barely force a smile.

"We're coming down," Mike shouted.

The elevator descended. Mike and Kaigani darted out ahead of the others. The two threw their arms around Ember with such force, it knocked her two steps backward.

"How?" Ember said. "How did you know to come here?"

"Yute told us," Mike said. "He caught us sneaking

around in his lab, he told us everything about you. He said if we wanted to find you and help you, we needed to go to Alaska—"

"He knew you'd come here to the Kantishna Hills," Kaigani said. "He was so convincing, we hopped in the Jeep and left that same night."

"Who was Kaiser shooting at up there?" Nika asked. "Was anyone hurt?"

Mike looked at Ember. "Yute saved you all just now, he kept Kaiser from nailing you. Kaiser shot him twice, but he rammed the bastard with his snowmobile. Yute. He sacrificed himself."

Nika cried out and cupped her hand to her mouth.

"He's dead?" Chief Willy asked.

"Don't think he's going to make it. The paramedics are with him now."

Nika pushed through the crowd to get to the elevator.

Ember gazed up at the ledge of ice, feeling weary to her marrow.

"All this sacrifice, all for nothing . . . I'm the very last. . . ." She hung her head. "I'd let Yute study me now, but it's even too late for that."

A bearded Chilkakot Indian gawked at Ember. "I thought it was supposed to be *He*-Who-Comes-Back."

"Me too," said a dark-skinned woman. "That's what our storykeeper taught us."

"Oh, this one has the power, all right," Chief Willy said, and put his hand on Ember's shoulder.

Ember shot a glance to Mike. "Old Man never said anything about this."

"Actually, he did tell me the same thing. The legend speaks of 'He-Who-Returns.' "

"Yes . . . *yes.*" Ember clapped her hands together. "There is something . . . someone . . . I've been missing. . . ."

She stepped out and away from the growing crowd of Indians, and spread her arms wide, palms upturned. Feeling, feeling, as if her body were an antenna.

"I am not the savior of the O-kwo-ke. Not me. I've never known what to do. The one who can restore them knows exactly what to do. He's here now."

He-Who-Returns, who are you? Where are you?

Her heart flew open like a window.

There is one here who brought me to life from an ancient embryo.

She spun around and raced for the elevator.

He-Who-Returns is Yute Nahadeh.

51

Yute lay sprawled on his back on top of a thick rubber drop cloth, draped by a silvery thermal blanket.

"Nothing more we can do," one man whispered. Ember nodded for them to move aside. Nika knelt by her brother, across from Ember. She held his hand.

Ember pulled back the thermal blanket. Dark stains soaked the red nylon snowmobile suit. His lungs gurgled and sucked with each rapid, shallow breath, like a bellows partly full of water.

Yute opened his eyes and reached, feebly, for Ember's hand. She pressed his cold hand between her hot palms.

"Ember . . . I—I'm the one. . . ."

"Shhh. I know who you are. You're meant to restore my people, like you restored me."

He shook his head. "You don't yet . . . understand . . . it's only now clear . . . the mystery . . . of my whole life." He panted and labored to speak, "Blend your heart . . . with mine . . . there's so much . . . to impart."

She lay down in the snow on her side, facing him. She placed her left hand under his head as a pillow and laid her right hand directly over his heart. The blood was sticky.

Ember let her awareness sift down, down into Yute, like sand flowing into the base of an hourglass. She snuggled her body closer to his. After a moment her heart fell through into the well of his heart, and she was no longer simply Ember.

She was a burly redheaded man in a sheepskin tunic. His right hand gripped a reindeer-antler staff bored with a hole resembling a mouth with carved rays of force radiating from the lips; a raised-scar tattoo of the same design adorned his forehead.

His name was Talu, Shaman Chief of the Water-Talkers, Killer of the Beasts.

Abruptly, his memories unfolded in a kaleidoscopic whirl.

Talu and a group of his hunters chanced upon a long-forgotten band of the Beasts. But when they rushed to attack, the people buried themselves in a cave. He chased a lone survivor, a woman, up a steep, rocky slope. With her was a large white wolf. As Talu closed in, the wolf spun and leapt upon him, bowling him over and down the slope. Talu lay still at the bottom, his throat torn open in a ragged gash.

The woman placed her hands on him as he struggled for breath, and they became one—and through her, he became her people, in a web of hearts. And he remembered their common ancestors, and understood their reluctance to fight. And he realized with great sorrow that he and his kind had murdered their own brothers.

The dying Talu commanded the Water-Talkers to preserve the tragic story, forever.

Then he made a silent vow: The Talkers will go on and on in the direction of words and knowledge, and one day there will be knowledge powerful enough to undo their terrible crime. In that future I will take birth, to restore what I have destroyed.

In the next moment detailed images of the microsurgical devices Yute had invented stood out lucidly in their linked awareness. Ember understood how the sperm and eggs of the goldens could be harvested and fertilized in vitro. Thousands of embryos could be produced and stored, and the embryos could be implanted in surrogate mothers from around the world. The golden race could be regenerated.

The connection began to dissolve like a dream. Ember opened her eyes and sat up.

Yute breathed faintly, almost imperceptibly. He opened his eyes and met her gaze.

"Do . . . you . . . forgive . . . me?" he asked in a whisper.

Her answer was to kiss his forehead as he died.

Epilogue

Ember hiked up the steep trail in the predawn stillness. She reached her favorite overlook and sat down on a springy carpet of reindeer moss. From her high perch on a treeless knob in the Kantishna Hills, her eyes swept across the vast tundra below in the dark.

She took U-Ma's small bone flute from her shirt pocket. Her fingers nestled on the holes worn smooth at the edges by her mother's fingertips, long, long ago. The flute sang five bright notes that chased each other like butterflies, flitting over the high cliff edge above the sea of grass. She let the flute play itself, a tremulous soprano melody, free of hurry; and after a time she heard her mother's ancient songs, and she kissed her mother through the music, their lips touching at the mouthpiece.

Ember's infant son began to whimper, and her breasts tingled with fullness. The baby cried louder and she felt a gush of warmth as her milk let down.

"Shhh, little one," she said, "you're getting me soaked."

She took off the child-carrier backpack, pulled him free, and unbuttoned her flannel shirt. Her mother's gold amulet dangled from a soft leather cord. Her son made sucking sounds as he nursed, one strong little hand playing with her other breast. She had named him Rayne to honor her ancient brother. His bright green eyes smiled at hers, the eyelids growing heavy as his round little belly filled with sweet milk. Ember felt a bond with every mother who had ever lived, and she sighed with thankfulness for Yute, whose science had made this miracle possible.

Light appeared on the eastern horizon and the bottoms of the clouds glowed pink. The sun rose with fanfare of birdsong; its warmth painted her face and eyes; a breeze ruffled her hair.

Rayne stopped nursing and snuggled against her breasts, a drop of milk on his lips, his blond fuzz soft against hers. Their bare skin reflected each other's color and heat. She stroked his fine red hair, fiery in the new light. The morning clouds shifted like burning logs.

On the rolling green plain, hundreds of watery mirrors received the sky among a brilliant patchwork of flowers: orange poppies, yellow buttercups, purple rice lilies, blue mountain forget-me-nots. A herd of caribou grazed on moss and antler lichens near the edge of a small glacier.

Swans called loudly overhead. Ember gazed up at a wide V of graceful white birds, sixty or more of them, flying with noisy musical whistles toward their breeding pond.

Layers of wind arranged the clouds in tiers. The lowest tier was coal-black and ragged, moving fast. The highest layer was fluffy and white and draped the eastern sky like a dog-wool cape. Between these layers drifted rungs of gray, purple, and mauve. The sunlight flashed silver upon a jet, writing a long, thin contrail across a lone patch of arctic blue.

Lights winked on in the village at the base of the hill. Ember breathed in deeply the aroma of the moist earth and sky of early spring. She bent her head and kissed her sleeping son. He smelled as vital as the dew at the dawn of creation.

Tears of joy blurred her vision and fell with the first sprinkles of rain.

"My son," she whispered, "we goldens—Heart-Listeners and Heart-Talkers—will live on, and our fragrance will be remembered, from generation to generation, without end."